This wasn't going at all the way she'd hoped.

He paused in a sla... first of the windows. hair, like embers in a his eyes.

He's meant for me.

The thought emerged from nowhere, fresh as a slap and seemed as true as it was dumbfounding. She stared at him, bewildered. She'd never had a thought like that in her entire life. An ache started up, a barbed, hopeless longing. It was as though she knew him, had always known him, all his foibles and flaws and passions, in moments quiet and playful. As irrational a thought as she'd ever had.

She would need to make a decision.

To her surprise, something besides her mind had already made the decision for her. She heard her own walking boots echo across the floor. Her blood was swooshing in her ears, so hard was her heart hammering away.

He turned away from the view.

Their eyes met.

The silence suddenly seemed so total she felt deafened.

A quick smile haunted his mouth again.

And suddenly it was too much. She could hardly bear the suspense.

"Well, Lord Dryden. You may as well get it over with."

The smile vanished. "I beg your pardon?"

"You're going to try to kiss me, aren't you?"

Romances by Julie Anne Long

Julie Anne Long

How The
Marquess
Was Won

AVON

An Imprint of HarperCollinsPublishers

AVON BOOKS
An Imprint of HarperCollins*Publishers*
10 East 53rd Street
New York, New York 10022-5299

Copyright © 2012 by Julie Anne Long
ISBN 978-0-06-188569-3
www.avonromance.com

First Avon Books mass market printing: January 2012

Avon Trademark Reg. U.S. Pat. Off. and in Other Countries, Marca Registrada, Hecho en U.S.A.
HarperCollins® is a registered trademark of HarperCollins Publishers.

Printed in the U.S.A.

10 9 8 7 6 5 4 3 2

Acknowledgments

I'm so blessed and grateful to work with such gifted, lovely (and frequently very entertaining) people: my dear editor, May Chen; the hardworking staff at Avon; my brilliant agent, Steve Axelrod.

And I appreciate more than I can say the readers who've loved my work and shared their enthusiasm for it with me, their friends, and the romance community at large over the years. This list is far from complete, but it's a start, and it includes readers, talented authors (both published and aspiring), and industry professionals: P.J. Ausdenmore, Manda Collins, Bette-Lee Fox, Sue Grimshaw, Beverley Kendall, Kathy Kozakewich, Janice Rohletter, Courtney Milan, Elyssa Papa—thank you! You're all wonderful!

And my *heartfelt* gratitude to Julia Quinn for her kindness and generosity in sharing her enthusiasm for my work with her readers. I'm a lucky author, indeed.

How The Marquess Was Won

Chapter 1

It wasn't unusual to see a man stagger into or out of the Pig & Thistle, Pennyroyal Green's pub. Nor was it unusual for the entrance door to fly open hard enough to bounce against the wall. After all, a half dozen ales into an evening a man's arms and legs could mutiny on him and do things like fling open doors with too much strength, pinch the bottoms of passing females, and refuse to hold him upright.

But Colin Eversea was tormenting his brother Chase with talk of cows *again*, and since Chase had a perfect view of the doorway, he looked up from his ale and studied the man now framed there. The breeze caught hold of the hem of his coat, rippling it fitfully. His trousers were tucked into Hessians; the toes were dulled with mud. His dark hair was pushed back over a high pale forehead, upon which Chase could see what appeared to be a fading bruise.

The man swayed almost imperceptibly. He frowned, as if he was puzzled to find himself there, or had forgotten why he entered. He turned, slowly, and stared with glazed eyes into the crowd in the pub. And then his hand slipped inside his coat . . .

. . . very much like a man reaching for a pistol.

Chase stiffened. Then half-rose from his chair.

And reflexively slipped his hand into his own coat and closed his fingers around the barrel of his own pistol.

His universe narrowed to the man's hand, pressed over a pristine linen shirt.

Seconds later, Chase saw one drop of scarlet ooze between the man's fingers. The man's head tipped back, and he dropped hard to one of his knees, and then the other.

"Colin!" he barked.

Chase nearly scrambled over Colin, jumping across the top of the scarred table, to reach the man before he fell.

Colin appeared on his heels, and Ned Hawthorne seconds later. With a sort of tacit coordination (it wasn't the first prone man they'd born out of a room) they scooped the man up and whisked him away to the storeroom behind the bar as if he were a delivery of potatoes, as a prone bleeding man was bad for business.

And if anyone noticed, they would just put it down to the fact that picking men up off the floor was common in the Pig & Thistle, too.

They closed the door of the room, and deftly, wordlessly, lowered him onto a pallet usually used for those needing to sleep off ale, and together they slipped him out of his coat. Chase and Colin were veterans of war. One never forgot how to tend to the fallen.

"Can you speak?" Chase folded the coat neatly and quickly. Old military habits of tidiness die hard. He handed it to Colin, who raised his eyebrows at its quality.

"Yes." The syllable was a gasp etched in pain.

He opened his eyes then. They were the color of whiskey; the face was refined, strong-boned . . . . strangely familiar.

"I'm Captain Charles Eversea."

"An Eversea. Thank God." The voice was hoarse but clear. "Not a Redmond."

"How refreshing. That isn't something we hear very often. And I thank God for that every day, too," Chase said. "You are?"

A hesitation. And then he rasped out his name. "Dryden."

Colin and Chase exchanged a wide-eyed look over the man's body. Christ. Lord Ice, himself. Julian Spenser, Marquess Dryden.

"Shot, stabbed?" They eased him back onto the pallet, and Colin handed Chase a knife he'd slipped out of his boot. Chase slit open the Marquess's shirt and gently pushed it from his shoulders.

"Shot." A gasp.

And indeed he had been. The ball was near his shoulder, and a swift, closer inspection told Chase it was close to the surface of his skin. Thank God. They might be able to retrieve it whole. The blood was already congealing about the wound.

"Who shot you?"

Dryden was breathing roughly. He shook his head. "There's a woman, you see . . . please tell her . . ."

"A *woman* shot you?" This was from Colin.

"She might as well have done." Humor through the pain now, the dry and gallows kind.

Two smart raps sounded on the door, a warning before Ned Hawthorne opened it. He handed whiskey and rags to Colin. "Sent for the doctor," he reported with something like resigned cheer, " 'case you lads 'ave need of 'im."

Then vanished out the door again. His family had
owned the Pig & Thistle since it was built centuries ago,
and the marquess would hardly be the first man ever to
mingle his blood with the sawdust on the floor.

"We're going to see about getting the ball out,
Dryden, so drink this. As fast as you can." Chase
shoved the flask into the man's hand.

"I don't . . ." Dryden stopped to gulp the whiskey,
winced, then blinked appreciatively. " . . . *love* her, mind
you . . ."

"No?" While his brother tore rags into neat bandage-
sized strips, Colin wrapped his fingers round Dryden's
wrist and found his pulse quick but strong, not thready.
Which meant he hadn't yet lost a dangerous amount
of blood.

"You're lucky, Dryden," Colin told him. We can
probably get the ball out and bind you up without
stitching it. But you won't be dancing the reel anytime
soon. Where the devil did you get these scratches on
your chest? And the bruise on your head?"

"Hate the reel," was all Dryden said, after a considering moment, ignoring the other questions. "I rather
like the waltz, however." He sounded wistful, drifting
now thanks to pain and the whiskey.

"Do you? Drink that whiskey, now," Chase ordered.

He gulped down more. His throat moved in hard
swallows. "She's not even *pretty*." The marquess seemed
intent on making a case.

Fever? Colin mouthed to Chase across the marquess's
prone body. Puzzled.

Love, Chase mouthed back.

"Beautiful, though," the marquess muttered grimly.
"Damn her eyes."

"Is she?" Colin humored.

"And dear God, but she's *so* . . ." Dryden shook his head, and winced. "She has a . . ." He pointed vaguely at his face, and then his hand flopped down and turned palm up. There were apparently no adequate words to describe this paragon.

"Nose?" Colin guessed. "A wen? A third eye?"

Chase frowned at his brother. "Ever been shot before, Dryden?"

"First time. Bayoneted once before, though."

"Ah. Well, you aren't going to like this next bit."

This got them a faint smile. "Can't imagine why. It's been delightful so . . . far." He took another long gulp of whiskey.

"I'm going to clean the wound, and then we're going to . . . do the rest. And trust me when I say I've done this any number of times before. You might faint, but we won't raid your pockets if you do. Go on. Close your eyes if you need to."

Chase was accustomed to giving orders.

Dryden's head fell back. His breathing was shallow now. "Don't want to close my eyes. She's all I see."

It was so startlingly frank and devoid in the sort of drama that usually accompanied such statements that the Eversea men momentarily froze with surprise.

And stared down at the regal Lord Ice speculatively.

The marquess's chest rose and fell, rose and fell. His eyes closed.

"She doesn't love *me*," he said softly, finally.

It sounded like a correction of a previous implication. As though he was defending her honor.

They were terrible words to die on, if that's what he was going to do.

Chase hesitated for a moment. "Get Adam," he ordered his brother under his breath.

Colin was surprised. Telling a man he was going to live and then sending for the vicar, their cousin Adam, seemed a contradiction in terms, but when Chase Eversea issued an order it was nearly impossible for anyone near not to obey it.

Habit intervened. Colin just sent him a look, nodded, stood, and obeyed.

Chapter 2

Six weeks earlier . . .

Phoebe Vale flung open the door to Postlethwaite's Emporium of Lady's Goods then threw her body against it, fighting with the wind to get it closed again. The bells looped to the door jangled frantically.

She paused to savor her view. Postlethwaite's was Pennyroyal Green's very own Aladdin's cave. Everywhere was color and gleam and fingertip-seducing texture: Cases held silver and ivory buttons, satin bows and silk flowers, fine silk fans and fur muffs. A wall was devoted to spools of satin ribbon and silk thread; petal-fine elbow-length kid gloves were fanned on an antique escritoire; Chinese silk shawls and wool capes lolled about the place with indolent elegance. And in the corner were the bonnets and hats, all breathtakingly fashionable and very, very expensive, huddling together on their stands like aristocratic gossipers.

One bonnet in particular throbbed at the periphery of her vision.

Her heart lurched with joy—*it was still here!*

And then she coolly, pointedly turned her back on it. She could feel it there, still, like the eyes of a spurned lover, on the back of her neck.

"Good afternoon, Miss Vale. Run all the way here, did ye?" Mr. Postlethwaite's voice carried across the shop. He was standing behind the counter. "I was just sorting the mail."

"Well, you know how it is, Postlethwaite. Papa won't allow us to use the carriage until he's had the gilt on the coat of arms repainted."

"Tsk. Now canna have a carriage without the family coat of arms shinin' from the door, can ye? *However* will the world know ye're inside?"

"How you understand me, Postlethwaite! We are always in such accord!"

"And when you marry me, lass, we shall live out our days in bliss."

"In time, my dear Postlethwaite, in time. I am sowing my wild oats, as you know."

They grinned at each other. They both knew the only thing Phoebe was sewing was her own dresses, often twice over after picking out the stitches and turning the fabric to get more wear out of it. And Postlethwaite was a quarter of a century her senior if he was a day and had only a horseshoe-shaped patch of hair left on his head.

"Windy today," she told Postlethwaite idly.

He cast an eye up at her through his spectacles, studied her briefly, then dropped his gaze again to the mail. "Niiivver would 'ave guessed," he murmured dryly.

Phoebe bit back a smile. She planted her hands on the counter and peered into the mirror over it. She *was* a bit of a disaster. Her cheeks were scarlet, her eyes were brilliant and watery, and her fair hair was escaping in wild maypole streamers from beneath her bonnet.

"I've the London broadsheets for ye, Miss Vale. A bit in here about me rival for yer hand."

"Lord Ice?" she said with idle and utterly feigned disdain. Her heart quickened. "What *has* he done now?"

"Wagered ten thousand pounds on a horse race . . . and won."

She sniffed. "The man will do anything to elicit a gasp."

"And it says here he bought one pair of gloves at Titweiler & Sons in the Burlington Arcade. And now all of the ton must have a pair. And they cost one hundred pounds!"

"I imagine the ton would leap from London Bridge if the marquess did it first. Mind you, *he'd* land on a cart carrying a feather mattress when he did it, whilst the rest of London would splatter."

There had in fact been turmoil in the ton when the marquess had acquired four matched black horses with white stockings to pull his new landau. For a time, a black horse could not be had at Tattersall's for anything less than a king's ransom, and owners of black horses took to posting sentries at their stables at night against enterprising Gypsies who would steal them, then paint on white stockings and sell them.

The broadsheets were Phoebe's secret vice. By day she lectured restless young girls in Latin and Greek and French and history. By night, in bed, she pored over ton gossip the way she'd first gulped down the tales of the Arabian Nights—both seemed equally fantastic, part of another universe entirely. The broadsheets were how she knew, for instance, that Lord Waterburn was known for outlandish wagers, and that the Silverton Twins were the most wickedly glamorous young ladies of the fast set, and that Lisbeth Redmond, a young lady she'd once tutored, was now considered a diamond of the first water.

But it was the formidable Lord Ice Julian Spenser, Marquess Dryden, who haunted her imagination. She knew all about him: he dressed only in black and white, he regularly shot the hearts out of the targets at Manton's to remind the bloods of the ton how foolish it would be to *ever* challenge him; he tolerated only the finest, the most singular, the most beautiful, in gloves, in horseflesh, in women. He was said to be cold and precise in all things: the making of money, the acquiring and dismissing of mistresses, and, as was rumored to be next, the finding of a wife.

He made reckless things, horse races and blood-chillingly high wagers, seem so sane and effortless that in a rush to emulate him, London bloods broke their necks or lost their fortunes.

While Dryden always emerged with his arctic dignity and his enormous fortune unscathed.

Every man wanted to be Lord Dryden.

And if one believed the broadsheets, every woman wanted to be *with* Lord Dryden.

Postlethwaite finished sorting the mail. "Ah! Two of them addressed to the academy today, my dear Miss Vale! And wouldn't you know, both are for you."

"Probably yet another proposal from the marquess, for he is *most* persistent, despite the fact that I have explained again and again that I am promised to you. And the other would be an invitation to yet another ball."

Postlethwaite leaned forward. "And what will ye be wearing to *this* ball?"

They never tired of this game.

"Oh, I suppose I'd wear my primrose silk, the cream kid gloves, and my necklace—the one with the little diamond." She brought her hand up to her throat and tapped the base of it. "And . . . my second-best coronet,

I suppose. I shall look as delicious as a meringue! But likely as I shall send my regrets, as their last do was such a bore." She lowered her voice to a confiding hush. "Have I told you what happened?"

"No!" Postlethwaite's voice dropped to a hush, too.

"So many young men wanted to dance the waltz with me that two of them came to blows. And one of them called the other one out and . . . well, I fear there was a duel."

"Never say a duel!"

"Oh, I'm afraid so. They fought with pistols at dawn. And one of them was *wounded*."

"Scandalous!"

"I always seem to cause duels," she said sadly.

"Canna say as I blame them, Miss Vale. You were born to break hearts."

"Hearts? Not mirrors?"

They grinned at each other. For if Phoebe Vale was a beauty, no one had yet pointed this out to her. Compliments were generally confined to her complexion, which admittedly was very fine. She'd danced but one waltz her entire life, during a party held in Pennyroyal Green's town hall, with a spotty young man who was either too bashful to look her in the eye or too grateful to be so close to such excellent cleavage to do anything other than worship it with his gaze.

But men *had* indeed come to blows over her more than once. She was inclined to blame too much ale at the Pig & Thistle. But the men of Sussex knew something they couldn't articulate: they wanted to be close to Miss Phoebe Vale the way they wanted to be close to the fire on a cold night, and they kept their distance for the very same reason. She threw off sparks.

And the sparks were in large part the reason she did

indeed own one very beautiful thing: a pair of surprisingly fine cream-colored, gold-trimmed kid gloves, a gift from a bold and unlikely admirer who had shown her definitively that, *why* yes, she did indeed enjoy being kissed, and that no, she could not settle for an ordinary man. She'd even begun entertaining the notion of falling in love when he'd suddenly disappeared. She congratulated herself on the fact that he hadn't taken her heart with him. Phoebe had learned long ago the consequences of fully surrendering it to anyone, as in her experience, disappearing is what people did.

Since him none of the young men she met fired her imagination or stirred her heart; none of them—and not once had she thought of this as arrogance, merely as an act of charity—seemed equal to her or worth pledging her life to. She would make none of them happy should she marry them.

And besides, her destiny lay elsewhere. And she knew that at least one of the letters waiting for her contained her future.

The bell on the door jangled again and two giggling girls jostled each other for entry and then threw themselves bodily at the door to close it against the wind, then elbowed each other a bit more just for the pure pleasure of it once they got inside. "Oy, you stop it now, Agnes, or I tell you I'll—"

They saw Phoebe and went immobile. Their shoulders flew back so swiftly it nearly created a wind, their spines stiffened, their hands folded into neat little knots against their thighs, their eyes widened with doelike innocence.

They regarded her mutely.

"Good afternoon, Miss Runyon, Miss Carew," she said kindly.

"Good afternoon, Miss Vale!" An angelic chorus.

"Are you looking forward to your holiday?"

"Yes, Miss Vale."

"And will you be returning home to visit your families or staying on with us at the academy?"

"Home, Miss Vale." In harmony, once more.

"Are you here to *buy* gifts for your families?"

"Yes, Miss Vale."

Miss Runyon had been accused of being light-fingered, and her harried father had installed her at Miss Marietta Endicott's academy when she was ten years old.

Coincidentally, about the same age Phoebe had been when she'd been taken there.

"I will show you some excellent things, and all can be had for a ha'penny. Buttons and bows and the like," Mr. Postlethwaite assured them as indulgently as if they were fine ladies, for this was in part what made them *behave* like ladies, both he and Phoebe knew. She in fact knew how to manage recalcitrant young ladies so well it was almost unfair. Then again, she knew a little bit about being one.

He emerged from behind the counter and handed the two letters to Phoebe. "Do 'ave a look at the seal of *this* one, Miss Vale," he murmured, with an upward wag of his eyebrows.

He tapped it with one finger and handed it over.

An elegant and unmistakable *R* was pressed into red wax.

Well!

Curiosity a bonfire, she took herself back to a sunny corner of the shop—she was of course *entirely* unaffected by the proximity to The Bonnet—after all, one could admire scenery without needing to own it, was that not true?—and slid her finger under the seal while Postlethwaite helped the girls choose gifts.

My dear Miss Vale,

I hope this finds you well and turning young hoydens into young ladies with as much alacrity as always. I apologize for the sudden nature of this message, but I should be delighted if you would join me for two days at Redmond House when I visit, beginning on Saturday. Mama and Papa are in Italy, as you know, and Mama is under the impression that I will not have a suitable friend or chaperone present for the duration of the visit, since my cousin Miss Violet, as you know, has lately become a countess and it is likely she will be in London with her husband. Mama will happily pay you for your time and Aunt Redmond approves. I have a surprise to share with you, too! I will tell you all about it when I see you. Oh, do say you'll come!

With affection,
Lisbeth Redmond

Well.
Well, well, well.
She'd once been engaged to tutor Lisbeth—niece to Isaiah and Fanchette Redmond, cousin of all the rest of them—in French. Phoebe spoke five languages fluently and was a more than competent teacher, but Lisbeth had been impressively resistant to learning. She preferred to acquire information by simply asking for it. But she was charming enough company. And her two-month stay with Lisbeth was how Phoebe knew about things like primrose satin and coronets. Her stay

with Lisbeth Redmond was also indirectly the reason Phoebe had once been kissed (and if the Redmonds had known this, she *certainly* wouldn't have been invited) and the reason she'd decided to leave the country.

Because staying with a family like the Redmonds—and they were so *emphatically* a family—had emphasized how she belonged nowhere, to no one, wasn't particularly wanted, and would never have the things the Redmonds had. It would be not only invigorating, she'd decided, but *essential*, to start her life over somewhere else entirely, someplace of *her* choosing, since the tide of fate had rather chosen everything for her to date.

Still. She *could* use a little extra money.

Not to mention a night or two in a featherbed, and excellent meals served on silver, and—

She would mull the invitation.

She knew who the other letter was from and what it would say. She would read it later in her rooms at the academy, and mull that, too.

She looked up when a shadow fell over the letter from Lisbeth. *Odd.* The day had been so astonishingly clear, so scoured by wind, it seemed unlikely a cloud would ever gain purchase in the sky.

She turned her head toward the window. And she nearly swayed with shock.

An enormous, pristine black landau had come to a halt in front of Postlethwaite's. Phoebe shielded her eyes against the sunbeam that bounced off the glittering glass and gold lamps and ricocheted off her beauty-loving heart before returning to set the coat of arms—gold leaf, from the looks of things—aglow. One of the horses gave its head a coquettish toss and restively raised a fine leg.

The horse was black.

Its stockings were white.

And Phoebe's heart jumped into her throat.

Because . . . Mother of God . . . hadn't the door just jingled . . .?

She held her body very gingerly when she turned, because if she *was* dreaming, she didn't want to accidentally jar herself awake.

She saw him, and the air in the room became thinner, headier, as though she'd been jerked up high and deposited on a mountaintop. He seemed taller than . . . anyone. And suddenly all the hats and ribbons and buttons and gloves seemed like gaudy props arranged on a stage, awaiting just his arrival all these years.

He swept the shop with a glance, taking in ribbons, gloves, Phoebe, hats, watches, her students, reticules, shawls and Postlethwaite, in that order and with equal dispassion.

His coat and boots were black.

His shirt and cravat were white.

And his voice, a baritone edged with smoke, was exactly how she'd imagined it.

"Dryden," he said.

As if it was the answer to all of life's most important questions.

Chapter 3

His name echoed all by itself in the shop long enough for everyone to begin wondering whether they'd imagined he'd spoken.

Up went one of his black eyebrows. Like an arrow.

Phoebe saw this in the mirror over the counter. Her view was now of the man's back, which rivaled the Alps for majesty. His shoulders narrowed to a waist in a line so fundamentally masculine she'd never been more unnervingly aware she was a woman. When he shifted his feet, she could almost sense the lovely slide of muscles beneath the black coat he wore with the same casual grace a panther wears its pelt.

Phoebe's students stood frozen in the corner like statues of girls for sale. Their eyes were so round they were more whites than pupil.

Postlethwaite darted a glance at Phoebe from over the top of his spectacles. She gave the slightest of nods in confirmation. *You're not hallucinating.*

"Mr. Postlethwaite at your service, my lord." His bow was deep and really very elegant, she thought, even despite the tiny cracking sound his spine made on its way up again. "You honor my humble establishment, indeed! What can I do for you today, my lord?"

She attempted to steal a glance at Dryden's gloves, the

ones that had allegedly cost one hundred pounds. But he'd pulled them from his fingers and bunched them in his fist. He lifted off his hat and held it, pushed his dark hair back from a high pale forehead. The candle flames of the chandelier swinging overhead danced, reflected in the polished toes of his boots—made by Hoby, she knew, because the broadsheets said so.

His bearing was almost aggressively erect.

He either didn't notice or didn't care that she was staring at him. Perhaps it would have been more notable if she *hadn't* been staring. She wondered if charisma—and his poured from him in veritable rays—was simply a patina formed from the accumulated stares of countless people over years.

"I should like to see your selection of silk fans, if you would, Mr. Postlethwaite."

His tone was brisk, impersonal, and surprisingly kind. But she heard restraint thrumming through it. He was clearly aware of his impact and was making a concerted effort not to frighten the rabble and freeze them like rabbits before wolves. After all, frozen people could not do his bidding.

Herself and Postlethwaite being the rabble, of course.

She half resented the loss of the game she played with Postlethwaite. Because it was clear that this was the sort of man who could never be a figure of fun.

But just in case she *was* dreaming, she succumbed to an impulse to reach across her body and pinch her own arm.

Too late she realized the marquess had a perfect view of her in the mirror over the counter.

He swiveled his body a quarter turn.

She felt his attention like an explosion of light smack in her solar plexus.

His cheekbones were high and stark, and somehow this made his gaze seem particularly potent, as though he were calmly viewing a siege from the crenellations of a castle. His eyes were clear, just a shade darker than whiskey.

Not a gentle face. Nor a safe face.

And not a face one could get accustomed to in a glance.

Three or four or fifteen more glances of the lingering sort, perhaps.

She touched a hand to her wind-ruddied face, as if it was a wand that could change her into a princess before his eyes.

He turned away without a change of expression.

Which was when she began breathing again.

"Of course, of course, my lord." A whiff of glee had entered Postlethwaite's voice. "I've a lovely selection of silk fans, from plain to ornate." He gestured to a case in a shadowy corner of the shop near the girls, far away from sunlight that could yellow or fade painted silk. "I hope you find something that pleases you."

Fat chance, Phoebe thought.

Postlethwaite bustled out from behind the counter and strutted across the floor. "May I ask what brings you to our town, Lord Dryden?"

"I've been invited to a party." She'd never heard the word *party* sound so ironic. "I am also here to visit Miss Endicott's storied academy on behalf of my niece."

Storied? Was it *really*? Was the niece the recalcitrant girl? And would he be attending the Redmonds' party? But where else would he be going?

"Miss Vale is a teacher at the academy." Postlethwaite made a vague gesture in her direction. The marquess dutifully turned.

She took advantage of the moment to show off her curtsy, while he devoted another tick of the clock to her. "An honor to meet you, Lord Dryden." Her tones were low, and, she liked to think, dulcet.

His long firm mouth turned up only faintly. Perhaps he calibrated smiles according to rank. This time she saw surprising faint shadows of fatigue beneath his eyes.

"Miss Vale." He gave her a bit of a bow. "I'm to meet with Miss Endicott at the academy."

The faintest conclusive emphasis landed on the words *Miss Endicott*. Likely he was accustomed to females of all sorts flinging themselves at him and hoped to discourage her from doing the same.

"Of course." Too late Phoebe heard the hint of irony in her voice: of course *you'll* be meeting with the *most important person* at the academy.

She could have sworn his eyes glinted swiftly. A flash, there and gone. Then again, it could just as easily have been the reflection from the gold leaf on his carriage's coat of arms.

When he turned away from her again to follow Postlethwaite toward the corner where the fans were kept, she made an emphatic nudging motion with her chin and raised her eyebrows at the frozen girls.

They stirred to life and curtsied as prettily as two little flowers drifting to the ground. The marquess gifted them with a brief and utterly charming smile and a little semi-bow which they would remember forever while he, Phoebe was sure, promptly forgot them.

When he'd passed Miss Runyon gripped Miss Carew by the elbow and silently slapped the back of her hand to her forehead, and began to buckle her knees in a faux swoon.

In order not to laugh, Phoebe fixed her with a quelling frown and motioned with her chin to the counter. The girls hastened to obey, each of them biting down on their lips to prevent giggling.

"Please do take your time with your selection, my lord," Postlethwaite told the marquess.

Phoebe doubted the marquess was tempted to do anything other than precisely what he wanted to do.

The bells on the door jingled yet again.

In walked an enormous blond man. Big and pale as a Viking, rectangular where the marquess was rather more . . . tapered. He whipped off his hat and swept back fair hair, and planted himself in the center of the room.

"Saw your carriage, Dryden." Almost a monotone, the voice, so low was it, as if nothing, nothing could divert him from his ennui. But so aristocratic it could have been carved from diamonds.

A flick of the eyes over his shoulder from the marquess. "Waterburn."

Phoebe had the distinct impression the marquess was stifling a resigned sigh. *Intriguing.*

Waterburn was the viscount known for whimsical wagers of staggering amounts. He'd once wagered five hundred pounds on a race between crickets, or so she'd read in the broadsheets.

Waterburn strolled deeper into the shop, pale eyes lighting upon ribbons, hats, and light fixtures like a Bow Street runner searching for evidence of a crime. "I think we may have been invited to the same party."

"I am stunned." The marquess's tone was ironic.

Waterburn smiled.

The marquess was now inspecting two fans he'd chosen from Postlethwaite's collection the way Leonora

Heron, one of the Gypsies who camped on the outskirts of Pennyroyal Green, pored over the tarot cards when she *dukkered* for paying visitors.

Envy washed over her, spiky and hot and surprising. Who? *Who* was special enough to warrant that sort of care in selection?

"Lord Waterburn." Postlethwaite was compelled to bow again. "Mr. Postlethwaite at your service. May I bring tea for Your Lordships?"

"None for me, but thank you for offering, Mr. Postlethwaite." This came from the marquess.

Waterburn's idle gaze lit upon Phoebe. She tried a smile and a nod. He dipped his great head unsmilingly, and turned away again.

For heaven's sake. She was growing a little tired of feeling like part of the decor.

Her students were rustling with the packages and preparing to leave. "Good day, Miss Vale. I hope you have a lovely holiday."

"Thank you, ladies. I hope yours is lovely as well. But please don't forget to read your Marcus Aurelius, or you will find yourselves behind in your lessons upon your return."

"Of course not, Miss Vale! I am looking forward to it *greatly!*" Miss Runyon lied passionately.

And off they went with a jangle of bells, letting in a rush of wind that fluttered the ribbons on the bonnets and lifted up the horseshoe of hair remaining on Postlethwaite's head, and then the door was shut once more.

Phoebe took one last hungry look at the bonnet that would never be hers and folded her message from Lisbeth so she could tuck it in her reticule along with her other letter.

Which was when the large blond lordship drifted,

much like a galleon, over to the marquess. "Ten pounds says even *you* cannot get a kiss from the . . . *la insegnante*, Dryden."

Insegnante? But . . . *insegnante* was Italian for *teacher*.

Waterburn jerked his chin in her direction.

She went numb with shock. *He means for the marquess to kiss me!*

She whirled immediately around again and began fondling the lavender ribbon on the bonnet, and listened.

"For God's sake, Waterburn. What need have I of a kiss from her *or* ten pounds?" the marquess murmured, sounding bored.

"But that's just it. She hardly looks *kissable,* wouldn't you agree?" Waterburn insisted. *"Un*kissable, in fact. And yet it's said, Dryden, that you can get one anytime you please from anyone you please. I say . . . well, from the looks of things, you *cannot."*

From the looks of things? What things? The tips of her fingers turned white and bloodless from gripping the ribbon.

The marquess's voice had an edge now. "Don't be ridiculous. It would be child's play."

Oh.

Mortification scorched the entire surface of her skin. She couldn't breathe for it. The bonnet blurred in front of her eyes.

As Postlethwaite's hearing wasn't what it once was, he seemed entirely unaffected. He was now happily counting money, which jingled in his palms, and whistling through his teeth, which likely drowned out scandalous murmurs.

"Then it's a wager, Dryden. And we *know* you never lose wagers."

Phoebe held herself still, as though she'd just taken a great fall. Trying not to breathe or feel, the satiny ribbon in her fingers an alien contrast to her abraded pride. She stared at the bonnet she coveted and would never have, while a man she'd once coveted and would never have dismissed the notion that she might be *kissable* and painstakingly selected a gift for another woman. Whereupon he would climb once again into that behemoth of a carriage and be driven to the academy whilst she ran up the hill again, doing battle with a wind determined to tear off her old bonnet.

Bloody *aristocrats*.

How very disappointing to discover they were mortal and childish.

The marquess straightened abruptly. Reminding Phoebe once more of just how unfairly tall he was.

"This one, Mr. Postlethwaite." He'd chosen the painted fan. It was ivory silk, scattered with a few pale pink blooms twined with very fine, pale green thornless stems. Exquisite.

Naturally.

"Very good, sir!" Postlethwaite all but vaulted the counter in his eagerness to assist.

Not one of the men had looked at her again.

"Thank you for the mail, Postlethwaite," she said crisply, managing to sound cheery enough. "Good day."

She left the shop trailing a hand in a farewell wave before he could answer. She gave the legendary carriage a good shunning as she swept past it, when every fiber in her being wanted to feast her eyes, and maybe pat a glossy horse. She dove back into the wind. It was uphill to the academy from Postlethwaite's. She was suddenly aware that much of her life had always been precisely, metaphorically like that: uphill into the wind.

It was a very good thing she found uphill climbs invigorating, then. Even fortifying.

And the wind soon took the rest of the marquess-inspired mortification flush out of her cheeks and then set to work scouring it red again, putting the Sussex back into it.

Chapter 4

The seats of his landau were as plush as his last mistress's thighs, but when Jules leaned back and closed his eyes, his thoughts were hardly sensual.

And besides, his last mistress had tried to kill him with a vase.

He half dozed, eyes lowered, but as usual his responsibilities ran through his mind like beads on a rosary. He'd hired excellent people to work for him, to worry for him, to manage his properties and oversee his investments, and yet vigilance remained almost a pleasurable vice. He found it difficult to release. He hadn't slept solidly since he was seventeen, when his reckless Roman candle of a father, in his final spectacular act, had gotten himself killed in a duel over a woman . . . who wasn't his wife. He'd loved her, he told the ton at large. And love was worth dying for.

All this, of course, after years of steadily losing properties and money and stature in games of chance.

And by all accounts, having the time of his life doing all of it.

He'd left behind debts, disaster, and disgrace, all of which Jules had methodically righted. The years had been harrowing; but he was clever and strategic and shrewd and coldly, ruthlessly determined. He never put a foot wrong. He'd regained family property, amassed a new fortune, and gained untold power and influence. His dignity was unassailable, seemingly impenetrable.

And while his father had been a glorious, gorgeous wreck, at the mercy of his impulses, in the end, despite his ancient title, a subject of mockery . . . *no one* dared mock Julian Spenser.

He ran his thoughts over another bead. His family was safe and comfortable. His sisters married well. Crises and needs came and went; they turned to him to solve them, and it was what he did, because he did it best.

And then there was bloody Waterburn. Who was really a minor irritant, but seemingly omnipresent. Like a gnat, if a blond giant could be said to resemble a gnat. He'd never forgive Jules for winning the favors of the lush Carlotta Medina, or, for that matter, for being Julian Spenser: always ahead of him in school, promoted ahead of him in the army, a better shot, and by all accounts, a better lover, whose cool discrimination—not to mention the looks he'd inherited from his father—women found maddeningly compelling.

Of course, in hindsight, the victory was rather hollow, since Carlotta had been fiery and acrobatic in bed and really quite unmanageable out of it. Mad as a hatter, demanding and spoiled and very confusing, all told. An alarming episode.

Not that he didn't sometimes still imagine Carlotta in bed, and for that he would always be grateful.

Women. He smiled to himself.

No wonder everyone wanted to be Lord Dryden.

The *irony* was that not even Lord Dryden was really Lord Dryden. And this, too, mostly suited him.

And almost no one remembered his father now.

No one, of course, but Isaiah Redmond. Because Isaiah Redmond held the final piece of land that Julian wanted.

Needed.

But over the years Julian had acquired the vision and finesse of a chess master, assessing the social and business landscape in order to make the proper moves at precisely the right moment, the ones that assured his victory, the ones that assured he got exactly what he wanted.

The fan was part of that. He fingered the tissue-wrapped package. It was an excellent choice for a gift, an excellent place to embark on his new campaign. He knew a quiet satisfaction.

Only one thing stood between him and the estate in Sussex that had been his mother's dowry.

Perhaps he would finally rest when it was his.

As it inevitably would be.

He lowered his eyelids, closing out the rolling Sussex landscape, but he didn't sleep.

Phoebe raced up the stairs to her room, clawed the ribbons of her bonnet undone and flung it aside, jerked her chair out from her desk, whipped out a sheet of foolscap so swiftly Charybdis, her striped cat, shot to his feet from his feline languor on her bed. He collapsed again, yawning, when he saw it was only her.

They'd both been scrawny underfed ill-tempered scraps prone to rebellion when she'd dragged him here from London as a young girl. Both had become refined and filled out and grateful for their comforts.

But both were still wild at heart.

Charybdis was in fact a fluffy trap. He liked to sleep upside down, his tempting soft belly exposed to the

world. When unsuspecting visitors reached down to
sink a hand into all that downy fur—*SNAP!* He closed
all his limbs and clung with teeth and claws and
wouldn't let go. It had proved embarrassing more than
once. Also, very funny. It kept curious students from
even considering exploring her room.

Bloody aristocrats, she thought. Why would I want to
spend another moment in their presence? Especially if
he might be there.

She plunged her quill into the well of ink and began:

Dear Lisbeth—

*Thank you so much for your kind invitation, and as
delightful as it would be to see you again, I fear I will
not be able to—*

She jerked her head up from her foolscap when the
tap sounded at her door.

She sighed gustily enough to send her half-written
message fluttering, pushed back her chair, abandoned
her work, and flung the door open.

The maid standing there leaped backward, perhaps
to get out of the reach of the flames shooting from
Phoebe's eyes.

With an effort, Phoebe composed her face into more
placid planes. Mary Frances, who was short and round
and had springy rusty red curls, offered the sort of
wobbly conciliatory smile you might show an armed
looby to discourage them from lunging. She dipped a
little curtsy.

"Beggin' yer pardon, Miss Vale, and sorry to inter-
rupt yer important work," she peered curiously past
her into the simple room, at the two thick rag rugs,

the bed covered with an eccentric quilt she'd stitched
from dresses and pelisses she'd dismembered when she
couldn't coax any more wear from them. "Miss Endicott would like a word with you before she leaves."

Phoebe drew in a steadying breath. Mary Frances
thought they were all very clever and did important
work here at the academy, which was rather sweet and
soothing.

"Thank you, Mary Frances."

Miss Endicott was about to leave on holidays, too,
she knew, but she'd left the running of the academy in
the hands of senior teachers Mrs. Bundicraft and Mrs.
Fleeger.

Phoebe turned to the oval mirror nailed up over her
bureau and gave her fine, fair hair a cursory smoothing, shook out her skirts and gave *them* a cursory
smoothing, and then hurried down the long hallway
and darted down the winding stairs, one hand sliding along that deliciously smooth banister polished by
generations of recalcitrant young ladies doing that very
thing, just as she had when she was young.

She came to a halt in the doorway of Miss Endicott's
office to avoid colliding with a big black wall.

The wall turned around slowly and proved to be the
marquess.

"Ah, there you are, Miss Vale." Miss Endicott managed to make it sound as if she'd been waiting for her
all afternoon. She was dressed for travel in an elegant
gray wool dress and matching pelisse and a splendid
gray-lavender felt hat. A packed portmanteau sat atop
her great polished desk. A trunk was lined up next to
it on the floor.

"I'd hoped you'd show the marquess at least one of
the upper-floor classrooms, as I must leave at once or

miss the mail coach, and my sister, I assure you, will never forgive me if I arrive an entire day late for our visit as she has a full program of entertainments devised." She pulled on a pair of gloves as she spoke. "I felt it of value that His Lordship should speak with one of our teachers in residence. He mentioned he had the pleasure of making your acquaintance in Postlethwaite's."

Miss Endicott's eyes were small, blue, and piercing. She was another in a long line of Miss Marietta Endicotts who ran the academy with the skill of a general, the finesse of an orchestra conductor, and business wiles that might make even Isaiah Redmond blush. She was in fact very kind, a secret all the girls in the school eventually uncovered.

Mind you, it took a good deal of digging to uncover it. And she was kind, but never weak. *Implacable* was in fact a better word for her.

A decade or so had accustomed Phoebe to the gaze, and yet she had never been able to defy it or lie to it. Not once. And she'd once been able to defy *everything*.

Her skin heated again from a mix of emotions and sensations, none of them compatible.

"Of course," Phoebe said evenly. "We had the . . . pleasure."

Miss Endicott paused in her glove pulling-on and stared at her with mild incredulity until Phoebe dipped a desultory curtsy in the general direction of the marquess. He returned the favor by nodding in her general direction.

Neither of them had looked at each other.

The marquess in fact showed no sign of being affected by her presence at all. The same suppressed impatience rolled in waves from him, the kind that made one want to shift their feet or fidget, do something, any-

thing, as long as it was his bidding. He was casting his
eyes over the furnishings of Miss Endicott's office and
lightly slapping his hat against the palm of his hand.
Whap . . . whap . . . whap. As if marking off how many
more precious minutes of his life he'd need to devote
to his tedious visit to a school for girls.

"I shall be grateful if you would show me a classroom, Miss Vale," he said at last.

He was exquisitely polite. Though he likely would
have said "I should like you to stuff it, Miss Vale," in
the same tone.

He was looking at her now.

"I shall be happy to do it." She could be exquisitely
polite, too. Still, she directed this to his left eyebrow, to
avoid looking straight into his gold eyes.

He nodded, as if there had never been any question
of this. He turned to address Miss Endicott.

"My sincere thanks, Miss Endicott, for your time,
and I hope you enjoy a safe and pleasant journey."

"Thank you. I expect to, Lord Dryden," she said
briskly, and no journey would ever dare defy Miss
Endicott by being anything other than pleasurable or
uneventful.

So Phoebe curtsied to Miss Endicott, too, but Miss
Endicott swept past her, gave her a kiss on one cheek,
followed it with a little kid-clad pat as if to drive the
kiss into Phoebe's very soul, and then tugged on the
bell for a footman.

She stared after the departing headmistress.

Phoebe supposed it was evidence of the fact that she
was no longer strictly a green girl that the headmistress
saw naught amiss with sending her to the upper floors
alone with a handsome marquess.

She was only twenty-two! For heaven's *sake*. And in

a single day she'd received a letter asking her to chaperone a girl hardly younger than she was, and had then been deemed unkissable.

"If you would follow me, Lord Dryden."

She spun on her boot heels and aimed for the staircase. She was tempted to scale them two at a time, to bolt away from him. Over the years, Phoebe had learned to keep her rebellious impulses in check by shoveling in information the way one fed coal to a furnace. She was an excellent teacher, but primarily because she understood recalcitrant girls so well it bordered on unfair. Certainly she could keep those impulses in check now.

He followed her, and in seconds was flanking her, despite her insultingly brisk pace. She sensed he was politely matching his pace to hers. He called to mind a tethered stallion who had decided to humor her with temporary docility.

Her pace accelerated. She risked a glance over her shoulder. She saw a short white hair—his own?—clinging to the arm of his coat. For an instant it made him seem unbearably human. Accessible. An absurd notion, no doubt.

She knew very well how to spout pleasantries and to charm. Still, she stubbornly refused to speak.

So he did. "I'm given to understand that teachers here at the school advocate solving the problems of . . ." He was delicately searching for a word.

"Recalcitrance?" she completed brightly.

". . . very well, then, recalcitrance—by filling the girls' minds with facts?"

Odd. He sounded . . . well, she might have said half-amused. Perhaps skeptical.

"Engaging intellectual curiosity, Lord Dryden, and

instilling intellectual discipline, keeps them too busy to misbehave. Though naturally they *will* try."

"Naturally."

"All, shall we say, *misguided* high spirits, can be transmuted into grace and confidence and respect, if such is expected of them, and such is extended to them. And if much is expected of them."

"Ah. Quite the philosophy. A straw into gold sort of thing?" He sounded ironic again. And doubtful. And weary.

Which made her wonder about the girl he was proposing to install here.

"If you wish. May I inquire for whom you are investigating our premises?" She did have a duty to the young lady who might soon be joining their numbers here.

She was impressed with herself so far. She was very, very polite. She was very, very prim. No nun would ever be so sedate, so proper, so disinterested.

It would all be so much easier, of course, if he didn't smell so wonderful.

Starch and very good tobacco, maybe a bit of . . . horse? But she liked the smell of horse. A hint of sea breeze, as if he'd actually walked for a bit out in the hills. He smelled manly. He smelled like wealth.

She wouldn't have minded in the least *licking* him, and she'd never had a thought like that in her entire life.

Unkissable, she reminded herself.

"My niece was caught smoking a cheroot. Twice. Among other things. She's twelve years old and her father is on his third wife in six years, and the latest one cannot tolerate her. I'm given to understand that the feeling is mutual. I'm here on business for my brother, who is away in Northumberland at present.

Since I'd planned to be in Sussex I offered to do . . . reconnaissance."

"Her third mother? Good heavens. The poor thing. I suppose you should be grateful she hasn't taken to drink."

He turned his head toward her sharply. She sensed he was uncertain whether to smile or frown, and was tempted to do the former, but was uncertain of *her*.

Perhaps it *had* been a bit too impulsively said. And she'd gotten such excellent control over her impulses over the years.

"Do the girls emerge quite ruined for marriage after you stuff them full of knowledge?"

And *now* she suspected he was sending out a subtle foray to test her wit . . . or marital status. And again, here was that suspicion that he was so bored with the proceedings that he'd decided to do anything at all to divert himself, and that included goading her.

Perhaps he was attempting to charm her in order to make her more *kissable*.

"I should imagine most of our girls emerge less tolerant of fools, if that's what you mean." She added, "Ha-ha!" unconvincingly when he looked genuinely startled.

"You've naught to fear, Lord Dryden," she placated hurriedly, remembering that regardless of where she wound up living in the world, she liked Miss Endicott and the academy could use the marquess's money. "We're proud of the diversity of skills imparted to the young ladies here. They will leave prepared to raise families, run large households, play the pianoforte, embroider, and pore over their husband's books to ensure their Men of Affairs aren't stealing from them. In short, we prepare them to manage nearly any circumstance."

"Or nearly any man."

That was so quickly said she didn't have time to bite back a surprised laugh.

He smiled then. No baring of white teeth, mind you, just a curve of the lips, a show of dimple, a crease at the corner of his eyes. But suddenly he reached out and drew a casual finger along the fine moulding lining the hallway. Like a boy might do. Almost as though he was *enjoying* himself. Relaxing into her company.

He wouldn't find any dust, of that she was certain. The school employed a battery of maids.

Unkissable, she reminded herself.

She wondered again if the party he was attending was hosted by the Redmonds.

"And languages," she added pointedly. "We try to make certain our girls can speak at least one other language fluently. Such as Italian. For instance. Which I speak. Fluently."

"Do you?" he said absently. "Languages are useful. Tell me, since you speak so many languages . . . do you know what . . ." he tipped his head back in thought and recited carefully, as if from memory '¡Esto es lo que pienso en su regalo, hijo de una puta!' means? I believe it's Spanish."

Mother of *God.*

He turned to her, eyes wide and hopeful.

It was Spanish, all right.

"Were the words . . . shall we say, shouted at *you,* by any chance, Lord Dryden?"

"They might have been," he allowed benignly.

She studied him closely; his face was blandly patient.

"Because it means '*This* is what I think of your gift!'"

It actually meant, "This is what I think of your gift, you son of a whore!" and she was positive the devil knew this full well and likely spoke Spanish fluently. Given that he'd allegedly once had a temperamental Spanish mistress.

Or so the broadsheets would have one think.

"Huh! Imagine that." He sneaked another sideways look at her. Inviting her, *daring* her to laugh.

Oh, bloody hell. The trouble was, she was picturing *this man* with his mistress, which effectively sent her thoughts scattering like billiard balls. She took a deep breath.

A mistake! In came the scent of him again, and her head swam.

This wasn't going at all the way she'd intended.

"We were speaking of curriculum," he prompted mildly. When it seemed she would never speak.

Mary Frances was scurrying toward them from the far-end of the hallway, bearing a feather duster. They could see her eyes from ten feet away, big and round and more white than pupil thanks to the marquess.

She bustled past them after a nervously dipped curtsy, then darted back to dust the portrait of the current Miss Endicott, as if it was omniscient and would clear its throat if she shirked an opportunity to do just that.

"Of course. And *speaking* of our demanding curriculum, Lord Dryden, it's the reason we prefer to admit only the cleverest girls. I imagine Miss Endicott told you we conduct interviews to ascertain our pupils will be equal to what we present in the classroom."

"I imagine the cleverest girls are often the wealthiest?"

She had a sense of him now.

"It's serendipitous how often this is true."

His sudden delighted, wicked grin cracked like

lightning against the surface politeness of the conversation. It made . . . *everything* . . . better.

Just as quickly it vanished again.

"Mind you." Her words emerged hoarse, as if his smile had interfered with her ability to breathe. She stopped to clear her throat. "Mind you, we feel it necessary to inform the parents of every girl of fine family that we also admit the occasional girl who hasn't a farthing to her name or any pedigree to speak of, and we educate all of the girls equally. We find this helps to build the characters of all the girls present."

He stopped abruptly to stare up at a nicely done Sussex landscape with genuine appreciation. One of their former students had painted it.

No mediocre pictures hung in the hallways of Miss Endicott's Academy. She wouldn't stand for it.

"By exposing girls of privilege to ruffians?"

"And by exposing ruffians to girls of privilege."

"Much the way jewels are tumbled and polished, I suppose," he surmised. "Through . . . friction."

He tossed a sly look over his shoulder.

Good heavens, but that was dry. She liked it very much.

It also sounded, to her sensitized nerves . . . like an innuendo. Like he was indeed building up to . . . something.

Get a hold of yourself, Vale. She drew herself up to her full height and straightened her shoulders, a sort of unconscious attempt to make herself larger and more intimidating, the way certain South American lizards do.

She knew about South American lizards because she'd read about them in Mr. Miles Redmond's books. She read about everything, really.

"I prefer not to think of it as friction, Lord Dryden. Rather, as exposure to . . . different surfaces."

Good God, but *that* sounded a little erotic, too.

Then again . . . perhaps she'd meant it to.

The effect was dramatic. He turned. His pupils flared interestedly. His mouth didn't smile at all.

And good God, those eyes were potent when he wasn't blinking.

Un-kiss-a-ble, taunted the Greek Chorus in her head.

She hastened to clarify, "They aren't necessarily ruffians, you know, simply because they're poor. Many are simply girls who may have . . . experienced a different start in life, or may have encountered a bump in . . . shall we say, destiny's road."

She'd regretted it as it was on its way out of her mouth. What a *purple* way to say it.

There was a little silence.

"Destiny's . . . road . . ." he finally repeated thoughtfully. Just in case she missed how ridiculous it had sounded the first time.

His eyes glinted insufferably.

He was daring her again not to smile. As if he knew, he knew precisely who she was beneath the primness and was determined to extract her true self from her before he departed.

She realized then that at some point she'd folded her hands behind her back. Why? To prevent them from touching him? She wasn't *quite* that reckless.

Then again, it was also entirely possibly she'd never been quite this tempted.

Their eyes reflected deviltry back to each other.

Child's play, he'd said, she reminded herself. *Why should I want a kiss from her?* It echoed in her mind. *Child's play child's play child's play.*

She repeated it in her mind until her flirting impulses were drubbed into a humiliated stupor.

Child's play? Oh, we shall see, Lord Dryden.

He must have sensed a change in the temperature of the conversation, for he suddenly became brisk and very official again.

"The school's reputation precedes it, Miss Vale. And the academy has a generous benefactor in Mr. Isaiah Redmond."

"And in Mr. Jacob Eversea."

The patriarchs of Pennyroyal Green were not averse to having a school in their midst, as long as it was a respected, well-run school stocked with girls whose fathers had titles and political connections.

She moved on, and he followed, and they at last reached the end of the hallway. The door to one of the main classrooms was open wide, and out of it poured the scent of linseed oil and a wash of lemony light. The maids had clearly only recently efficiently completed their work and departed. The marquess paused, peered in. He could hardly find fault with the sight of glowing wood floors and rows of dusted, polished tables and chairs, or the three arched windows reaching to nearly the height of the ceiling set into the back wall. The sun poured through them. Bookshelves lined the wall inside the door. A handsome globe presided over the front of the classroom. The enormous, unadorned fireplace at the far end was cold now and the hearth swept clean.

The room was resoundingly empty, thanks to the impending school holiday.

She hovered in the hall behind him while he peered in. As though he was contemplating whether to go inside or not.

And that's when her heart accelerated like a carriage pushed downhill.

Because if he was going to win a *wager*, so to speak, this would be the perfect place to attempt it. And if *she* was going to make a point . . . well then, once again, this would be the perfect place to attempt it.

Time stretched torturously. Her heart beat a good one thousand times if it beat once in the silence that followed.

She stared at his feet. She gave a start when they shifted . . . and he quite casually strolled into the room.

His shining Hoby boots echoed portentously on the floor. He paused in a slant of sunlight sent in through the first of the windows. She saw red hidden in his dark hair, like embers in a coal fire. Lines at the corners of his eyes.

He's meant for me.

The thought emerged from nowhere, fresh as a slap and seemed as true as it was dumbfounding. She stared at him, bewildered. She'd never had a thought like that in her entire life. An ache started up, a barbed, hopeless longing. It was as though she knew him, had always known him, all his foibles and flaws and passions, in moments quiet and playful. As irrational a thought as she'd ever had.

She blamed the dramatic lighting. Surely once he stepped out of it the feeling would go away.

He wasn't looking at her. He was quietly surveying the grounds through the window. It was a quintessentially Sussex view of low rolling green hills and trees which were rapidly losing their leaves as autumn got under way in earnest. This wasn't the side that faced the sea. There wasn't much to remark upon. Or criticize.

And yet still he stood there and said nothing.

Was he trying to lure her in with silence?

She would need to make a decision.

To her surprise, something besides her mind had already made the decision for her. She heard her own walking boots echo across the floor. Her blood rang in her ears, so hard was her heart hammering.

He turned away from the view.

Their eyes met.

The silence suddenly seemed so total she felt deafened.

She wondered if he was actually bracing himself for the moment of . . . lunging? How did one get a kiss from a teacher for ten pounds? Surely he ought to have been charming her toward that eventuality? Surely he ought to be standing closer in order to snake one of those long arms around her and—

And suddenly it was too much. She could hardly bear the suspense.

"Well. I see nothing objectionable and *much* to recommend the school," he said finally.

Was *that* an innuendo?

"Your endorsement is ringing, Lord Dryden." Suspense, and resentment, and pride, and that fruitless yearning was turning everything she said dry, dry, dry.

But he seemed to like it, oddly. A quick smile haunted his mouth again. She liked what smiles did to his eyes, and how it felt to be looked at by him. She contemplated for a wild instant that he might be . . . shy. She knew the difference between distracted and awkward, between indifferent and preoccupied, and though he was clearly a man at home in his skin and in the world, he seemed at something of a loss here.

Perhaps it had to do with the gulf between their classes.

Or perhaps he was steeling his nerve to get a kiss from the schoolteacher, when he really hadn't the will to do it. Let alone for a mere ten pounds.

Mere for him, that was.

Oh, for heaven's *sake*. She could stand it no longer.

"Well, Lord Dryden. You may as well get it over with."

The smile vanished. "I beg your pardon?"

"You're going to try to kiss me, aren't you?"

Chapter 5

The marquess froze. His face was an immobile blank for an instant. He parted his mouth. He closed it again. He parted it again.

And then gave his head a little shake.

"I *beg* your pardon? Why would you think . . . I beg your *pardon?*"

She'd made him *stammer*.

"Well, here we are alone. You've a reputation for accepting and winning wagers. But I suppose the primary reason I think that is that I *heard* your friend urge you to do it. Ten pounds, I believe the wager was. Imagine! You could buy the finger of one glove for that amount."

Such a fascinating play of emotions chased each other across his face. Guilt and comprehension and horror and irritation and an undeniable prurient curiosity and . . .

She didn't expect to like the expression that at last settled in:

Good-humored defeat.

"Well, *announcing* it certainly takes all the fun out of it."

And there were a number of things she could say. And she knew what she *shouldn't* say.

"*All* of the fun?"

She'd said it, anyway.

Silence. And then:

"Miss Vale?" he said carefully.

"Yes?"

"Are you . . . flirting with me?"

"Would it surprise you if I said yes?"

"Well . . ."

She was laughing silently at him. "Because I'm plain, and I shouldn't have such skills at my disposal, and because you've only learned one way to play the game, and it involves *you* applying the charm and the maiden capitulating? Don't you ever *tire* of it? Of things always being the *same*?"

She clasped her hands in front of her, leaning into the question with mock earnestness.

He floundered. "Yes—no! That is, you're not plain."

Jules didn't know whether this last was true or not, but out it had come. And certainly it was the wisest thing to say under the circumstances. Surely if she was a beauty he would have *noticed*?

"Oh, I *know*. My complexion is very fine. So I've been told. Often enough to believe it." She was wickedly amused.

Jules was shocked to realize that this chit was *toying* with him.

He took a moment to compose himself. He couldn't recall the last time he'd *needed* to compose himself. There was no question that Waterburn's wager had inserted itself in his awareness like a burr. He found Waterburn altogether a damned burr.

He'd thought she was quick, which he approved of. She didn't lack wit. He'd sensed a suppressed energy about her since he'd seen her in Postlethewaite's, but he'd thought then it had been contained passion for a bonnet. She'd been staring at one as though it were an oracle.

He didn't want to kiss her.

Did he?

But now this girl thought he was actually feckless. Which was ironic, given that fecklessness was a luxury he'd never known. And bloody hell, but now he was assessing her complexion and trying to prevent her from noticing that he was doing exactly that.

And in the light filtered in through the high windows . . . well, comparisons to pearls would not be inaccurate. She radiated health and luster and . . . life. She did rather glow.

"It isn't *unappealing*," he allowed.

"Oh, now. You needn't gush."

He felt the smile begin and then slowly take hold; he couldn't help himself.

"Should I apologize for my species for trotting out the same compliment again and again? Isn't it better than having none at all?"

"When you hear the same one again and again, it's difficult not to come to the conclusion that it's the only thing of note about one's person."

She still sounded amused. As if it was all the same to her. He didn't think he'd ever encountered a more self-possessed female. Then again, doubtless she'd honed her confidence on the characters of unruly young ladies. What challenge would a marquess pose in the face of that?

"Have pity on us. We cannot all of us be poets. We think it's what women expect to hear, and so we do our duty. Consider the possibility that your admirers are so dumbstruck by the wonder that is your complexion they can see nothing else."

"Oh, excellent theory! I shall give it due consideration."

"Your eyes have gone unattended in compliments?"

"Are you about to compliment my eyes, Lord Dryden?"

"I wouldn't dare. You'd find my compliment wanting and I shall feel a fool."

She smiled at him, thoroughly delighted. Perhaps even a little surprised.

He found himself smiling in return, absurdly gratified to have pleased her.

A moment ticked by during which only smiling took place, and which the air itself seemed peculiarly effervescent, and breathing it made him feel weightless.

Why hadn't anyone complimented her smile? It was very good. Her eyes—whatever color they may be, and he still wasn't certain whether they were green or gray—lit with it as surely as though they were lamps, and dimples appeared at the corners, reminding him she was a schoolteacher, as they seemed as charming and necessary to her smile as punctuation to a sentence or bookends to a row of . . . books.

Hardly poetic, but at least it was a metaphor.

"Perhaps the fault *is* all mine." She tapped a finger to her chin thoughtfully. "Or perhaps it's just that I've met no men who've imaginations worth firing."

It sounded like a flirtation gauntlet thrown down.

"That could very well be," he allowed, very cautiously.

What sort of men was a schoolteacher likely to meet? Farmer? Vicars? Other teachers? Soldiers? Was she *daring* him to charm her?

He was a *marquess*.

A marquess who, coincidentally, liked a dare. Almost as much as he disliked entanglements. And wagers foisted upon him.

"Have you been to London?" he asked her.

A peculiar hesitation. "Yes."

"One can meet . . . a wide variety of people in London."

She found this very funny. "You're proposing I diversify my experience of men in order to hear better compliments? Fear not. I do plan to go abroad. Very abroad. I ought to meet a good many types of gentlemen en route."

Deeper and deeper he fell into the conversation, fascinated despite himself. "Where do you plan to go?"

Another brief hesitation.

"I should like to go to Africa."

"Africa!" She may as well have said the moon. What on earth did one say to this? Missionaries did go on missions to Africa. He imagined they needed teachers.

"To . . . work?" He delivered the word gingerly, after a pause.

She burst into laughter.

It was the best thing he'd heard in a very long time, that laugh, better than any opera or musicale, better than birdsong or the sound of hooves clattering around a racetrack or the sighs of a mistress or any of his other favorite sounds. Her eyes vanished completely and her head tipped back and he could even see molars. He basked, astonished and pleased.

"Oh, my goodness, Lord Dryden. You should have seen your face when you said the word *work*. It's not counted among the deadly sins, you know. But I thought, yes, that's what I would do there."

"With . . . missionaries?" He frantically riffled his

brain for anything at all he knew about Africa and why people would go there. "Perhaps to teach?"

"Yes."

"Because . . . you are so saintly?"

Imagine that. Now he *was* flirting a little.

The smile she gave him here was the very opposite of saintly. Slow, and crooked and pure imp.

She didn't say a word. The smile answered for her. And to his surprise, he felt that smile at the nape of his neck, and in places lower on his body.

"Or perhaps it's because you have need of reforming?" He'd lowered his voice.

She dodged that question, too.

Losing your nerve, Madame Schoolteacher?

"I want to see the world, quite simply."

"Some people start with Italy. Or Brighton."

"I thought perhaps I would begin at the far end and work my way back."

He laughed. He was officially enjoying himself. "I was simply taking a guess, you know, regarding the work. The possibility remained that perhaps you were going with your husband for his own duties, or to take in the climate, which is like living atop a stove, from what I understand. And a woman should not have to . . ."

He realized what he was about to say and stopped himself.

"Work? It's all right. I shan't tell anyone you used the dreaded *W* word multiple times in front of me."

". . . if she has a husband, brother, or father to care for her."

"Precisely," was all she said.

So she'd none of those in her life? Who then, did she have? Surely she was young enough—or old enough—

to have any or all of them. She possessed all of her limbs and she wasn't otherwise deformed. Surely she could have married by now if she'd wished to. Perhaps she was a widow? She didn't look or act the part.

"It's just . . . well . . ." She took a deep breath. "Honestly, Lord Dryden, aren't you ever bored with the same pleasures and pursuits? Don't you ever feel . . . *confined*?"

Imagine anyone asking him such a question.

"What makes you think I indulge in the same pleasures and pursuits often enough to bore of them?

"I read the London broadsheets."

Oh.

"It hasn't been all unrelieved *debauchery*, you know. I am particular about my pleasures."

"You don't say."

His mouth tipped up at the corner. "I have a number of pressing duties."

"Attending to your estate*s*." She lingered on that final *S* with gentle mockery.

Well, it *was* true he had as many estates as he had titles. More, in fact. His responsibilities were legion. His skill at delegating them was unparalleled. Because he of course, with an unerring instinct, hired the very best men for the jobs.

Would that he could hire men of affairs to manage his *family*.

"They are an ever-present responsibility, yes. The gossip sheets don't write about the fact that I've arranged for new drainage ditches in my Hereford estates."

"Is that so?" She sounded fascinated. "Drainage ditches?"

"Or that I've acquired an excellent herd of sheep and am profiting greatly from wool."

"Wool is one of England's finest resources."

"And I served as an officer in the army."

"Very impressive. I've been told that war is boredom interspersed with violence and terror."

So she *had* known a few soldiers. In *what* way had she known the soldiers? he wondered. He could imagine the soldiers serving under his command being enchanted with her. It was the lively women they met on the Continent to whom they were ultimately grateful for making the war more bearable, not necessarily the beautiful ones.

"Oh, that's not all it is. If a man *really* applies himself in the army, he can learn an untold number of curse words and catch all manner of diseases. Not to mention acquire a few interesting scars."

"Have you any diseases?" Unflatteringly, she sounded more curious than concerned.

"None that have a prayer of killing me or you in the course of this conversation."

Her smile appeared again, starting slowly and spreading. He liked the slow smile, because then it seemed to last longer, and light her face gradually, and it was like watching the sun rise. Or watching a . . . beginning. Of any kind.

He was perilously close to feeling . . . well, *happy*, for lack of another word . . . in an unusual way, and yet his nerves felt pulled taut as harpsichord strings. It had been some time since he'd felt surprised by a conversation. Let alone a conversation with a woman. He couldn't anticipate what she would say next, and this wasn't true of anyone else he knew.

Then again, he didn't think he'd ever had a conversation with a schoolmistress.

Confined.

And now that she'd said it, he could almost feel the sides of an invisible box all around him.

"And a man can make friends for life, too, in the army," he said evenly, feeling the need to defend the institution. "It's helpful to know who will die for you."

"And do you know?"

"I do know. Do you?"

Odd, but he thought a shadow darkened her eyes then. Whatever it was, it was there and gone just as quickly. And he'd learned in the space of this conversation that her eyes disguised very little.

"Friends are important," she agreed, instead.

He raised his eyebrows to let her know he knew full well she'd dodged the question.

She regarded him evenly and gave him back nothing but a pair of similarly raised brows. He suspected she would have grave difficulty ever hiding her thoughts completely, given how her eyes lit with humor and intelligence. The person she was, a crackling, complicated one, seemed to shine through.

He really ought to attend to the business at hand.

"Are *you* often bored, Miss . . . ?" Bloody hell. He'd breeding enough to be ashamed at the loss of her name.

"Vale," she reminded him, sweetly. Not offended. Amused.

He couldn't help it: he was genuinely curious. It had never occurred to him that any of the women with whom he was acquainted might be bored enough to bolt to Africa, of all places. They seemed so *occupied*, with things that mystified and often charmed him but when taken altogether, or God help him, *discussed* in his presence, sent him into the sort of foot-shifting, eye-darting, finger-drumming panic that not even having a pistol aimed his way could achieve. The minutiae of aristocratic womanhood. Embroidery and modistes and the like.

And this was a woman who *worked*. Why should she be bored?

"I am grateful for my work at the academy. The girls are a pleasure and Miss Endicott a very fair and kind employer. I suppose one must be cursed with an imagination to be bored."

"And you are cursed with such?"

He asked it neutrally. Carefully. Because he was acquainted with one or two "imaginative" women. They wrote florid poetry and read horrid novels and sang with an excess of passion during evening musicales, attacking the pianoforte keys like pouncing animals and pulling faces. They often took the form of mistresses who threw vases at one's head when one took their permanent leave of them by way of a quick, polite farewell and an expensive gift.

"Perhaps."

"Hence Africa. The imagination caused it."

"I suppose." She clearly wasn't eager to expound. He wondered if she was bored with *him*.

"Your imagination has an impressive reach."

"Or my boredom an impressive scope."

He smiled again.

She drew in a short sharp breath. There was some emotion she was suppressing at that moment, he was certain of it. Something very like pain. She dropped her eyes and sent them in search of something else to fix upon, which turned out to be the globe. He had the strangest sense that she was waiting until whatever she'd felt to pass, and it involved not looking at him.

"Perhaps it's the company you keep, Miss Vale."

She looked up. "I keep excellent company," she reproved.

They stared evenly at each other.

Who? he wanted to know desperately, suddenly. And he felt a twinge of . . . surely it wasn't jealousy? For this was what prevented him from asking.

It was strangely exhilarating and dangerously too comfortable to look her in the eye.

"I shall take that as a compliment, given my presence here."

"Please do feel free to take it however you wish, Lord Dryden," she said politely. "Shall I presume you no longer wish to kiss me?"

She'd deftly snatched the conversation from him, steered it with coquetry, and now here she was casually dropping the word *kiss* into it again, like one spilling a grenade onto a pillow.

It detonated in his mind a moment later.

And all he could think about was what it might be like to kiss her, and how unlikely it seemed now that she'd called him on his ambivalent game.

He wasn't certain whether he liked her. Though he was fairly certain he liked this conversation. At the very least, he wouldn't soon forget it.

Or her.

"If you'd like to get kissed in the future, might I suggest a different type of conversation?" he suggested dryly.

"It's not so much about whether I'd like to simply *get kissed* or not," she explained mildly, not at all offended or nonplussed. "Perhaps I'm particular about who does it."

His eyes went to her mouth then, for how could they not? Small and . . . pillowy, he would have described it. The palest shade of pink. Half of a heart sitting atop a generous lower curve.

Something familiar and yet very surprising sizzled along his spine. Like a lit fuse.

She noticed him staring. That half-a-heart tipped up at the corner.

"*Have* you been kissed before?" He for some reason *needed* to know.

"Why? Are you worried you'll pale in comparison should *you* kiss me?"

Christ, but she had a volley for everything and a very direct gaze, and he suspected she knew full well the effect she was having on him. He supposed her eyes were . . . green? They were clear and large and her lashes were blond at the tips and her eyebrows were fair near to invisibility and shaped like little wings. She was altogether comprised of muted shades, which a man ought to find soothing.

She was anything but.

"You'll forget you've ever been kissed before once I've kissed you."

The words were quick and fierce.

He actually *saw* her breath catch, and then she went so still. And though he was certain she was even now silently cursing the fact, a faint flush slowly invaded her—admittedly *fine*—complexion. It was like watching dawn flood into the pale sky.

In short, he'd managed to shock both of them. The words had somehow managed to bypass reason on the way out of his mouth. And this rarely happened.

So she was *not* impervious to him as a man. Nor was she as worldly as she'd like him to believe. Perhaps it was just that she flung flirtation at men as a way of keeping them at bay.

What was she afraid of?

He wasn't certain how much he cared.

And having chased the conversation to an unnerving crescendo, a fidgety, awkward little silence ensued between them.

"I might be more persuaded of the truth of that, Lord Dryden, if I wasn't certain you'd said that very thing to a legion of women in your lifetime," she finally said lightly.

Though he thought he detected a hint of a question in it.

He wasn't going to take that question up.

The trouble was, he was fairly certain he hadn't ever said such a thing before to anyone, ever. He was shocked he'd said it at all. If he wanted a kiss from a particular woman he generally got one without taxing his powers of persuasion overmuch. He was the Marquess Dryden, he was wealthy, and he looked . . . well, he looked the way he looked. He imagined he could count himself fortunate to have inherited his father's eyes and not his character.

But if even his *original* thoughts rang like clichés to this woman, then impressing her was going to be—

Had he really begun to think in terms of *impressing* her? The schoolteacher?

It was time to remember who he was and why he was here.

"Alas. And here I thought it had the ring of spontaneity." He took pains to sound bored.

She tipped her head slowly to the side, perhaps to examine him from another angle, one she found less *boring*, but if she came to any conclusion her expression didn't betray it.

And then one of her shoulders went up, came down. She wasn't even troubled enough to *shrug* completely.

He ought to be amused. Instead, he was silent. He was uncertain how to speak after they'd banked the conversation to such a pitch.

She had no trouble speaking. And once again he had cause to admire her self-possession.

"I've a group of young ladies to instruct this afternoon. Miss Endicott is very fair but strict and I shouldn't like to be tardy." She was all gracious, deferential, distancing apology.

She took his silence for acquiescence. Then she turned and continued up the hall while he remained still. And perhaps because his equilibrium was shaken, he noticed a dozen distinct little things about her at once, as though she were a faceted gem turning into the light: Her neck was long and white, and her narrow back flared into a pair of pleasingly consequential hips, and the hair that traced the nape of her neck shone every bit as fine and golden as his sister's most expensive embroidery silks, which was as florid as he was willing to allow his metaphors to become.

All of this seemed unduly significant. He was wary and fascinated, as though he'd stumbled across some undiscovered species.

When Phoebe returned to her room, she sat down at her desk, and looked down at the letter she'd begun earlier.

Then crumpled it into a ball and hurled it over her shoulder to Charybdis, who effortlessly caught it in his paws.

And because she was wild at heart, she selected another sheet, dipped in the quill.

Dear Lisbeth,

Thank you for the invitation. I should be very happy to join you for a few days. I very much look forward to seeing you again. Thank you for thinking of me.

With affection,
Phoebe Vale

Chapter 6

She smoothed her walking dress and reached out a hand, immediately seized by a footman. She managed to step down from the carriage the Redmonds had sent for her without showing her stockings and garters to him, though doubtless his expression wouldn't change at all if she did, so trained were they.

"Phoebe!"

Lisbeth rushed down the marble steps of the enormous house, swept her into a hug, shot out her arms to examine her face with fulsome affection, and then pulled her back to plant a kiss on each of her cheeks, which struck Phoebe as very continental of her.

It took a moment for her head to stop spinning when it was all over.

"I'm delighted to see you! You look wonderful, Phoebe! Very healthy!" she declared.

"Why, thank you! Every girl dreams of looking healthy, Lisbeth."

Lisbeth missed her irony, because Lisbeth was a literal creature.

But she was fundamentally kind. Lisbeth had doubtless taken note of Phoebe's walking dress, correctly identified it as the same one she'd seen the last time Phoebe had visited two years ago, and resisted the temptation to issue the rote compliment which was the traditional part of exuberant greetings exchanged between young women everywhere. Phoebe's dresses were adequate at best. They both knew it.

"And I you! I must thank you again for thinking of me. You're so beautiful, Lisbeth!"

This was true, and she could say it with only a little hitch of envy. Two years had melted away the vestiges of Lisbeth's girlish plumpness. She'd wide-spaced blue eyes and a nose like a delicate blade and a mouth doubtless compared a hundred times over to blossoms this season alone.

It was obvious she'd gained confidence and poise and exuberance—maybe just a little too much of all of them—from all the attention and activity and had become a bit like a child overexcited by Christmas festivities.

Lisbeth linked her arm with Phoebe's and marched her into the grand foyer of Redmond House, while silent, bewigged, liveried footmen bore her trunk away with the same solemnity they'd carry a state coffin.

But they didn't carry it up the marble staircase, which was where the family and distinguished guests would be sleeping.

Phoebe watched as they proceeded through the foyer and disappeared after bearing left, which was a door that opened upon a courtyard . . .

. . . beyond which were rooms that were used for staff.

Not the housekeeper and footmen, per se. The governesses and tutors and men of affairs and visiting bailiffs and the like. People who *worked* for the Redmonds for a living. She wondered how many other Redmond *friends* had been installed in those quarters.

Lisbeth followed the line of Phoebe's gaze.

"Aunt Redmond has ordered rooms to be prepared for you in the South Wing. They're lovely! They really are!"

Fanchette Redmond was scrupulously aware of the boundaries of class. It had likely never *occurred* to her to install Phoebe on the floors with the Redmond family.

Phoebe wasn't surprised. Well, not very surprised, anyhow. Still, it required a moment's worth of composure-gathering before she could speak.

"I'm certain it will be beyond compare, and perfectly suitable for me."

Lisbeth nodded, as if this went without saying, and that was the end of the topic. "I'm so happy you could join us at such short notice! We shall have a lovely time of it. Only think, Phoebe! We'll have some distinguished guests for a few days, too, and wait until you meet them! Your jaw will surely drop. I've decided we shall go on a walk to sketch the ruins if it doesn't rain, so I hope you've brought your sketchbook. Uncle Isaiah has arranged for a surprise for all of us, he says, as an evening entertainment. Dinners will be lovely— we shall be having my favorite, lamb in mint!—and we shall all go to church together on Sunday. And just wait until I tell you my news. Well, it is not so much news as a hope, but I *do* think things will be different after the ball. And we are to have a salon this evening, where our guests can meet each other, so you'll wear a very good dress and I'll even send my maid over to do your hair."

Phoebe was reminded that Lisbeth possessed a brain but never saw a need to exercise it, and she was content to ask Phoebe for the answers to anything she grew curious about. And it was pleasant to walk alongside her and listen to her chatter the way it was pleasant to sit in a garden and listen to birdsong. Too much of it would drive Phoebe to distraction, as she liked conversations to be directed and occasionally *about* something, but she ought to manage through three days of festivities.

And if Lisbeth considered her a friend, very well then, she would consider Lisbeth a friend.

Despite the fact that they slept in very different wings.

And despite the fact that Lisbeth would never be truly privy to Phoebe's deepest thoughts, and would in fact be startled speechless if she heard them.

"Here, Mrs. Blofeld will direct you to your rooms. Come downstairs in two hours, do! We're having a gathering for guests in the salon."

The room *was* pleasant. Even if she could hear snoring through the wall. Possibly a bailiff who had come to report to his liege, Isaiah Redmond, about the condition of one of the other Redmond properties.

The carpet was thick. The bed was, too, and filled with feathers. She gave the pillow an exploratory punch. More feathers! She thought of Charybdis, who would have loved napping atop it, but he was being cared for by Mary the maid of the academy. A writing desk was pushed beneath a window, and while the carpet was hardly Savonnerie, a term she'd learned from the broadsheets, it was nothing like the rag rug that covered her floors at Miss Marietta Endicott's school.

She hung up her dresses in the wardrobe, which took no time at all. And then she lifted her sketchbook from her trunk. She sat down, and idly flipped open a page. After a moment's hesitation, her charcoal flew across the page in bold, nearly unconscious, almost urgent strokes.

Just in case she never saw him again, it seemed important to capture his image, lest she forget it.

And when she was finished, he seemed made of darkness and flame, angles and hollows, which was ironic for a man whose nickname was Lord Ice.

She quickly turned the page, hiding him from herself, and tucked the sketchbook into her trunk again.

Two hours later Phoebe dutifully took herself downstairs and followed the sound of voices to the salon, a big warm room dominated by a hearth carved with cherubs and autumn vegetation, and sprinkled about with a variety of settees and a few gas lamps, as Isaiah Redmond liked the modern innovations.

She donned her neutral social smile and slid into the room surreptitiously, hugging the wall. It was crowded with guests, all of them dressed in the first stare of fashion. The first person she saw was patriarch Isaiah Redmond. He was tall and older and handsome but had eyes sharp as chisels. He had a reputation for being an unforgiving man, she knew, and it was generally assumed he was dangerous if crossed, but these qualities were gilded in deceptively easy charm. She'd heard the murmured rumors—who in Pennyroyal Green had not?—about the lengths he would go to in order to achieve his ends. The mutters were particularly voluble when it had come to Colin Eversea's near-demise on the gallows. Some even said he'd driven his oldest son and heir, Lyon, to disappear. But most everyone in Pennyroyal Green laid the blame for that at the feet of Olivia Eversea and the legendary curse that claimed an Eversea and a Redmond were destined to fall in love once per generation—with disastrous consequences. Olivia Eversea herself laughed it off as nonsense, but not even Waterburn ventured to record a single whimsical wager regarding the likelihood of a wedding in the betting books at White's. He was as fond of winning as anyone else, and he knew the odds were against him. The beautiful Olivia appeared to be aspiring to spinsterhood.

Phoebe scanned the room, grateful there was no chance of seeing Olivia *here*. She saw Jonathan Redmond at once, for he looked more like his brother Lyon every day. Next to him was the familiar handsome face of his friend Lord Argosy, a frequent guest in Sussex, and who often joined Jonathan at the Pig & Thistle and at church.

Her heart accelerated when she saw the big bored blond hateful Waterburn . . . for if Waterburn were here . . .

She rubbed her palms along her skirts, as they'd gone damp. He'd said to the marquess that he suspected they were invited to attend the same party. She hardly dared look, but she sensed him before she saw him. Or rather, saw his unmistakable . . . back. Jonathan and Lisbeth were perched on a striped settee, and Lisbeth appeared to be talking. The marquess was leaning toward her, the better to hear what she had to say.

He turned slightly, perhaps sensing the intensity of a particular gaze between his shoulder blades.

And when he saw her he turned abruptly. Straightened slowly to his full height.

And went still.

Lisbeth merrily laughed at something then, perhaps her own joke, and the sound echoed in Phoebe's ears like shrill cascading bells. And noticing the marquess had turned away from her, Lisbeth gave his arm a playful tap . . .

With a cream and ivory fan.

Scattered all over it were pale pink blossoms and twining, fine green stems.

Phoebe stared at it until it blurred before her eyes. A ringing started up in her ears. And for an instant—a bloody *ridiculous* instant—it felt as though the bottom had dropped from beneath her world and she pressed her back against the hard wall to feel something solid, to keep from sliding to the ground.

Well, of course. The marquess purportedly wanted only the finest. The most beautiful and rare and singular.

And he was rumored to be seeking a wife.

And according to the letter she'd written to Phoebe . . . Lisbeth had a surprise to share with her.

Apparently his silence and inattention had gone on too long. For Lisbeth looked up at the marquess, and then sharply followed the line of his gaze.

A momentary puzzlement flickered over her face, but then she must have decided that the marquess was staring because Phoebe looked decidedly out of place. Because Lisbeth beckoned cheerily with little scoops of her hand.

Phoebe remained rooted to the spot. Her feet wouldn't seem to carry her forward.

Lisbeth beckoned with more vigor.

And somehow Phoebe got to the other side of the room, step by step. She felt like a recalcitrant bull being dragged by a rope and hoped it didn't look that way.

"Phoebe, would you be a dear and fetch my reticule for me? It is upstairs in my bedchamber. I want the one I left atop my bed."

What the *devil* . . . ?

Phoebe stared at her.

Lisbeth gazed back at her. Her face pleasantly expectant. And when Phoebe remained silent, her expression became just a trifle insistent.

She wasn't a *servant*. She hadn't been hired to run about and fetch things. At least, this hadn't been mentioned in the letter.

She suspected Lisbeth knew this full well. Clearly she was testing her social power. Or making a point about Phoebe's presence to the marquess.

"I'm Lord Dryden," the marquess said, when it seemed Lisbeth would forget her breeding and forgo an introduction.

Phoebe curtsied. "Pleased to make your acquaintance, my lord." She heard her own even, pleasant voice as though she were hearing it through a layer of glass. "It seems Lisbeth wants her reticule. If you will excuse me?"

She turned abruptly and departed the room the way she came in. Swiftly and unnoticed.

By all but one person.

A funny thing, but the moment Miss Vale left the room seemed darker. Though it was afternoon, and the sun was pouring profligately in through the tall windows, as if the Redmonds felt entitled to more sunlight than everyone else.

Jules excused himself with no explanation, with a warm smile for Lisbeth, and promised to return. She looked beautiful holding the fan. She would have looked beautiful holding a hedgehog, but it satisfied him to match the gift so splendidly to the woman, and to give it to a woman who had been so blushingly pleased to receive it.

He only fully realized where he was going when he

turned the corner and stopped short in the entry, just so he could watch the back of the woman he hadn't been able to forget.

Miss Vale was heading toward the stairs, but appeared to be in no great hurry. Her hips swayed subtly when she walked. He watched them as though they were a mesmerist's pendulum. Her dress was covered in minute faded gray checks. It was as serviceable as any day gown could be. He let his eyes travel the length of her, imagining her legs beneath them, and what manner of garters might be holding up her stockings.

His eyes stopped at the fray at the hem, and the faint, very fine white line there created by hundreds of applications of an iron, and the picking out of stitches so she could turn the dress and re-sew it to get more wear out of it.

And that thought bounced his gaze up and away and back to the walls. He frowned.

He was baffled. She was a *schoolmistress*. If she'd ever laid claim to any gentility, likely it was a generation or more removed by now. England was aswarm with women just like her, a class existing on the fringes of the aristocracy and one incident of bad luck away from poverty, respectable but only just. And for heaven's sake, every woman's hips swayed to *some* degree. Apart, that was, from his aunt Lady Windemere's. She trundled over ground like a miniature barouche and was considerably better sprung.

She paused by an alcove window. Despite the fact that she'd been dispatched to fetch a reticule posthaste, as if she was a maid. He silently approved of her little rebellion. He couldn't imagine what Lisbeth needed with a *reticule* during an afternoon soiree.

Phoebe stared out onto all the rolling green she'd

come to know over her years in Sussex, and thought: perhaps if she recited Marcus Aurelius in her head the sheer effort would intimidate misery from taking hold. She felt like a *fool*. And she never felt like a fool. Surely a fool wouldn't know her Marcus Aurelius?

Tucked into the alcove near the window, she could see and hear the gathering, but they could not see her.

She went still when she heard the footsteps behind her.

"I didn't know you'd be attending this house party."

She'd know the voice anywhere. In the dark, in a crowd, in a dream. Still, when she turned slowly, her heart bounced right into her throat.

He'd followed her. She was certain of it. Misery vacated immediately.

Heel, she told her heart sternly.

"I suppose I am not so much attending as . . ." She changed her mind. "Well, I can't imagine when I'd have an occasion to mention it to you. Lisbeth invited me."

"Hmm. Lisbeth is much too old to have a governess dancing attendance upon her, Miss Vale, and I know none of the Redmonds attended your school. Her mother isn't present, and the Countess Ardmay hasn't yet arrived, and I've known Miss Lisbeth Redmond for two seasons now, and . . ."

The Countess Ardmay? Who the devil—

Oh! Violet Redmond. Now married to an earl.

"So. Am I correct in assuming that you're a . . . shall we say, paid companion of sorts . . . for the next few days?"

She smiled faintly. "You've managed to make that sound so . . . unsavory."

"Because I knew it would make you smile, saintly creature that you are."

She tried not to laugh. She really ought not. She ought to fetch a damned *reticule*.

"You've the right of it. Lisbeth's mother was unable to attend the festivities, and she thought it best Lisbeth have a companion near her age present. Lisbeth invited *me*. I once tutored her when she was younger, and we became friends after a fashion. And now I suspect my job is to protect her from the likes of you."

He liked that. His eyes brightened. "Ah. Are you a decoy? Like a wooden duck set free on a pond during hunting season?"

"Are you suggesting that you're *drawn* to me, Lord Dryden?"

He smiled slowly.

She smiled slowly.

The two of them together . . . well, really. They spurred each other on, and it was surprising, and delightful, and very dangerous, really, how quickly it ignited.

"You cannot be much older than she is, Miss Vale."

"Are you fishing about for my age? But again, you've the right of it. Imagine that! You're clever as well as rich. But I am apparently deemed much wiser in the ways of the world and less likely to be lured into, shall we say, *foolishness*."

"Ah, now, that *is* a pity."

She tried not to smile, and failed. "It is quite true, I fear. I've had so many years of practice resisting foolishness, you see, it's become second nature."

A warning. And a dare.

He acknowledged this with one of those smiles, swift and crooked that snagged her breath.

"So what do you do in the capacity of paid companion?" He leaned back against the wall, as if settling in for a chat.

Oh, God. That would *never* do. She nervously darted her eyes toward the gathering. Then toward the stairs.

And then, God help her, she leaned back, too.

"Well . . . it's not entirely clear. I expected I would primarily smile, make pleasantries, listen to Lisbeth and tolerate Jonathan. It's an improvisational position, really. But she's sent me to fetch a reticule. I fear this may set a precedent for my duties throughout the rest of the party."

"Lisbeth makes it a pleasure and not a duty," she hastened to add. "She is very sweet and kind and charming."

"She *is* charming," he agreed, after a moment.

She wished he didn't sound so fervent.

"Perhaps you ought to go and speak to *her*, then." A little too tart. Blast.

He was amused by her irritation. "I *have* spoken to her."

"And you've said everything you have to say? That's a shame. I was under the impression that conversation perpetuates itself, if done properly."

He looked back at the gathering, and spoke after a hesitation. "Nobody speaks to me the way you do."

He wasn't bantering now. They were both surprised by his honesty, clearly, judging from the moment of silence that followed.

"Perhaps because nobody else here will be going to Africa ere long and they all likely care what you think of them."

"Ah. Of course. I'd forgotten. You're going to *Africa*. Heaven knows, the privilege of burning beneath the hot sun is a costly one, hence the reason you took up the extra work as a paid companion."

"Right you are!" she said cheerfully.

"You see, Miss Vale? I do comprehend the principles of work."

"Perhaps you should cease troubling yourself over the concept of work, Lord Dryden, and stick to what you do best."

"And what do you imagine *that* is, Miss Vale?"

Oh, God. She'd never known a grown man could . . . purr. His tone caused a series of vivid images to burst into bloom, all prurient, none of them suitable for sharing with anyone, ever.

"I try not to *imagine* anything at all about you." Her voice had gone a little hoarse. *Damn.*

"Do you know what I think?"

"I suspect you're about to tell me."

"I think you haven't stopped thinking about me since we discussed kissing."

In his mouth, the word *kissing* was a weapon. It pinned her like a butterfly.

"Of course I stopped." *Long enough to dream about you.*

His little smile told her he knew she was lying.

She glanced at the stairs again, and back at the gathering, where Lisbeth was deploying the fan with an air of secrecy and hauteur, as if she'd just been crowned.

With great effort, Phoebe herded her scattered composure.

He must have sensed she was about to bolt, because he said the very thing that would stop her in her tracks. "I've been wondering about you, Miss Vale."

She sighed. "Honestly, Lord Dryden, I will *loan* you ten pounds. It's exhausting to witness you working so hard just to get a kiss."

She'd thought he'd be amused. His eyes flared something almost like exasperation, irritation. "I swear to you. I never officially took Waterburn's wager. But if he should issue it *again*, Miss Vale . . ."

And now he'd unnerved her. He sensed it, as intuitive as an orchestra conductor, he eased the conversation in another direction; he didn't allow the pause to stretch.

"And I'm the head of a large family, you know. Sisters, a brother, nieces, nephews, cousins. Many of whom are to some extent dependent upon me. I am essentially the patriarch. It's work just to stay sane."

But he sounded as though he was making a point.

She said nothing. She was watching the gathering. Jonathan must be teasing Lisbeth, because she'd gone a vivid shade of pink, and not in a fetching way, either.

The marquess followed the direction of her gaze.

"The fan reminds me of her," she said abruptly. She'd wanted to impose a safe distance.

"That's why I chose it."

Somehow it was the worst thing he could say. The delicate pink, the grace, the fragility, the fine stems bearing the flowers—he'd thought of Lisbeth in detail, in terms of colors and character. She wondered what that might be like to be so cherished, so *noticed*.

"Exquisite and pink and fair and rare?" she said lightly.

"Delicate and particular and *expensive*." He smiled faintly. "Oh, and everything else you said, of course. Hasn't anyone ever given you the perfect gift, Miss Vale?"

His tone was almost gentle, which made her irritable, because to her ears it smacked of condescension: Why should *she* have received a perfect gift, when she was a schoolmistress/paid companion?

She considered the kid gloves now wrapped in tissue, tucked away in her trunk. They were the finest thing she'd ever owned, which was a mixed blessing, in that they made all of her other things seem rather plebian and really weakened her fortitude when it came to coveting things she could never afford to buy on a teacher's salary, which was in all probability how her lust for that one particular bonnet had seeped in. She would wear them this evening, feeling quite subversive, considering who had given them to her.

Yet, as she stood here before the marquess, it was difficult to conjure the face of that man. She could not think of them as a *perfect* gift. She suspected the giving was more by way of a whim from someone who had passed through her life like a shooting star, brilliant, fleeting, furtive, gone, than an expression of true ardor.

Nevertheless, they were cream-colored *kid*, for heaven's sake. She'd never seen anything near as fine or anything quite like them in Postlethwaite's. She liked them very much, indeed.

"I suppose that depends on the spirit in which the gift is given. I suppose I should like a gift that makes me feel . . . known."

Instantly she felt abashed.

The marquess seemed struck by the words. He turned to her. "Known . . . ?" he repeated, thoughtfully.

"A gift . . . unique to . . . me, I suppose. To my tastes and interests. Not necessarily expensive. Just . . . something meant just for me." She shrugged with one shoulder to dismiss it as nonsense. She felt shy and foolish to have said it.

He was still thoughtful. "Do you think any of us ever really *knows* anyone?"

"Philosophy, Lord Dryden? And yet it's daylight and everyone is still sober."

He gave a short laugh. But he didn't seem amused. "Do you know . . . I'm *never* reckless?"

This surprised her. He sounded bemused, vehement. And yet it was a word the broadsheet enjoyed using in front of his name. To describe a wager, or a horse race, or an investment.

What she wanted to say was, "What do you call standing near me and saying words like *kissing* while another young lady deploys your expensive gift?"

"What about the horse race in which you wagered ten thousand pounds?"

He made an exasperated sound. "It was a very fast horse racing against slow horses. I knew this definitively. And my instincts are excellent. Have you considered, Miss Vale, that what you read in the broadsheets is . . . an *interpretation* of me? That they report on my comings and goings and pastimes like so many anthropologists and draw conclusions about my character from a scattered few things? And that perhaps they've got it wrong?"

She took this in. "If it's wrong, why do you allow it to continue?"

"It provides hours of entertainment for the ton. I see no need to correct impressions. Sometimes it's useful not to be known."

"Magnanimous of you."

His mouth twitched. "Mmm. Use more words like that, please. Schoolmistress words. Long, impressive ones." He'd made the last three words sound like an innuendo.

"Will incorrigible do?"

"Odd, but it sounds like flattery when you say it."

"I assure you, it wasn't meant to be."

"You seem to have a gift for it, teaching. I do admire the way you made those young ladies hop like subalterns in Postlethwaite's shop. I wish I'd thought to threaten the men under my command with Marcus Aurelius."

"Oh, I wouldn't go so far as to call it a gift. I can impart knowledge and employ strategies to keep girls in line precisely because I was a girl once like . . . just like they were. I know what works, and how to engage them. So I scarcely feel I can take credit for it."

"You are too modest."

"I assure you, I speak truth."

"Will you miss them when you leave for Africa?"

She smiled faintly. "Oh, yes, I suppose I will. For a time. But I've been a teacher for four years only, and I suspect they'll forget *me* soon enough. I'm confident the ones I've taught will eventually make socially advantageous marriages and in all likelihood rule their households with velvet fists. Teaching is something that just . . . happened to me. Though I am grateful for the position and I do enjoy it."

"Something that just happened to you," he repeated, after a moment. Thoughtfully. As if it was something he intended to remember. "Nevertheless, I maintain you have a certain natural authority, and trust me, I recognize that sort of thing when I see it."

"In other words, *I'm* not delicate or expensive."

He smiled at that. "Is that the real reason why you're running so far, far away? So you can choose what you want to be or do?"

She jerked her head toward him, astounded. *"Running?"* she said between her teeth. When she could speak again. *"Away?"*

Judging from the way his eyes brightened, he was obviously silently congratulating himself on being so astute.

"I have never run from anything in my life. And what on earth can you mean by 'real reason'?"

"This is what I mean. Of all the choices of all the things you can have in the world, is Africa really your first? *Africa?* Not a husband, not a family?"

"I never said I objected to a husband. Recall our discussion of the variety of men I am destined to meet."

"You just don't think you'll find one in England."

"Perhaps not."

"In aaaalll of England. No likely husbands."

She shifted impatiently. "Why the interview, Lord Dryden?"

"Why the circumspection, Miss Vale?"

"Because if I dodge it long enough I'm hoping to bore you into abandoning the topic."

He gave a short laugh. "Patience is *nothing* to me when I want something."

She was tense as a drawn bow now. Want. Want want want. *Want* was the reason she was here at the Redmonds' at all. She wanted to be here because he was here, and she wanted to be talking to him, and she wanted him to leave her alone, and . . .

What precisely did *he want* from her? And why?

"Per*haps*," he said slowly, as though the inspiration were only just dawning, "your life story could be your gift to me."

The sudden cold little knot in her stomach told her she didn't like the direction the conversation was taking. "Oh, honestly. I'm hardly Scheherazade."

Too late she realized the comparison might be unfortunate, given that it was a story of a vengeful Arabic despot who beheaded three thousand virgins until he found the one—that would be Scheherazade—whose storytelling amused him enough to spare her life. For 1,001 Arabian nights she told him stories. Upon which the violent old sod fell in love with her and married her, but not until she'd had three of his babies.

"Sche*her*azade," he repeated wonderingly, giving each syllable a fascinated emphasis. Amusement and a certain prurient speculation was written all over his face. "Another long and excellent word. You're quite the reader, Miss Vale, aren't you? And I don't mind remarking that's a rather scandalous story."

She sighed. "It's a well-known tale." That she'd forbidden the younger girls at the school to read until they were older.

"And as intrigued as I am by what you might have in common with the story's heroine, I'm hardly going to demand that you tell me 1,001 stories for 1,001 nights in a row. Nor is your very life at stake. All I want is *one* story. The story of your life. Succinctly."

Bloody hell.

It was really the last thing she wanted to give him. Because she didn't want to watch his face change when he heard it.

She tried to sound bored, flippant. "But surely you already have everything you need."

He looked amused. "It isn't so much about *needing* it, Miss Vale. I want it. I want it because I value the rare and singular. I have that in common with the despotic Arab king of the story."

"But *her* stories fascinated a king who was arguably homicidal. My story, I assure you, is very mundane."

"Oh, I doubt it."

"Why should you doubt it?"

And curiously, he hesitated. As if he was actually giving careful consideration to what he was about to say, or considering whether to say it at all. He looked back toward the gathering, his eyes touching on the people there, one by one, as if taking inventory, but she didn't think he actually saw them. When he spoke, his words settled over her like mink.

"Because it's yours."

She didn't look at him. For an instant it was difficult to breathe, and she almost closed her eyes against the sudden surprising onslaught of emotion. Dangerous, dangerous. The voice, the request, the man, the perfect, perfect words. Dangerous and clever. Because in truth she'd never truly belonged to anyone, her story had never particularly meant anything to anyone, and his words had slipped past her battlements and ambushed a need she'd long ago exiled. She'd almost—mercifully—forgotten it existed.

She hadn't lied about one thing: Her story *was* mundane . . . in some circles.

"But you haven't yet given a gift to *me*, Lord Dryden."

Flirting was an excellent way to dodge a question. Then again, he brought it out of her. The way rain brought out the flowers. Or heightened the stench in St. Giles, for that matter.

His head went back in surprise, and then came down again on a little smile. "Well played. Very well, then, Miss Vale. A gift for a gift. I will give *you* a gift once you give one to me. For I find I am forever giving gifts but seldom receiving them. What do you say?"

This struck her as odd. But a moment later, she thought she understood. In all likelihood everyone assumed he had everything he wanted. And then again, he was so legendarily particular about the things he acquired everyone dreaded the judgment rendered by silence and one of those upraised eyebrows. *This? You deign to give* this *to me?*

She silently watched Lisbeth across the room. She was now speaking to Lord Argosy, who had become, so rumor had it, a veritable *rake*, complete with *genuinely* reckless wagers, which, unlike the marquess, he often lost, and an affair with a scandalous widowed countess. He laid all of this at the door of the notorious Miss Cynthia Brightly, who had allegedly broken his heart by marrying Miles Redmond instead of him. She couldn't help but notice that despite the air of ennui he'd adopted, he seemed to be enjoying himself very much indeed. He hadn't yet acquired an air of dissipation. His golden curls were glossy. His eyes bright.

When contrasted with the marquess he seemed . . . unfinished. A boy, playing at being a rake. When contrasted with Lisbeth, they seemed like . . . part of a set. The way a silver breakfast service, the teapot and the jam pot and all the little spoons, all clearly belonged together. From her perspective of belonging nowhere and to no one at all, they all looked so different and yet so very much the same.

She was certain she would be a source of fascination for the marquess for about as *long* as he wondered about her.

"I was born in London," she said.

The marquess's head swiveled toward her.

She pretended not to notice she was fixed in his gaze. She idly continued surveying the crowd from a distance, tapping her foot as if listening to spritely reels in her head.

"And?" he prompted.

"*And* if we know each other for 1,001 days, Lord

Dryden, perhaps you'll hear the rest of the story."

She eased away from the window and tossed an enigmatic smile over her shoulder as she dashed for the staircase.

His gratifying expression of bald, astonished admiration was the last thing she saw.

She got up the stairs and stopped, and pressed herself against the landing wall, because that's when her bravado gave out. She laid one cold hand against her throat, amazed at the hammering speed of her heart. But the fact that she was warm everywhere was a helpful reminder that she was, indeed, playing with fire. She suddenly wished she had a fan.

The fan of course reminded her of Lisbeth.

Ironically, that proved effective, indeed, in cooling her temperature.

She went up to fetch Lisbeth's bloody reticule. The stairs seemed inordinately long.

Chapter 7

Dinner that night was a peculiar, delicious, lonely punishment, as she'd been relegated to the far end of the table next to a nearly deaf elderly gentleman who shouted mundane pleasantries at intervals to her, causing her to shout back agreements, which made everyone look at her with faint astonishment each time she did, whilst Lisbeth and the marquess were at the other end, side by side. Phoebe felt it keenly as a lash every time his head turned to address something to Lisbeth.

His eyes met hers four times—Phoebe counted.

He'd been the one to catch her gaze. And she'd been the first to look away every time.

Out of preservation: of her pride, her heart, and her sense of mystery.

Later that evening, she'd stalked to her room across the courtyard, seized her sketchbook, flipped it open, and tried again. This drawing featured more detail. She now knew about the little white scar near his mouth, for instance.

In the end, she'd made him look regal and saturnine, which wasn't quite right. She wasn't getting it quite right because he remained out of reach, just as he had at dinner. She stuffed the sketchbook with great dissatisfaction in her trunk, and flung herself backward on her bed.

She woke up after a night of fitful dreams and to her chagrin found herself still dressed.

It rained the whole day.

Not torrents, but it was a steady, discouraging rain. Phoebe soon learned this meant she would be imprisoned—that was, *pleasantly ensconced*—in one of the Redmonds' myriad plush, heated parlors with Lisbeth, embroidering and listening to Lisbeth natter on while all the male houseguests disappeared to God knows where to do God knows what. She suspected they were at the Pig & Thistle drinking and throwing darts—the younger ones, anyhow. The marquess had retreated with Isaiah Redmond after a brief appearance at the breakfast table, to discuss money, or whatever it was that men of their ilk and means enjoyed discussing.

Fanchette Redmond joined Phoebe and Lisbeth for a time, bringing her embroidery hoop and an icy, vague imperiousness with her. She stitched a few flowers, consulted the mantel clock, and then disappeared again with a pleasant impersonal smile, much to Phoebe's relief. And to Lisbeth's, too, she suspected. Lisbeth didn't chatter nearly as much when Aunt Redmond was in the room. One was tempted to assume she was a vapid woman, given her blond beauty and limited conversation and the offhand affection with which her children clearly regarded her, but Phoebe had never felt comfortable in her presence. Even in church, when she sat several pews away. Vapidity, she suspected, was an excellent disguise for many qualities, few of them safe ones.

"Music this evening, Phoebe." Lisbeth's eyes were

sparkling with delight. "Uncle Isaiah has arranged for a surprise!"

Oh, God. Phoebe very much enjoyed playing pianoforte, but she had skill and no real talent, whereas Lisbeth, who had been planted before a pianoforte since she could walk, was actually very good. She didn't look forward to this being reemphasized.

Lisbeth correctly interpreted her expression.

"Silly, you likely won't be asked to play, but you may turn the pages of my music, as I expect *I* shall. If that's the sort of thing my uncle has in mind. But I don't think there will be time. Neighbors are coming from miles around for just a few hours this evening—Uncle Isaiah has engaged Madame Sophia Licari, the famous soprano, to sing for us!"

She clapped her hands together and beamed beatifically.

Phoebe had read of Signora Licari, of course, in the newspapers. "Is she a very wonderful singer?"

"Oh, my goodness. Haven't you heard her sing, Phoebe?"

The answer to this ridiculous question was of course "No."

"Her voice is a marvel, and she's so very haughty and beautiful and a little bit frightening. She is said to . . ." she lowered her voice to a hush ". . . take *lovers*."

Lisbeth was flushed with her own daring and the sheer sophistication of such a word.

"Never say lovers! *Imagine* an unmarried grown woman taking lovers."

Lisbeth missed the irony.

"Scandalous, I know, but she is very worldly and sings so well no one seems too mind."

Perhaps I ought to take up singing, Phoebe thought. "Particularly the men, I should imagine."

"Phoebe!" Lisbeth pretended to be scandalized, because she suspected she was supposed to, but in truth Phoebe suspected no one spoke to her of such things, and now she was curious.

Because there followed a little silence.

"Do you think the marquess does that sort of thing? Jules?"

Jonathan and Waterburn and Argosy wandered into the far end of the room and flung themselves down before the fire on settees. She hoped for the sake of the maids they weren't muddy, too.

Phoebe was feeling mischievous. "What sort of thing?" So it was Jules, was it? The diminutive of Julian.

She *wasn't* going to discuss the marquess and mistresses with Lisbeth. For God's sake, Lisbeth could read a broadsheet as well as anyone else. Perhaps she would hand her own stack over to Lisbeth with the appropriate pages marked and sternly inform her, "You will be tested." Invariably the mistresses were coyly described as breathtaking. One young man had broken an ankle tumbling out of an opera balcony in an attempt to get a look at the marquess's latest one.

"*You* know . . . do you think *he* . . ." She widened her eyes and gave her eyebrows a wag.

"I'm afraid I don't take your meaning." She was doing a brilliant job not laughing.

Her eyes were wide, wide, wide. Keeping company with Lisbeth was honing her ability to take passive revenge.

"*Takes. Lovers,*" Lisbeth said irritably, emphatically. And a little too loudly, because all the male heads swiveled in their direction.

Phoebe furrowed her brow. "Takes them where?"

Lisbeth was scarlet now. "Now I think you are teasing me." She sounded wounded. Lisbeth was much too literal a creature, and took herself a trifle too seriously, to know what to do about teasing. She found it incompatible with her status as diamond of the first water.

Which meant Jonathan *enjoyed* torturing her, because she invariably became red and began squeaking, while Phoebe took little pleasure in it, because Lisbeth didn't play along, and Phoebe liked conversations to be between equals, if at all possible.

"I'm certain he does. Or has. Honestly, all men of significant means do, Lisbeth."

It was certainly the truth. It was also hardly the sort of thing anyone's mother would want a paid companion to say. She was also aware her motive in saying it wasn't entirely benign. Let Lisbeth toss and turn with uncertainty at night, too, she thought.

Lisbeth was subdued for a moment, considering this. In the end, she seemed to take it in with a certain amount of equanimity. After all, men did all manner of things that women were simply expected to endure even if they didn't condone them.

"Of course he wouldn't do such a thing when he is married." It sounded like she was asking Phoebe another question.

Phoebe almost rolled her eyes. Who had allowed this girl to grow up so ignorant of men? She had Jonathan for a cousin, for heaven's sake. And her other cousin, Mr. Miles Redmond, had written a book about his South Sea travels that famously described affectionate native women who went about wearing nothing above their waists all day.

But she was reminded that Lisbeth liked to acquire information by asking for it.

"Of course not," Phoebe humored. "What on earth would he need with a mistress if he had a wife?" Phoebe said it for the sake of amusing herself. For all she knew it was true with regards to the marquess.

This mollified Lisbeth.

"Everyone would like to see a match between us," Lisbeth confided on a lowered voice. She was flushed with pride and awe.

Phoebe slowed the stabbing of the needle in and out of cloth.

Not everyone.

"What do *you* want, Lisbeth?"

For God's sake. They were scarcely two years apart in age. She was a young woman, too. She shouldn't have to adopt a soothing maternal tone, as if she were a governess, or someone to whom men and sex and the like were uninteresting or unavailable. But her innate sympathy, curse it, did battle with her wits, and her wits wanted to flay Lisbeth.

She flirted with the idea of flaying her with wit and fleeing to Africa, but decided against it.

What did Lisbeth want? Did she even know? Or was she just a vehicle for the desires and ambitions of her influential family and the marquess?

"I think . . ." Lisbeth tipped her head back and a dreamy smile drifted over her face ". . . nothing could be more glorious than to be married to him. He's very . . . very . . ."

She paused, seemed lost in a reverie.

Yes, he is. Very.

". . . sweet."

God, no. Did *she* ever have the wrong end of the stick.

Phoebe accidentally snorted. Then turned it into a discreet cough. Lisbeth stared at Phoebe with mild concern and something like curiosity. She'd never do anything so gauche as to snort. She was probably wondering how it was done.

But perhaps he *was* sweet to Lisbeth. And treated her with deference and kindness and delicacy, the way one would a well-bred prospective wife or an expensive Chinese vase.

Other women were for flirting with. And making love to.

"And he's impressive," Lisbeth added. "He is quite the best catch in all of London."

"He *is* impressive." *Catch? You make him sound like a mackerel.*

Lisbeth perhaps caught a whiff of something too enthusiastic in Phoebe's tone. She looked up at her from her embroidery and regarded her with mild bemusement.

"That is, from what I can tell." She'd decided echoing Lisbeth was working out nicely, for it saved her from expressing opinions or lying.

"And everyone knows he will settle only for the very best," Lisbeth added.

Settle. Did one actually "settle" for the best?

"Is that why you admire him, Lisbeth?"

She looked up, earnestly surprised. And almost reproving. "Don't you think it's why he admires *me*?"

Implying that naturally *she* was the best that could be had.

Clearly she'd thought *Phoebe* had gotten the wrong end of the stick.

* * * *

After dinner, another one in which Phoebe was installed at the nether end of the table and forced to listen to intermittent bursts of laughter from the other end while the elderly neighbor squire next to her dozed quietly, his chin tucked into his chest, the women and men separated politely, as they normally did—to recover from each other's company?—and then the lot of them were ushered into the smaller ballroom, where chairs, at least a hundred of them, were aligned in rows, and guests, local aristocracy, Londoners who had made the trip to the country, and people of whom the Redmonds were simply fond, began arriving, milling about excitedly. Phoebe wore one of the two finer gowns she owned—it was a dove gray silk, and entirely frill-free apart from a shining silver cord beneath the bosom— and her fine gloves, which she liked to think rather elevated her ensemble to something close to what all the other glamorous guests were wearing.

The small ballroom was very warm, but then the temperature in the house was generally sultry, at least by contrast to the conservative way they heated Miss Marietta Endicott's academy.

The marquess, who had been at dinner and seated by Lisbeth again but who seemed unusually distracted, remained noticeably missing even after the rest of the male guests reappeared.

Lisbeth seemed to have noticed it, too. She was waving the damned fan about as if she could invoke his presence with it, as if to remind herself that he had indeed given it to her. She smiled politely for all the guests, and exchanged pleasantries, but she was clearly growing increasingly agitated.

Which is probably why she said, "Phoebe, would you please run and fetch my shawl?"

"Run" and "fetch." Phoebe spoke five languages fluently, and this girl was asking her to run and fetch.

"Perhaps you'll want your own as well," Lisbeth allowed, magnanimously. "Fetch that, too."

It sounded like a bloody whim to Phoebe, as the house was warm as the inside of a closed hand.

Phoebe regarded Lisbeth evenly.

And said nothing.

Lisbeth stared back at her, pleasantly anticipating her dash to do her bidding.

When a man appeared and began to settle sheet music against the pianoforte, the crowd rustled and murmured with anticipation. Phoebe didn't want to miss a note of the music.

"Of course," Phoebe said at last. And sighed inwardly.

She spun on her heel. She half stalked, half ran up the stairs and retrieved Lisbeth's Chinese silk shawl from Lisbeth's Abigail. And then she dashed down the stairs, slipped with cat-like speed across the foyer and stepped out into the chilly night to dart across the courtyard to her own room. *Bloody Lisbeth.*

"Where are you going in a tearing hurry, Miss Vale? Dare I hope the salon is on fire and the musical evening has been canceled?"

Chapter 8

She came to an abrupt halt and whirled, looking for the voice.

"Here," he said helpfully.

Ah! There he was. He was really not much more than a shadow leaning against the pillar, illuminated by a sliver of moon and the chandelier light pouring out of the windows. A few lamps were hung amongst the eves along the courtyard walls to aid the passage of servants and staff through the dark, each hardly more brilliant than a firefly. He was moodily smoking a cheroot near one. A few hapless insects circled it, moving in and out of the nimbus of light.

"Yes," she said. "The house is all aflame, and I've decided to abandon the lot of them to their fates."

He laughed softly.

"Don't you like sopranos, Lord Dryden?"

"Oh, on the contrary. I like them very much indeed." He sounded darkly amused.

He sucked at the cheroot as though it were the source of all oxygen. Finally the tip glowed like a demon eye. He exhaled a stream of blue smoke toward the flawlessly clear night sky.

She coughed melodramatically as it drifted back down again.

"My apologies," he said insincerely.

"If you love sopranos, then if I may be so bold as to ask, Lord Dryden—"

"Fancy *you* asking permission to be bold."

"—why are you out here alone smoking a cheroot? I thought things among the Redmonds were usually done in a proper order. Which means that after dinner the gentlemen retreated for manly drinks and cigars whilst the ladies talked about you, and now we're to reconvene to listen to a singer."

"Talked about me," he repeated. "Amusing."

"It was." No one had said a word about him, at least within Phoebe's earshot.

He smiled slightly. He seemed to be pondering his answer.

"I am smoking," he finally said, "because I needed an occupation while I stood out here."

She laughed.

He stirred, turned toward her, smiling, as though turning toward the sun. And then he went so still, and the smile faded. And that bemusement, that tension they always created between them, settled in. If she peered hard enough, doubtless she could see galaxies reflected in his clear eyes. The moon was now scarcely a presence in the sky, obscured by cobwebby clouds, but stars were flung thickly all over that blue-black canvass.

And as he wouldn't relinquish her gaze, she seemed unable to move past him.

Her shawl would have to wait. Ironically, she began to wish she had one and was tempted to sling Lisbeth's round her. The air nipped at her bare arms. "She is the finest soprano on the Continent, they say. Signora Sophia Licari."

"She is at that," he agreed with grim amusement.

"She also . . ." he exhaled more smoke ". . . has excellent aim."

Excellent . . .

Oh!

She struggled not to laugh. "I think I begin to understand, Lord Dryden. Pray tell, did she once say something to you along the lines of, oh . . . '*ciò è che cosa penso al vostro regalo*'?"

It was Italian for "this is what I think of your gift, you son of a whore!"

She suspected he knew. He was worldly, indeed.

"You weren't lying when you said you spoke a number of languages, were you, Miss Vale? Perhaps you should forgo Africa and offer to spy for the crown."

He was irritated.

She was greatly entertained. "Are you afraid she'll hurl one of the Redmonds' heirlooms at you should she get a look at you? There are so many to choose from in the parlor."

"I shouldn't like to tempt her. Though it was years ago, mind you, and perhaps she has forgotten me." His tone, and his roguish smile, implied that this would in fact be impossible.

She shook her head slowly in awe of his arrogance. Still, it was very difficult not to smile.

He sighed. "In truth, I wouldn't want to be the cause of an awkward scene, and the possibility exists that Signora Licari might be tempted to . . . express herself . . . in something other than song. And I shouldn't like any of the guests present to recall my *involvement* with her and introduce the topic after one too many glasses of port. It is not my wish to humiliate . . . anyone."

"Anyone," of course, being Lisbeth, who would disintegrate in horror and bewilderment should the marquess's former mistress—an actual mistress present!—begin hurling things and shouting in Italian.

Nor would he want to jeopardize a promising future as a partner in business with Isaiah Redmond.

And as usual when it came to him, a dozen emotions competed for her attention. Curiosity got the better of her. "What did she throw?"

"Do we *need* to continue to discuss this?" He was uncomfortable, which merely made it funnier.

"Well, it's not so much something I need, as something I want. And when I *want* something . . ."

He gave a soft laugh. "It was a humidor. It was over in seconds. The corner of it shaved a strip from the side of my hair."

"It didn't!"

He grinned. "Of course not. But I'll admit to a skipped heartbeat when I saw it go sailing by. Fortunately, my sense of self-preservation was honed during the war. I ducked; it struck a vase, which shattered, and which my man Marquardt subsequently swept up without a single change of expression. And then Signora Licari stormed out. I'd given her a very handsome necklace along with a polite speech about how it was time to part ways, and she threw a humidor. What do you make of that, Miss Vale?"

She took a moment to picture the scene, enjoying particularly the notion of the graceful marquess diving in defense, maybe throwing his hands up over his head, taking cover behind a settee . . .

Only what he deserved, likely.

"Lord Dryden, it *strikes* me that—"

"Interesting choice of word."

"—you consistently . . . associate . . . with women—"

"Associate!" He found this very funny. "*What* a delicate choice of euphemism."

"—who are possessed of fiery temperaments. Which is interesting, when yours is so very . . ." she searched for just the right word ". . . contained."

His reaction was immediate and wholly unexpected. He went rigid. His head turned toward her so swiftly she took a small step backward.

When he spoke, it was so coldly she was reminded uncomfortably that he was titled, wealthy, feared, and respected. For very good reasons.

"Very what?" Each word was given equal anvil weight and delivered slowly. He pronounced the *H* in what perhaps a little too emphatically.

"Contained," she repeated bravely, matching his gravity, wondering why on earth he should find this troubling. For it wasn't untrue. And it wasn't an insult. Necessarily.

He stared at her for a moment. Then narrowed his eyes, which was unnervingly like being viewed through crossbow slits.

And then turned away from her and of course reacted by remaining . . . contained.

His posture, even as he mimed holding up the pillar, was flawless. No sloping shoulders for *him*.

He drew deeply upon the cheroot.

He spoke after he exhaled more smoke. "Explain."

"Have you considered it's the very thing causing the women to react so . . . profoundly? The containment?"

He gave a short humorless laugh. "I'm entertained by the care you take with choosing words, Miss Vale. I'm still not certain of your meaning."

"If you are so very . . . *cool* all the time . . . very poised, if you will, very controlled . . . Well, consider . . .

for example, consider how a fire must burn hotter and higher to compensate for a cold temperature in a room. So if you bring an association to an end very coolly and *politely*, as you've just said, shall we say, tempers may . . . boil over. Things may be thrown."

"And that's what I am?" he asked sharply. "Is that what you think? I'm cold? Hard? The broadsheets think so."

"No." The word was emphatic and immediate and soothing; she sensed she'd drawn blood, hurt him somehow. But in truth, it was a thought she'd entertained about him before. *"No."* Instinctively, she softened her voice. "I do know the difference between . . . cold . . . and an abundance of caution."

More carefully chosen words.

He was a clever man. But he wouldn't tolerate the implication that he was vulnerable, that he was self-protective, for *everyone* knew he was invulnerable. Impenetrable. His nerves were steel, his heart was a fortress, his mind was a trap, and et cetera. His legend was built upon it.

He exhaled shortly. It wasn't quite a sigh.

"I'm hardly *dis*passionate, Miss Vale."

"Oh, I didn't think for a moment that you were."

He looked sharply. He knew her innocence was feigned, that it was provocation cloaked in careful words.

He smoked thoughtfully for a moment. She rubbed at one arm. It might be tropical inside the Redmond house, but it was most definitely autumn here in the courtyard.

"You see, Miss Vale . . . I was responsible for a great deal at a very early age. I was seventeen years old and still at school when my father died, leaving me with

debts and enormous responsibilities and everyone in
the family flailing and looking to me, like so many
baby birds with their mouths open, to save them. I
needed to make decisions, important ones, difficult
ones, on behalf of my family and . . . impulsiveness
was a luxury. One learns things when the circumstances are dire. One learns precision, for one thing.
And timing. For a wrong move could have brought
it all crashing down. And I paid the debts. I built the
fortune. I ensured everyone associated with my name
thrived."

The marquess was trying to *explain* himself to her.

Estates, she'd said mockingly. Suddenly she saw
them for what they were . . . ballast. Slung about the
neck of a seventeen-year-old blue blood. Huge tracts
of lands, great houses, and families, for that matter,
didn't run *themselves* profitably through magic. He'd
cared for everyone from the beginning. He'd managed.
He'd looked out for everything and everyone associated with his name and done them proud. And he'd
never stopped.

She was ashamed she'd teased him.

"The wrong man could have brought it all crashing
down," she told him. "A different man might have collapsed under the weight of the responsibility."

He widened his eyes in surprise, as if the option to
allow it to crash down around him had never occurred
to him. Then he gave a short laugh. No humor in it, but
it was a bit wistful. "It was like walking a tightrope at
times," he said absently. Perhaps reflecting on that time.

"And now?"

"And now . . ." He tipped his head back in thought.
"Now it's almost second nature." He gave another ab-
breviated almost-laugh. "Doing the right thing at the

right time for the right reasons." He glanced sideways at her. "Almost," he added cryptically.

The man who never put a foot wrong. Who was grace personified. Who was particular and "lucky" and "reckless." Who'd become a legend as a result of all of these things, who was admired and imitated but never matched.

No one understood what his legend had cost him.

Her stomach knotted. She felt the sides of the box he voluntarily occupied as if it had been lowered over the two of them. And for an infinitesimal moment she felt grateful not to be him.

"You must have been frightened at times."

He seemed to consider this. He shrugged with one shoulder. And then he reached up, deftly captured a moth in one hand before it could dash itself to death in the lamplight.

"I think it's remarkable," she added softly. "What you've done."

"Perhaps. But you see how amusing I find it that I'm considered *reckless*. I am never . . ." He freed the moth with a wry twist of his mouth, knowing it would try for the light again, as it was its nature. ". . . reckless."

She saw how very true this was. How a juggler, a tightrope walker, must learn precision and timing . . . or perish.

"You should be very proud," she said softly. Surprisingly, vehemently. "Of everything. Your family is fortunate indeed to have you."

"I am," he said offhandedly, after a moment. Sounding surprised that it was ever in question. "And they are."

He turned to her with a half smile.

It made her shake her head. She was certain, somehow, the arrogance was native, not something he acquired along the way. She liked it.

"I promised my mother I'd restore all of the lands that had been sold to pay off debt. Little by little, over the years, I've rebuilt my family's legacy and honor. How fragile it is, really, when what was built over centuries can be torn asunder by one man. Only one more tract of land remains to be reacquired—an expanse of Sussex not entailed to the title that my father lost in a card game. The estate that occupies it was part of my mother's dowry, and her childhood home. I wonder if you can guess who owns it."

She didn't have to guess. She knew it must be Redmond property.

"Is there a condition associated with the land?"

He looked up at her sharply, surprised at the astute question, perhaps. He smiled, faintly, and the smile seemed almost bittersweet. "Of course. Little in life is unconditional, and naught is unconditional when it comes to Isaiah Redmond. But I'm a man who understands actions and consequences and business. I can't in truth object. And the condition . . ." he paused ". . . it's not an onerous one." He turned to her, and delivered the words carefully. "The property is attached to another dowry."

Not an onerous one. The condition, she knew with clarion certainty, was Lisbeth Redmond.

She was speechless. He was going about the business of marriage the same way he'd gone about the business of his life. Purposefully.

"The question remains . . . who takes care of you, Miss Vale?"

A sly ambush of a question to distract her from what he'd essentially just admitted.

She dodged it. "I might ask the same question of you, Lord Dryden."

He seemed genuinely puzzled. "Oh, I've a host of servants. Marquardt, I suppose, in particular. And the likes of Sophia Licari—"

"*Not*," she said softly, lest he expound along those lines because she really didn't want to know, "quite what I meant. And not quite the same thing."

He was about to acquire a wife who would need looking after and coddling, as she was sheltered, delicate, and demanding. Yet another person for him to take care of.

To whom did he surrender his burdens? He probably didn't know how to surrender his burdens.

He looked at her a moment longer, then looked away. "With regards to my *containment*, as you've called it . . . in my defense, I never told any of those women who threw things that I loved them."

Oh, for God's sake. Men.

"Well, there you are, then. Of course they would never *dream* of falling in love with you in absence of a declaration. How dare they hurl things at your head?"

He laughed. Sounding very much like a wicked little boy.

"They're *human*, you know," she said huffily. "Not everyone has the advantage of your sort of self-control."

"Hold." The warning note was back in his voice. "Do you think for an instant I think of them as otherwise? As *objects*?"

"No, I just—"

He leaned away from the pillar, took a step toward her. Apparently he needed to stand very straight to make his point.

"Miss Vale, it's a business arrangement that suits

both *humans* right down to the ground. It is entered into voluntarily, and I am generous and attentive and *much more skilled*, I'll have you know, than even any rumors you may have heard about me. I doubt Signora Licari would tell you otherwise. And though I cannot prevent hurt feelings, sought-after women are often as arrogant as the men who seek them, and I can assure you that the main thing hurt is pride when an *association* comes to a close."

She suspected he knew she wasn't nearly as sophisticated as he was, and was using words like "much more skilled" as a weapon.

"And humidors. And vases," she managed.

"On occasion, yes."

And then all at once it was strangely difficult to breathe. *"Much more skilled."* The reaction was delayed and potent and she knew he'd wanted her to think about it. In seconds, she'd discovered that she'd swum out into deeper waters than she'd ever crossed.

He watched her.

She spent a silent moment flailing inwardly before she spoke.

"Nevertheless, my point is . . . they're . . ." she gestured ". . . women. They're not . . . Mr. Isaiah Redmond, with whom you can conclude a transaction with a shake of the hand and a hearty thank-you. You can apply the rules of business all you like, but emotions are . . . emotions are anarchic. They resist . . . legislation. Even by you."

Too late she realized she sounded a trifle vehement.

He stared at her. "Know a little something about anarchic feelings, do you, Miss Vale?" There was that voice again. So low, so soft it was like a breath against the back of her neck.

Odd that she should say such a thing, when she was the one who had drummed her own wildness into compliance with facts and order. She was a fine one to lecture him.

"No," she lied.

Which made him smile crookedly.

"I swear to you I have never given a diamond necklace to *Isaiah Redmond*," he said finally.

And then they both smiled, picturing *that*. Vehemence dissipated into the air like smoke.

He sighed. "I accede you may have a point regarding my ability to . . . end associations gracefully. Congratulations, schoolmistress. You've imparted yet another lesson."

The question was out of her before she could stop it. "Have you any associations now?"

There was a silence. A peculiar hesitation. She could have sworn the question startled him.

And then he fixed her in his gaze.

"No." It sounded like a careful word.

He seemed to be waiting for her to say something more.

She was afraid that *he* might say something more.

And then into the silence someone who played pianoforte very well, perhaps an accompanist who traveled with Signora Licari, launched something beautiful and complicated.

The recital had begun.

Chapter 9

The music twined around Phoebe, and in moments held her fast, in thrall. She *yearned* to know the next note, the next phrase. It was a fresh and delightful shock when each was lovelier than the next. Anticipation ramped and ramped.

The voice slipped in almost unnoticed, like an interloper into a party. It insinuated itself between notes, and then surreptitiously, then ever more boldly, climbed, and climbed, and climbed . . . until it soared above the music. Brazen and glorious.

Dear God . . . the sound of it . . . it hurt, *hurt* to hear, such was its beauty. She felt *swollen* with it.

She reached out and clutched the marquess's sleeve without realizing it. As if to prevent herself from launching skyward. "What is it? The song. Please tell me what it is," she demanded on a whisper.

He looked down at her hand. And then down into her face.

If she had known his breath had caught when she'd reached out for him . . . if she had seen his expression . . . then she might have backed away, confused by the unguarded confusion and hunger there.

Or she might have flung herself into his arms.

She was owned by the music. She'd closed her eyes.

"It's Galuppi's *L'Olimpiade*," he whispered, finally. It was his turn to soothe her, understanding she was overwhelmed by the newness and splendor of it. "The libretto is Metastasio. *L'Olimpiade* is about an . . . amorous competition, shall we say. From the Trial of the Suitors."

An amorous competition? she thought. Well, *that* was a little too close to home.

For a moment she couldn't speak. She *suffered* from the beauty of it.

So she did what she usually did to ease suffering: she requested information.

"The Trial of the Suitors? An opera based on *Herodotus*?"

"Herodotus." He shook his head. "She said Herodotus," he said to the sky. "Another splendid word. Have you read everything there is to read, Miss Vale?"

"I read. Frequently. Tell me, please."

"Yes. Herodotus."

Her eyes were open now. He held very, very still. As though a lovely bird had lit upon his arm and he didn't want to frighten it away.

And at last she sighed with deep happiness.

And then smiled and gave her head a little shake, as if trying to clear her head of laudanum.

"Goodness," she finally said, very inadequately.

"You've never before heard opera, Miss Vale?" His voice was gentle, and she didn't think she'd heard him sound truly *gentle*. She wasn't certain she liked it, because gentleness was sometimes perilously close to pity, which she could not for an instant tolerate. But there wasn't a shred of irony in it.

"No." It was awestruck and almost plaintive, the

word. She gave a short rueful laugh. "I just . . . I had no *idea*. I'm sorry. I didn't mean to . . ."

He shook his head, and her words trailed off.

They listened together as his former mistress's voice clambered like a monkey up over impossible scales, soared like a bird, really made a mockery of the notion there might be limitations to what a human voice could do, every bit of the acrobatics achingly beautiful, her voice so enormous an army could have marched with Signora Licari into Jericho and accomplished the same thing as Joshua, sans trumpets.

"It simply takes one that way, sometimes," he said softly. "It doesn't take everyone that way, but some."

She suddenly became aware that she could feel his breath, smoky and warm, on her cheek when he spoke. How did they come to stand so close? She didn't move away.

"I remember the first time I heard an opera," he continued. "It was—"

"Shhhh."

He grinned, a bright flash in the dark.

Sophia Licari's voice gamboled up a scale, then tumbled down it again in a series of remarkable, acrobatic trills. It taunted and demanded, teased, implored, and finally it came to an end on a note that by rights ought to have shattered the chandelier and sprinkled the gathering guests with crystal.

The crowd gathered in the Redmond ballroom thundered its approval.

Phoebe felt both exhausted and fulfilled. "Clapping seems inadequate," she murmured.

"Oh, it is, I assure you," he murmured, as *he* wasn't at the mercy of any sort of spell. "She would prefer obeisance. And I will tell you this, Miss Vale. She sounds like a goddess. But she's a human, by God. A vessel, if you will. An expensive, demanding, easily bored vessel for an otherworldly talent, who snores as loud as she sings and bathes less often than one might suspect."

She laughed, and then bit her lip to punish herself for laughing. "For shame! You oughtn't tell me things like that. It's not gentlemanly."

"I gave her a gift and showered her with luxuries and she tried to kill me. I just . . . everyone is human, Miss Vale. No one is flawless. We all have foibles, and beauty is in the eye of the beholder. And the beholder oftentimes gets it wrong."

Was he trying to convince her or himself? Was he trying to tell her something important?

Or did *everyone* in the ton have the wrong of it, when it came to him?

"I don't imagine you do obeisance well, Lord Dryden."

"Right again," he said with grim cheer. He wistfully studied his cheroot, which he'd smoked down to a nub. Contemplating perhaps whether to give it another suck.

It was only then she noticed she was clutching his sleeve. She relinquished it, abashed.

"I'm sorry," she whispered foolishly. "I didn't know I had . . . I'm so sorry."

"Don't be," he said, with a soft vehemence all out of proportion to the circumstance. "Don't be," he added more softly, as if correcting himself.

She could smell him now, that heady, unique manly scent of him. She could feel the heat radiating from him, as if he were a fire burning low. It was both soothing and disturbing.

She could not recall the last time she'd reached out for anyone, for safety or protection or sharing.

But protecting people was apparently what he did. In between dodging hurled humidors.

He spoke, very softly, paving over the unnerving moment. "I know I'm supposed to pretend to dislike or merely tolerate opera, as it's considered the manly thing to do. But I find it . . . transcendent. That is, when a true talent is behind it. And there is a veritable universe of difference, mind you, between opera and most musicales. I find musicales . . ." he searched for the proper word ". . . distressing."

Phoebe couldn't help but laugh at that. And the laugh fully restored her to her body when the music had all but taken her out of it and shook off the last of her awkwardness.

"Do *you* play the pianoforte, Miss Vale?"

She laughed. "You should *hear* the trepidation in your voice, Lord Dryden! Yes. I play competently at best. *But* I enjoy it very much," she warned him. "Doubtless you would suffer through my playing. You may yet need to do just that during your visit here."

"Oh, for you I would be polite for the duration. I wouldn't yawn or scratch or shift so much my chair squeaks."

"I am relieved to know it."

He nodded graciously.

She smiled, and wrapped her arms around her shoulders again. Without the shelter of music, the night began to nip at her exposed places. In more ways than one.

He shook one arm out of his coat, and was preparing to get out of the other sleeve in order to drape it about her shoulders.

She realized what he was doing and took a startled step backward.

He froze. One arm in his coat, the other out. And then wordlessly, expressionlessly, he reinstalled his arm into his coat.

They were silent now, awkward again.

His hands fumbled at his cheroot. They weren't quite shaking, but he hadn't command over them. He looked down at the spent thing accusingly.

The man who was known for grace.

She suspected they were both a little shaken by how *right* the gesture seemed, how spontaneous and innate. He wanted to protect her.

She'd shied away.

She was a schoolteacher and a paid companion and he was a marquess, and really, he oughtn't to hang his coat over her shoulders any more than he ought to hang it over the cook's shoulders. And she'd never really known how to let someone take care of her, anyway.

"Lisbeth plays pianoforte very well," he mused after a moment, sounding a little too hearty and casual. "One might even say she possesses actual talent."

And money. And beauty. And prospects. And family. And beautiful clothes. And a fan that reminds you of her.

Does she have your heart?

Or is your heart subject to "business arrangements" only, too?

"That she does," she agreed softly. Because she was above all things honest, and because it was the right thing to say and do in the circumstances.

The *safe* thing to do.

Nonsense. It was the cowardly thing to do, she told herself, suffering.

Suddenly Lisbeth's Chinese silk shawl burned in her hand. She turned her head nervously back toward the door. Bloody hell! How long *had* she been gone?

He must have sensed she was poised to bolt, because his voice came quickly.

"I've never told another soul about the vases and the humidor and . . . the like."

She froze.

She drew in a breath, and her suddenly racing heart made the breath shudder out when she exhaled. A part of her was furious and impatient. It was very unfair of destiny to arrange for her to be alone in the dark with a soul-stirring man and soul-stirring music. She was only human, too, and though she was strong she had nowhere near his fortitude. She wanted to stomp her foot.

Don't burden me with your friendship. Don't gift me with your thoughts! Don't seek me out. Nothing good will ever come of this. I'm only twenty-two! I haven't the answers. I just wanted to be near you.

"Perhaps you told me because I'm . . . safe."

I'm nobody. I wouldn't dare gossip. I'm leaving the country.

Even she didn't think that was true. She did, however, want to hear what he would say about it.

He lifted his head slowly. And as she followed the clean line of his profile with her own eyes, it felt as though it were being etched into her heart, one curve, one angle, one hollow at a time.

When he spoke, his voice was soft again. Mildly incredulous.

"Oh, you're not safe, Miss Vale."

Meaning rippled out from the words. Like water disturbed by the skip of a stone. They contained warning and promise, bemusement and bittersweet irony.

And because, despite uncertainties and gulfs, they

were both rogues at heart, their smiles were simultaneous, crooked, slow.

She shook her head. Wonderingly or warningly or exasperatedly, she wasn't sure.

The space between them, both the distance and the nearness, just shy of inappropriate, was suddenly fraught with meaning. It seemed ridiculous, when really, by right of natural law, she ought to be in his arms.

And then something spritely and raucous began on the pianoforte, and she jumped.

"I'll go inside and listen to her now." She was all bright babble now. "After all, I didn't jilt Signora Licari, and her voice is beautiful and rare. And loud. At least you shall know when it's safe to return, because it shall be apparent when she stops."

He sighed, acceding to the broken spell. "Is she staying beneath this roof tonight?"

"One can hardly send a famous soprano to the Pig & Thistle to sleep in the room behind the bar. But I understand she has another engagement in London, so she'll be leaving straightaway. Perhaps even this evening."

"Perhaps I should sleep at the Pig & Thistle."

"There's always the barn."

He grinned suddenly again, looking like a boy. She wondered if he was relieved that the moment had been shattered, too.

How long *had* she been gone? The length of an aria, at least. However long an aria was. And now the panic was a thing with claws. She hadn't the time to fetch her own shawl now. She held up Lisbeth's shawl. "Lisbeth might be in there shivering even now. So—I—"

She spun on her heel and almost dashed. She could

hear her own footsteps, and it worked on her nerves as though someone or something was in pursuit of her.

My own desires, she thought melodramatically.

She was nearly to the door when his voice rose, called after her.

"Where in London, Scheherezade?"

She turned and walked backward a few feet before deciding to answer. He was asking where she'd been born.

"Seven Dials."

Mull that out here in the dark, Lord Dryden.

"And you owe me a gift," she added.

Her heartbeat matching the staccato beat of her footsteps, she disappeared into the house.

Chapter 10

She hadn't realized quite how cold she was until she burst again into the heat of the house and began to rush back to the salon, her slippers nearly skidding over marble. She deliberately slowed her pace to the sedate one expected of a schoolmistress/paid companion, straight-spined and square-shouldered, one foot in front of the other and . . . well, how about that. Very like walking a tightrope.

Interesting that she should have that in common with the marquess.

She peered around the parlor doorway to get her first glimpse of the soprano. Signora Sophia Licari stood next to the pianoforte, one hand resting atop it as though it were a beast trained to do her bidding and simply awaiting her next command. She was a gorgeous beast herself, a lioness, with masses of golden-brown hair piled up high and stabbed into place with sparkling pins. Her dress was a melodramatic crimson and very snug. Her bosom was majestic. Her waist tiny. Her eyes were all but closed, her long, long lashes lying over her cheeks, as her head tipped back as inhumanly glorious sound poured from her.

The diamonds around her throat were as subtle as a breastplate on a Viking warrior.

They didn't look like the sort of diamonds the marquess would choose, which would naturally be tasteful, expensive, and blindingly pure. Perhaps she'd moved on to another protector. In all fairness, Signora Licari didn't look like the sort to hurl a humidor out of outraged pride. Her dignity, like the marquess's, was a palpable thing. And there was an otherness about her that Phoebe was certain was apparent to everyone who saw her: *I am not ordinary*, it announced. *Rather, I am extraordinary. Proceed at your peril, mere mortal.*

But he was no ordinary man. Even goddesses like this one had succumbed to him.

I would never take the loss of him lightly, either, if he'd ever been mine.

But here was the thing: even as he'd spoken about her, she'd been certain he'd never truly belonged to Sophia Licari. She knew it the way she knew the color of her own eyes, or the freckle next to her mouth, or that the sun would rise again.

Because he's meant for me.

She huffed out an impatient breath, blowing the dangerous, ridiculous thought away.

Phoebe peered in at the audience, savoring it with unguarded wonder. She would tell Postlethwaite about it later: how the rows of beautiful people looked lit by the Redmonds' gaslight and enormous chandeliers, their cheeks flushed from the extravagant heat and all those bodies snugly packed together on velvet-cushioned chairs. Lord Waterburn was fast asleep, head thrown back, mouth open, arms crossed over his chest. Jonathan Redmond and Lord Argosy were in the back row pretending to pay rapt attention, but their hands were moving surreptitiously, and she suspected they were playing some kind of card game balanced on their thighs. She saw Jonathan hand over a rolled-up note of some kind, likely a pound note.

Her intimidating hosts, Isaiah and Fanchette Redmond, were ensconced in the front row, seemingly riveted by the performance.

Isaiah reached for his wife's hand, brought it over to his lap.

Phoebe was fascinated by the gesture. Was it staged for the guests, or was he indeed moved enough to clutch his handsome, frightening wife's hand? It was such a *human* thing for a man like him to do.

Lisbeth was leaning forward as far as she could, as though the music was a beam of light.

She hadn't noticed Phoebe standing at the entrance at all.

Phoebe smiled ruefully. She was pleased Lisbeth had lost herself in the music. But no matter how often she looked at her, she never became less beautiful or appealing or less perfectly suited to be the wife of a marquess.

Or less determined to *be* the wife of a marquess. She was clutching her fan as if it was the marquess himself.

The song ended with a note Signora Licari teased into lasting a quavering eternity. She must have lungs like bellows, Phoebe thought admiringly.

Signora Licari regally ducked her head when applause crashed around her.

Phoebe took that opportunity to scurry into the room and slide into her chair next to Lisbeth. She nudged her gently, and Lisbeth's hand absently reached out for the shawl. She scarcely glanced at Phoebe, so enraptured was she by the glorious creature that was Signora Licari. Too enraptured, with any luck, to notice the marquess's continued absence.

"Thank you. Did you *hear* her, Phoebe? Isn't she *marvelous*?"

"I've never heard anything quite like it. Thank you for inviting me so I could hear her." She said this quite sincerely. No matter what, she would never forget it.

Lisbeth turned then, eyes wide with surprise, indecision, and the expression she finally decided upon was benevolence. "Oh, Phoebe. I'm glad that I could share it with . . ."

Her face blanked peculiarly.

She blinked.

She lifted her shawl to her nose . . . and lowered it slowly again to her lap.

And then she leaned forward abruptly and sniffed the air near Phoebe.

Phoebe reared back.

Lisbeth stopped sniffing. Her lovely brow furrowed, as if she was undecided about what she was about to say.

"Phoebe . . . ?"

"Goodness. Is aught amiss, Lisbeth?"

"You . . . you smell like cheroot *smoke*." This last part she said on a reproachful hush.

Christ!

Phoebe's stomach plummeted. She stared at Lisbeth.

Who stared back at her. Looking troubled but vaguely hopeful, like a child who hopes to be reassured no monsters are under its bed.

Phoebe wanted to speak. Really she did. A number of excuses occurred to her and she would have produced any of them, if only her mouth and brain were in communication, not clubbed into a stupor by guilt and terror. Her mouth simply wouldn't move at all.

"It's not Phoebe, it's probably me, you goose." Jonathan leaned over back of her chair so suddenly both girls jumped. "Besides, *she* can't afford the kind of cheroots we all normally smoke."

He was teasing, she knew; she saw the glint in his eyes. But then he flicked a glance at Phoebe. She saw his eyes travel to her gloves and linger, and widen infinitesimally. Some expression—surprise?—she couldn't quite identify twitched across his face, there and gone. He looked up into hers, and his expression was still kind.

She still hadn't quite recovered from the urge to faint. But she produced a smile that probably looked as sickly as it felt. She rejoiced in the fact that her mouth could move again, at least.

"I suppose you're right." Lisbeth sniffed at Jonathan. "You do rather stink, Jon." She wrinkled her nose, sniffed her shawl again, frowned—only Lisbeth could make a frown seem pretty—shrugged, and then decided stoically to drape it over her shoulders.

And Jonathan helped her in a very gentlemanly and cousinly fashion. As if tucking the question of the cheroot stink decisively away.

And as he did he looked up at Phoebe. He didn't wink at her. But something speculative and—dare she say it?—sympathetic lingered in her eyes. Odd, but she'd never thought Jonathan Redmond capable of appearing enigmatic. Or of being complex.

But then she thought of Isaiah Redmond reaching for his wife's hand. And the marquess walking a tightrope. The one thing she'd been able to count on her entire life was her cleverness. She was so often *right*. It was humbling and disorienting to realize that she in truth knew nothing at all. One only ever saw a fraction of someone, whatever it was they chose to show you, and extrapolated a whole person from that. And saw them through a prism of one's own prejudices.

Does one ever really know anyone? the marquess had asked her.

The pianoforte music started up again. Phoebe and the smoke were forgotten as Lisbeth folded her hands rapturously beneath her chin again and curved her mouth into a little smile. It looked to Phoebe very much like another pose she'd practiced in front of the mirror.

When Signora Licari opened her mouth to sing, Phoebe could feel her voice vibrating in her chest, as though her heart was singing along. And she ducked her head and, with great hope, surreptitiously sniffed her own shawl. She said a silent hosanna. It, too, smelled like smoke.

Which meant it smelled like him.

She closed her eyes and surrendered to a moment of weakness. She imagined the weight of his coat draped over her, warming and protecting her, simply because she belonged to him.

The church bells hadn't yet rung, the sun was barely a suggestion in the sky, but Mr. Postlethwaite had already hung out his sign and was just about to take his first sip of tea. He sighed with happiness instead when the bells on his door danced and in walked Lord Deep Pockets.

He peered out the window. No carriage today, alas, advertising to the world his presence and luring curious crowds who would want to, need to, buy something where Lord Dryden had purchased something. He'd instead tethered a horse—an enormous black one, as glossy as the toes of the man's boots—outside the shop.

Which Postlethwaite assumed was the marquess's version of arriving incognito.

He replaced the teacup in his saucer with a clink, and bowed low and deep.

"A pleasure and honor to see you again, my lord. Did the lady appreciate her gift, or have you had an opportunity to give it?"

"I believe the lady sincerely did appreciate it, and thank you again for your assistance, Mr. Postlethwaite."

Postlethwaite was tickled by the opportunity to speak so formally. "May I help to find something else? We've a selection of gloves for gentlemen."

The gloves again! Jules could have sworn there was a devilish glint in the shopkeeper's eye.

And then the marquess said the words he'd been dreading uttering. But the compulsion could not be denied, and he wasn't fundamentally a coward.

"I find today I am in need of a bonnet."

Mr. Postlethwaite was silent.

And then his eyes crept toward the marquess's hairline.

"It will be a gift for a *woman*, Mr. Postlethwaite."

"Of course, sir."

The marquess wished the "of course" sounded a bit more sincere. He'd scarcely been in the shop for more than three minutes and already his dignity was fraying.

But he'd actually lost sleep contemplating and rejecting strategies with the seriousness one might plan a military campaign. And *while* he planned, he tried to ignore the fact that he'd decided to do this was wholly irrational, and that he'd never yet done anything irrational in his life.

But there was no question that he would do it.

In the end, it all came down to whether he could imagine giving the instructions to a footman or to his valet for the purchase he wanted to make. And he simply couldn't countenance it.

"Would you like to peruse the bonnets for a time, my lord, or did you have a particular one in mind? I can show you—"

By way of answer, the marquess merely raised one finger: *Hold*. Because the only way he could be certain he had the right one had to do with . . . geography.

Mr. Postlethwaite watched, riveted, as the marquess followed the instructions he would have needed tell a footman, as carefully and methodically as if he were walking off a treasure map:

Stand in the corner of Postlethwaite's shop, the one brightest at three o'clock in the afternoon. Likely it is not so bright at half past seven in the morning. Align yourself directly opposite the mirror behind the counter, because that's where she was standing when you first saw her. Make sure you can see yourself clearly in the mirror.

Then turn around quickly again, and seize the bonnet immediately to your right. The ribbons on it are a sort of deep lavender, and the silk flowers are various shades of purple.

With a certain amount of triumph and ceremony, he lifted it off the stand.

Yes. This was the one. Fine-woven, deep gold straw, it would frame her face. That was the extent of his guess regarding the reasons for her passion for it. He hadn't the faintest idea whether the color of the ribbons or flowers would suit her; he suspected she knew. Women invariably did. All he knew it might as well have been the grail for the way she'd been yearning after it with her eyes when he entered the shop.

Women, he'd thought then.

And now he was wildly, humbly (humble wasn't one of his usual conditions) grateful he'd noticed, because he for some reason had never before wanted so desperately to please someone.

"Ah. A lovely bonnet, that one. And it's a bit dea—"

He'd been about to say "dear," but the marquess severed his sentence with a mere look. The very notion that something might be too dear for him, let alone a bonnet, was absurd.

And Postlethwaite was almost surprised to immediately find himself behind the counter, as much to do the marquess's bidding as to put a little distance between him and the intensity radiating from the man.

"It's a fine thing you've rescued that particular bonnet. A certain young lady was about to stare a hole clean through it before I sold it."

"It's a very good thing, then, isn't it, Mr. Postlethwaite, that I rescued it from such a fate?"

The room was cool, the gray light filtering in through the parted curtains told her it was just past dawn, and her chest was too *light*. Perhaps it was because a fat striped cat wasn't sprawled atop it. She patted her hand along the bed searching for fur; she recalled where she was when she heard the soft clanking sound of the maid building up her chamber fire.

The maid heard the rustle of her sheets as she sat upright.

She smiled shyly. Her white cap was sliding off of her head, and she pushed it back and put a coal thumbprint on her forehead when she did.

Phoebe smiled back. And then the maid was upright

and quick as a wraith at the door again. Keeping fires
burning and candles lit around the vast house was a
Sisyphean chore.

She paused. "There was a box for ye at the door,
miss. I brought it in."

And she was gone.

A box? Phoebe leaned forward in her not-quite-
for-servants bed and looked about her not-quite-for-
servants chamber, and saw it. Large, and round, of the
sort that might contain a . . .

. . . might contain a . . .

She practically toppled out of bed and lunged for it.

She recognized at once it was from Postlethwaite's
shop. Had *Postlethwaite* sent a gift to her? This seemed
very unlikely, unless he'd undergone a conversion to a
mysterious religion and had decided to divest himself
of his possessions. He attended services every Sunday
along with the rest of the town, but his allegiance—
after his Maker—was to the almighty pound note.
Phoebe harbored no delusions that he might be fonder
of her than he was of profit, though she was certain she
ranked highly enough in his esteem.

She sat cross-legged upon the carpet spread out
before the new fire and tucked her bare toes beneath
the hem of her nightdress.

And then with a certain amount of ceremony she
shimmied up the lid and began to paw gently through
layers of tissue.

She thought she glimpsed purple.

Oh, God.

She was so overwhelmed she needed to stop entirely for a moment. She paused, glanced stealthily back
toward the bed, half expecting to see her sleeping form
in it, still dreaming.

She began unwrapping again, the tissue rattling in her shaking hands. Her head was a bubble, light, floating.

When she uncovered her first glimpse of gold straw, she cast her eyes toward the ceiling and mouthed *Hallelujah!*

As she did, a half sheet of foolscap, ragged-edged, tumbled out of the box.

She took it up in awkward fingers and read. The note said, in a script she'd never before seen, tall, emphatic, and very neat:

I should like to know you.

A signature was hardly necessary, and there was none.

Joy was a sunburst in her chest. She gave a short, wondering laugh, feeling wholly mischievous, alive.

She'd demanded a gift. And he'd actually given her a gift.

She thought she'd better open her eyes again quickly, lest the bonnet disappear.

Better yet—she lowered it onto her head and carefully—and quickly—tied the ribbons. There. It felt at home there.

Like it was made for her.

She didn't know how she would send word down to Lisbeth that she would be spending the morning gazing at herself in the mirror. Because it was really all she wanted to do.

She stood up now, and did just that, turning her head this way and that.

How had he known?

It was yet another lesson that threw off her equilibrium. She'd thought the marquess had walked into Postlethwaite's and reviewed the shop with dispassion at best, or judgment at worst. But he'd swept it more the way an army scout takes in the lay of any battlefield, taking note of everything, including the plain disheveled young woman gazing with unrequited loved at a specific bonnet.

I should like to know you.

She tested a number of theories, because she always wanted to know the why of things. She considered whether it was a game for him, if he was indeed a bored aristocrat distracted by novelty she presented, or by how she could dodge and feint with words like any talented fencer. Whether he was looking to form another *association* in the absence of one . . . though she was hardly his type. He wanted the finest. The best. The Signora Licaris of the world.

But she now knew something no one else in the ton truly understood: he wasn't a frivolous or reckless man. He did nothing without a reason. Surely the bonnet represented . . . a *strategy* . . . at the very least.

Theories flitted in and out of her mind, but it was no use. They were all eventually incinerated in her joy. Like moths in a flame.

No one talks to me the way you do, he'd said.

She thought of the marquess scooping a moth out of the air and releasing it again, only to watch it head straight for the lamp again.

Helpless not to risk its whole existence for light and warmth.

Chapter 11

Phoebe was wrong. Jules had no bloody idea why he'd purchased a damned bonnet.

And *nothing* had ever troubled him more than this realization.

He'd only just become aware that he'd been on a kind of trajectory, as though he'd been shot from a catapult without his permission. It had culminated in him buying a bonnet. He'd been *helpless* not to buy the bonnet. And he couldn't trace how he'd arrived at that moment, the moment where became at the mercy of something immune to his reason, and he disliked this as much as he disliked regret.

Because one of the symptoms seemed to be restless pacing. He was *not* a meanderer by nature, a person who moved purposelessly to expend energy. But he'd arrived in the churchyard before the bells even rang to call the town to services, and this was precisely what he did: walked among the ancient crooked headstones, counting the number of Redmonds and Everseas who had died in the town since 1500. Quite a few people named Hawthorne were buried there, too. Two or three Endicotts. Someone named Ethelred. He wondered how many of them had killed each *other* while a discreet messenger engaged by Postlethwaite ferried his gift over to Redmond House, with instructions to hand it to a footman, who would then deposit it with their odd silent discretion outside the chamber door of Miss Phoebe Vale.

Finally irritated by the pacing and by the evidence of mortality all around him, Jules went inside even before the bells were rung and took a seat in the Redmond pews.

He hadn't been a churchgoer since it had been a compulsory childhood activity. The pews were still as hard as penance itself, and dug themselves with what he suspected was meant to be a purifying pain into his thighs and into an awkward place on his back. It was a squat little church, probably one of the first things built when the first Eversea and Redmond took a crack at each other's skulls in 1066, and it contained a delicious hush, seasoned by thousands of prayers, births and deaths and weddings.

Moments later there was what could only be described as a sedate stampede, primarily of women, and he watched them avidly, with burning eyes. Mostly he watched their heads. His palms were actually *damp*. He surreptitiously pressed them against his thighs. He'd never been more enthralled by bonnets, more aware of their staggering variety of flowers and ribbons and shapes.

And he'd never seen so many shining female faces instantly pointed raptly in one direction in a church. He followed them, expecting to see the North Star or a grail of some sort. Instead, a lanky chap with silvery fair hair and long, fine-boned handsome face and the sort of blue eyes that projected across the room like sunlight through stained glass windows stood up there. He wore his cassock with the same panache as the marquess wore Weston. As though he was born to it. And something about the way he looked out at the congregation . . . something about the way he stood . . . made Jules suspect he had a sense of humor.

He nodded at Jules, who nodded back.

In came the Eversea contingent, Jacob and Isolde, the infamous Colin and his wife. He was acquainted with them, but not well, and everyone—that meant the whole of England—knew who Colin was.

When he saw Isaiah Redmond enter he thought his heart would stop. He was followed by Fanchette Redmond, Jonathan and Lord Argosy, Lisbeth . . . where his eyes lingered, for she had that beauty that caught one's eye like a hook, and who couldn't help but respond to it? She looked like an angel reporting for duty. Lisbeth saw him, and her eyes brightened and her smile was white and precisely measured, as though she had a specific smile for every occasion, like a doctor has tools for surgery.

But he couldn't help it. He looked past her, eagerly and . . .

Hallelujah! She was wearing the bonnet.

His heart leaped like a spectator at a triumphant cricket match.

And she really did look wonderful in it, but then again, that could have something to do with the smile she was wearing along with it. It was all of a piece to him. She walked in her own light through the door of the church.

She cast her eyes up at him from the shelter of the bonnet and found him, of course, immediately. Because his gaze could have burned a hole through her.

Their gazes locked, lingered. He thought her cheeks went rosier. But her smile was such a thing of pure, saucy delight he only noticed when the bells stopped ringing that he'd gone breathless. He suddenly had a terrible suspicion that his cheeks were rosier, too. Dear God. Because he was definitely warm.

Her eyes darted to the left. And to the right. And then, as surreptitiously as she was able . . . she *saluted* him.

He grinned.

Lisbeth noticed none of this and naturally thought the grin was all for her and beamed radiantly in his direction, tipping her head fondly.

Which caused an immediate mass swiveling of heads to get a look at whom her beam was directed.

He was aware of the collective rustling of silk flowers and muslin shifting on the polished pews, like a breeze through wheat. He could almost hear the muscles in necks creaking with the strain of turning in order to gulp down the sight of him. All those eyes. He was accustomed to eyes, but he could hardly snuff out his grin in an instant without injuring Lisbeth's feelings, or at the very least, confusing her.

Oh, God.

And yet he wasn't a beamer by nature, either. When *he* smiled people tended to buckle with relief or fawn. It would never do to allow the world at large to think he was suddenly easily pleased. A gratuitous *smiler*, for heaven's sake.

He decided he'd best turn it into something like un-specific beneficence. He rotated his head much the way one might swing a lantern to search for smugglers off the coast. Isaiah and Fanchette and Jonathan Redmond were all caught in the beam of it. Jonathan flinched and looked tempted to throw up an arm. Likely he was hung over and startled by the glare.

Phoebe had ducked her head. He had the distinct impression she was biting the inside of her cheek to keep from laughing.

And at last, all the heads swiveled back to the handsome vicar, restless for their weekly long look at him.

Adam Sylvaine, the new vicar of Pennyroyal Green, had the perfect voice for the job, at once soothing and conversational, commanding and resonant. And he was speaking today on, of all things . . . covetousness.

More than one bum shifted uncomfortably, certain he was talking directly to them but forgiving him at the same time, given that he was what many of the ladies in the congregation coveted.

The marquess's wasn't one of the shifting bums. He was staring at the back of a bonnet. He was riveted by the few inches of fair neck exposed between a lace collar and the straw curve of the hat. It seemed the most significant few inches of skin he'd ever seen. The glittering fair hair that traced it mesmerized him, and all he could think now was what it would be like to put his lips there, just there, in that sweet bend between her chin and throat. To touch his tongue to the silkiness. And watch the gooseflesh rise over her arms, and her nipples peak beneath the muslin, and—

Hardly the sort of thoughts one ought to have in church. And for good physiological reasons. He shifted; the pew obligingly dug punitively into his back and he returned to admiring the Redmond profiles, like one ordered to read scripture.

It was decided (by Lisbeth) that they would all go out for a long healthy walk with sketchbooks after church to see the ruins, and return for a hearty breakfast. She secretly thought she looked well when her cheeks were pink with exercise, and she was quite right, of course. She did.

The men were less enthusiastic about the healthful walk than they were about the opportunity to shoot something, grouse or some such. So they congregated on the groomed parkland and waited for Jonathan, who ambled slowly toward them from a distance. Plodding at his side was what appeared to be a dog. A very fat hound.

As they drew nearer, it was clear the hound was ancient. It had gray round its muzzle and huge watery eyes.

"What is that?" Argosy was suspicious.

"It's a dog," Jonathan said defensively.

"Well, it's barely that. What is the dog in aid of? It can hardly fend off attacking beasts. Has it any teeth? It might not be able to hold a game fowl."

The dog gazed up at Argosy with eyes full of soulful contempt.

Jules eyed it critically. "It seems to have been enjoying a quiet retirement before you rousted it, Jonathan."

"When one goes out hunting, one ought to have a dog," Jonathan insisted. "And father has his own hounds out on a shooting party with the neighbors. How are we going to flush birds?"

Jules shrugged. "Very well, if this is all the hound we have. It may surprise us with hidden talents."

Their party trudged forth. The ruins were at the end of a long hike through a very fine wood, growing increasingly thick the deeper in they walked, and since they were enjoying a crisp, clear autumn day, there were no complaints for quite some time. Just cheerful chatter from Lisbeth and pleasant acknowledgment of her chatter from Jules, who nodded and added "you don't say?" in appropriate places while devoting most of his energies to admiring the back of Phoebe Vale and the bonnet.

The complaints began to trickle in as the wood thickened, when it seemed Lisbeth had meandered off course in her insistence that her ruins were in a particular direction, and when it became clear that Waterburn and Jonathan and Argosy had been optimistic to bring muskets as the hound wasn't likely to flush anything. Game foul were likely watching it trudge by and snickering beneath their wings.

The path narrowed, so that they could only proceed two by two, and when Lisbeth and Jonathan began to bicker about the proper direction, Jules dropped back and strode alongside Miss Vale.

Silently, for some time. She said nothing.

He said nothing.

But she was wearing a small, secretive, impish, and very pleased little smile.

"I like your bonnet very much, Miss Vale," he said finally.

"Do you? It's new, you know."

"Hardly new. I'm given to understand that a certain young lady nearly stared holes in it before I purchased it. You can count yourself fortunate it remains intact."

She smiled. "One might say the same thing about you, my lord, given how a gathering tends to stare at you."

He laughed. Lisbeth, from far up ahead, turned her head over her shoulder and sent him a look from between her lashes. He thought he'd seen Miss Violet Redmond use that very look on suitors. It was an excellent look, indeed. He smiled reflexively and she turned again, satisfied with the attention for the time being.

He turned to discover that Phoebe had neatly ducked out of sight behind a tree. He ought to feel guilty for being so complicit. Instead, he was nervous for another reason entirely.

Jules, with great trepidation, asked the question he'd been dreading. "Is it the right bonnet?"

She let him suffer for a second or so. Or at least that's how it seemed.

"It's the right one."

He just nodded. Too relieved, too elated—in truth, too confused—to speak. He just wanted to admire her in her bonnet. The desire baffled and irritated him, and all at once he felt a peculiar pressure welling.

"Tell me, Lord Dryden . . . does it suit me?"

She was flirting. Suddenly it felt like torture, because he was so strangely raw and exposed.

"I don't know," he said irritably. "Is it meant to improve you?"

She swiveled toward him, eyes wide with shock.

"Because nothing could," he added.

Her mouth dropped in astonishment. Blotchy scarlet rushed her complexion. One would have thought he'd shot her.

Oh dear God!

He realized belatedly how wrong it had sounded.

"No! God . . . that is to say . . . nothing is necessary to improve you. Nothing could possibly make you better . . . than you already are."

It was a staggering compliment, both in its clumsiness and magnitude and its sheer honesty. It had been forged somewhere inside him immune from sense.

He was appalled.

Silence fell hard. Once again, he'd managed to shock both of them.

He wished he could unsay it. The aftermath was too unnerving.

He looked ahead at Lisbeth and Jonathan and the hound, at Argosy and Waterburn, and tried to remember how he'd felt about things, about anything at all, before he'd arrived here in Pennyroyal Green. He considered how much simpler it would be to return to that time, and knew it was already too late.

And then Phoebe drew in such a long fortifying breath he could almost *feel* the crisp air entering her lungs so aware was he of her. He finally got up the courage to steal a glance. The words had made her face luminous, and set her eyes ablaze. But her eyebrows were faintly troubled.

She said nothing.

He found that lavender ribbon tied beneath her chin unaccountably moving. Such a pretty thing for someone who'd hailed from Seven Dials, the most notorious district in London. No wonder she'd yearned for it.

"So. Seven Dials," he said almost brightly.

She smiled a small smile and shook her head slightly at his tone.

"How does one go from Seven Dials to Pennyroyal Green? Were you a delightful orphan child scooped up and born off by a generous benefactor?"

"I was not. I was a thoroughgoing termagant. I was very unpleasant and wild. Though I suppose I *was* scooped up."

"Imagine a thoroughgoing termagant using phrases like 'thoroughgoing termagant.' When you were scooped up, you were only . . ."

"Ten years old. They had to put out a snare like a wild

hare to catch me on the streets of St. Giles. They left a crust of bread as a lure. I dangled by one ankle up in the air for a time until they cut me down and whisked me off to Miss Marietta Endicott's for reforming."

He was so delighted with this image he couldn't speak for a moment. "You didn't. They didn't."

"Very well. Metaphorically speaking, then. Why do you want to know?"

"Are you going to begin demanding more gifts for snippets of your tale? Because I warn you, I cannot surpass the one I've given you. And a bargain is a bargain, Miss Vale. I'll have your story, please."

She smiled one of those slow smiles that took over her whole face. She was clearly trying not to laugh.

Lisbeth turned her head around then, her hands full of autumn flowers. White lacy things, lady's-tresses, he thought they were called. She held them up to her cheek as if to test for softness, and tipped her face against them. It was an enchanting image, marred only by the fact that he suspected she knew it was enchanting. She smiled saucily and pranced forward to catch up to Jonathan and Argosy.

That was when he'd noticed that Phoebe stopped and looked about interestedly, ducking behind a tree again, so Lisbeth couldn't see her.

He bit back a smile.

"I think wild sage grows about this area," she said suddenly. "It smells wonderful, you know."

"It might. It does. You were saying about your childhood in Seven Dials?"

"I wasn't."

"Oh, for heaven's sake. Are you really so invested in preserving your mythology?"

"As invested as you are in preserving yours."

"And yet I told you things. About humidors and the like."

"Our lives were very different, Lord Dryden. I don't think you'll—"

"Understand? Don't condescend to me, Miss Vale. You're afraid I'll judge you. The way you judged me."

This actually made her a bit angry, he could see, because her pace accelerated and her jaw grew tense and she seemed very focused on whatever was straight ahead of her.

"Very well. It was a very long time ago, mind you. And I was ten years old."

"And your parents?"

"Well, they left, didn't they? One at a time." She'd said it brightly, but the breathlessness in her voice told him it had been difficult for her to say it.

"Did they?" He tried not to soften his voice. She, he suspected, was the sort who would grow restive if subjected to overt sympathy.

"Papa first. We lived in rooms above a pub. He just . . . stopped coming home. Mama was arrested for picking pockets and was transported, or so I was told, by the prostitute who kept rooms upstairs. All I know is that she disappeared one day, too. I didn't want to go to the workhouse and so I fled and lived with a series of other . . . characters . . . until someone, a gentleman who I believe now was someone's man of affairs, determined I was clever and swept me away to Sussex, kicking and biting, I might add. I was installed at Miss Marietta Endicott's academy. I still don't know who my benefactor was."

Christ.

It was a good deal to absorb, but he couldn't remain silent too long or she would know how it had affected him: like a swift kick to his gut. Would that he could undo all of that for her, remake her life with safety and family.

"Do you have any other relatives? Any brothers or sisters?"

"None that I'm aware of."

"You've no one."

He instantly regretted saying it just like that. For she blinked as surely as if he'd jabbed a finger into a wound.

"Oh, I wouldn't say that," she said a moment later. "I've a cat."

This took him aback. He took the view that cats were work animals, and occupied a place just slightly above the vermin they caught. They lived in barns.

"What is its name?" He wanted to know about *her* cat.

"His name is Charybdis. He came with me from St. Giles. He's a bit elderly for a cat, now, I suppose. Still quite spry, however."

"You named your cat for a . . . a sea monster?" From somewhere in the mists of memory of Eaton days he wracked his brain to remember the mythology. *Between Scylla and Charybdis,* so the saying went, when one was between two unattractive choices. Charybdis was a nymph-turned-sea monster, daughter of Poseidon, who gulped down ships.

"That's how they knew I was clever." Very dryly said. "My cat's name. Quite a mouthful."

"But how did you learn to read? Let alone Greek mythology?"

"An apothecary in St. Giles by the name of McBride gave me a picture book of myths that had . . . well, let's just say, it came his way through one of his customers. I suspect he told one of his customers about me, too, which is how some tender-hearted person decided I should be sent to Sussex and Miss Endicott's. And my mother could read—I don't know where she learned, but I always took it for granted that she could—and I would follow along with the story as she read it to me. I suppose I must have learned my letters that way. All I know is that reading came easily to me, and I liked it."

"Why didn't you name the kitten something precious, like Daphne, or Apollo?"

"I suppose it's because I always wished I had an ally, someone to protect me, and Charybdis the monster was the most fearsome thing I could imagine. Even more fearsome than The Watch or the drunk men who fought in the streets and, well, you can imagine. I supposed I had little faith that even the Greek gods would be much of a match for the likes of St. Giles. I wanted something truly *nasty* as a familiar."

More dry humor.

But Mother of God, what must she have seen as a child?

St. Giles was violence and darkness and noise and rot; sagging drunks leaning against sagging buildings and dying in alleys from gin poisoning. Criminals committed their thievery in other more affluent parts of London and fled to St. Giles like rats into holes.

He looked at her, fine skin, worn walking dress, new bonnet . . . and the thought was unbearable: she'd been so afraid she'd needed a kitten for a talisman. He almost couldn't breathe from imagining it.

He understood now that her unique light, the light he basked in, existed by virtue of all those shadows. And the shadows were what made her seem more real than everyone else, threw her into relief.

She was right. He didn't know what to say to her.

And until he'd met this woman, he'd never in his life been at a loss.

"Is Charybdis very fearsome, then?" What a coward. And yet it seemed safe enough to keep talking about the cat.

"Oh, yes. Very." Oddly, she sounded sincere. "He has a good deal of striped fur. One of the other teachers is feeding him while I'm here."

"And what will he do when you go to Africa?"

"Why, come with me, of course."

He saw Waterburn turn his great blond head toward him. Then narrow his eyes thoughtfully.

"Seen anything you'd like to shoot?" he called to Waterburn, devilishly.

Waterburn shrugged, bored. The hound swiveled its big head disinterestedly at the sound of a raised voice, and trudged onward with a world-weary, put-upon seen-it-all gait. Honestly, dog, how unbearable could life in the Redmonds' stables be? Jules wondered dryly.

When he turned back around, Phoebe had vanished. Completely.

Chapter 12

He swiveled his head about madly.

Lisbeth frolicked ahead of Jonathan and Argosy, looking like one of those lacy white flowers she'd just plucked up. Tendrils of dark hair escaped artfully from her bonnet and lay as eloquently as sixteenth notes against the white of her neck.

"It's this way, Lord Waterburn. Isn't it, Jon? Since you claim to know. Jules, I cannot wait for you to see it!"

She turned her head, sent a smile over her shoulder. It was a breathtaking angle for her, all cheekbone and long throat. Her eyes flashed blue.

He smiled again. "I cannot wait to see it," he echoed.

There were ruins simply bloody everywhere in this part of England. They were all to some extent picturesque. The things one did for women.

"No, not that way. There's a haunted hunting box that way, Lisbeth," came Jonathan's voice, "and best mind yourself or someone will mistake you for a deer and shoot you."

"Oh, Jonathan!" She was irritated. "That would never happen. I'm all in white. I hardly look like a deer."

"A unicorn then."

"But who would shoot a unicorn?"

And so they disappeared, bickering, from view.

What the devil—? A woman couldn't just vanish into thin air. He scanned the pathway. Oaks had dropped their loads of leaves, but hawthorns were everywhere thick and rustling with tiny hidden creatures.

And then he saw the narrow passage between a hawthorn and the trunk of a large oak.

He peeked through.

And there she stood, in an almost magical clearing, a circle of lush meadow grass not yet killed by frost bounded by, hidden by, hawthorne and oaks and trees that hadn't yet lost all of their leaves.

She was dappled in the shadows of leaves when she stood up, smiling, with a handful of green clutched in her fist.

"You see?" she presented, triumphantly. "I was right. Sage does grow here. And it smells heavenly."

She pressed it to her nose and inhaled deeply.

He watched her close her eyes to isolate herself with the scent. All at once every corner of his being seemed filled with light.

He'd gone mute.

"There's a region in France that claims sage helps in the easing of grief. They plant them around tombstones in their cemeteries," she explained.

"How did you . . ." he tried.

But there really was no point in asking. She read things, she knew things, and out they came, little surprises. It was strangely like unwrapping little gifts, not all of which he appreciated. She clung to facts and information, like flotsam in a shipwreck. They'd saved her.

Mutely, he looked at her. Too full to speak. Her eyes were green. He knew that decisively now. A more facile man would have compared them flatteringly to something—leaves or moss or emeralds or some such—but all he would truthfully be able to say was that no one he'd ever known possessed eyes quite like hers. It had little to do with their color. It was in the way that over the course of mere days he'd found himself saying things just to see how they would change: how humor would kindle them, and kindness soften them, and anger make them flash, and how he felt when the light of them was turned on him. How he wanted to hold up his hands before them and warm them.

"I read about it," she told him anyway. She looked down at the bundle in her hand, indecisively. And then: "Here." She extended it to him. "A gift for you."

He stared it. All at once too many thoughts and impressions jostled for the exits, and none could escape in the form of words. So he did as she ordered. Slowly, wordlessly, he reached for them.

And as she began to surrender them, her fingers brushed his.

He stopped breathing.

He'd once seen a man struck by lightning. He'd watched as the bolt held him helpless, motionless, arcing his body. Having its way with him.

It wasn't unlike that.

Breathlessly, dumbly, they both stared at the place where their fingers met. Stunned to at last, at last, be touching. Skin to skin.

He dropped the herbs and seized her wrist. "Enough."

The word was low and dark. And it thrummed command and something like a plea.

Slowly, slowly, she levered up her head, as if spooling courage on the way up. Her jaw was taut; her eyes were wide when they met his, but comprehension flickered in them.

The air suddenly seemed full of snapping sparks. One would have thought *he'd* captured a unicorn, for God's sake, for how enervated he felt.

As he watched, a flush painted her from her collarbone upward. Beneath his thumb, placed over a pale blue vein in that silky hand, her pulse raced.

He turned her palm up. He wished he could be certain she was the one who was trembling, for *one* of them was. Her hand was achingly soft, too vulnerable. It was cold, which struck him as poignant. He wanted to warm her. He needed to warm her.

And so he brought her palm to his mouth.

He softly opened his mouth against her skin, touched his tongue there, burned her with a kiss that was at once chaste and perhaps the most carnal he'd ever given.

Her head tipped back hard; her eyelids shuddered closed. She made a soft sound, a gasp of shock and pure sensual pleasure.

Mother of *God*.

He lifted his head with some effort. He curled her fingers closed over the place he kissed her, as if handing her a keepsake.

He knew he ought to. And yet he found he couldn't relinquish her hand.

"Look at me, Miss Vale." His voice a low demand.

A moment's hesitation. She opened her eyes. He was absurdly thrilled to see them again. They were dazed and starry and wary. The sun haloed her, and the light both set her aglow and obscured her. As he stared, he withstood bolt after swift bolt of impression, each distinct and pure and primal:

Who kissed you first? I will kiss the memory of it away. I will run him through with a sword. I can't recall kissing anyone before you. I am ruined. I am happy. I'm afraid. I need to leave. You need to leave.

He was holding her hand as though it was a Fabergé egg. Which rather contrasted his expression, which, little did he know, was edging toward the thunderous.

"I didn't know I was going to do that," he said finally.

"Do you always know what you're going to do?" Her voice was a low husk.

"Always," he said shortly. It sounded like an accusation.

A heartbeat's worth of silence passed.

"What are you going to do now?" And in her whisper was both sensual challenge and trepidation.

They could hear the distant voices of Jonathan and Waterburn and Lisbeth and Argosy, all still bickering happily, but they seemed as consequential as the birds rustling in the trees. Dangerous to think that way, he knew.

He heard his name: *Jules!* Cheerfully sang out by Lisbeth.

The rest of their party could come upon them in seconds or minutes. He was just clear-headed enough to realize that arousal could tinker with a man's sense of time enough to doom the pair of them to discovery.

And yet.

He drew in a long breath. Exhaled at length.

Phoebe must have seen his plans in his eyes. "Don't," she urged on a panicked whisper. "You'd best not. Please—"

He took hold of her other wrist, gently, as if she hadn't spoken at all, and Phoebe let him take it, because his touch turned her bones to water. And as he pulled her toward him, he gave his head a regretful, incredulous little shake, as though neither of them had a choice in the matter, as if he were at the mercy of momentum. Which appeared to be true, as her head was already tipping back to meet his lowering lips, and later she could not have said how that had happened, only that his will in that moment was hers.

His lips landed softly on hers at first, the merest bump of his warm firm mouth against her soft one. And then he coaxed hers apart with his. More shocking than the kiss was the *relief*, as though she'd longed for this her entire life, for him, for this kiss. It nearly buckled her knees. Her body seemed to know precisely what to do and what it wanted, and her sense dissolved against the onslaught of sensation. Her breasts crushed against his hard chest, the button of his shirt was cold against the skin of her collarbone. His mouth like cognac, the kiss spreading like slow fire through her veins, until she was molten. When her body blended against his with such wanton ease he might as well have been the missing part of her, he loosened his grip on her wrists, clearly satisfied she was going nowhere. She wasn't quite sure what to do with her hands, so she settled them on the front of his shirt and slowly curled her fingers into it. The linen was hot from being next to his skin. And this seemed so unbearably erotic she moaned low in her throat, a shameless animal sound, pure need.

And when she did he muttered a hoarse word that may have been *Christ* or an epithet or her name, something raw and helpless and very enthusiastic. He shifted abruptly so that his hot hands were sliding over her back to cup his hands beneath her arse and lift her with shocking deliberateness against his cock.

And through the fine fabric of her twice-sewn dress, she felt him: enormous, inexorably male, shockingly hard. His hands were furling up her dress; she felt the air on the backs of her stockinged calves. Their lips clung and parted, then returned more hungrily, their tongues twined and tangled, teeth once clashed gracelessly. But the kiss never seemed deep enough, penetrating enough, because what he wanted was more than a kiss and she wanted what he wanted, and she was at the mercy of that.

Help. The word rang in her head, though she didn't know whom she was entreating or what she wanted. She was endlessly spiraling, in a fever induced by the heat of his body, the taste of him. His cock was so hard it hurt to be held against it, and yet she pressed herself closer, as close as she could, because every time she did pleasure cleaved through her, built upon itself, doubling, trebling, until she was trembling with urgency.

And suddenly her head was bare. She felt the air on her hair, the back of her neck. Her bonnet had been knocked free and was bouncing around the back of her neck.

His mouth traveled to the place her pulse thumped in her throat, bare to him now. He made a desperate sound in his throat, and his lips traveled lower, and she arched backward to abet him.

His mouth had just skimmed the bones at the base of her neck, so close, so close to the swell of her aching taut nipple, when:

"Oh, *Juuules!*" Lisbeth trilled again.

Her voice echoed. *"uuu . . . uuu. . . . ules . . ."*

Christ! That voice was close now!

They froze in the midst of what amounted to climbing each other.

"Phoooeeeebeee!"

Now without the echo.

The marquess stepped back so abruptly she staggered forward.

He righted her by clapping his hands on her shoulders.

They stared at each other. His eyes were dazed and hot. Their breathing was a low roar.

A breeze rattled the leaves on the trees, and to Phoebe it sounded like so much ironic arboreal applause.

Finally, gingerly he lifted his hands from her shoulders, as if worried she was so kiss-drunk she might topple. Or disappear like a mirage the moment his touch left her.

Satisfied, he lowered his hands to his sides and seemed to, with an effort, hold them very still.

She touched her fingers to her lips. They burned; she'd taken from him as savagely as she'd given. It was an excellent sort of pain. Her skin felt everywhere feverish.

But she left the other hand on his chest, and watched as it rose and fell, rose and fell, with the bellows of his breathing. And as if she couldn't help herself: she slid it inside his shirt, between the gaps in his buttons . . . over his hot skin.

He hissed in a breath. "Phoebe." His voice was hoarse, curt. A warning. He wrapped her wrist in his hand again.

But in case she never kissed him again, she wanted to feel for herself what she'd done to him. And wonderingly, she savored the hammer blows of his heart against her palm.

Until he gently, gently, lifted her hand away. Gave it back her.

And unwrapped his fingers from it, one at a time, prolonging the time he was touching her.

Until they were no longer touching at all.

Which seemed wrong all of a sudden.

She considered that one of them ought to say something, but she could think of nothing appropriate, and couldn't imagine what he might say that would be at all the right thing. The language she knew—the King's English, and all the precious facts she'd acquired over the years that could be used to explain or sum up or keep the world at bay—were useless here. This was another language entirely.

"Juuuu-*ules*!" Lisbeth sang out. Her voice seemed closer now, but it was impossible to know just how close, given the way sound tended to ricochet off and pool in the little valleys between the hills, the way the breeze picked it up and dashed it about through the trees, playing tricks. "Phoeeeeebeeee! Where have you got to?"

She still sounded brisk and playful.

But they were startled seconds later to hear the crunch of footsteps and the *huh huh huh* of the old hound.

Bloody hell!

Jules and Phoebe realized at once they were essentially trapped in the clearing. And one of them had an erection and the other one was pink in the face and in the lips and her bonnet was askew and her dress was hiked up in the back.

Only an imbecile would come to the wrong conclusion about what they'd gotten up to.

Thus began the frantic hissing whispers.

"Your dress is—" He gestured broadly.

"Your hat . . . !" She pointed at his head.

"*Your* bonnet!"

Jules's hand shot out and he tugged her dress

down from behind, gave it a cursory hurried patting
to smooth it while she tried in vain to untangle her
bonnet ribbons, which seemed to have entwined with
her hairpins.

"Thank you," she said on a frantic abashed whisper.

"Not at all," he replied under his breath.

For heaven's *sake*. Why on earth were they being
polite?

The hound gave a rusty, disinterested bark from
what sounded like an uncomfortably close distance.

They were both a little wild-eyed now.

"Your—is still—" he hissed urgently, gesturing at
his own head.

She clawed at her bonnet ribbons again, but they
were knotted hopelessly. She nearly lynched herself trying to free it. Her hands were trembling and
useless.

Woof! the dog said again. And they heard the crackle
of footsteps, too, over leaves and twigs.

"Smell something, old boy?" Waterburn's voice now.

Rank fear, Phoebe thought. *Or perhaps mortification
has a smell.*

"Do you hear voices, Lord Waterburn?" Lisbeth
called. "This way, I think."

Phoebe abandoned her bonnet efforts instantly.

"We can't both stay here." She was light-headed with
panic.

"Too right. You stay. I'll go!" Jules lunged to the left,
ready to plunge through a hedgerow.

She seized his elbow. "No! Not that way! You'll end
up in a bramble. I know the woods, so *I'll* go—"

He seized her elbow as she lunged to the right.

It was like a reel gone violent.

"For God's sake, we can't *both* go crashing off like deer through the underbrush," he hissed.

And Jules knew with despairing, crystalline clarity he'd been wise to avoid the illicit affairs other men seemed to find so invigorating. He'd only barely gotten an illicit affair under way and his dignity was already in jeopardy, what with the beaming in church and the bonnet purchase and now this. He *cherished* his dignity.

An "affair"? It was just a kiss.

Well, two kisses.

Nevertheless, two kisses in a clearing did *not* qualify as an affair. And as embarrassment was *hardly* an aphrodisiac, it was unlikely to become one. So he told himself.

"You're not as familiar with the woods," she pointed out. "I grew up here in Sussex."

"*I* might get *lost*?" He'd gained an octave, which wasn't easy to do when one was whispering. "*I* might? These woods are dense and it isn't safe for a woman to wander about alone. You will stay and I will go." He said this curtly and dismissively and pulled away from her grasp.

If she'd been a cat, her fur would have been erect with outrage. "I never just . . . *wander*."

"For the love of *God*, woman . . ." he growled. He clapped an exasperated hand to his forehead, which sent his precariously perched hat tumbling off.

He spun about, lunged for it, missed, bounced it futilely a few times off of his fingertips, and one final valiant lunge to capture it merely served to bat it across the clearing.

It cart-wheeled merrily over the ground and came to a rest well out of his reach.

Just as the top of Lisbeth's shining head and her exquisite profile came bobbing into view over the top of the hedgerow.

"Erk!" was the last thing he said before he threw himself to the ground and slithered on his belly over the wet grass, aiming like a lizard for the hedgerow. His boot heels were just disappearing from view behind it when Lisbeth appeared, humming happily to herself. She was followed by Waterburn, who was followed by the hound.

Phoebe was frozen. She felt certain she would never forget the image of a marquess vanishing like a lizard into a hedgerow.

"Phoebe does wander off now and again on walks all by herself," Lisbeth was telling Lord Waterburn, "but she knows this part of Sussex fairly well, so I shouldn't worry. I thought I heard voices right about here. Didn't you hear them, too?"

The ensuing noncommittal syllable from Waterburn could have meant anything. Phoebe doubted he was expending very much concern over whether she might have gotten lost.

She could almost feel Jules's triumph radiating from behind the hedgerow: *You never wander, Miss Vale?*

"I walk but I don't get *lost*," Phoebe called out loudly, cheerily, pointedly . . .

. . . and prematurely. Because: Bloody hell! His *hat*. She'd forgotten about his hat!

It throbbed with significance on the ground like a great poisonous toadstool right where Lisbeth would see it the moment she entered the clearing.

She snatched it up, wondered why on earth she would do that since having it in her hands was hardly better than leaving it on the ground, then thrust it behind her back in both hands as Lisbeth burst into view and came to a surprised halt at the brink of the clearing.

Lord Waterburn's towering blondness hovered over the top of the hedgerow and his boots crunched to a halt as he dispassionately surveyed his surroundings. He was still cradling the musket. Likely he considered the day a sort of purgatory, one in which he was destined to wander and wander and never shoot anything.

"Well, there *you* are, Phoebe!" Lisbeth sounded pleased. "It *is* just you?"

Chapter 13

She took a cursory look about the clearing to ascertain the truth of this, but it was clear she'd already drawn that conclusion. And Phoebe knew a quick, sizzling irritation that Lisbeth didn't at all doubt she was alone and not doing anything untoward with anyone, let alone a marquess. She was tempted to touch her still-burning lips again to prove to herself she had indeed been kissed, because the mere appearance of the glowing and no doubt eminently kissable Lisbeth made it seem an impossibility.

And she *would* have touched her lips, if she hadn't been holding a beaver hat behind her back.

The three new arrivals—Lisbeth, Waterburn, and the hound—regarded Phoebe for a silent bemused instant.

Jonathan and Argosy's laughter came to them distantly.

Then the dog sighed and tipped over with a snort and began to doze.

"I thought I heard more than one voice," Lisbeth said finally.

"Oh! Well, likely you just heard me . . . singing." Phoebe's voice fluted from nerves; she cleared her throat to restore her usual pitch. "A duet. I like to sing both of the parts when . . . when I'm alone. To feel less alone. Signora Licari inspired me."

Perhaps that was laying it on a bit thick.

Lisbeth clapped her hands together, which made Phoebe jump, since her nerves were a bit sensitive. "Singing! What an excellent idea! Perhaps we should all sing, and if Jules is lost he'll be able to hear us."

"I will not be singing," Lord Waterburn said flatly.

"*Does* he often get lost?" Phoebe couldn't resist asking, "The marquess?"

"Never," Waterburn said, and shifted the musket into his other arm and looked at his nails, as if they were infinitely more interesting than she could ever be. *You've still five of them*, Phoebe was tempted to say snidely. "Would get you killed in the army, getting lost would."

She could practically feel the rays of satisfied vindication pouring over the shrubbery.

A quick sideways glance told her the marquess had rolled over on his back. If she looked very closely, she could see his boot toes pointing up at the air, gleaming.

She imagined herself lying next to him, his arms around her, staring up through the trees at the blue sky and suddenly she couldn't breathe as a fresh wash of lust swamped her.

She nearly swayed with it. What had *happened* to her? What had he unleashed?

Was it permanent?

"What a lovely clearing you've found, Phoebe. Odd that I haven't seen it before. It's downright *magical*, isn't it?" Lisbeth spun slowly, arms outstretched, head tipped back, embracing it, and she was so fair and flushed and glossy that the gesture didn't seem at all contrived. She looked like a nymph surveying her domain.

Phoebe wondered how quickly his heart was beating. And whether a squirrel had ambled over to sniff him, or whether insects had decided to have a look at a prone marquess, and were perhaps crawling for the intriguing openings his nostrils and ears presented.

She *almost* smiled.

"Oh, and look, there's your sketchbook, Phoebe. I've finished naught in mine. Let's have a look at yours!"

Her sketchbook! Bloody hell!

It was soaking up grass and dew a few feet away from where she sat, closer to Lisbeth than to her. From where she stood she could just make out her quick, impassioned charcoal of the marquess. He looked angular and tempestuous and the masses of dark hair she'd given him resembled nothing so much as flames and smoke shooting from a burning building. The sketch glowered up at the sky much the way the real marquess was likely doing right now.

Really more of a reflection of her own feelings than of the man himself. And this was incriminating indeed.

Oh, God. Lisbeth started merrily toward the sketchbook. Time torturously slowed. *One step. Two steps.* The crunch of her friend's boots over the grass rang in Phoebe's ears like the crunch of her own bones. Phoebe stared helplessly into her doom. Short of throwing herself bodily at her friend's ankles, there was nothing she could do to stop her from reaching the sketchbook first.

And then out of the corner of her eye, she saw the musket gleaming. Inspiration alighted like an angel, and she blurted:

"If you saw a grouse right now, would you prefer to shoot it or sketch it?" she blurted.

"Sketch it," Lisbeth said at the same time Lord Waterburn said, "Shoot it."

"Because I think I saw one right over there by that tree! The . . . the tree that looks like an old man." She pointed in the opposite direction.

Her friends whirled in unison, and when they did Phoebe hurled the marquess's hat like a discus over the hawthorn hedge and made a lunge for her sketchbook.

There was a startled grunt from over the hedgerow.

Lisbeth and Lord Waterburn whirled back around.

Lisbeth stared at Phoebe, who froze in something perilously similar to a pointer position.

What looked suspiciously like . . . like *suspicion* . . . creased Lisbeth's brow.

Behind her Lord Waterburn's face scrunched infinitesimally, registering distaste—but a bit insultingly, not surprise—at the notion she might have made a grunting noise.

There was no hope for it. She was going to have to grunt.

"*Ugh*," she said, as she lunged gracelessly, seized the corner of her sketchbook and dragged it across the grass safely into her hands.

When she was upright again she saw the vestiges of a wince vanishing from Lord Waterburn's face.

She clutched the sketchbook to her bosom. Her heart was thudding sickeningly.

Lisbeth studied her for a silent moment, a bit nonplussed by Phoebe's sudden lunge.

"I don't see the resemblance."

Phoebe felt faint. "Resem . . ."

"To an old man. The tree." Her gaze was fixed.

Phoebe had seen a man aim a gaze down a rifle just like that.

"Oh." Relief swamped her: *not* the sketch. "Don't you? I suppose I thought so, since it's gnarled, and bent, and . . ." She gave up when she saw Lisbeth's expression go patient and tolerant, complete with humoring upraised brows. "Fanciful of me, I suppose. Something about this clearing, perhaps. Magical. As you said."

Carnal, was more like it. Dangerous. A trap!

Lisbeth gamely turned back toward the tree to give it another examination.

"I see it a little bit around the north side of the trunk," she allowed charitably. "Perhaps that knot might be construed as a nose?"

Waterburn snorted.

She really is a lovely person, Phoebe thought despairingly. She glanced down; her charcoaled marquess glowered back up at her. He *was* smudged.

She glanced down at her bodice; it was smudged, too. And then a horrible possibility occurred to her: she may have inadvertently pressed a perfect charcoal image of the marquess to her bosom. She might as well have sewn a scarlet *A* for herself.

She slapped the sketchbook back to her chest.

For heaven's sake. *Gather your wits, Vale,* she told herself.

It seemed desperately unfair how quickly life became chaotic, given the years she'd spent ensuring it was orderly.

"Yes! I suppose I was imagining the knot as nose." She lowered her arms just a few inches and sent a wistful glance down at her sketchbook. "It's just as I thought. My sketchbook is ruined. The pages have warped from the damp."

Lisbeth clucked sympathy. "I'm sure your drawings were very pretty, too," she indulged. "Now where do you suppose the marquess has got to?"

"Perhaps he got lost for the very first time."

She said it with deviltry in mind, and specifically for the person flattened behind the hedgerow, but she heard uncertainty, and something very close to query, in her voice. *Damnation.* She was the one who was *lost.* She'd collected knowledge like gemstones, amassing her very own treasure chest in the absence of a fortune. She buffed and polished all the rough corners from the young ladies at school with facts, just as her teachers had more or less refined her. Her reputation and comportment were considered faultless. She was held up as an example for all the young ladies.

And now she might be sporting a charcoal marquess on her bosom and she'd just grunted twice.

If she'd correctly interpreted the expression on the marquess's face right before he gripped her wrist . . . he was lost, too. At the very least, he was confused.

No man had ever looked at her that way before. And no matter what happened, no matter what continent she lived on, she would never forget it. She half suspected it would be the last thing she saw every night before she slept.

But a man who'd lost his moorings was liable to do anything, she thought.

"Well, let's help him find *us.*" Lisbeth was purposeful. "What song were you singing before we arrived, Phoebe? The one you took in parts?"

Twigs cracked as Lord Waterburn's boots shifted restlessly.

Oh, no. Phoebe stared at Lisbeth blankly while her mind whirred. She knew so few songs, really, in their entirety, and her voice was tolerable at best.

But she was on a quest to distract Lisbeth, and suddenly she knew just the way to do it.

"The . . . the one about Colin Eversea! I learned a

new verse from a young lady at school. It's very funny
and . . . and . . . bawdy."

That last word was a reckless inspiration. She presented it almost defiantly.

Lisbeth blinked as though she'd flicked water into
her eyes.

Lisbeth and Waterburn eyed her for a silent nonplussed instant.

A finch peeped somewhere in the hedgerows.

Apparently it wasn't a word anyone associated with
her, or particularly wanted to associate with her, judging from the carefully bland expression on Waterburn's
face.

Next I'll try the word whore *in a sentence,* she thought
wildly.

"Oh, do let's sing it now!" Lisbeth said finally, as
though Phoebe had just broken wind and they'd all just
chosen to ignore it. The Redmonds were bloodthirsty
when it came to the Everseas, thanks to the business
with Lyon, and eager to perpetuate the worst of their
reputations in song. "I'll start, and then you can sing
your new baw . . . your new verse," she humored. "Do
let's!"

Oh, God. She'd now have to invent a bawdy verse on
the spot. She'd never had to improvise so much in her
entire life as she had in the last five minutes.

Improvise being another word for *lie,* of course.

Lisbeth took a deep breath, and flung her arms out,
and with gusto began, *"Ohhhhh, if you thought you'd
never see, the end of Colin Ever—"*

With shocking speed, Lord Waterburn sighed,
cocked the musket and fired straight up in the air.

A cloud of tiny startled birds burst from out of the
shrubbery like so much shrapnel and disappeared into

the sky. Phoebe and Lisbeth jumped and waved away musket smoke and coughed.

Woof, the dog said disinterestedly, after a moment.

When the smoke cleared Waterburn was greeted by a pair of baleful stares.

"That should flush Dryden out," Waterburn said mildly, finally. "He'll follow the sound. Not to mention Jonathan and Argosy."

"Was that necessary?" Lisbeth finally said reproachfully. "You could have just refused to sing."

A lazy smile tugged up one corner of Waterburn's mouth. "What fun would that have been? And I *did* refuse."

Interesting, Phoebe thought almost sympathetically. Waterburn really *was* bored. He was tolerating a good deal more than they had realized. But what he made up for in fortune and manners he lacked in imagination. So he was perhaps destined to suffer at the hands of the likes of Lisbeth, who took for granted that men would indulge her, enjoy or pretend to enjoy her company, and happily consent to holding her embroidery silks or carrying her picnic basket or otherwise being steered to wherever she wanted them to go, like a mule. Because she was beautiful and young and wealthy.

Until, of course, she married. In which case, her husband would do whatever he wished and she would do whatever *he* wished her to do.

Women really were afforded so few windows of power. Perhaps she couldn't fault Lisbeth for seizing the moment while she could.

And how perilously close she'd been to giving away whatever power she did have . . . to a man.

"Well, I do wonder where he could have got to," Lisbeth fussed, irritable now. "You must have seen him,

Phoebe, for you both seemed to vanish at about the same time."

Oh, dear. Phoebe darted a glance toward the shrubbery. The boot toes had disappeared. Jules must have taken advantage of the musket roar to scramble—or slither—away.

"I . . . fear I didn't see him. And I didn't vanish, I just found a clearing," she pointed out, trying for good humor, and stammering when Lisbeth's blue eyes fixed on her unblinkingly. "I didn't see him. I suppose I thought he was with you. And I'm sorry, but I don't know which direction he took." It wasn't strictly a lie. Not at the moment. "I was distracted, you see, when I saw this clearing, I was drawn toward it. And then I began sketching and—"

She reared back when Lisbeth stepped abruptly toward her. So close she could see the tiny fine, fine hairs on Lisbeth's upper lip.

"How on earth did your bonnet become *so* askew, you silly thing."

Phoebe blinked. Lisbeth had never said such a thing to her before. She was patently *not* a silly thing, had never been, and everyone knew it. Everyone in fact counted on it. And while the words had the *ring* of affection, the question was strangely uninflected.

Lisbeth reached out and made a great show of rearranging Phoebe's bonnet, unknotting the ribbons, freeing them from her hairpins, drawing them smooth between her fingers, her gaze unnervingly direct and uncharacteristically inscrutable. Phoebe remained as motionless as a rabbit before a wolf. Phoebe was certain that if Lisbeth were later interrogated about the number of hairs in her eyebrows she would surprise everyone with a correct answer.

"I must have knocked it askew on a branch," she managed faintly.

While she submitted to having her bonnet rearranged, it occurred to her a word or two from Isaiah Redmond could remove her from her position at the academy and render her forever unemployable in England.

Whereupon she'd have no place to go—she hadn't yet enough money saved for her journey to Africa—and would be ruined in nearly the blink of an eye.

She maintained what she hoped was an inscrutable expression. But now her palms were perspiring.

Lisbeth gave a brisk satisfied nod when she got her friend neatly wrapped and tied, precisely the way she liked her.

Which was when they heard the rustle of something significantly larger than a finch moving about in the woods nearby. Before they had time to flinch there came a voice.

"It's Dryden, not a wolf or a bear. Don't shoot, Waterburn."

The marquess parted the hedgerow with as much dignity as anyone bursting through a hedgerow could muster, and emerged.

His hat was restored to his head. And he looked otherwise crisp.

The dog lifted its head, stared at the marquess with an expression remarkably like Waterburn's disdain, gave an obligatory *woof* and rested its head on its paws again.

"I heard the musket shot, and didn't want to miss out on any game shooting, if that's what was finally happening."

Lisbeth's face was lit up like a star, as if the marquess emerging from shrubbery was a surprise arranged just for her.

"No, Lord Waterburn threatened to shoot us for singing."

Waterburn had no patience for such whimsy. "I did no such thing," he said flatly.

"*I* might have done, however," the marquess teased. "Depending upon the song."

Lisbeth dimpled beautifully while the marquess smiled at her and Phoebe suffered.

He was patently refusing to look at her and she likewise refused to look at him.

She wore a fixed, benign smile that had served her in countless social situations, the sort of smile that could offend no one, signify nothing, reveal nothing, and sent her gaze around the clearing in search for something neutral to light upon. For anyone happening upon the scene would have thought that the marquess and Lisbeth had eyes for no one but each other.

She settled upon the hound. She met its brown eyes. It blinked slowly in what she liked to think was sympathy. Neither of them wanted to be where they were at the moment.

"Don't shoot without us!" came Jonathan's voice from a distance. "Where the devil *are* you?"

"Where did you get to, Dryden?" Waterburn asked laconically.

"Get to? I think we've been parted but, oh . . . fifteen minutes." With a single fluid motion, he retrieved his pocket watch, flipped it open with his thumb, reviewed the time, and replaced it. "Fifteen minutes," he confirmed. "I enjoyed the exploration. Enviable lands."

Fifteen minutes. She'd manage to upend her orderly life in *fifteen minutes*.

Although it might have been symbolically put to rights again the moment Lisbeth retied her bonnet, for all she knew. A moment of recklessness, never to recur.

She looked at the marquess then; it was impossible not to, since everyone, including the hound, was doing it.

And then he looked at her.

She couldn't read any conclusions in his eyes, though it seemed to her he had trouble looking away from her. There was tension about his mouth. Then, doubtless he'd had more practice with disguising his thoughts than she had, and so she looked down.

"You've a great stripe of green on the front of your shirt, Lord Dryden," Lisbeth said. "Did you take a fall?"

Lisbeth was suddenly a great one for noticing when things were out of order, Phoebe thought peevishly.

"I took a fall," he confirmed evenly. After a hesitation doubtless only Phoebe noticed.

And Phoebe didn't know whether it was the sort of fall Lucifer took, or the sort poets wrote about when love struck, or even if it was an innuendo at all, because she suspected everything was destined to sound like an innuendo from now on.

But now that she'd been kissed it was like someone had taken a hammer to her China pig full of ha'pennies and now she had a job of sorting the glittering things from the dangerous shards.

They all began to file out of the clearing. The marquess hovered an indecisive moment. Then turned and quickly bent to pluck something up off the ground.

"What did you find, Jules?" Lisbeth asked. "Are you gathering darling buds?"

"Nothing quite like that," he told her, and smiled to distract her from her question, because his smiles did rather send women into a daze, as he stuffed the bundle of sage in his pocket.

Chapter 14

Jules handed the shirt with the great green stripe of grass to his valet, who took it without question or a change of expression, having seen much more dreadful things on shirts before.

The marquess had a full dozen identical clean ones in his trunks.

If it had been Marquardt, his London manservant, it would not have gone unremarked. Acerbically. But his valet did cast his eyes upward and allowed them to linger, almost mournfully, near his hairline.

Which caused Jules to swivel abruptly toward the mirror.

Bloody. *Hell.*

He sighed. Well, it had admittedly been an excellent throw. The velocity had done the damage. He touched the small darkening lump that only he and one other person would recognize as the shape of a hat brim.

He looked like a ruffian. And a fool. He was beginning to feel like the latter for many reasons, and not once, not *once* in his life had anyone accused him of being such a thing. Foolishness had never been an option in his life. He hadn't acquired the knack for it.

He should have known. Kisses, he'd learned through hard experience, complicated things, unless they were a means to a foregone conclusion or part of an ongoing sensual entanglement.

He'd never had a kiss quite like that one. One he hadn't planned. One that had seemed so . . . necessary.

One that had nevertheless solved nothing.

One that had led to him flattening himself behind a shrubbery and later, sneezing a tiny winged insect out of his nose on the walk back to the house. It had lodged there while he lay flat on his back, staring up at the crisp blue Autumn sky, contemplating his folly, listening to Miss Vale prevaricate wildly. He was almost sorry he hadn't heard her invent a bawdy new verse to the Colin Eversea song.

He'd walked back to the house accompanied by a chattering Lisbeth, whom he listened to indulgently, enjoying her lightheartedness and easy cheer and her elegant loveliness. All of which were obvious and pleasing and none of which challenged him, and all of which could be fielded with a nod here or cheerful word or tease there, even as his mind was consumed, troubled, clouded, giddy, with something else entirely.

Behind him had walked a mildly bitter and mostly taciturn Waterburn, who was swinging no dead fowl at all and resented it so thoroughly it was almost audible, and Jonathan and Argosy, amiably debating the merits of Argosy's new high flyer.

Phoebe walked behind all of them, quietly, which seemed wrong. The behind part, and the quiet part. She was not the sort who should be quiet or should trail anyone.

She said she was worried about the health of the hound, who might expire at any moment and shouldn't do so alone, so she kept pace with it. A ridiculous excuse that all accepted without question.

Jules sat down hard on the edge of the bed, and tipped his forehead into his hand. Then winced and jerked it up again.

He inspected the bruise in the mirror again.

Aesthetically, it was lovely. Currently a mottled reddish purple, darkening by the second to a more majestic shade of indigo. He impatiently raked his fingers through his hair and brought it down over his brow in a rakish forelock. The bruise disappeared.

He inspected the result.

He looked like a damned dandy.

Very well: he would consider the absurd new hair penance.

And so it was a somewhat chastened marquess, newly fueled with a resolve not to lose his mind over a schoolteacher, which he could *surely* manage, who went downstairs for the soiree, cheeks scraped smooth by a razor, body scrubbed, cravat fluffed, trousers spotless, coat crisp. Looking every inch the Marquess Dryden who caused spines to straighten and conversation to lull when he appeared, the way all the gazelle lifted their heads alertly when a lion appeared at a watering hole.

"Would you like to watch me dress, my lord?"

She propped up the smeared charcoal sketch of Jules, the Marquess Dryden, against the headboard. On the theory that pretending insouciance might actually make her feel insouciant.

"Shall I wear the green silk?" A question which amused her, because she only had the two nice dresses and she'd already worn the other.

She laid the dress gently on the bed, and then she shimmied out of her day dress while the smeared marquess looked on.

She splashed about in the lavender-scented basin until she felt clean and scented, and slipped into her dress. She tied a green ribbon around her throat, twisted up her fine, fair mass of hair and pinned it, then pulled two saucy strands down to dangle near her mouth, and inspected the result in the mirror.

Well. Her nose hadn't become any more retroussé, nor had her cheekbones suddenly become poetry, and her eyelashes were still thick but fair unto invisibility, apart from their golden tips. In other words, if she were lined up next to Lisbeth Redmond, she would hardly cast her in the shade.

But if someone had told her, in that moment, that she was beautiful, she would not have accused them of being drunk.

It was the fault of the kiss. Her eyes were brilliant with secrets, her skin glowed like a lantern.

Oh, she knew he had plans, and that his plans had dictated the course of his life and that he fully intended they would dictate his future. She knew his plans did not include her. And she might spend the entire evening holding a reticule and fetching things for Lisbeth.

But given the way the rest of the house party had proceeded, she had no reason to believe this evening would be ordinary or unexpected.

And so out onto the tightrope she walked, blowing the smeared marquess a kiss as she departed.

Jules slipped into the salon as unobtrusively as he could manage, taking up a spot against the hearth. Behind the screen a fire burned merrily and superfluously, and the back of him began to heat uncomfortably. Even as lofty as the ceilings were, enough humans were already milling about the room and it was bordering on stuffy. A tray-bearing footman appeared at his elbow so quickly and silently he almost jumped. The footman was offering port. It wasn't at all what the marquess wanted to drink but he took it. Holding it would give him an occupation.

He'd been seen, despite his attempt at unobtrusiveness. He knew it, because he could practically hear, as usual, the neck muscles straining not to crane in his direction. He intercepted numerous glances sent from beneath lowered female lashes, acknowledging them with a faint smile that caused hearts to leap.

He looked about for someone tolerable to have a comfortable, noncommittal conversation with. But he didn't see the Earl of Ardmay, lately and rather swiftly married to Redmond's daughter, Violet. Isaiah Redmond was across the room, simultaneously charming and inspecting a gentleman who had the clammy awestruck look of the newly wealthy, eager to impress Redmond and to be included in his circle of rarified influence. He was just the sort who might be persuaded to join the Mercury Club, Isaiah's investment group . . . should he be found acceptable.

Isaiah would be at his side soon enough, he knew. The Redmonds, until the King decided to bestow a title on them or the Everseas—he was forever dangling one—craved the aristocratic connections. An earl *was* now in the family, but he was hardly the sort of earl Isaiah had always dreamed of.

The Marquess Dryden was another story altogether.

He saw Lisbeth perched on a striped settee. Effortlessly, achingly pretty in gauzy white, a diamond sparkling at her throat, a coronet in her hair, destined to hear a dozen compliments comparing her to an angel or a nymph or some such ethereal creature tonight.

He wondered if *she* ever tired of her compliments, or if the assortment she received ranged widely enough to divert her.

But he was conscious of looking at her the way a man admires the main course . . . dutifully. While looking forward to the dessert.

Dessert was sitting right next to Lisbeth.

And she hadn't yet noticed him. Or so it seemed. She was wearing a green dress that had been the rage two seasons ago. *Willow,* he thought they'd called it. And it was simple—cut square at the neckline and low enough to reveal a tantalizing, pale swell of bosom, puffed at the sleeves, ribboned beneath the bosom in a darker shade of green. Her slim white arms were covered in a surprisingly fine pair of cream kid gloves up to nearly the elbow. She'd tied a narrow matching ribbon around her throat and dressed her hair up high. Tendrils of it traced her jaw, and he followed them down, down, past her lips, to where they tickled, lightly, her collarbone.

What he *should* have thought was: She looks every bit of what she is—a country schoolteacher, invited to attend a party out of charity, a paid companion to Lisbeth. For she did.

But what he thought was: *I haven't yet touched her hair.*

And from that thought a dozen more spiraled in an exhilarating, carnal rush: there was a *universe* of her he hadn't yet touched or tasted. The whorls of her ears. Her collarbone. That vulnerable bend of her elbow revealed just above the long gloves she was wearing. The shadowy valley between her breasts. Dear God, her *breasts.* The curve of her shoul—

"What *are* you looking at, Dryden?"

Jules gave a start. Waterburn had materialized and planted himself against the hearth and followed the line of his gaze with his usual unerring instinct for annoying Jules.

Waterburn answered his own question. "Are you looking at that grunting governess creature?"

Grunting? "She's a schoolmistress," he said shortly.

Waterburn shrugged, as if the entire lot of working class females was interchangeable and he couldn't be bothered to distinguish between them.

"Why do you ask? How was I looking at her?" He took great pains to sound amused and ironic. But tension pulled the bands of muscle across his stomach taut. Surely Waterburn saw nothing incriminating. Inscrutability was one of his chief qualities. And certainly now that he had a forelock his expression would be even more difficult to decipher.

Waterburn inhaled, apparently giving this actual thought. "Well, it's a *bit* like the way you looked at Countess Malmsey when she wore the blue dress the night of the Mulvaney ball—"

He paused to allow the requisite moment of reverie.

"Ah, yes. That blue dress," the marquess allowed, dutifully, as the blue dress was legend now and it almost considered bad form not to say just that, the way one followed a sneeze with "Bless you." It had been a splendid dress, and he would have wagered a guinea her modiste had sewn her naked into it, to the humble gratitude of every man present.

"—and a bit like the moment before you intend to fire a rifle. Rather . . . oh, *purposeful*, I suppose . . ."

He sounded both pensive and insinuating.

Jules opened his mouth, preparing to scoff.

"But noooo . . . that isn't quite it, either."

One of those footmen appeared and Waterburn gave

a start and frowned. But then he took his port gratefully. "Silent as cats, those chaps," he muttered, when
he left. "Need to drink just to calm my nerves with
them sneaking about. Wonder if Redmond uses them
as spies. No . . . you looked . . . you looked . . ."

He was looking at Jules now with those pale eyes.
Jules had clenched his teeth in anticipation, actually
interested in what the man would say. As though Waterburn, of all people, was a sage come down from the
mountaintops bearing prophecies.

But he wanted to know: *How* do I look? What on
earth *is* it I'm feeling? Because God only knew he had
no idea.

". . . worried," Waterburn concluded at last.

Jules gave a disdainful snort, and sipped at his port.
"I'm worried I won't get a stronger drink tonight."

Then pulled it away from his lips and eyed it resentfully. The port was thick and cloying and sweet. He
would have liked something stronger, something that
bit back. He wanted a punishing drink. A thin, clear,
angry one.

Did he look worried?

But God help him, Waterburn wasn't finished. Jules
was tempted to plant his foot in the man's instep and
go in search of a more comfortable conversation.

"Well, no," Waterburn admitted. "That's not it. Not
exactly. But the mere fact that I cannot quite identify
your expression . . ."

He let the sentence dangle. Took a sip of his own
port, looked at it, and nodded in happy approval.

Jules just sighed, and shook his head, implying world
weary, mild amusement. He deliberately inspected the
rest of the room, his eyes lighting on one person at a

time, causing more than one woman to absently touch a hand to her hair, or turn her best profile toward him unconsciously.

It was a glittering gathering, the sort of which he approved, in which he reveled, in which he felt at home. It was his native environment; it reminded him of his place in the world and all he had done to keep it. And yet he was as interested in everybody here as a shopkeeper was in counting the number of potatoes left in a bin. In a day's time they had become just that mundane. Troubling.

Waterburn swirled the port around in his mouth. Swallowed. Gave his lips a smack.

"Do you find her . . . *Miss Vale* . . ." He said her name almost satirically. He appeared to be carefully considering the end of his sentence. ". . . *appealing*, Dryden?"

Jules turned slowly toward Waterburn. Whose tone was reminiscent of the careful one his mother had used to address his ancient great-aunt Calliope, Lady Congdon, when she'd blithely arrived at the dinner table one night wearing nothing but her chemise and one slipper.

"Because if it's novelty you're seeking, Dryden . . ." Waterburn lowered his voice. "Well, there are other brothels besides the Velvet Glove. For instance, Madame Elaine near the docks employs a young lady who supposedly sports a tiny beard, and another one who is so double-jointed she can wrap her legs round her own head not to mention *yours* if you're clever enough to ask—"

"For the love of *God*, Waterburn. She's a woman. She possesses all of her limbs, her form is not . . . unpleasant . . . her features are all present and accounted for and I don't find her bosom wanting. And I wasn't staring. I'm truly sorry you're so bored. There will be cards later this evening. Perhaps losing your fortune to me will prove diverting."

He realized too late this was both a confession and an obvious lie, in light of his recitation of her qualities. As tempered as he'd made them sound.

Waterburn stared at Jules, his eyes wide in genuine surprise. Then he narrowed them shrewdly.

Then widened them again and swiveled his great chiseled head to level upon Phoebe a speculative gaze.

"If you just need a place to rest your eyes, I would have thought you'd choose a beautiful woman, Dryden."

Dryden wondered if this was a calculated statement. For it seemed very wrong to want to call Waterburn out, but the impulse burst into flame and he felt his hand curl tightly around his port, and his lungs tighten with anger.

Beautiful. Jules once thought he'd understood what the word meant. He now believed it overused. Some word needed to be kept in reserve for the rare, the arresting, the surprising . . . the magical. Or a new one invented.

Phoebe laughed at something then. It made him immediately restless. He wanted to be near her and feel the laugh pour like tiny sparks over his senses. He suffered, because he wanted to be the one who'd made her laugh.

"Precisely," he said to Waterburn absently.

Waterburn's curiosity was now flourishing. He was staring thoughtfully at Phoebe, too, with not a little bemusement. He called to mind a museum patron told he *ought* to appreciate a particular painting.

"*Ahhh*hhhhh!"

Waterburn drew it out into two syllables. So suddenly Jules jerked his head toward him. "Do you know,

Dryden . . . I think I see now. Yes, I think I do."

"See *what*?" Jules said irritably.

"Why, my partner for one of the waltzes this evening. And I salute you, you clever devil. I never would have had an inspiration if not for you."

He eased away from the mantel with those words and merged with the crowd.

And when Waterburn passed a mirror, he paused. Then drew a lock of his blond hair down over his brow, studied himself, and nodded in satisfaction.

Chapter 15

Phoebe never suspected her trip to the ratafia bowl would turn out to be one of the most eventful trips she'd ever taken in her life. She'd been sent by Lisbeth, of course, but she hoped to eat a tiny sandwich while she was there, too, because the dancing would begin shortly. And she was certain Lisbeth would expect her to hold her ratafia and accompany her to the withdrawing room when beckoned and hear her assessment of her partners and the music and she'd hardly have time for a sandwich.

The events began with Lord Waterburn, whom she'd begun to silently refer to as Hadrian's Wall. A little bit of schoolmistress humor. He seemed to be a vacuum of the sort where amusement went to disappear.

For days she'd watched his expression twitch between boredom and disdain and back again, broken only by the occasional fleeting smile, which one might be forgiven for mistaking for gas.

He was smiling now.

She eyed all those teeth suspiciously. She'd never seen them bared in her direction before, and she was wary, as she'd done nothing in particular to earn it. He also, suddenly, sported a forelock. She stared at it, puzzled.

And he was so close she could see dimples, a small crescent nestled inside a large one, at the corners of his mouth, and the lines at the corners of his eyes. Not unattractive. Still, she felt strangely uncomfortable viewing his face in such detail.

"Good evening, Miss Vale," he said with a bow.

"Good evening, Lord Waterburn." She curtsied.

He didn't continue on his way to wherever he'd been going before he intercepted her. He remained still, neatly blocking the view of the rest of the assembly and the ratafia and the tiny sandwiches.

It occurred to her then that *she* was his destination.

And now she was beginning to feel uneasy, since he'd obviously viewed her as something little better than an object until now. She wanted to peer around him yearningly toward the little piles of food, but considered it might be rude. She prepared her polite social smile, since she could hardly offer him a neutral expression while he was beaming at her. It was as useful as her old gray cloak, that smile.

On it went.

Until he cleared his throat. "Miss Vale, I wondered if you might be so gracious as to do me the honor of . . ."

Her smile congealed in shock.

" . . . dancing the first waltz with me. The orchestra is meant to play three of them this evening, I understand. If it isn't . . . too much trouble, I should be happy indeed if you would accept."

Trouble? Had Lord Waterburn been knocked on the head?

He waited. The smile remained.

A *waltz*. A waltz with a *viscount*. Not only that, but he'd requested the *first* waltz . . . suggesting it would be just one of the three she would be graciously, strategically bestowing throughout the evening. As though he might have *competition* for the others.

It occurred to her for one wild moment that the marquess might have mentioned she was giving out kisses at this house party, and that Waterburn hoped to get one by waltzing with her, and then maneuvering her out into the garden.

No. The marquess wouldn't dare compromise his dignity or reputation by admitting he'd kissed a *schoolmistress*.

Not only kissed her, but *liked* it.

Perhaps this day simply had a theme: the sudden and inexplicable.

Which would explain how she answered. "I believe I *will* be that gracious," she said carefully, slowly.

This pleased him, judging from the way the smile grew.

"And Lord Waterburn . . . it shall not *trouble* me at all." *Unless you intend to talk to me during it.*

She smiled, too, cautiously, whilst she peeked surreptitiously at the glass he was holding. It appeared he'd been drinking the port. How much of it? she wondered.

Or perhaps his request was a result of a . . . dare?

Nevertheless.

She was more than equal to anyone's *dare*, as she could not be maneuvered out into the garden for a bit of fondling or whatever the dare might entail; she was far clever for that. And knew just where to trod on or kick his person to, er, discourage him.

But she rather looked forward to dancing a waltz. She would simply account it another experience to entrust to her journal, a once-in-a-lifetime type of thing,

and simply enjoy the waltz with Hadrian's Wall the
way she might enjoy a ride in a high flyer. Or in his
case, something considerably larger. A landau, perhaps.
With four shiny black horses harnessed to—

"Thank you, Miss Vale."

He was studying her almost . . . avidly, if she had
to choose a word. Absently, she brought a hand up to
rub between her eyes, to ascertain whether she had
sprouted a third one, or perhaps a horn.

With an effort she brought it down again. She struggled not to frown, as he likely needed to be encouraged
to smile. His smile lit his eyes. And they were pretty
eyes when they were lit. There was indeed a person,
perhaps a not entirely intolerable one, lurking behind
them.

Next he'll compliment my complexion.

"Until we dance," he said instead.

"Until we dance," she agreed solemnly.

If he noticed her eyes glinting wicked humor he
showed no sign. He bowed and stepped aside, and as
though he were a great boulder rolled away from the
mouth of a treasure cave, the marquess was revealed.
He was leaning against the hearth directly across from
her, a good ten feet or more away. In contrast to the
beaming viscount, he appeared darkly preoccupied
and unfortunately incongruous, as the hearth was covered in carved cherubs and they cavorted just above his
head. "Satyr with cherubs," she might have titled it, if
he'd been a woodcut. The expression on his face hinted
that if they'd been real cherubs buzzing about he would
have shot them out of the sky with a bow and arrow.

Her heart stopped. Then resumed beating considerably more quickly.

His hair was pulled rakishly down over his pale

brow. A puzzlingly devil-may-care decision, given that devil-may-care was the last thing he was purported to be.

When their eyes met her social smile faltered. Because as usual she didn't see him so much as *feel* him, like a hand brushed over the fine hairs on the back of her neck. The parts of her he'd touched seemed to tingle with the memory of it, and the parts he hadn't touched ached at the oversight. The result was she was very likely flushing, at least judging from her temperature.

She offered a tentative smile. She contemplated offering a cheery ironic wave. She doubted he would appreciate it.

For a moment she worried he was simply going to brood in her direction, and she suspected no one brooded with more potency than he did.

But then his mouth tipped slowly up at the corner. Rueful, enigmatic. As though he wasn't ready to commit to feeling a particular way.

She'd kissed that mouth this very afternoon.

She suddenly felt feverish and shy and awkward, as if all of her limbs had grown two sizes. She was aware she'd dressed her own hair, that she owned no jewelry, that her dress had a spot near the hem, that her slippers were thinning at the soles.

She glanced sideways, guiltily, at Lisbeth, who was awaiting ratafia. The coronet shone in her dark hair like a substitute halo. She was chatting gaily to yet another friend who had come to pay homage.

When Phoebe glanced back at the marquess he swiftly lifted that rogue lock of hair, pointed at his forehead and mouthed:

Good aim.

She clapped a hand over her mouth. Dear God, he

was sporting a *bruise*! So *that's* where she'd clocked him with his hat!

And this explained the forelock.

He grinned, swiftly, just like a boy. Oh, God. That grin might as well have been a lariat looped around her heart.

But she pulled her hands away from her mouth. Her eyes were watering with mirth, which was probably wicked, when she really ought to have been mortified she'd maimed him. She bit her lip to keep from laughing.

He dropped his hair again and put a finger against his lips.

She took another step, a tentative noncommittal one that could have taken her toward him or toward the ratafia table. A test of sorts.

He visibly tensed. His smile faded and a strange wariness set in.

She halted. Her spirits plummeted into awkward uncertainty.

And then to her astonishment he vanished. Obscured from view by another pair of dark coats and fluffy cravats.

She tilted her head back and discovered Jonathan Redmond and another gentleman she hadn't yet met, though she'd certainly noticed him, as it had been impossible not to. Handsome, even more dazzling than Argosy, and a dandy, this one, in a waistcoat striped in gold, a cravat tied in the fashion equivalent of a Gordian knot, and chestnut curls as loose and abandoned as his trousers were snug.

It was the trousers she'd noticed when she'd first arrived in the salon. Or rather, what was contained therein. He'd been the recipient of so many sidelong glances since he'd stepped into the parlor she doubted anyone would be able to relate the color of his eyes, but would have been able to accurately estimate the size of his masculine blessing.

"Miss Vale. I don't believe I've introduced Sir Geoffrey d'Andre to you yet this evening."

As if an introduction of this sort had been an *inevitability*. What on earth was happening tonight?

"A pleasure to meet you, Miss Vale," he murmured. He drawled, as though he had a mouth full of something thick and delicious, perhaps honey.

She curtsied and held out her hand for him to bow over. When he moved to bow over it a waft of scent came with him: expensive and spicy and yet still pleasantly male and exotically—to her, anyway—aristocratic.

"I am quite pleased to meet you, too, Sir Geoffrey."

She stared at him. His face was sharp at the chin, prominent at the cheekbones, hewn at the jaw. He was preternaturally handsome, as though his ancestors had bred with nothing but other beautiful people specifically to arrive at him.

"Ah, well. It's my understanding you'll be joining the dancing this evening, Phoe—Miss Vale?"

This came from Jonathan, who looked as mystified as she felt. She had the sensation that he'd been enlisted *specifically* to make this introduction. She wondered if he, too, thought it might be the result of a dare. She was his sister's paid companion, after all. Albeit one who'd smelled of cheroot smoke the other evening.

"To my great delight, yes. I will be joining the dancing." She tried not to sound defiant.

Sir d'Andre smiled at this. He looked . . . Well, for some reason her answer seemed to *enchant* him, if the sparkle in his eyes was any indication. This seemed a rather extreme reaction to what she considered a simple statement.

It could hardly have anything to do with her dress, which she'd worn innumerable times to mostly resounding indifference. Maybe once a woman is thoroughly kissed by a marquess she radiates a certain *je ne sais quoi*, she thought. Something only aristocratic men could sense, the way the highest of pitches were said to disturb the ears of dogs.

"I wondered if you would be so kind as to share one of the dances with me, Miss Vale. In fact, do I dare hope you'll favor me with a waltz?"

Favor me. How they did talk, these titled men. Did they think it was expected of them, all these "dares" and "favors" and so forth? Such a lot of words to issue a simple request.

She couldn't say she disliked it. It had the ring of ceremony, if not sincerity. And in truth, though her life hadn't lacked for order since she was ten years old, it was sorely lacking in ceremony.

"You may do more than hope, Sir d'Andre. I'd be quite pleased to favor you with a waltz. The second one, as my first is taken."

It was the first time she'd ever uttered that sentence in her entire life. It was rather astonishing how quickly and easily she took to pomp.

And though her gravity was almost entirely comprised of irony, he didn't seem to notice. Perhaps he considered it all a part of the ritual. Or perhaps in his experience all women spoke just that way.

And that's when a certain giddiness began to creep into her spirits. She felt like an actress in a play who'd decided to recklessly veer from the script.

Ah! Perhaps that was the theme of the day. *Recklessness.*

Or perhaps veering from the script?

"I shall look forward to it, Miss Vale."

Trousers bowed, gifting her with a slow smile on the way down, and then gracefully backed away with Jonathan Redmond, leaving her path to the ratafia clear again, and once again revealing the marquess against the hearth.

Who was no longer smiling. Who in fact looked rather saturnine.

She darted a look about the room to ensure no one was watching her. And then she surreptitiously turned her palms up, a gesture of wonderment, and widened her eyes: *Aristocrats are descending upon me!*

He gave a quick, involuntary smile. A quirk at the corners of his mouth.

She took a deep breath. And tried another brisk confident step forward toward him.

She froze. For his smile faded again. And his expression took on something that looked very like a warning. It was subtle.

But she felt it like a slap.

He never would have dared aimed that expression at Lisbeth. Or any of the other women in the room. *She* was to keep her distance, apparently.

And then he vanished again. And this time he disappeared courtesy of a bemused-looking Lisbeth, who was flanked by two identical brunettes wearing white.

Four brown eyes beamed not entirely benign curiosity at her. Two pairs of bow-shaped lips turned up in identical enigmatic smiles. Their hair was intricately dressed up and decorated with shining combs and curls bobbed playfully at their temples. Since she hadn't yet imbibed a single drop of ratafia, she must in fact be seeing two separate girls. Identical twins.

Oh, good heavens! These must be the infamous Silverton sisters!

They were beautiful as a pair of pixies.

They curtsied, and she did the same.

"I wondered where you'd gotten to, Phoebe! I came to fetch my own ratafia." Lisbeth smiled. But her tone was the same tone Phoebe had used before on her pupils when they did something disappointing.

She contemplated a strategy. "Forgive me, Lisbeth, but I know you'll be delighted to hear why I was waylaid. I've been asked to join the festivities!"

"But . . . weren't you already doing that?"

She sounded genuinely confused. Phoebe contemplated telling Lisbeth that *watching* her dance did not qualify as *participation*, necessarily, and wasn't nearly as diverting as Lisbeth might think.

"Well, you see . . . it's a funny thing, but I've been asked to dance. The waltz. Twice. I thought it would be impolite to refuse."

This was met with more silence. "But do you know how to dance the waltz, dear?"

Dear? Lisbeth had landed rather hard on the *D*. One might have thought she'd said it through clenched teeth.

"Of course, dear." Well, she was certain it would come back to her, anyway, once she got the waltz under way.

Lisbeth's teeth appeared and yet her eyes seemed entirely unaware that she was smiling. It reminded Phoebe unnervingly of the first time she'd met Mr. Isaiah Redmond. She didn't think there was ever a time when Isaiah Redmond wasn't . . . *planning*. That his mind invariably efficiently rolled along on an entirely different yet parallel track from the one his conversation took, and very few people noticed.

Two throats cleared prettily and simultaneously.

"The Silverton sisters have asked to make your acquaintance," Lisbeth remembered, and sounded bemused, and a frown shadowed her brow.

"This is Lady Marie Silverton." The girl on the left curtsied.

"And this is Lady Antoinette Silverton." Lady Antoinette curtsied.

Marie . . . and Antoinette? Oh, good heavens. And why on earth would the infamous Silverton sisters *ask* to meet her?

It was then that Phoebe decided simply to surrender and treat the entire day like a dream. In dreams, events happened for no discernible reason and in no logical order. One simply drifted through until the chime of a morning clock ended it.

So she made her curtsy a particularly pretty one, deep and graceful, because she was beginning to enjoy the theatricality of the event.

"Delighted to make your acquaintance," she said to both of them.

"Mama wasn't being whimsical or macabre when she named us Marie and Antoinette," Antoinette explained. "She's just rather stupid."

Phoebe was speechless.

Their eyes glinted at her. Like animal eyes, shiny and inscrutable above their smiles. She couldn't read their intent. And there seemed to be one, or a test of some sort. The silence was the waiting kind.

"Have you siblings named Antony and Cleopatra?"

Two pair of identical eyebrows immediately shot upward.

So . . . apparently she wasn't supposed to say *that*. The palms of her hands went clammy inside her gloves. She wondered if her waltzes could be revoked.

She was so tense that when the twins burst into peals of laughter, she jumped.

A cascade of bells, the laughter was, merry and abandoned, nearly buckling their petite frames. Lady Marie laid her fingers on Phoebe's arm familiarly, so overcome with mirth was she, and her curls wobbled as though they were laughing, too.

She turned to her sister. "He was right!" she said cryptically to her sister, as her sister was saying to her, "Antony and Cleopatra! Ha ha ha!"

They turned identical expressions of such wicked delight upon Phoebe it was difficult not to feel warmed. She approved of wicked delight. Though she could not for the life of her understand what on earth had charmed them so.

A dream, she reminded herself, *doesn't have to make sense.*

Lisbeth looked as though she'd swallowed an insect. "We should so enjoy your company at the card table after the dancing, Miss Vale. And never fear. We don't play very deep."

"I *adore* playing shallow," Phoebe gushed.

Where on earth had that statement come from? She'd never gambled in her life with anything other than walnuts with other teachers at Miss Marietta Endicott's academy, and she had only five pounds in her reticule with which to do it. She could ill afford to lose it.

"She adores playing shallow!" Lady Marie and Lady Antoinette repeated rhapsodically into each other's pretty faces. As if Phoebe was quite simply too endearing to be endured.

"Excellent. We shall collect you during the ball," Lady Marie vowed, and they departed in tandem, trailing little waves of their kid-gloved hands, leaving her alone with Lisbeth.

"I shall look forward to it," Phoebe called after them gaily.

She might be at the mercy of the tide of events, but she felt as giddy as a seal being tossed about in the sea. It was *lovely* to be so fervently wanted, whatever the reason. It was balm after the wall the marquess had thrown up with his wary expression.

Lisbeth stared after the Silverton sisters, a faint puzzled crease in her brow. "I told them you were a schoolmistress . . ."

The unspoken part of the sentence being, "But they wanted to meet you anyway."

"Perhaps they feel a lack in their education, and hope I can tutor them over the card table."

Lisbeth was, as usual, literal. "I shouldn't think the Silverton sisters have ever felt a lack of any kind. And they are very popular." Lisbeth's tone was still abstracted. "Very."

"I am not surprised, as they seem charming, indeed."

Lisbeth didn't appear to be listening to her. "With whom shall you be waltzing, Phoebe?" Lisbeth asked suddenly.

"Lord Waterburn and Sir d'Andre."

She nodded absently. "Mmm. The orchestra will play three waltzes this evening. I've given away two of mine already, too."

The moment was so peculiarly taut they could have plucked a note from it. And as if on cue, the crowd parted, and their view was of the marquess again.

Lisbeth smiled at him.

Which meant he was forced to abandon his brooding and the cherubs and come forward to make his bow to both of them.

Phoebe was shocked her heart didn't echo like a drumbeat over the hum of the salon conversation.

"Miss Vale and I were just discussing how we'd each bestowed two of our waltzes already. And we've each one yet to give away."

He didn't look at Phoebe. And she knew that he didn't because he would not be able to stop once he did.

"I should be more than honored if you would share the waltz with me, Lisbeth."

"I am delighted to do it."

"And oh, look, there's Jonathan. Perhaps we can persuade him to dance the other waltz with you. Since you will only be here until tomorrow, you might as well enjoy the night, wouldn't you say?" she asked brightly, suddenly, as if she was coming to terms with the peculiar notion that Phoebe would be waltzing at all, and including Jules in this magnanimity, as if Phoebe was their shared problem. "And then I can wave to you as we whirl by in the ballroom!"

Persuade. As if Jonathan would need to be bribed to take a schoolmistress for a twirl.

Lisbeth was already tripping lightly off in pursuit of her handsome cousin, who looked unnervingly more and more like his older brother Lyon Redmond every day, and who took one look over his shoulder and picked up his pace, looking very much as though he was fleeing Lisbeth.

The marquess was gone. Without him, the cherubs on the mantel now seemed smug and sinister, as if they knew secrets she did not. As if they'd stolen him away and were holding him for ransom.

Ironically, now that she at last seemed free to find a sandwich, she'd lost her appetite.

She wouldn't mind a drink or two . . . or three . . . of ratafia, however.

After all, she told herself ironically, it *was* a party.

Chapter 16

She'd nearly forgotten how to waltz.

She'd been stiff at first. And then her body recalled that the key to the whole thing was surrendering the lead to someone else. This did not in any way come naturally to her. And there had been a moment when the toe of her slipper had snagged in the hem of her dress, but Waterburn was so large he didn't seem to notice at all. He'd flexed his big arm, like a man steering a boat might make an unconscious adjustment to an oar, and suddenly she was balanced again.

She felt less like a partner than an accessory, like a reticule.

She decided she didn't need to make conversation. He was the gentleman. It would be up to him. She would listen to the music and allow the ratafia and the twirling to conspire in making her feel very pleasantly drunk.

"Your . . ." he examined her person, and apparently decided upon ". . . ribbon . . . is very fetching."

"Are you at a loss for compliments, Lord Waterburn? I mean to say . . . it's a *ribbon*."

She smiled winsomely at him. She'd stood over the table and drank three cups of ratafia in rapid succession, and this, and the likelihood of never seeing Waterburn again after this day, and the marquess and Lisbeth gliding and spinning in almost criminal splendor in her peripheral vision was making her a trifle reckless.

"But no one else here is wearing a ribbon," he pointed out.

"No, they're wearing diamonds and pearls. Oh, apart from that bloody great ruby round the throat of that large woman over there. It is a ruby, isn't it?" She craned her head inelegantly.

His eyes went wide when she said "bloody." He craned his head, too, suddenly curious. "I should say so. That's Lady Copshire, after all."

"Mmm. Of course. Lady Copshire."

"It suits your eyes. The ribbon." Perhaps he thought grunters would naturally say things like "bloody" and had come to terms with it.

She gazed up at him so limpidly he seemed startled. "Lord Waterburn?"

"Yes?"

"It strikes me that life is very short, and I fear I cannot bear any more talk of my ribbon. I might in fact do something desperate to stop it."

He barked a shocked laugh. "You *are* an original. My apologies, Miss Vale. I fear I became mired in my compliment. My admiration was sincere, if clumsy."

Well, that was very nearly a pretty speech. She was perilously close to being charmed.

"Why don't we discuss something else, then? What is it like, being a teacher?"

His eyes glinted, and his voice lowered to a hush, as if he'd asked something taboo.

Oh, for heaven's sake. She nearly rolled her eyes. "Oh, every day is like a day in Eden. I can imagine nothing more glorious and satisfying than shaping young minds and reforming young characters."

He considered this somberly. "I believe you are teasing me, Miss Vale."

"I might be," she allowed just as somberly. "I just might be. What is it like, being a viscount?"

He seemed surprised. "I have never given it any thought. I suppose it's like asking, 'What is it like being human?' I just . . . *am* one."

She noticed he hadn't seized the opportunity to think about it *now*, either.

"Oh, I believe I understand, Lord Waterburn. Why would one reflect upon one's role in the universe when one can instead be racing a phaeton at breakneck speed or losing copious amounts at the gaming tables or just generally having a *wonderful* time?"

He was so pleased with their accord that he tightened his grip on her hand, which made her wince a little. "Too right, Miss Vale! Too right! Life is for living, not for *pondering*. I might add that as a viscount I find that I am ever seeking new . . . diversions."

Oh, dear. He'd lingered suggestively on the last word. When he glanced down at her bosom and up again her suspicions were confirmed: he'd meant it as an innuendo.

This was a man who thought she was a grunter, who'd scarcely even noticed her as a person, let alone as a woman. What had happened between this afternoon and this evening to change his opinion of her? It was the marquess who had sustained an injury to his head, after all. Not Waterburn.

He would need to be considerably less sober to compliment her *breasts* outright, she suspected, but for one reckless moment she considered steering him down that road, for it would be almost too easy to do it. What had she to lose?

She sighed so gustily it seemed impossible he wouldn't feel her ribs rise and fall beneath his hand. For it was exhausting to contemplate. Like treading water. He was simply too . . . *simple*. A cipher, upon which she could manufacture an entire conversation.

Though she knew she probably shouldn't make such careless assumption. Not everyone or everything was as they appeared on the surface. If naught else, she'd learned that during this house party.

"Do you enjoy having a lot of money?" she asked him instead.

He gave another woof of startled laughter. "How can one not enjoy having a lot of money?"

"I cannot say, as I'm content with what I have." She thought she sounded pleasingly and loftily enigmatic. Of course this wasn't necessarily true. She was certainly *grateful* for what she had. But she'd never even considered returning the bonnet to Postlethwaite's, for example.

She simply wanted to tax Waterburn's big blond brain to make the waltz more interesting for *her*.

Alas, apparently she'd said something so provocative he fell pensively silent.

For a moment it was pleasant to be spun around, to hear graceful music played by competent musicians and not have to speak to him. But then out of the corner of her eye she again saw the marquess and Lisbeth sweeping across the floor, the two of them in black and white, their two shining dark heads elegantly matched, Lisbeth's dress floating out behind her like so much mist over the moors. She could have sworn everyone on the periphery of the ballroom floor had clasped their hands in beaming indulgent admiration of the two of them.

I am content with what I have? It was a bald lie. A lie with talons. She savagely envied Lisbeth the hand resting on her waist, enfolding Lisbeth's hand as though Lisbeth was something precious and worthy.

She jerked her head back to her dancing partner.

Her cheeks were burning now, and the ratafia was beginning to churn as they turned round and round. Perhaps a *circular* dance on the heels of too much drinking hadn't been the most sensible choice she could make.

The viscount's eyes were gleaming at her. "I have never known anyone like you, Miss Vale."

She sighed. She almost pitied him. "Likely because I am a *teacher*," she pointed out. "And you are a viscount. And viscounts tend to meet other viscounts and the like."

Even this bit of practicality he seemed to find profound. "And you've never married?" He sounded mystified.

"I am twenty-two years old. It is perhaps a bit too soon to use the word *never*."

Every time she said something, he blinked as though she'd shone a bright light in his eyes. And there was always a peculiar moment's hesitation before he responded. She was reminded of a young Italian girl she'd once tutored, who needed to carefully translate English words into Italian and before she spoke aloud her English answers, so conversation with her always featured a bit of delay. Clearly there was nothing in Waterburn's experience to prepare him for someone like her. He needed a Rosetta stone for translating Rabble into Aristocracy and back again.

"But *come* now, Miss Vale . . . wouldn't you rather be wealthy? To be showered with gifts and—"

She halted his sentence with the hike of one shoulder: a shrug. Simply because she knew it would make his eyes widen in astonishment.

They did.

"And . . . have you . . . suitors?"

He might as well have been a naturalist along the lines of Mr. Miles Redmond interviewing a native. He seemed almost afraid to hear the answer, suspecting it might call into question his entire existence.

"Countless," she lied.

It was while Waterburn was absorbing the troubling notion that she might be inundated with suitors *because* of her laissez-faire attitude toward wealth that Phoebe at last caught the eye of the marquess.

The chandelier struck light from his guinea-colored eyes. They saw her, flared swift with surprise, then went hot. She would have *given* a guinea to be able to toss her head insouciantly and look away again, to laugh merrily up into the face of her partner and then heave an obvious and contented sigh.

But the moment their gazes brushed she felt that lightning-strike sizzle at the base of her spine. There was nothing else in the room. There was no one else in the world. They searched each other's faces for answers to some question they could hardly formulate. She found no answers in his. But there was some small compensation in knowing he was equally in thrall, for he didn't look away, either.

And then he was forced to look away, because he stumbled.

She winced. It was a rare and momentary hiccup in grace. Likely no one who wasn't *avidly* watching him would even have noticed. He took two confident little steps forward to correct his rhythm and catch up to his partner.

Which would have done the trick, if Lisbeth hadn't just taken two little steps backward to accommodate his stumble, all the while beaming up at him sympathetically.

Forcing *him* to take two more polite little steps backward to match her pace.

Just as Lisbeth, eager to correct her error, did precisely the same thing. At the same time. Again.

Forcing him to launch into a sort of lunge reminiscent of a long jumper to avoid crushing Lisbeth's foot under his, which is where it had wound up.

While at the same time Lisbeth tried to leap out from beneath his boot by pulling with all her might to the left.

And this, tragically, was when gravity lost its patience and destiny exercised its rights and everything went straight to hell and into legend.

The marquess teetered to the left, then teetered to the right, and Lisbeth's slippers futilely scrabbled in place, but when they began to tip in earnest, the marquess made a desperate decision: he flung Lisbeth away from him to safety.

So it was Jules who crashed to all fours on the floor of the ballroom.

Lisbeth spun past Phoebe like a blurry muslin roulette wheel. Her eyes and mouth O's of shock.

Phoebe burst into laughter. She quite roared with it. It was rude, she knew, but she simply couldn't help it. The ratafia . . . ! And Lisbeth's expression . . . !

Someone gave Lisbeth a little push in the opposite direction and she had enough momentum to go spiraling back to the marquess. Who had righted himself nearly instantly and deftly caught her, sweeping her into the *one, two, three* rhythm of the waltz again as if nothing had happened at all. As if he indeed had *planned* all of it.

Phoebe was able to watch all of this thanks to her own mountainous partner, her head turned one way watching whilst her body below was waltzing. If she began to trip she imagined Waterburn would merely lift her off the floor, give her a shake to untangle her legs and set her down again.

Waterburn wasn't laughing. When she returned her eyes to his face, his were narrowed shrewdly. He'd been watching the entire episode as if memorizing it.

"He doesn't normally drink to excess," the viscount mused. "So *that's* not it . . ."

"Perhaps he *did* drink to excess for the first time." She didn't believe it. "Perhaps he just stumbled. Everyone makes mistakes."

"No. He doesn't. And he never does anything without a reason. He certainly doesn't *stumble*."

He sounded both fascinated and speculative and bitter and so utterly certain that Phoebe wondered where *she* fell in the spectrum of things the marquess had done.

And then it was quite sobering to know that this was what the ton at large thought of Jules, and what a burden it must be for him.

Chapter 17

If she'd had to summarize, she was forced to admit the evening had been glorious.

She'd won ten pounds—*ten pounds!*—at the disreputable game of five-card loo, instigated by Lady Marie and her lovely echo, Lady Antoinette. She half suspected they'd lost deliberately, as they seemed to find it charming when Phoebe won. She'd danced reels as well as all three waltzes, including the very last dance of the evening, the Sir Roger de Coverley. The young men had clamored for a chance to dance with her.

She drank too much. She laughed a good deal. And the marquess seemed everywhere on the periphery of her vision, though this might have in fact been an illusion.

She paused in the courtyard to admire the moon. Just a curved sliver of light, like the door of heaven had been left slightly ajar. She fancied it would be slammed shut after today, and today she'd slipped through. She'd had just a taste. And she'd long ago learned not to hold on to anything too tightly, for the pain when it was wrested away could not be born.

She wanted to remember every detail about this day, for when she lay awake at night, telling herself stories in order to help her sleep in the wilds of Africa.

"A bit like the Sword of Damocles hanging up there, isn't it?"

She didn't jump, possibly because the ratafia had quite blunted the edges of her nerves, and partly because, given the events of the day, she'd half expected him to appear out of the shadows anyway. In fact, if she'd had a wish, in her heart of hearts, it was that he'd appear out of nowhere and they would be alone again . . . and here he was.

But she was growing nervous of the cascade of wishes coming true today. In fairy tales, granted wishes generally resulted in grave consequences. A punishment for wanting too much, or wanting the wrong things.

Still, it didn't stop her heart from turning a cartwheel. And then thumping on much more quickly than before he'd spoken.

He'd waited for her. Of that she was certain.

"And here I was thinking it looked rather like the door to heaven just slightly ajar, Lord Dryden. But your observation does give one a bit of insight into *you*."

He laughed softly. "And yours gives one insight into yours, Miss Vale. It's about escape, isn't it?"

"Mmm. Perhaps. And perhaps *you* fear the consequences of what you really want."

She heard his breath catch. She'd struck home.

"I won't deny it," he said, finally.

The admission was a gift. He wanted *her*.

But she couldn't so easily forgive the expression on his face this evening as she'd stepped toward him. Or forget hearing him request a waltz from Lisbeth as she stood there, pawned off upon Jonathan.

Who'd turned out to be a delightful dance partner. But who now looked so like Lyon proximity to him was a little unnerving.

"I wondered, Miss Vale . . . if you'd promised your fourth waltz to anyone."

"There were only three waltzes."

"I'm not certain parliament has yet ruled the number of waltzes allowed during a given evening. Or when they should take place. Doubtless we won't be strung up if we add one more."

No "honor me with" or "if you would be so kind as to." No pomp, no ceremony. She was tempted to decline on the basis of that alone.

That, and she was fairly certain she shouldn't touch him again. She could get to needing to touch him. She'd seen what *needing* things had done to people. And she, quite frankly, didn't want to need anyone ever again.

"No music is playing," she pointed out.

"I'll hum, if you like."

This won him the smile he'd been aching to see.

"You had an opportunity to dance the waltz with me earlier."

"I took pity upon Lisbeth. I felt certain all of yours would be taken eventually."

She snorted.

"And they were taken, weren't they?"

She tipped her head, and he watched her reflect on the evening, and a dreamy smile spread over her face. As she spoke, she was almost breathless.

"They *were*. It was the most . . . *amazing* thing."

He felt her awe as surely as it was his own, this girl from St. Giles. He reveled in her pleasure. "I'm glad," he said softly.

"Glad?" As usual, she was alert to hints of condescension.

"That you got in some waltzing practice before *I* dance with you. I shouldn't like to be tread upon."

"I see. It was all strategy, on your part, not dancing with me. A viscount asked for the *honor* of dancing with me." She still sounded amazed. "That was the word he used. *Honor.*"

"Did he, now?" he said softly. "And well he should have."

For a moment they regarded each other in silence. And when he spoke, his voice was soft.

"I should be deeply, humbly grateful, Miss Vale, if you would be so unthinkably generous as to honor me with a waltz. Right now."

She mulled this offer, while the crickets played the opening bars of the waltz.

"Well, before I raise or dash your hopes, Lord Dryden, I best take a look at my dance card . . ."

With a flourish she held up her hand and examined an invisible card.

He was ridiculously breathless with anticipation awaiting her verdict. She allowed a strategic moment to pass, to punish him, which perhaps he deserved.

"You are in luck, Lord Dryden. My fourth waltz appears to be available," she informed him loftily. "And you may have it."

"This is very good news, indeed. Shall I hum, or shall the crickets be music enough for us?"

She was silent, mulling. "Crickets." She sounded shy again.

"Excellent. For I should feel a fool humming. I cannot carry a tune."

He bowed low as any courtier before any queen.

She curtsied as deeply as she could, grateful her knees didn't crack, aware that she could feel the chill of cobblestone now against the bottom of her slipper. The soles were wearing a bit thin.

And she took his hand. He folded his reverently over it. He settled the other at her waist.

"Shall we?" he said softly.

And he set the two of them in motion. *One, two, three . . . One, two three . . . One, two three.*

Odd how this didn't seem at all absurd, the two of them sailing in stately, broad circles in a deserted courtyard. Their heartbeats, the crickets, the rhythm of their breathing, their feet landing on the cobblestones comprised their orchestra. Keeping time was somehow effortless.

"You've some experience, now, Miss Vale, and some comparison. Come now, tell me the truth. How is my dancing? Keeping in mind that the debacle you witnessed tonight was entirely an anomaly and entirely your fault. And you laughed! I was wounded. Sorely wounded."

"It wasn't *entirely* my fault. How did you know I was laughing?"

"Because I could *hear* it."

Oh, dear. "Tell me it wasn't funny and I shall apologize. Tell me you are injured and I shall feel terrible remorse. It's just . . . if you were me, and watching it all . . . and Lisbeth's eyes were so very *round* . . ."

"Shhh. Don't laugh again. Very well. It *was* funny. The only thing injured was my pride. So how do you find my dancing now?"

"Mmm . . . Well, *while* you dance very well . . ."

He smiled. A glittering flash in the shadowy dark, an echo of the moon. "I sense a qualification pending."

". . . I fear it's not so well as Trou—as Sir d'Andre."

"Impossible," he said firmly.

"I feel I must be truthful above all things, Lord Dryden, and Sir d'Andre has a certain indescribable flair. Perhaps it is in the way he *turns* in the dance . . ." she mused, as they swept in a circle. ". . . or the way he glides . . . perhaps it's the fit of his *trousers* . . ."

"You noticed them, too?"

". . . or perhaps it is related to *velocity* . . ."

"Ah, but what I lack in velocity I can make up for in . . . elevation." He lifted her off her feet entirely, and she stifled a little burst of laughter.

She weighed very little; he felt effortlessly strong.

The realizations settled in for the two of them a moment later, and they were both moved in ways they couldn't explain. Resulting in a silence.

Dryden didn't think he'd ever done anything quite so whimsical before in his life. He'd never wanted to.

They were moving in sedate pattern now. Slowing, somehow, like a watch winding down. He looked down into her eyes. Clear as pools. Which he knew was certainly a cliché, but it fit, and he liked it. She was watching him with an expression he could not decipher, but the intensity of it gave him the sense she was memorizing him.

One, two, three. One, two, three.

Somewhere a nightingale, unable to contain itself any further, burst into song.

"Tell me, Miss Vale. How often do you do *exactly* what you want to do just because you want to do it?"

One, two, three. One, two, three.

It was twice around the courtyard before she responded. "I can think of one time in particular." She sounded just a bit breathless.

He'd hoped she'd say something just like it. Because he knew his next line. "Did it happen this afternoon?" Conversational, his voice. And silky.

The tempo continued to slow and slow. Twice more around the courtyard before she answered.

"It might have done," she allowed. Whispering now. *One, two, three. One, two, three.*

Closer and closer they drew to each other. Slower and slower. As though some invisible thread was inexorably spooling them together with every rotation of the dance.

"What do you want to do *now*, Miss Vale?"

The question was both a caress and a demand.

He could feel tension humming in her body where his hand rested against her waist. He breathed in, because he was greedy to discover things about her. Anything. This time he discovered she smelled of soap and sweetness, of the lavender no doubt her dress lived in, packed in trunk in tissue, when she wasn't waltzing in the moonlight.

"It isn't fair, you know, Lord Dryden, to ask such questions. I haven't the words for it. You shouldn't make me say it."

The space between them was now entirely gone as if it had never been. His cheek was against hers now. Nothing had ever felt so natural. His breath, even and warm, washed over her throat. She closed her eyes. Her senses were drunk on brandy and smoke and the crisp scent of linen, on the feel of a cool masculine cheek and the rasp of his whiskers over the vulnerable skin of her own.

She was the one who stopped moving altogether first.

He still gripped her hand. His hand still rested at her waist. The waltz could begin again at any time. They held each other, just like that. Only breathing now. In and out. In and out. They breathed in time with each other.

"Aren't you curious about what *I* would like to do?"

"You told me earlier today that you always know what you're going to do."

"I generally do," he agreed on a whisper. "And this moment is no exception. For example, *this* . . ." and now his breath was in her ear ". . . is what I would like to do now."

The breathed words alone were enough to stand the short hairs on the back of her neck, send gooseflesh raining over her arms, and ruche her nipples. But then he turned the last word into a whisper before he dipped his tongue into her ear.

And pressed a hot, open kiss in that hidden, silky place beneath it.

Her breath snagged.

And then it shuddered out on a single word: "*Oh.*"

She ducked her head, tucking it into the crook of his neck. She could taste his throat. The salt and sweetness of it, if she opened her own lips.

". . . and this." His tongue returned to trace, oh so delicately, the whorls of her ear.

She'd closed her eyes against the shivers of pleasure, each a quicksilver rush through her entire body.

"Good heavens, Miss Vale, but you're squeezing my hand rather tightly."

"Devil." It seemed odd to laugh when her body was a riot of new sensation.

"Am I?" He sounded puzzled, but she could hear the laughter in his voice. "That seems all wrong. Given that this strikes me as heavenly."

"Oh, dear."

"Oh. I'm sorry." His voice was husky. "Was that too predictable? How does my hyperbole compare to Sir d'Andre's? Did he make you laugh, Miss Vale?"

"No. His tongue was never close enough to my ear."

"It's my *tongue* that made you laugh?" He sounded affronted. "And not my wit? And here I was setting out to *arouse* you. Though I suppose it's a good thing his tongue was never close to your ear. I might have been tempted to shoot him."

"It would hardly be a fair fight," she murmured. "I doubt he can move very quickly in those trousers."

Her voice was a distracted murmur against his chest. In large part because somehow, at some point, he'd wrapped his arms around her, and his hands were traveling in long, feathery strokes over her shoulder blades, above where her dress laced, where her skin was bare and chilled by the night air.

She could feel him smile against the top of her head. "He's handsome." It sounded like a question to her.

"He is." There was no point in disagreeing.

She'd looped her hands around his neck. And his hands, over the fine fabric of her gown, left little comet trails of sensation over her skin. Sighing, she surrendered to the pleasure.

So different from the *collision* of bodies this afternoon. She didn't think his caution had anything to do with a concern for her virtue. Given the events of the afternoon, he could be forgiven for thinking she might hand her virtue to him on a platter with just a little urging.

If she didn't know better she would have guessed he was uncertain. Perhaps for the first time in his life. The man who always knew what he was going to do.

"Do you know . . ." He gave a soft laugh. "All I could think about tonight was what it might be like to touch your hair?"

It was yet another extraordinary thing to say.

It was overwhelming. She closed her eyes and shook her head slowly, in wonderment. As he dragged his fingers softly, softly along the outline of her, the swell of her hips, the nip of waist, then traveling up to skim her breasts, deliberately dragging over the hard beads of her nipples pressed against the silk of her bodice. And when they did, her body arched into his touch as if shocked; her breath snagged in her throat. He didn't linger; instead his hands continued their journey, glided over her collarbone, then came to rest at the nape of her neck.

And then his fingers stroked the silky hair there. Again, and again, his fingers like feathers.

"And?" she whispered.

He hesitated. "It's soft."

His voice was gruff.

It's yours, is what he meant. And she knew it. She could have been sporting pig bristles on her head or some such. He'd wanted to touch her hair because it was hers.

He cradled the back of her head in his hand and tipped it back and brought his mouth down to hers.

The kiss was hot, languid, thorough. He kissed her the way he might kiss a longtime lover, with no preamble. It invaded her. And within seconds she was trembling, and all but aflame.

He sensed the need in her and took swift clever advantage. His fingers played over the laces of her dress; and then expertly, as if he'd done that very thing a thousand times before—there was a thought she didn't wish to entertain in the moment—he loosened them. And such was the madness of the moment it seemed right, logical, even necessary.

His mouth played over her ear, traveled the length of her throat, quite distracting her from the fact that his hands were gliding over her shoulders and easing the bodice of her dress away from them. Down, down, down. Only distantly was she aware she was increasingly bare, because his warm hands never left her skin and the kiss . . . the kiss never ended.

Her blood was fiery liqueur.

He slipped his hands into her dress along her back, and when he touched her skin he half groaned, half sighed her name, and her breath caught. His trembling fingers slid along either side of her spine, fanned open over her waist, sliding beneath the silk of her loosened bodice until his knuckles brushed beneath the velvety undersides of her breasts. And there he lingered, teasing, teasing, allowing her to guess just how much pleasure could be had from her own body. Quicksilver shivers of pleasure fanned everywhere through her. Until she was writhing, arching into his touch, and when she'd had enough teasing she arched up against his hands.

He swore softly, closed his hands over her breasts. He cupped the weight of them in his hands, lifted them, dragged his thumbs hard over her nipples.

"My God . . ."

She'd had no idea. Lightning strikes of pleasure coursed through her again and again.

He nipped at the base of her throat, while he clung to her.

"I want you," he whispered, sounding astonished, almost angry. "So. *Much.*"

With frantic, shaking hands she drew his shirt from his trousers and slid her palms beneath it. Slipped her hands over his hot skin, dragged them down over where his cock strained against his trousers, found his buttons. Hungry for the feel of his skin against hers. Caught up in a maelstrom of her own making.

He could take her here, and they both knew it.

He covered her hand with his, stopped her, gently but firmly.

"Phoebe," he murmured. He rested his forehead against hers. Their breath gusted audibly, mingled.

He slipped his hands from her dress and tucked a hair behind her ear.

"Phoebe . . ." he began. And then he spoke quickly, his voice low, taut, urgent. "I can give you everything you could ever desire. Gowns and pelisses and boots and bonnets. A beautiful, elegant home, a featherbed, a carriage. The finest food. Servants to do your bidding. Opera singers to sing just for you. I can make you safe and warm. And I can give you untold pleasure. Imagine the *untold* pleasure. Night after night of it. This is . . . scarcely a hint. I know so much. So much."

What was he saying?

Her heart leaped in hosanna.

His mouth moved to her throat, and he whispered there. "So much. Can you imagine how it will be for us? Imagine it," he murmured into her ear. "Our bodies, bare entirely, my body moving inside you. The things I can show you, Phoebe. Do you want me?"

She couldn't speak. She was weak from the pictures he'd painted, from hope and astonishment.

"Do you *want* me?" he demanded on a hoarse whisper.

"I want you." She choked.

"I promise. You will see me often—whenever you please."

Wait.

She went rigid.

He went on. "Where do you want to live? Tell me, and I'll buy a house for you in London and see you whenever I can . . . a house wherever you want. And it will be yours, always, no matter what happens . . ."

She felt the plummet and the landing so physically the breath left her body. She nearly put her hand up to ward off the blow, as if the ground was rushing up to meet her.

And still he was kissing her throat, as if he hadn't yet realized he was kissing a statue and not a woman.

She couldn't believe how steady her voice was when she spoke. She heard it through a ringing in her ears.

"And where will your wife live?"

His hands stopped moving.

She pressed her hands against his hands, gently but firmly pushed them away from her body. And then she pulled out of his arms, backed up three steps.

"So what you propose is . . . a business arrangement."

"If you . . . if you wish to call it that." He actually sounded confused by her indignation.

"When *I* throw a humidor, Lord Dryden, I don't miss. And I have no need of diamonds."

"Phoebe . . . I have never been dishonest with you about my plans. I've upset you . . . please tell me why."

The bastard was confused.

"You don't know me at all." She said it slowly, astounded that she thought he had.

The cool air was a slap to her feverish body. She wrapped her arms around her torso. They were a poor substitute for his. Already she felt bereft. She shook her head roughly.

"At least . . . take my coat . . ."

"As a souvenir?"

She sounded so bright, so brittle. Like the hard jagged edge of a broken porcelain cup.

Possibly a porcelain cup hurled at the marquess's head.

He flinched.

Good.

The two of them were patently ridiculous now, with their clothing in disarray, his trousers open, her dress unlaced, the aftermath of an absurd fever. What had she expected, anyway? The past several days had been comprised of one magical moment layered upon another. She'd gotten spoiled and complacent. For a moment in time she'd expected his narrative to end the way Cinderella's story had, and not the way a Greek myth would. With the poor molested nymph turning herself into an olive tree or some such to free herself from one of the god's clutches.

She couldn't do that. But she could go to Africa.

She pulled the top of her dress up to cover her breasts, pushed her sleeves up over her shoulders.

"Good night," she said firmly.

His hands, hovering where he'd last touched her, as if she'd indeed been a mirage, finally dropped to his sides. And from where she stood, she could see his face go closed and hard and inscrutable.

She'd hurt him. In all likelihood, more specifically, she'd hurt his pride. It was a survivable wound, of that she was certain.

And a self-inflicted wound, Lord Dryden.

"Very well," he said softly.

If he'd said nearly *anything* at all more she might have stayed. She might have been persuaded. If he had tried. But it was so clear that there were only two options for him. She fit into one box and Lisbeth another.

She gave a short sardonic laugh and shook her head, slowly, to and fro, like a teacher disappointed in a pupil. Even as the shards of her heart clogged her throat.

And then she turned, skirts whipping across her ankles, and fled across the cobblestones, hearing her own footsteps echo over them.

Chapter 18

Phoebe, awakened by a maid poking up the fire, tossed her a quick smile over her shoulder.

And then she sank back down onto her pillow. Argh. A mistake. Her head felt like a throbbing boulder.

She was amazed, given how her dream had ended, to find herself still in a featherbed in the Redmond house. She ought to be barefoot, dressed in rags and staring in bemusement at a pumpkin and four mice.

"You've a message, Miss Vale."

Hope, the traitor, catapulted her out of bed, and she nearly skidded to the tray upon which the message rested.

And then balanced herself, because she came very near to casting her accounts as her stomach spent some time sloshing to a halt.

She didn't recognize the seal.

She slid her finger beneath it.

And she read it once. And then again. And then looked at her reflection, puzzled.

For it seemed the fairy tale had acquired a second act.

We would be delighted if you would join us in London, Miss Vale. We've festivities planned—two balls and a party. Don't worry about the proper dresses!

We've lots! Do say you'll come for at least a fortnight.
You may bring your cat.

With great affection,
Marie and Antoinette

With great *affection*? They were an exuberant pair,
those two wicked pixies.

She stared at it. But this . . . this was a fairy tale she'd
never before read, and she had no idea what she ought
to do. There was no precedent.

At the moment she was alone at the breakfast table
but for Lisbeth. The service was informal, tureens of
food plunked on the table rather than on the sideboard in acknowledgment that most of the guests had
departed the night before: eggs, kippers, fried bread,
marmalade, coffee.

"Is aught amiss, Phoebe? Your face is so funny."
Lisbeth lowered her voice to a near-whisper. "Should
I avoid the kippers? Do you need the chamber pot?"

Phoebe looked at Lisbeth. Lucky Lisbeth. Whose
own face would under no circumstances ever be construed as *funny*.

"It seems I've been invited to London to stay with the
Silverton sisters. And to attend . . . parties and balls."

A silence.

Lisbeth went very still. "But . . . I'll be staying with
the Silverton sisters in London. Papa and Mama gave
me their permission to stay with them for at least a
fortnight, as Mama will be visiting my cousin in Dev-
onshire. Papa will be in London. They invited *me*."

"Well, then." Phoebe offered a noncommittal smile.
"They invited the both of us."

Another silence. And then Lisbeth tried for a smile,

and failed. It was more of a grimace. She fingered her teaspoon with feigned casualness. "And you've been invited to attend the same parties and balls . . . I'll be attending?"

Another uninflected sentence, pitched a bit higher than usual.

"I'm uncertain. Do you normally attend the same parties and balls as the Silverton sisters?"

"Yes," Lisbeth said carefully.

"Well, then," Phoebe said again. And smiled another neutral smile. And in a morning where she thought everything would be covered in a fine gray haze of heartbreak, she found herself perversely enjoying Lisbeth's discomfort.

Lisbeth placed her spoon down very gently, lining it up precisely in its place. As though she wished she could do the same with Phoebe. Line her up where she *belonged*.

"They're a bit . . . fast, you know. The Silverton sisters."

Oh, I *know*, Phoebe thought with a sudden surge of reckless delight.

She didn't respond.

Another little silence.

"And when you go to these balls you will go to . . . dance?"

To hold your reticule. "Presumably."

Lisbeth stared at her. And though no furrows appeared on her snowy brow, her abstracted eyes made it clear that she was struggling, as Viscount Waterburn had done just the night before, with translating *her* experience of Phoebe—the companion, the schoolteacher, the person she ordered about and upon whom she bestowed occasional largesse—into the sort of person who received coveted invitations. Their worlds were *parallel.* They could not intersect. It was quite simply a natural law, as far as Lisbeth was concerned.

I shall be a schoolteacher in my thoughts until the day I die, Phoebe thought.

"I should love to see you in London," Lisbeth claimed, finally. "It will be such fun! But will you have the proper clothes?"

She flicked Phoebe over with a look that seemed to take in every worn fiber of her dress, the faintly yellowing lace at the collar, even the minute fray at the hem. It was a second's worth of breathtakingly scathing pity.

Entirely supplanted by an expression of sympathy a second later.

Oh, *well* done, Lisbeth, she felt like saying. It was a look that Phoebe suspected had always been in Lisbeth's arsenal but had never before been deployed, at least in her direction. It was effective. All the Redmonds seemed to possess the innate ability to terrify and judge with the twitch of an eyebrow or a flinty second's worth of inspection from their perfect eyes.

Phoebe's own character was forged in a particularly effective furnace, however. She was shaken, not bowed.

"I'm told I oughtn't to worry about the proper clothes." Phoebe said this evenly.

"Everyone worries very much about proper clothes in London," Lisbeth said in all seriousness.

Jonathan staggered into the breakfast room, then flung himself noisily into a chair, lowered his chin into his palm, reached for the silver coffeepot with his other hand, closed his eyes again, aimed for his teacup, and poured.

And poured.

And poured and poured and poured.

The coffee waterfalled gently over the rim of the cup,

into the saucer, onto the tablecloth. He'd dozed off.

"Jonathan!" Lisbeth squeaked.

His eyes snapped open, and he smoothly hoisted the pot and eyed his brimming saucer and the tablecloth in some surprise.

"Don't squeak, Lisbeth. It hurts." He placed the coffeepot gently, gently down again, rubbed at his eyes and yawned cavernously.

"Will you please pass the sugar, Miss Vale?" he said very politely, though his voice was shredded from tobacco and all the happy drinking and shouting he'd done over the dartboard at the Pig & Thistle the night before after the ball.

Phoebe pushed it over to him.

"My thanks," he said with great gravity. He tonged three lumps into his coffee.

The housekeeper appeared at the table and froze when she saw his sloshing saucer and the brown ring round it on the snowy tablecloth.

And then she lifted the saucer deftly and bore it away without spilling a drop.

A moment later she returned bearing a tray of kippers and hovered behind Jonathan.

Jonathan's eyes went wide when the scent wafted up to him; he visibly paled. He put a hand to his mouth like a swooning maiden.

"Would you care for some kippers, Master Jonathan?"

"You're a sadist, you are, Mrs. Blofeld," he declared darkly, through his hand. "Take them away at once."

She smiled and bore the tray away, having made her point about the tablecloth.

"Phoebe has been invited to London by the Silverton sisters, Jon," Lisbeth told him brightly.

"Capital!" he pronounced immediately.

"Isn't it?" he asked, mildly bewildered, when Lisbeth and Phoebe remained silent and it became clear that the silence contained layers and layers.

"I haven't decided whether I ought to go," Phoebe said.

"Of course you ought!" he rasped. "Balls and parties, excellent music and food and drink, dancing, escorted to and fro by the naughty Silverton sisters—I cannot imagine a finer way to *OW!*"

He jumped. The coffee slapped at the sides of his cup but none escaped.

And thusly Lisbeth made her position on Phoebe's presence in London clear with a boot toe to Jonathan's shin.

He frowned blackly at Lisbeth. His mouth opened. And then he closed it again, composed his face smoothly.

His eyes went speculative.

While she and Lisbeth pretended nothing of the sort had taken place.

There was no sound for a time but for the clink of a tiny silver spoon against the sides of his porcelain cup. He winced and went at his stirring with more precision, avoiding the porcelain. All the while he was watching the faces of the two girls.

Phoebe found herself herding her scrambled eggs around her plate, as though they were recalcitrant sheep. She wasn't hungry.

"Choosing just the right first bite, are you, Miss Vale?" he asked.

"I like to push them around a bit before I eat them. It intimidates them good and proper."

"Ah." He smiled benignly.

She eyed him warily. Handsome devil. A bit bleary-eyed and bristly this morning. Nevertheless, he would be breaking hearts in earnest this season and every season until he decided to become leg-shackled. He also never resisted a mischievous or beastly impulse. It was the job of siblings and cousins everywhere, after all.

Lisbeth sipped at her tea delicately. She settled it down with a clink into her saucer. She still looked altogether ruffled. Phoebe was reminded of her cat, who abhorred it when anything was moved from its usual position. She'd dropped her pillow on the floor once from her bed, and Charybdis had warily circled it as though a meteor had landed in her room.

Lisbeth disliked disruption in the pattern of her world.

Jonathan looked from Lisbeth's face to Phoebe's and back again, like a billiard player assessing a shot.

"Did our marquess leave this morning?" Jonathan asked idly.

Excellent shot.

The corner of his mouth tipped slowly, slowly up in a smile, that spread all over his face, because obviously he'd drawn some sort of accurate conclusion from the expression on their faces.

"Pity Violet isn't here," he sighed to no one in particular.

Presumably Violet would have congratulated him on identifying a . . . sensitivity. And exploiting it.

"I've missed her," Lisbeth declared. "Though she has made a brilliant match, and I'm quite, quite happy for her."

"Oh, what balderdash, Lisbeth," Jonathan yawned. "Violet wreaked havoc upon your nerves, and you know it. Admit you're relieved she's not here. *You* are *much* too well-behaved." Jonathan made this sound like a cardinal sin.

For some reason Phoebe felt as though the reference to *behavior* was addressed to her. Something about the emphasis on the word *you*. Then again, everything was funneling into her ears through layers of guilt and disappointment at the moment.

"I can misbehave!" Lisbeth protested, sounding nine years old.

Jonathan snorted. "Don't be ridiculous. You don't know how. Al*though . . .*" he took a long, long sip of coffee ". . . you *might* make a brilliant match yet! Just like Violet's." He gave an exaggerated wink. "There's still time. You *might*. One never knows." He managed to inject a little doubt into his tone.

"Of course I will make a brilliant match!" Lisbeth was pink in the cheeks. "Why shouldn't I? *Everyone* thinks I will marry the mar. . . . There's no 'might' about it! How can you say that?"

A nerve, a terribly raw one, had apparently been struck.

Jonathan regarded her sadly. And then sighed, and carefully set the coffee cup down in the saucer, and leaned forward and took her hand between his.

"Here is the thing, dear Lisbie," he said, with great gravity. Lisbeth hated being called "Lisbie." "You are much, much too easy to tease. It's wearisome. And yet I feel I must keep at it, for your own sake."

And then he dropped her hand and leaned back again.

Phoebe laughed, and rapidly turned the laugh into a cough.

Jonathan turned to her, eyebrows upraised. "Which

balls will you be attending with the Silverton sisters—and Lisbeth—Phoebe?"

"I don't know. And I haven't decided whether I'm going."

"Of course you must go," both he and Lisbeth said at once. One slightly less sincerely than the other.

"I will dance at least one time with you if you go," Jonathan promised.

"In *that* case," Phoebe said. "If you warn me ahead of time, I shall know when to run."

Jonathan looked at Lisbeth and made a "See how it's done?" gesture with his hands in Phoebe's direction.

Lisbeth stuck out her tongue at Jonathan, which seemed to please him.

"Really, Lisbeth," Fanchette Redmond, who had chosen that moment to enter the room, reproved. "What would your mother say?"

Lisbeth went scarlet.

Poor Lisbeth. Phoebe did feel a surge of pity. No wonder her personality seemed comprised of a series of attractive postures. Censure was around every corner. Acceptable behavior had been proscribed for her, and she was a hostage of sorts to her own beauty.

Phoebe tried to make herself as unobtrusive as possible by going still and sipping at coffee, like a wild creature freezing before a predator. She suspected Mrs. Redmond barely approved of her presence at the table. It wasn't a personal issue; Mrs. Redmond understood the world as orderly and stratified and she liked to know everyone's place. Occasionally order wriggled out of her velvet grip, such as when her son Miles had married Cynthia Brightly. Or when her eldest up and disappeared.

Nevertheless, she never ceased trying.

She was wearing a topaz-colored riding habit and pulling on gloves. Still such a pretty woman, so soft-looking for her age, so flawlessly turned out. Her clothes made Phoebe's heart ache with a fleeting yearning and they were as intimidating as armor.

One new bonnet had opened up a floodgate of love for beautiful clothes she'd long learned to suppress at the school on the hill.

I can buy you anything you want.

That could very well be true. Of course, she'd never be received in the same homes that received Fanchette Redmond.

It occurred to Phoebe then that she wasn't too terribly removed in philosophy from Mrs. Redmond. She understood now the value of . . . a *place*. She wanted to know where she was welcome and where she was not.

Argh. She hated *wanting*. Especially when what she wanted was as obtainable as the moon.

She looked down again at the girlish, breathless invitation with a certain wonder. There was no harm in fleeting pleasure, she told herself. And there was pleasure to be had in being wanted—for her *company*, and not as a . . . business arrangement.

And though she could now buy passage to Africa, she *could* also afford to give herself a reckless, glittering, send-off. But she might very well see the marquess in London.

Correction: She *hoped* she would see the marquess there.

Because he wanted her, and he couldn't have her, and she wasn't so magnanimous or large spirited as to hope he didn't suffer over the sight of her.

Besides, it was beginning to look more than likely that someone else would want her, too. When no one ever, in truth, really had. Hope was that other thing she'd traditionally shied from, and yet here it was, just a little seed of it, poised to sprout with a little encouragement.

Jonathan noticed the dawning smile before she even knew she was smiling. "And will you be going to London, Miss Vale?"

"I'll be going to London," she announced. "Will you please pass the coffee?"

"A good many more opportunities for governesses and the like in London," Fanchette pronounced dispassionately.

Phoebe looked up at her, and she was aware that she and Lisbeth were wearing nearly identical expressions. Lisbeth's contained a hint of vindication.

"'And the like,'" Jonathan repeated, amused, as his mother left the room.

She thought he'd winked, but then again, the aggressively polished silver might be making him squint.

Chapter 19

The very next day, the Silverton sisters actually *sent a carriage* for Phoebe at Miss Marietta Endicott's academy. That was how eager they were for her company.

It was a landau. Not quite as grand as the *marquess's* landau, at least judging from the outside, of course, but still so large and plush inside she nearly bounced to the ceiling with every rut in the road. And there were more than a few between Sussex and London. She'd packed Charybdis into a large comfortable cushioned basket with a lid. He registered his objection to this with a steady nerve-grating keening.

Every now and then a striped paw shot out of the top of it and waved around. She'd give it a pat and he'd tuck it back in.

"You'll like London," she promised him. "You used to live there."

She was trying to reassure herself.

She'd packed a single trunk with all of her clothes, including two walking dresses, her only two dresses appropriate for balls and parties, the green one and the soft gray one, which looked very well with her eyes, and one spectacularly fine bonnet nestled in its own box with its original wads of paper, as if it were an egg or a loaded pistol.

Lisbeth hadn't invited her to ride along in the Redmond carriage, as, she explained, there was no room, given that Jonathan and Argosy were coming along, too, and they hadn't planned on another party from Sussex.

"But I shall be delighted to see you there! What fun we all shall have!"

Jules strolled into White's more out of habit than desire, because he needed something familiar to orient himself in the ton again after the fever dream of the previous few days.

It was the day after the first time he hadn't gotten precisely what he wanted, and that was Phoebe Vale in his bed.

The world looked different and he couldn't say exactly why. Everything was as it ever was. It was evening, a Tuesday, and the club was thick with smoke and conversation. Drinkers drank, gentlemen took refuge from wives behind newspapers; footmen moved among the crowd with trays. As usual, Colonel Kefauver, long retired from the East India Company and veteran of any number of battles, most of them foreign, slept in his usual high-backed chair, legs splayed, snores fluttering up his cobweb-fine gray hair at soothing intervals.

Jules handed his hat and coat and walking stick to the footman. And even before he was seen, a restless rustle began, a disturbance in the atmosphere, like an approaching storm, a sense that something exciting might be about to happen, that caused postures to straighten and heads to turn and fingers to drum.

The two young men sitting in the bay window immediately stood and went in search of other chairs.

Jules stared after them. They were both sporting forelocks.

He frowned briefly and gave his head a little shake. He sensed everyone harking in his direction. And this was usual, too. He began to feel a semblance of peace settle in, if not contentment. It amused and gratified him, and it was a solid place from which to launch his future.

"Brandy," he told the footman, not necessarily because he wanted something to drink but because he wanted something to hold.

And he settled in at the bay window, because of course that was by far the best table and when he was present, it was his by default.

Which was when he saw Waterburn's great wall of a back standing alongside d'Andre, and three or four other men, all of whom were huddled over the betting books and negotiating something with great earnestness.

"Two hundred pounds says we'll do it within two *days*—"

"Two hundred? Are you mad, Waterburn? No, no, no. It needs to be *interesting*, and more . . . specific. And we need a defined period of time."

This apparently caused a moment of silent mad pondering.

"I have it! We shall do it in . . . tiers! I'll wager *you* . . . two hundred pounds for the first appearance of a nickname for her, but it has to be within two weeks . . . if one appears, you win."

"Excellent! I'll take that wager." Waterburn scribbled something. "I'll wager *you* five hundred for word of hothouse flowers being sent to her."

"Mmm. I don't know, old man. Difficult to prove."

"Nonsense. We'll just ask the girls to verify it. And they have to be from someone with a title. And obviously not one of us."

"I like it. And . . . let's say . . . one *thousand* pounds for a duel challenge. Upon which we shall call it ended and tell the whole ton what we've done so no one need actually be shot."

Waterburn snorted.

"Very well. I win if it happens by the end of the month, in two weeks time. You win if it doesn't."

"Done and done. And when you lose, I shall buy you supper, old man."

They giggled like schoolboys and clinched whatever the bet was with a single firmly pumped handshake. A few other young men clustered about to see what the fuss was about.

Jules watched them idly. He avoided the betting books as though they were spreaders of disease. He wasn't a whimsical or theoretical wagerer. He liked games of skill or a good horse race or pugilistic match. He wagered occasionally, spectacularly, and invariably won.

He refused to be his father's son.

Across the room, a newspaper lowered to assess the giggling, and Isaiah Redmond appeared. He saw Jules and nodded.

He nodded, and with the toe of his boot, nudged a chair away from the table in invitation. Redmond smiled and folded his newspaper in neat thirds, and rose to join him.

Waterburn and d'Andre turned around, saw him. He stared at them.

They bowed.

When they were upright again, he noted to his amazement that they were both sporting forelocks.

"DAMNED Cossack! I'll show you whassawhassa . . ."

Everyone gave a little jump.

Old Colonel Kefauver was given to bellowing in his sleep.

A new member of the club had spilled his drink. "You won't do that after the first few times," someone reassured him, as a footman hurried over with rags.

Colonel Kefauver snorted and muttered and was soon asleep again.

Redmond took the seat across from Jules.

"I must thank you again for your hospitality, Redmond."

"On the contrary, it was an honor to host you, Dryden. I want you to know that I've spoken to my solicitor. It was the first order of business when I returned to London."

"Excellent. I thank you."

"I think the transfer of the estate can be arranged. But I should like to discuss an additional investment."

Jules gave a half smile. "I would expect nothing less."

Redmond nodded, smiling. "The Mercury Club is involved in railroads, as you know. And they're our future. Your involvement with us would be more than welcome.

Jules nodded noncommittally. "I should of course like to hear more about it. If you would send over some information with your man of affairs I'll happily review it straightaway."

Isaiah nodded. "Of course. Shall we meet here again in a few days time, then, to discuss it?"

"I should like nothing better." Jules smiled.

Isaiah lifted a glass to him. "My brother's fondest wish is to see his daughter make a splendid match."

"Lisbeth is a charming girl," Jules offered with gravity. "I'm quite honored to be taking her riding in The Row this afternoon."

"She's a prize." Redmond sounded like he was agreeing, but Jules suspected it was more of a correction.

And really, as far as the two of them were concerned, quite literally the truth.

London looked and smelled much the same as it had when Phoebe had last seen it, when she was just a girl. She sniffed out the carriage window, gulping in air like a curious hound: the coal smoke and sea, the stench of rotting food, the scent of something fresh borne in by a breeze off the ocean. She liked it.

The Silvertons owned a town house on St. James Square. Phoebe was greeted like a long-lost relative, pulled into an extravagant cheek-kissing embrace by each of the fragrant and surprisingly strong little Silverton sisters. Two footmen bore her trunk upstairs, to where the *family* slept.

Not the servants.

Just to be certain, she watched them all the way up to see if they made any wayward turns.

Lady Marie reached for the lid of her basket and lifted up a corner before Phoebe could stop her. "Oh, and look you brought your precious little puss—*oh!*"

She reared back when Charybdis's arm whipped out of the basket and took a swipe at her.

He pulled the paw back into the basket, having made his point.

"Behave yourself, Charybdis," Phoebe admonished insincerely, as the odds of this were unlikely. "He likes precious few people," she said by way of apology. "He's very discriminating," she added, strategically. Suspecting this would appeal to the twins.

Her suspicions were confirmed instantly. "We shall win him over, I just know it," Antoinette avowed. "We'll just have to keep him apart from Franz."

"Our mama's Pekingese," Marie clarified.

Oh . . . dear.

"I imagine we ought to keep him away from Captain Nelson, too," Antoinette mused to her sister.

"Our mama's parrot," Marie clarified.

Neither one of them seemed to be envisioning the sort of carnage Phoebe immediately did.

"I shall keep him closed up in my room."

She issued a silent apology to the cat. One of them was going to have more fun on this particular holiday than the other. And it wasn't Charybdis.

"And you can take him out into the little yard once or twice a day for . . . you know." Marie wrinkled her nose. "It should be just fine for a few days. We won't tell Mama." She leaned toward the basket again and lifted the corner, crooning. "And we will feed him kippers, won't we, little Charyb—"

The paw whipped out again and took another swing. Marie and Antoinette leaped back shrieking and giggling.

"He'll take off a limb," Phoebe warned them.

"He won't!"

"Of course not. He's actually very sweet." *Sometimes. Well, to me, anyway.*

"Well, you and your little pussycat will want to get the dust off and settle into your room, for *we've the Kilmartin ball to attend tonight!*"

They bounced on their toes and looked so delighted that Phoebe laughed. These were girls who attended balls, from the sound of things, nearly every night, and still the prospect thrilled them.

"I've only the two dresses," she reminded them.

They seemed just as charmed and mystified by this as before. They exchanged looks and repeated, *"Only the two!"* with a sort of secret delight.

"Well, wear the one we haven't yet seen, and we'll kit you out in our own dresses if you need more for the other things we've planned." She winked. Visions of phaeton races and gambling flashed before Phoebe's eyes. "We've *lots* of dresses."

They nodded vigorously, simultaneously. Curls swayed hypnotically.

Well, and why shouldn't friendships be forged just like this? Phoebe wondered, caught up in the giddiness of it all. Why shouldn't she just be thrown into the deep end of the social swim, swept up in the current of it, dashing off to one entertainment after another, never slowing to mull or exchange meaningful *life secrets* and the like? It was only a few days out of her life. And it would be *just* the thing to help her forget the mar . . .

Oh.

Down the stairs, tripping lightly, came the startlingly lovely vision of Lisbeth Redmond, wearing a blue wool riding habit and the jauntiest, most graceful hat in creation, over which a peacock plume arched. She looked very sophisticated and expensive, and Phoebe immediately felt every inch the provincial. She stopped herself, deliberately, from swiping a restless hand over her face. She was certain it was shiny from her long journey, and that her hair was disheveled.

Lisbeth paused three steps from the bottom of the staircase. As though the foyer was suddenly a moat awash with alligators.

"Phoebe! You've arrived! How splendid!"

There was a peculiar delay between her words and

her smile, as though the two were unrelated. And she didn't fly from the stairs and sweep her into an exuberant, theatrical embrace this time, either. She ventured down the final stairs and it could be said that she almost approached Phoebe . . . *gingerly*. Phoebe was again reminded of Charybdis, who suffered turmoil when any of his familiar things were moved even a foot away from where he expected to find them. Days went by before he forgave her for moving her bed away from one wall and against another in her room at Miss Endicott's academy.

She half expected Lisbeth to sniff her warily.

"Good day, Lisbeth! It's wonderful to see you. I'm very happy to be here."

Ladies Marie and Antoinette beamed their approval.

"So lovely to have you with us this time, Phoebe!" Lisbeth lied. "I wish I could linger for a time, but I've been invited to go riding." She swept an illustrative hand over her elegant riding costume. "In The Row."

Phoebe knew what The Row was. Because of course little dramas and encounters, love affairs and snubs and all manner of excitement took place on horseback and in carriages all of the time there. The broadsheets gleefully reported them.

The twins leaned forward conspiratorially. "She's going riding with the Marquess *Dryden*. He'll be riding a black horse. With white stockings! Naturally."

Five minutes. Honestly. She'd scarcely been their guest officially for *five minutes*. The mere sound of his name opened the ground up under her feet.

The drop was sickening and sudden. The giddy atmosphere went gray and flat. How had she thought she'd be able to endure the notion of him and Lisbeth together? How had she thought she could forget all of it in a giddy social swim?

She arranged a pleasant smile upon her face, but it felt so wrong she was worried she'd bared her teeth like a mare, instead. She almost put a hand up to her face to adjust it.

"Do you ride, Miss Vale?"

She didn't know who'd asked. Her ears were still ringing.

"No," she said.

"We shall stay here with *you*, then!" Antoinette declared. "And we will not follow our Lisbeth and her beau, though the temptation is great, great indeed, to *spy*." She winked. "She is quite the thing, you know, thanks to the marquess. It makes everything ever so much more delightful, for everyone wants to be with *us*!"

Interestingly, Lisbeth seemed less delighted with this pronouncement. Her triumphant smile faltered into something uncertain, almost irritated. Phoebe suspected Lisbeth had become so enamored of her own glory that she was struggling with the notion that it might be the reflected variety.

But then she tossed her head and gave a cascading little laugh and a winsome shoulder shrug. This set of mannerisms, and the brittle, arrogant confidence she likely associated with sophistication, was new to her repertoire. "Everyone says he wants only the best!"

The Silverton sisters laughed, too, delighted and certain of their collective supremacy and beauty and wealth, tipsy with the pleasure of it.

Phoebe didn't think Lisbeth was entirely joking.

It was so unutterably strange to hear these people discuss Jules as though everything written about him in the broadsheets comprised the whole of his character.

Did *nobody* know him? Did nobody want to? Did he intend to marry himself to this creature? And spend the rest of his days with her?

Panic and sadness and loneliness—on his behalf—threatened to pull her under. She nudged it rudely away. *He'd* chosen this route. He had boxes for everyone and everything, and boxes made him happy and comfortable.

Lisbeth was clearly more comfortable in the presence of Phoebe's silence. "What's in the basket, Phoebe?" she said magnanimously. "Did you bring a picnic along with you, or perhaps little cakes?"

Lisbeth *loved* little cakes.

Lisbeth smiled beneficently, but flicked Phoebe with a look that she was sure counted the particles of dust clinging to her walking dress and the worn toes of her boots and the shine on her face.

Don't say it. Don't say it. Don't say it.

"Why don't you have a look?" Phoebe inveigled. Saying it.

She saw Marie and Antoinette's eyes flare wide.

Lisbeth reached out and lifted up the lid.

Charybdis threw a great furry arm out of the basket and took a wild swing, hissing like a cobra.

Lisbeth shrieked and leaped back and Phoebe shut the lid again.

Marie and Antoinette needed to hold each other up, so buckled with mirth were they. Peals and peals of laughter echoed through the marble foyer.

"Ferme la bouche! Ferme la bouche!" From its perch, Captain Nelson the Parrot shrieked its objection to all the noise.

Lisbeth was white in the face. Two tight little lines

bracketed her mouth. She held one hand in the other, as though comforting it, though Charybdis had entirely missed her. She stared at Phoebe with a look reminiscent of her Uncle Isiaah, and one her ancestors likely wore before ordering executions or assassinations. Apart, that was, from the little smile.

"It's a cat," Phoebe said mildly.

Thusly a swiping paw was equivalent to a drawn sword. The subtlest of duels had just been called.

The butler appeared in the foyer, and every girl swiveled toward him expectantly.

"The Marquess Dryden is here."

Chapter 20

Jules knew the route to The Row from St. James Square well; he knew it, in fact like the back of his hand. He was surprised, however, to find that they'd arrived and he hadn't recalled one moment of the journey.

"You've scarce said a word, Jules," Lisbeth teased. She sat her gray mare beautifully. She'd likely been hurled up into a saddle before she could walk.

"Haven't I?"

This surprised him, as his thoughts had been so noisy. Perhaps it was because he'd suffered a shock.

And he was usually entirely in command of such circumstances. He had instead remained silent, and taken in the pale Lisbeth, who was tense about the jaw but resplendent in a blue riding habit; the Silverton sisters, who were pink-cheeked and whose brown eyes held the residual glitter over some mischief or private joke . . .

. . . and Miss Vale.

Shiny, a bit disheveled, holding a hissing basket.

He'd spent a day acclimating himself to the idea of a life without her, of nursing his unlikely rejection, of pulling the components of his life around him like a snug blanket . . . and the bloody woman appeared in

London. And like a green lad he'd simply stood dumbly in the Silverton foyer, said nothing, and stared at the wrong woman for too long.

Until Lisbeth proprietarily touched his elbow and led him toward the door.

"Handsome riding habit." Compliments were a lifesaving reflex. "Blue suits you."

"Thank you."

He really ought to attempt more of a conversation. They were in The Row now, and the day was crisp and, for London, anyway, marvelously clear. He knew they were being watched by everyone in the vicinity who possessed eyes, and he peripherally recognized nearly everyone who rode by. He didn't really *see* them, however. And he greeted no one, though tentative smiles were offered. And fell away when he didn't respond. Wondering, nervously, what they might have done to offend the powerful marquess. And thusly he effortlessly and obliviously ruined the moods of a number of equestrians.

"Did Miss Vale accompany you to London?" He knew this wasn't the sort of conversation he should have. It was the only thing he was currently capable of saying, however.

Lisbeth seemed puzzled by the question. "Oh, no."

"Did she simply call upon the Silvertons for a visit?" he pressed. Perhaps a little too urgently.

A peculiar hesitation. "She was invited, if you can countenance it by the Silverton sisters. They sent for her."

What about *Africa*? He'd thought she'd be preparing to leave. People ought to be in his life or out of it, he thought self-righteously. Not lingering on the periphery like a mirage, slipping away when one reached out.

There was a *reason* he liked black and white as a combination of colors.

"Do you know why they sent for her?"

Lisbeth looked mildly amazed by the question.

He was unforgivably poor company presently, he knew. He was also aware that it hardly mattered, as Lisbeth likely didn't notice when he was good company or poor.

This suddenly made him feel bleak.

"Because they're easily bored," Lisbeth said intelligently enough. "You haven't yet complimented my new mare!"

"How remiss of me. Perhaps she left me speechless."

And Lisbeth laughed, having coaxed him back into the sort of conversations she enjoyed, about things, and about herself, and about the people they knew.

She talked a good deal as they rode around, and she graciously greeted with a nod members of the ton, including, naturally, Waterburn, who was out riding with a Lord Camber. His Aunt, Lady Windemere, trundled by in a barouche that he'd helped pay for. She blew him a kiss and winked. She was seldom entirely appropriate, his aunt.

The hour passed without his involvement, it seemed.

Back at the Silverton town house, he reined in his mount and loosely tethered it at the gate, and then lifted Lisbeth down from her horse.

He felt surprise, and a moment of real pleasure, when his hands spanned her narrow, taut waist. It had been some time since he'd thought of her as a woman, with all the delicious things this meant, and not as a beautiful prize.

Had he *ever* thought of her as a woman?

Perhaps he had no right to feel bleak, since he'd made

as much effort to know her as she'd made to *know* him. And yet she probably thought she did know him. As a series of adjectives employed by the broadsheets.

He resolved to do better. She deserved better.

So in the spirit of this, and because he was a man, and because she was a woman, he lingered ever so slightly to look in her eyes as he lowered her to the ground again, and was gratified by her blush.

She seemed so young.

She was only two years younger than Phoebe.

His hands lingered momentarily at her waist. She was closer to him than she'd ever before been.

And then she stiffened suddenly and recoiled.

He released her immediately. "Lisbeth . . . is aught amiss?" Was she the sort who shrunk at a man's touch? He was appalled to have offended her.

"No. No! That is. I apologize. I thought . . . I thought I smelled . . . smoke."

He frowned slightly. He sniffed the air. He smelled London, which was a cornucopia of scents and stenches, all of which reached his nose, swept along by sea breezes. "Of the coal variety or the burning building variety or of the cigar variety?"

"The latter."

The girl could certainly go for a long while without blinking, he'd noticed. She'd blue eyes, very dark blue.

"Ah." He smiled. "Your uncle and I smoked cheroots at White's. Likely it's what you smell. My apologies if it's so very overpowering—I would have worn a different coat, you know, but I was in such a hurry to see you." It was a sin, it really was, how he knew the right things to say. "I know it's a *singular* blend, but is it truly offensive?" he teased gently.

Her relief was instant. She was almost dramatically

reanimated, softened from the hard mask her face had become. She smiled, charmed.

"Of course! That's what it is. Were they Uncle Redmond's cheroots? He smokes a particular and expensive brand, or so Jonathan would have me believe."

"I'm certain he *does* smoke an expensive brand, but I shared my own with him. El Hedor, they're called. Imported from Spain by a pair of gentlemen who keep a tobacconist's shop in Bond Street." Recommended by a former mistress. He'd kept them in the humidor hurled at him by Signora Licari. "And I've no idea of the cost," he said disinterestedly. "They simply send them over to my town house once a month."

Of course he knew what they cost, he knew the cost of everything, but it contributed to his legend to say such things.

And it helped to remind Lisbeth how very, very wealthy he was, and that he wouldn't countenance even the whiff of a suggestion to the contrary.

"I shall think of you if I smell it again," she said.

Well.

He was taken aback. It seemed like such a nearly . . . romantic . . . thing to say, almost provocative. And yet somehow cryptic. And Lisbeth, in his experience, had always been more of a gracious *recipient* of attention. A basker in it. She accepted it as her due so prettily that one enjoyed giving it to her. But it might be the reason she'd never acquired any of the skills of a coquette, nor did she seem to come by them naturally as did Phoe— some women. Which might well be a merciful thing, as combined with her looks she might have nearly too much to bear. Rather like her cousin Violet, who'd been revered and feared by every blood in the ton until she'd married perhaps the only man he could imagine wed to

Violet Redmond, the unlikely Earl of Ardmay.

Then again, if she'd been more like Violet, Lisbeth might have been more . . . traitorous though . . .

. . . interesting.

He didn't allow it to show in his eyes. "Better you think of me than your uncle."

He'd struck the right note of flirtation. It wouldn't frighten her or tax her coquetry skills.

She smiled at him winsomely. Winsome smiles she did *brilliantly*. He was peculiarly relieved she didn't attempt more flirting.

A silence as her mare tossed its head. A groomsman appeared and led her away with a touch of his forelock, and neither the marquess or Lisbeth paid any note of him at all.

"Will I see you tonight at Lord and Lady Kilmartin's ball?" He should have asked this. But she did.

"Yes. I shall look forward to seeing how you stun the masses senseless with whatever dress you happen to be wearing."

She laughed at this. He was reminded guiltily that she wasn't without a sense of humor.

He felt guilty about asking the next question, too, and he took pains to ask it conversationally. Even as his heart pounded peculiarly. "And will your friends be attending?"

There was a moment's hesitation. She mounted the first step of the town house. He could almost sense the eyes peeping out between the almost-but-not-quite-entirely drawn windows of all the town houses. He expected to read something about it in the broadsheets tomorrow.

She mounted another step. Her peacock feather swayed in a breeze.

And then she cast a look over her shoulder through lowered eyelashes, angling her chin over her shoulder. A precisely aimed beam of her sapphire eyes.

"I expect many of my friends will be attending," she said. As lightly, disinterestedly as he'd asked the question.

He wasn't to know it, but she'd practiced that look in the mirror. A dancing partner had pronounced it "bewitching" and that was quite enough for Lisbeth to install it permanently in her quiver.

It was, in fact, such an excellent look that during the narrow second's worth of time she'd produced it and the time Lisbeth had mounted the next step, he'd stopped thinking about Phoebe Vale.

Who hadn't, not for one moment, stopped thinking about him.

Not entirely, anyway. He was ambient thought, the background against which all of her other thoughts played. Against which she heard all conversation. Experienced all sensation.

And her sinking misery had been replaced by something that by rights shouldn't really have cheered her. But there really was no disguising the wonderstruck look he'd worn when he'd seen her, and he hadn't said a word to anyone. *Not one word.* Until Lisbeth had steered him out of the house.

If nothing else, her pride was assuaged.

Assuaged pride would likely animate her enough to enjoy a ball. And she would see him, and she would dance with other men . . . and he might catch her eye, and accidentally fling Lisbeth across the room again . . .

She was cheering more by the moment.

Her room was *luxurious.* No governess had ever slept

in it, of that she was certain. The porcelain basin that held lavender-scented water was painted all over in tiny pink and red roses, and the carpets were a variety of shades of pink, from blush to crimson, patterned in more roses, nearly as plush as Charybdis's fur, and fringed. The curtains were heavy brocade and a sort of blush shade. It was an almost absurdly feminine room, but she loved it. She felt like the pearl in an oyster.

Lady Marie, who Phoebe had begun to think of as the Instigator, while Antoinette was the Enthusiastic Supporter, had brought up a blue ribbon to tie about Charybdis's neck and a kipper, his weakness. They were fascinated by the notion of winning over such a pretty, temperamental animal. After much coaxing and flattery and crooning of nonsensical things, he finally emerged from beneath the bed (which was of the fat, feathered variety, as lush as everything in the room) and consented to be stroked from his nose to his tail by both sisters, and even purred. They pronounced themselves enchanted. He ate the kipper, batted three times at the fringe on the carpet, and then sat down and hoisted one of his hind legs to lick between them, bored with all the women now that his needs had been met. So like a male.

Phoebe thought he'd take to the ribbon with as much enthusiasm as he would a noose. She was wrong. So far, anyhow. He looked very handsome and deceptively domestic, and was now lounging on her featherbed with the abandon of a pasha who'd come home after years crossing the desert.

The twins, faces uniformly shining with minx-like excitement, had finally backed out of the room and urged Phoebe to dress for the ball.

And she didn't know whether Lisbeth had returned

or not. Likely she had, for out her window, her view was of a brilliantly, uniformly orange sunset, and he would not have kept her out so long. The giddy enthusiasm of her reception and her queenly quarters was going a long way to both strengthen and weaken her. She was more resistant to blandishments and bribes than even Charybdis, though the girls would never know it, as she'd far more experience with saying the right thing and producing the right smiles and maintaining a guard. But she had to admit she felt herself sinking into their warm welcome and cheerful attention the way her bare feet sank gratefully, wonderingly, into the carpet. And it was very difficult not to do it.

She slipped into her dove gray dress, which was cut much like her green one, but was shinier and exposed more white throat and bosom. She thought with longing of the springing pin curls the Silverton sisters sported, and settled for brushing her hair until it gleamed. She pinned it up as she normally did, as she hadn't been offered the services of a Lady's maid.

In a fit of inspired whimsy, she plucked a white hothouse blossom from the vase in the corner and tucked it behind her ear. She pinned it in place.

She'd only the one pair of gloves. She pulled them on over her arms and inspected the result in the mirror.

The creamy kid of the gloves echoed the creaminess of her skin and the blossom; the gold trim round them colluded with her hair to make her . . . gleam.

It was absurd, but she very nearly took her own breath away, so surprised was she by her reflection. She imagined the expression in the marquess's eyes when he saw her . . . and hope was a shard in her chest. She breathed in deeply, breathed out, willing it away.

"You will stay here in this room," she told Charybdis. "Which means no molesting the parrot. No becoming acquainted with the Pekingese. I'm going to close the door now, but I shall return."

He yawned his indifference.

If the marquess attempted to claim a waltz . . . perhaps she'd do the very same thing.

Phoebe smiled and tossed her head and smiled with an entirely new bravado, and descended the stairs.

As it turned out, Lady Silverton, Marie and Antoinette's mother, was a vague, wispily pretty woman thoroughly bemused by her vivacious daughters. She showed no symptoms of being a concerned chaperone or an aggressive matchmaker, likely believing fate would take it in hand if she exposed her girls to enough titles, as it had with her. She greeted Phoebe with a vague furrow of her brow.

"You've met Miss Vale, Mama," Lady Marie lied wickedly.

"Have I?" She tipped her head and studied Phoebe, as if angling her brain in a different direction would aid her memory. She seemed puzzled by the flower.

"Of course," Antoinette added. "You told us you liked her very much, and told us you wouldn't mind having her to stay."

From behind her mother, Marie winked at Phoebe.

"It was very kind of you to invite me." Phoebe was astonished by how little goading into mischief she needed. "It was such a pleasure to meet you, Lady Silverton. I'm delighted to see you again."

"I say so many things," Lady Silverton allowed vaguely, pleasantly after a moment. "Welcome, my dear. Shall we? Your papa will meet us later."

Phoebe's confidence had flickered when she saw the other girls.

The beauty of their clothes found the chink in her armor, and she knew a fleeting, futile, fathomless yearning, the way she'd once looked at the bonnet in Postlethwaite's shop. Marie and Antoinette were hopelessly sophisticated in shades of rose silk, and Lisbeth was in evening primrose, magnificent with her hair and eyes. They were all wearing jewels, real ones from the looks of things, rubies on the twins and a sapphire on Lisbeth, and the three of them sported complicated hair, curled, twisted, sparkling. Lisbeth was wearing a coronet, her signature, as it approximated a halo.

"I would never have thought of wearing an orchid, Phoebe! You are a picture!"

This came from Lady Marie and the compliment seemed genuine, as did the twins' smiles and the sense of inclusiveness. Lisbeth, she suspected, smiled because it would have seemed wrong if she hadn't. But while Phoebe had half expected one of Lisbeth's pitying looks something speculative twitched across her face instead.

I must look well, indeed, Phoebe thought happily. *Well enough for me, anyhow.*

"My pink chamber inspired me," she told the girls somberly.

"My pink chamber inspired me . . ." Marie repeated slowly, wonderingly. Exchanging a rhapsodic look with her sister. They still found her enchantingly singular.

And off they went.

Chapter 21

In the carriage they all giggled at nothing at all, almost ceaselessly, as if the very air of the night was champagne and they took it in with every breath. Lady Silverton shushed them once.

"Surely you shouldn't laugh so very much." She sounded doubtful. "You'll burst your stays and ruin your dresses."

Which sent them into gales of giggles.

The Kilmartin ball promised to be a crush. Carriages had long since clogged the square so that no new arrivals could even get near, and now a river of silk-and-satin-clad humanity moved toward the town house, forced to disembark and walk gingerly the rest of the way. Footmen nodded at them as they passed (finally) into the house, and Lady Marie gripped Phoebe's elbow with breathless anticipatory glee, as if this were her very first ball and not just another of dozens she'd attended. No one glared at Phoebe as though she were an interloper, an enemy breaching class lines. The smiles aimed at her were all pleasant, even slightly bored. These people all knew each other and saw each other again and again at parties and balls, and yet here they were again.

Imagine growing tired of this, she thought.

And then she was swept inside with the crowds, exactly as if she belonged.

They burst into the enormous ballroom in a scented, shining little cloud. The Silverton sisters were ton royalty, as it turned out, and out of the corners of her eyes Phoebe felt as though she was running a gauntlet of smiles and curtsies and outstretched hands and fans held up before mouths so others could comment on them as they went by.

They're likely talking about me, Phoebe thought with dazed amazement. *I am the new girl.*

Postlethwaite might receive the broadsheets and save them for her, and she could say, "Oh, you can keep them, my dear Postlethwaite. I was *there.* In fact, page four, paragraph three is all about me."

"We don't greet simply *everyone,*" Marie explained as Phoebe was drawn through the dizzyingly gleaming crowd, while Antoinette nodded in earnest agreement. "That would never do."

And now she saw how Lisbeth had become the glittering, brittle social creature, all mannerisms. Giddy was the only appropriate mood. Superficial was the only appropriate, or even possible, conversation. And if one was beautiful, one would never be encouraged to display a personality at all, beyond smiling.

The Silvertons drew her through the room, pollinating various little clusters of people with their popularity, extracting the nectar of gossip and attention, and moving on again.

The flower behind Phoebe's ear was pronounced very original, indeed. Over and over. Until it became clear the word *original* was becoming nearly synonymous with her.

Eventually they encountered Lord Waterburn and Sir d'Andre, who were already flushed with heat, or drink, or both. They greeted the girls like prodigals.

"You must," Sir d'Andre said, "I pray thee, bestow one of your waltzes upon me, Miss Vale. It's all I dream of."

Phoebe tapped her chin thoughtfully. "Well, what do you think, ladies? Should I?"

"I *beg* of you, Miss Vale." He dropped to one knee, and seized her hand, in a pantomime of yearning.

Oh, for heaven's sake.

"And me, Miss Vale. I am so overcome by your unique loveliness. I yearn to look upon it again for the duration of a waltz. And to compliment your ribbon."

They were so *silly* it was difficult not to laugh. What a different man Waterburn had turned out to be from the bored, cold, unpleasant aristocrat she'd originally met. Clearly she'd leaped to conclusions about him the way she'd leaped to conclusions about the marquess.

She batted the thought of the marquess away as if it were a wasp on her periphery and returned her attention to the clowning of d'Andre and Waterburn. She was aware that everyone around them in the perimeter was watching with varying degrees of amusement.

"She says 'bloody,' too," Waterburn confided to d'Andre, on an exaggerated hush. "It's never sounded better, that word, than when it spills from her lips."

The two of them dropped to their knees, hands clasped before them in entreaty, to the great delight of the Silverton sisters and to the stiff-smiled suffering of Lisbeth. Phoebe made a great show of consulting somberly with the Silvertons, who pretended to weigh the benefits of waltzing with the two men.

"Now, d'Andre has the finer curls," Lady Marie reflected.

"But Waterburn, he's so large one scarcely needs to move at all. He does the waltzing for you," Lady Antoinette offered.

In the end, Phoebe capitulated, and graciously gave each of them one of the four waltzes. And they launched into paroxysms of gratitude and rose to their feet again, and departed.

And when they moved away, another crowd of men were hovering on the periphery and swelled forth, begging for introductions to Phoebe and for dances from all of them.

"You see? It's all such great fun," Marie said to her.

Phoebe couldn't disagree, though she felt a little winded from all the theatrics.

Ratafia was found for them by the handsome gentlemen and pushed into their hands. And then a gentleman who needed to one-up the others produced champagne, and Phoebe took a sip. Which led to three more sips.

She didn't mind in the least that she wasn't the Queen Bee. That role belonged unquestionably to Lisbeth this season, who could have auctioned off her dances and paid the national debt. Because within what seemed like minutes of their arrival, Phoebe's dance card was entirely full.

She gazed down at it, ran her thumbs over the names of men who wanted to be with her, knowing she would keep it forever, no matter what turn her life took.

And for the first time, a bit of doubt crept in about whether she might want to go to Africa, after all.

When she looked up again, it was to discover that the Silverton twins and Lisbeth had been born away, or had drifted away, like petals on a river of bonhomie. And in Phoebe's line of vision, just like the bloody North Star, was Jules.

He was quite inappropriately staring at her.

It was no good. No good. Despair and joy tugged her between them. Because in his usual simple black and white, he should have blended into the crowd like shadow and light. Instead, he stood out in stark relief, and everything in the room suddenly seemed like a gaudy prop, all those young men like silly members of a musicale chorus, clowns. He was the only real thing in the room. He would always be the only real thing.

She was almost abashed. She turned her head quickly away, worried that even despite the noise and crowd someone would notice the sheer potency of the beam of the gaze they exchanged. She knew she oughtn't speak to him alone. Not only was she an unmarried woman, he was the Marquess Dryden, for God's sake, and his every move was scrutinized and reported to the broadsheets.

She tried to flee. Her body, however, was in complete disagreement with her mind when it came to the marquess.

Jules found himself moving toward her, as surely as he was being furled by a cord.

She looked to him . . . like the moon and the stars. She looked like no one else in the room, and there were hundreds of women in the room, so many of them beautiful by anyone's definition. What was *wrong* with him that he only wanted to look at one of them?

And then he stood before her. "I didn't expect to find you here," he said finally.

"At the ball or in London?"

"Both, naturally. Given that Africa was your destination. Given that we said *goodbye*."

"Well, I was invited, you see. By the Silverton sisters. It seems they were quite taken with me. I decided to seize the moment. And good heavens, they've introduced me to so many *fine young men*, all of whom demanded dances."

She presented this with ironic defiance. But she couldn't disguise her own shy pleasure. She was radiant with her own success.

"Have they?" He was ridiculously torn between feeling genuinely pleased for her and feeling positively impaled by jealousy.

"Yes."

"Fortunate young men, indeed."

"So they all would have me believe," she said wryly. "The compliments have thus far centered about this." She touched the flower in her hair. "They all seem to think it's very *original*. And I just pulled it out of a vase in my room!"

He was peculiarly speechless. So full of competing emotions no words could emerge. He took refuge in a mundane question.

"How long will you be in London, Miss Vale?"

"A fortnight, I should think. I was invited for that long, anyhow."

"Who is minding Charybdis while you're in London?"

"Oh, I am. I brought him along. Why the interview, Lord Dryden?"

He knew the Silvertons kept a parrot and a small dog that Lady Silverton carried about like a reticule, said a silent prayer, and ignored her question. They stood together for a beat of fraught silence.

"Have you noticed something, Lord Dryden? All of the . . . shall we say, forelocks?"

They were *everywhere*. Even on a few of the older men who possessed enough hair to adopt it.

"I'd noticed," he acknowledged grimly.

"I wonder if they were *all* struck in the head by beaver hats," she mused.

He shot her a baleful look.

"Perhaps the hairstyle has a name. The Illicit Kiss. Or The Bruise. The Dryden?" she drummed her chin.

"What I like best about you, Miss Vale, is how you remind me of all of my finest hours."

She tried not to smile, and failed. "I was there for them."

"Perhaps because you were the cause of them."

Another statement that contained many layers of meaning.

Suddenly a woman went spiraling like a top across the ballroom, her dress spinning about her, while her partner dropped to his knees. At the periphery of the room, someone gave her a little push, and she went spinning back.

"The Dryden Waltz." Phoebe was delighted beyond words.

He shook his head slowly to and fro.

"Tell me, my lord, what is it like to be so admired that people attempt to imitate you?"

"Admired? I suspect I'm just the slate upon which they can write their own interpretation. It doesn't matter what I do. Forgive me, Miss Vale. I have an objective, and I must ask before the music ends. I wonder if you would do me the honor of danc—"

"—oh, I must stop you, my lord. I'm afraid I cannot. You see, I've given *all* of my dances away."

That gave him pause. "Did you now?"

She was trying to be haughty and failing, because she was in fact in awe of her own success. And he was, in truth, the only person in the world to whom she could confide her wonder. Who would share it and understand it.

It was a peculiar predicament. And yet all irritation and rejection and want dropped away momentarily, and they were friends, and he was proud for her. At some point he'd ceased being the commander of his own emotions. She'd usurped them.

"It was the most astonishing thing," she confided shyly. "All the gentlemen seemed to want to dance with me in particular. Perhaps because I am new?"

"No. It's because you are beautiful and special."

This widened her eyes and flushed her dark rose. She turned her head away from him abruptly.

"You are not a word mincer."

"No. Nor am I ever dishonest. May I see your dance card?"

"Don't you believe me?" She presented it to him with a flourish.

He ran his fingers down the list of names.

"Hmm . . . Waterburn? Bastard. D'Andre. Definitely a worthless bastard. Lord Camber, a thoroughgoing bastard. Lord Michaelson? Bastard. Peter Cheswick? Bast—"

She snatched it from him, laughing.

"I wouldn't dance a waltz with you, anyway, Lord Dryden."

"No?"

"You might accidentally lock eyes with Lisbeth Redmond, stumble, and fling me across the room to avoid crushing my feet."

She stared a dare at him.

Because they both knew full well that Lisbeth Redmond would not have him stammering or stumbling. Or diving into hedgerows. Nor would he be undressing Lisbeth Redmond in a courtyard at the Redmond household in the middle of the night. He in all likelihood wouldn't even seek her gaze from across a crowded ballroom.

"Has anyone ever told you your complexion is very fine, Miss Vale?"

She laughed. Shook her head to and fro.

Another silence ensued. And then at last the gathered tension broke like a storm.

"It feels very wrong to stand here and not touch you." His voice was a low fervent rush.

"*Don't*." She closed her eyes, shook her head roughly. "Please don't. You don't *see*, do you? You've a reputation for preferring the singular, the special, the finest . . ."

"Because I do."

"Do you see the trouble? And here it was I thought you set the fashion, Lord Dryden. It seems that fashion has outsmarted *you*. You would set me up in a house in London and make love to me and visit me whenever you can. But you never, never would to have danced with me at this ball, because I never would have been invited. All I have ever wanted is to *belong* somewhere. And if I became your mistress you would take that away from me forever."

Weakness and heat washed over him when she said the words "make love." "It isn't true, Phoebe," he said, his voice hoarse. "And imagine what I would *give* you."

"It most certainly would have been true had I said yes to your 'business arrangement.' And yet now you think you'd like to dance with me because everyone else sees it as acceptable."

The logic—and the illogic—in this was unassailable. And yet suddenly he was coldly angry. "Enough. What would you have me do? I have never been dishonest with you. Not once. You knew what my plans are. You're right, Miss Vale, in that our lives have been very different. And in much the same way as I cannot imagine what it was like for you to endure St. Giles, it's clear you can't imagine what it's like to be part of an ancient family, how important it is to me. My life isn't entirely my own. I rebuilt my family name and fortune. Marriage can never be a *thing of whim* for a man like me. My family history. My legacy . . . the people who rely upon me . . . These are not small things, Miss Vale. They are . . . the very roots of my life. *They're my blood.* They are . . . *everything.*"

She'd gone stark white, but two hot pink spots high on her cheekbones betrayed her fury.

"A thing of whim . . ." she drawled.

"I'll thank you not to mock what you clearly don't understand." He was cold, cold. Lord Ice.

"You cannot fit everything neatly into boxes."

"Oh, is that so?" he gave a short, sardonic laugh. "I cannot tell you how much I appreciate my continued education at your hands, Miss Vale. But here is the thing you, in all your cleverness, fail to recognize. You believe I should compromise everything I am and everything I want because some things don't *fit neatly into boxes.* And yet you're so self-righteously bloody unwilling to do the same for me. Who here is the hypocrite?"

She blinked as if he'd flicked something hot into her face.

He sensed, quite rightly, that if she'd had something to throw, he'd be wise in ducking right about now.

"Do you know what I think?" he drawled it conversationally. "*I* think you're afraid. I think you'd rather run away from me, and how you feel, and what you want, to Africa. And why should I endure the company of a coward?"

She reared back as if he'd struck her.

"In all likelihood Isaiah Redmond is keeping a very close count of the number of waltzes you dance with Lisbeth and would take it badly if you should waste more time with the novelty of the hour, the schoolteacher," she said coldly. "And Lisbeth is in yellow. Like the sun itself. You won't want to miss that. She looks beautiful."

"She always does," he retorted.

Through the crowd an eager looking Lord Camber came, belatedly, to claim her for the dance. And Jules found himself staring at the man as if he could stop him with a mere gaze, as if he stared hard enough the man would never reach her, never. The ballroom would freeze all around them, everyone in it flat as tapestry except for him and Phoebe.

And then he would take Phoebe into his arms and persuade her in a dozen ways, with his arms, his lips, that what she wanted was *him*, no matter what, no matter how, forever. But he'd never before encountered a force of will quite like hers. It was inconceivable that he would not be getting precisely what he wanted, because he invariably did. His pride was a raw wound. He felt like a bear in a trap.

"Adieu, Lord Dryden."

She sounded as though she meant it.

She curtsied, and went smiling toward Lord Camber without a backward glance, as if she danced with titled men as a matter of course.

He watched her go. And though he was certain his pride was the wounded party, damned if he didn't feel as though he were tethered to her, and as if his very heart were being pulled from his chest as she went.

Chapter 22

And since there was at last a lull in the storm of compliments, she decided to visit the ratafia table.

And she wove among the crowd wearing her useful, unspecific smile. Everyone looked familiar now and everyone was a stranger, but none of it mattered when they were united in gaiety, or so went her tipsy thinking. She sipped at her third—fourth?—cup of the evening. As she took a step backward, she bumped into someone, nearly sloshing ratafia onto an oblivious gentleman standing before her.

She turned carefully around. "Good heavens, I'm so sor—"

It was Olivia Eversea.

Phoebe froze, staring.

"Miss Vale, isn't it?" Olivia looked genuinely pleased. "How lovely it is to see another face from Pennyroyal Green."

"Oh, I agree!" Phoebe enthused. She'd learned how to gush this evening and it was becoming perhaps a little too second nature, but there was safety in it at the moment. "I do hope you're having a lovely time, Miss Eversea."

Phoebe never did know how to talk to Olivia Ever-

sea. She was so lovely and pale and *unnerving*, Olivia
was, though never anything other than pleasant, her
manners exquisite. All the Everseas possessed exquisite manners, even, rumor had it, when they were doing
things like dangling from the balconies of married
countesses or being sent to the gallows. And when her
path crossed with Olivia, in town or in church, they
were gracious to each other.

But unlike her gentler sister Genevieve, Olivia was
somehow fearsome. She was delicately lovely but she
was passionate about so many things, so very dedi-
cated to causes, so clever and brittle.

And this was why Phoebe didn't believe Olivia was
enjoying herself. She reached up a hand to adjust her
flower behind her ear.

Olivia went motionless. All the color fled her face.
And she stared at Phoebe's arm as though it was a
snake.

"Miss Vale . . . Where did you get those gloves?"

Oh.

It was as shocking as a knife attack.

The backs of Phoebe's arms went cold, and a ringing
started up in her ears, as she was pinned, surely as an
insect to a board, by Olivia's brilliant gaze.

She was entirely sober in an instant.

And as lying didn't come naturally to her, she hesitated too long before answering. No matter what, she
was *certain* Olivia would know she was lying, anyway,
so there was no point in attempting otherwise.

How did she *know*?

"Where?" Olivia's voice was hoarse now. Insistent.
She looked ill. "Who gave them to you?"

The crowd eddied around them, laughing too loudly,
reaching for more ratafia, toasting each other, noticing

nothing amiss about two frozen women staring at each other like animals about to lunge.

What in God's name to say to her? What could possibly take away that raw hurt and fury and shock?

"He never loved me," Phoebe managed, her voice a raw whisper. "Please believe me. He gave the gloves to me just . . . it was just because . . ."

Just because he couldn't have you.

She would never really know. Lyon was a man, after all.

I kissed him because I was flattered and because I wanted to be kissed and because he was a Redmond. He kissed me because he could. *And because he couldn't have you.*

She'd heard the rumors about Olivia and Lyon; it wasn't until she saw Olivia's expression that it became real to her, and it was disorienting, like seeing a myth come to life. *She does love him.*

She wished for an instant she'd never allowed Lyon to kiss her that night after the dart tournament, behind the Pig & Thistle. One second later she knew she would never, never apologize for it, for if she hadn't kissed him she might never have known the difference between a mere kiss . . . and a kind that created a universe comprised of two people. The difference, in other words, between kissing Lyon and kissing the marquess. She might regret Olivia's pain, but she would never apologize for a stolen moment of pleasure.

The silence stretched untenably. But Phoebe knew it wouldn't have mattered what she said.

Olivia's fine jaw had turned to granite. She gave her head a toss. And drew in a long, long breath, breathed out in a huff. Phoebe had the strangest sensation that she'd just born witness to the birth of resolve.

"Forgive me, Miss Vale," she said with admirable composure. "I'm certain it isn't your fault. I hope you have a wonderful time here in London." She laid a hand gently on Phoebe's arm, and she slipped into the crowd again and was gone.

Phoebe stared after her, composure rattled. She looked down at her gloves, that whimsically given gift, and wondered how Olivia knew. It seemed not even being a Redmond or an Eversea protected one from the vicissitudes of love. She had that at least in common with Olivia.

The thought held her motionless, despairing.

"Oh, please allow me to fetch another ratafia for you, Miss Vale. Yours is nearly gone."

She blinked. A young man—there had been so many this evening, she could not quite conjure his name—was standing in front of her and beaming.

"I should like that very much," she said.

And she pushed away the notion that she and Olivia and Lyon and the marquess might never get what they wanted. The best way to forget that, and Jules, was ratafia and compliments and dancing.

Jules danced with Lisbeth three times. Enough to prime the pump of gossip, enough to give the broadsheets fodder, enough to satisfy himself that he'd paid an appropriate amount of attention to her. Enough to convince Isaiah Redmond, should he indeed be taking note, of his sincerity. Because everyone knew the marquess did nothing without a reason. The dances, the flowers, the rides in The Row, were all paving stones set down along a path that would lead to matrimony. It was a dance everyone understood.

Unlike the one where a young woman was flung

across the dance floor and her partner fell to his knees.

"What do you want, Lisbeth?"

She looked startled. "Want? Do you mean, like ratafia or a little cake or a new gown?"

"No. I mean from life."

She seemed to struggle with the question, as if she'd been given something too large to hold in one hand.

"I'm not certain what you mean," she confessed, apologetically.

"What makes you happy?"

"Do you think I'm *un*happy?" She was trying to please him, he could tell, and he was very close to upsetting her with theoretical questions.

He knew a moment of genuine fear, a swift stab of it. A vision of a lifetime with a beautiful stranger. One he could please with gifts and compliments. One who would make him proud and wealthier. But one who would never learn his . . . language.

"No, of course not."

She still looked puzzled. "Do *you* want something in particular from life?"

At least she knew enough to ask the question.

But what he wanted was something he never, never would be able to tell her.

He would lie in bed next to her for the rest of his life, and never be *known*.

"Yes," he said gently, resignedly. "There is something I want from life. And I hope very soon I shall be made even happier."

It wasn't *un*true.

And he made sure he stared into her eyes when he said it, and she blushed prettily. His meaning was unmistakable.

"Have you noticed, Jules . . . We've started a fashion."

"*We've* . . . done what?" This was startling.

As if in answer to her question, some poor girl's partner just sent her spiraling across the ballroom while he fell to one knee.

And someone planted on the periphery gave her a shove back in the opposite direction.

"You see? A new sort of waltz. It's considered very daring. Because everyone wants to be like us."

He stared down at her, utterly nonplussed. "Lisbeth . . . you're aware that it was an *accident*? That I threw you across the room to avoid crushing your foot? I made a *mistake*."

"Surely not." She sounded genuinely surprised and a little troubled. "You are just being too modest."

"I am nothing of the sort," he said truthfully. "And no one has *ever* accused me of modesty. I do have flaws."

"But even your accidents have style."

"Lisbeth . . ." He gave up. "I suppose . . . it's in the eye of the beholder."

He ought to know better by now, but when he said it he watched Phoebe go sailing by in the arms of another man. Who looked as though he'd just won a million pounds, judging from his expression. Her flower was wilting, her dress was a bit crushed in the back, but her face was aglow and she looked to be laughing. Envy was serrated, excruciating.

He turned his head away quickly. Back to Lisbeth. Who had not stopped watching him for an instant. She'd followed his gaze.

"*What* is in the eye of the beholder?" She asked it with an edge he failed to detect.

"Everything is," he muttered.

* * *

Jules slipped into the library, thinking perhaps he might find a crowd of gentlemen and a decent cigar and some stronger liquor, and of course he did. He might find conversation about horses and hunting and shooting, too, which would be soothing after the lashing his soul and heart had taken this evening.

He wove through the cheerfully glassy-eyed crowd, through a haze of smoke, and helped himself to the brandy decanter, knowing his host wouldn't mind. He nodded to Gideon Cole, a friend and fine barrister who rivaled the marquess for smolder in the eyes of the women of the ton, and whom was leaning with the congenial Lord Kilmartin, the host, against the hearth. A gray-haired gent was bending Mr. Cole's ear, likely seeking out free legal advice. From across the room, he toasted the marquess with his own glass of brandy.

Just as Lord Camber strode into the library, flinging his arms wide.

"She danced with me! I just danced with The Original! She gave me a waltz! How many of you can say that?"

A chorus of cheerful, envious congratulations went up.

"I swear I shall be the first to dance with her at the next ball," someone muttered.

The Original, Jules thought. *One ball and Phoebe already has a nickname.*

The ground seemed to shift beneath his feet. As though he stood on shore and was watching Phoebe going out with the tide, deeper into the social sea, away from him.

What if one of these men, less beholden to history, less shackled to land and family . . . were to seriously pursue her? What if she decided this was the kind of life she wanted after all?

He was known for his coolness and control. Suddenly he wanted to hurl the glass of brandy across the room and watch it shatter, watch everyone jump.

Just like one of his temperamental mistresses.

He must have been wearing a black expression, indeed, because poor Camber intercepted it and flinched and his smile evaporated instantly. He reached up and fussed nervously with his new forelock, wondering what he might have done to offend the marquess. Jules considered scowling, just to frighten the young man good and proper.

He turned away instead, with effort, because at heart he was a gentleman and a fair player.

Which was when he saw something curious:

Waterburn and d'Andre exchanged glances, Waterburn gesturing with his chin at Camber. Waterburn rubbed two fingers silently together, and d'Andre sighed, and rooted around in his pocket, came out with some bills, and counted them out to Waterburn.

It looked very like Waterburn had won a wager.

Chapter 23

"**P**hoebe, wake up! There are bouquets down below for you. Five of them! *Five!* Five!"

Phoebe struggled to open her eyes. It was strangely difficult; she was wound in a thick, black web of sleep.

She succeeded after what felt like considerable effort. *Well.* Now that she was awake, she immediately went very still, shocked and a little fascinated by the ghastly pain in her head. A drummer had taken up residence in her skull and was playing with relentless, steady skill.

She opened her mouth to attempt to speak. Fur had grown on her tongue overnight. She felt a certain woozy fatalism: very well then. She would need to re-learn how to speak.

"How many bouquets?" She could still manage sarcasm. Even if her voice sounded like a dry caw.

"FIVE!" Marie and Antoinette bellowed. Oblivious to sarcasm.

Phoebe winced.

Clearly the Silverton sisters were more accustomed to nights like the one they'd just had than she was. She patted a hand across the bed, encountered Charbydis, still sleepy, fat and soft, then found another pillow. *Ahhh . . .* Lovely, lovely, soft, cool pillow. She dragged it languidly over and slid it gently, gently over her face.

"What timezit?" she murmured from beneath it.

"Eleven o'clock in the morning, sleepyhead! Get up, get up, get *up*! You must see your bouquets and . . . and an invitation."

"Invitation?"

She sat up abruptly and gasped as her brain sloshed forward in her skull. *Gah*. She put her hands up to her head to hold it motionless. It was like a pendulum knocking about in there.

"The maid is bringing up coffee. A whole carafe. That will put you right," Lady Marie said, sounding like a schoolteacher. The Silverton Academy of Debauchery, Phoebe thought. "So we can do it again tonight! Don't worry. You'll get used to it in no time!"

A carafe of coffee did indeed put her right, but she wasn't equal to breakfast. She watched in revulsion as the twins ate happily and gossiped about who wore what.

Phoebe's bouquets were lined up on the sideboard downstairs. Lisbeth was studying them with an almost scientific fascination. As if she was witnessing an impossibility.

The twins interpreted the bouquets—all of which were of the hothouse variety, and all of which featured flowers like the one she'd worn in her hair—and their senders for her.

"This one is from Camber. Quite respectable if a bit ordinary. Heir to a viscount. Cheswick . . . a nonentity. A minor baron. Oh, Wapping . . . mmm, not bad. When did you meet him? Oh, I recall: the reel. Argosy . . . ah, *now* you've credibility for certain, as he only responds to who and what is considered the first stare of fashion, dear. You are officially a success!"

Imagine that. Phoebe basked, bemused, in the information.

"Oh, and this arrived, too. It looks like weeds someone plucked out of a field and we were tempted to toss upon the fire. But a message arrived with it. No signature, mind you."

Phoebe stared at the bundle. Something in her face must have silenced the room for nobody spoke for a surprised instant as she gingerly took the "weeds" in hand.

It was a bundle of sage wrapped in lavender ribbon. *Bloody man.*

She slowly lifted it to her nose and closed her eyes.

She pulled it away from her nose quickly, as her stomach did an unpleasant lurch. She was still unprepared for strong smells.

Her hands fumbled at the note and got it open.

You're wrong. I do know you.

She wanted to crush it and hurl it at him, because he was right. About her.

Instead she sniffed the message. It smelled like sage, too. She folded it tightly in her fist.

"Is it witchcraft?" Lady Marie breathed. "They look like witch's herbs."

"Oh, for heaven's sake, Marie." Her sister rolled her eyes.

"Well, look at that bundle of weeds!" Marie was indignant. "I'm quite serious. The Gypsy woman Leonora Heron who camps near Pennyroyal Green will cast a spell for a shilling or two, and they use herbs that look just like that. You can make a rival for a man's love disappear, for instance."

"Can you?" Lisbeth and Phoebe said in embarrassingly quick and equally fascinated unison.

The Silvertons were startled. And then their bright little pixie eyes went speculative.

"Er . . . so I'm told," Lady Marie said after a moment, and studied her fingernails.

"It's just a bundle of sage," Phoebe told them. "The sort you pack your dresses in to keep them fresh. Sent to me by a woman I met last night. I imagine she thought I would find it useful."

She laid the bundle gently down next to her plate. She ought to burn it in the fireplace in her room. She knew that sage was used to purify houses of evil spirits in some cultures. She wondered if she could use it to purify herself of useless longings.

As this topic of storing dresses in sage edged dangerously upon housekeeping, the Silverton twins changed it instantly.

"Don't forget, Lisbeth, there's a bouquet here for you, too! But only the one."

They took a bit too much relish in saying it. But they gestured to the most spectacular bundle by far.

They were hothouse flowers, a profusion of pink roses and white lilies, sophisticated, delicate, tasteful, preternaturally gorgeous. Phoebe knew in an instant who had sent them.

"What does the message say?"

"I look forward to seeing you today."

—*Dryden*

"Effusive," Lady Marie commented, and her sister nudged her, amused.

"We're riding in The Row this afternoon." Lisbeth's face and voice were abstracted. "Jules and I."

"They're wagering on you now at White's, Lisbeth," Lady Marie volunteered. "Waterburn told me."

"Are they? What do the wagers say?"

"That you'll be engaged before the month is out."

"To anyone in particular?" Lisbeth actually sounded ironic.

"Very witty, my dear," Lady Marie congratulated.

And then Lisbeth startled Phoebe by reaching over and picking up the bundle of sage. She gingerly turned it this way and that in her hand. As if she was trying to decipher it. Her brow was shadowed.

"Where does this plant usually grow?"

"All over England," Phoebe said, mostly truthfully.

Lisbeth studied Phoebe the way she'd studied the sage. "Are you going to keep it?"

"Yes," Phoebe said.

They locked eyes.

And then Lisbeth put the sage down as abruptly as she'd drop a poisonous toad.

As it turned out, Phoebe's invitation was to join Lord Camber, he of the sincere brown eyes and solid chin, as well as Waterburn, d'Andre and the Silverton sisters, for a ride in The Row. As she didn't ride, Phoebe would be treated to a trip in his high flyer. Lisbeth was generously included, but she demurred, as she was going riding later with the marquess.

Or *Jules*, as she referred to him at every opportunity.

"I think I'll prepare myself for this afternoon," Lisbeth said finally. And excused herself from the table.

Snatching up her bouquet of roses on her way out of the room.

An hour later the doorbell rang, and Phoebe was nearly bounding down the stairs with the Silverton twins to meet Waterburn and d'Andre. She was wearing her best day dress, which was a sort of faded shade of gold wool and rather practical and demure, but she liked to think it looked well with her hair. Her boots had been so polished by the Silvertons' staff that she could almost forget the soles were wearing thin.

"I've news, gentlemen," Lady Marie told Waterburn and d'Andre with a sort of hushed glee. "Miss Vale received not one hothouse bouquet this morning . . . but *five*."

"You *jest*!" Waterburn's mouth dropped open. He exchanged a look livid with delight with d'Andre. "*Never* say I have competition."

"I fear the whole of the ton is your competition, Lord Waterburn," Phoebe teased.

"We shall fight Camber for you. Or perhaps race him."

Phoebe then watched as the men appeared to exchange money. *Men*. Likely settling some sort of wager or loan, given that this was Waterburn.

In The Row, Phoebe was goggle-eyed at the pageantry, and she didn't try to disguise it. The day was crisp and clear and The Row was swarming with handsome people in handsome clothing perched on handsome horses or driving beautiful carriages, calling to each other, waving, and gossiping, in all likelihood, as they passed.

Camber's high flyer was an almost outlandish contraption compared to the curricle driven by Waterburn, but she liked outlandish. She found it beautiful and very fast, both literally and figuratively. It told her definitively how Lord Camber defined himself and the set of friends with which he ran, and she didn't object in the least, though she found the contrast between it and her first impression of him rather striking. She sat beside him, wearing her glorious new bonnet, and felt like a queen, towering over the other carriages, which were lower to the ground. Two shiny-haunched bays pulled it.

They weren't quite as striking as black geldings with white stockings, mind you.

Nevertheless.

"I've won several races in this," he confided. "And nearly five hundred pounds."

The amount made her head swim.

"Well done," she decided to say, when she'd collected herself.

She noticed the heads of other riders swiveling toward them as they rolled by. She nodded regally from atop her perch as Camber called greetings.

"And look, Miss Vale. Everyone envies me because I'm with you."

It was such an extraordinary notion she didn't even care that in all likelihood Camber was with her because he wished to be envied. All afternoon she drank in admiration and envy like wine, until she was almost intoxicated enough to forget to crane her head for a glimpse of a man on a black horse with white stockings.

Almost.

An hour or so after the twins and Phoebe and the young lordlings had departed for The Row, whilst Lady Charlotte was dreamily working on her embroidery in the Silverton town house, Lisbeth working beside her, Captain Nelson the Parrot began shrieking one word, over and over.

"Singe! Singe! Ferma le Bouche! Singe!"

Lisbeth looked up, startled. "Is the parrot shouting what I think he's shouting?"

"He's shouting something about a 'monkey.' He's

telling a monkey to shut its mouth. Daft old bird. He'll stop in a moment. Never fear." Lady Charlotte continued embroidering.

"Singe! Charlotte! J'ai faime!"

He sounded insistent and shrill.

Lady Silverton sighed, and settling down her embroidery and scooping Franz the dog up in her arms, as she scarcely ever made a move without him, she drifted down the stairs.

"Good Heavens, my *dear* Captain Nelson, what on earth is troubling—"

She froze at the foot of the stairs.

Clearly the poor parrot didn't know the French word for cat, but he'd arrived at what he clearly considered an excellent substitute.

Charybdis was crouched below its perch, motionless apart from his fat, supple, switching tail, which *was* rather like a monkey tail. He and Captain Nelson were riveted by each other, their eyes locked with mutual, fascinated antipathy. Charybdis was keening low in his throat, his eyes huge and as green as parrot plumage.

The parrot was telling him to shut up.

"Charlotte! Singe!" the parrot squawked indignantly. It sounded very much like "I told you so!"

"Good heavens! Now where did that creature come from? We don't have a cat. Although, my goodness, it's wearing such a pretty bow, now isn't it? Heeeere, puss puss puss . . ."

Lady Silverton stepped off the stairs, and had just put her feet on the marble of the foyer when:

"GrrrrrrrrrUFF!"

Franz made a heroic leap from her arms, looking like nothing more than a flying squirrel. It was his first-ever break for freedom. He landed on the marble and for a few seconds his claws scrabbled futilely for purchase and he slid sideways. When he finally managed to correct his course he made straight for Charybdis.

"*Yap!yap!yap!yap!*"

Charybdis sat up interestedly from his crouching position. Likely he thought Franz was just a noisier-than-usual rodent.

SMACK!

Charybdis landed a blow to the snout, sending silky, slippery Franz spiraling across the floor like a weathervane in a stiff wind.

"Oh! Oh! Oh!" Charlotte squeaked, futilely trying to snatch him up again.

Franz finally lost momentum, righted himself, staggered forward, and blinded by his own hair ran confidently into Captain Nelson's perch. Which rocked violently to and fro.

"*Merde!*" the parrot shouted with dignified disgust, and he flapped across the room to land on Charlotte's shoulder.

Which is when the doorbell rang.

The footman, apparently inured to chaos, opened it. And Charybdis, perhaps smelling something alluring from his wild kittenhood, and perhaps with a cat's loathing for confinement and passionate love for an open door, was out of the house and down the stairs like a musket shot.

"*What* the devil was that?" Jules stood in the doorway, dressed for riding in The Row.

"Why, it was a cat, Lord Dryden, if you can countenance it," Lady Charlotte said. "Though my parrot seems to think it was a monkey—isn't he funny? *Singe*, he said. Over and over. We don't have a cat, at least not that I can recall, so I cannot for the life of me tell you how it got in—"

Jules swore something so heartfelt and profane that Lady Silverton gasped and crossed herself and snatched Franz up as though he was a talisman.

And he turned and bolted out the door just as fast as Charybdis had.

"Did you see which way the cat went?" Jules asked the footman. Who, at first was speechless when confronted with the sheer force of the marquess's presence, at last mutely pointed to the left.

Jules ran for it. The cat could have crossed the square by now; they were quick and slippery little beasts. It could have slipped through the gates into a garden; they were lithe as wraiths. It could have leaped aboard a hack and could very well be on its way to the docks by now.

It was a *cat*. It could be anywhere.

He halted deliberately. For *that* was no way to think for a man who made decisions and choices with precision. It would be, he decided, where he found it.

When he found it.

He was distantly aware he was leaving muttering in his wake, the breeze from his swift passage practically lifting the tails of waistcoats and blowing the hats off the heads of men passing by. He heard stifled, amazed laughter, just the once. He was aware he'd abandoned Lisbeth and he would in all likelihood be late for a critical meeting with Isaiah Redmond at White's. They seemed frivolous concerns in the moment.

He stopped passersby again and again with the same question: "Have you seen a cat wearing a blue bow? Striped, has lots of hair?"

Perhaps unsurprisingly, no one answered him immediately. They stared, rattled by his intensity, wary of the ludicrous question, of *him*.

He'd never seen that expression directed at him before in his life.

"'Ave you lost a wager, then, Lord Dryden?" one man asked, who clearly recognized him, and would likely gossip about it.

Jules scowled, which caused the man to take a step back.

"Would that I knew where yer pussycat has got to, Lord Dryden," he said fervently, and backed away.

Jules heard "no" after "no" after "no." The sun was lowering; a benign amber began to spread over the buildings, gilding wrought-iron gates, setting windows to dazzling.

He looked toward the horizon and he cursed it, threatened it. By God, he would *intimidate* the night from falling before he found the cat.

He was breathing heavily by the time he touched a stocky gentleman in a cheap blue coat on the shoulder.

"Have you seen a cat wearing a blue bow? Striped, has lots of hair?"

The man didn't even blink. He looked almost pleased to at last have been asked.

"Aye, that I did. It was 'avin' a bath out 'ere and I stop to try to pet the wee pretty bugger and 'e 'jes keep runnin'. 'E went that way, Your Lordship. Like a streak 'e was. Five minutes ago now?"

He pointed toward the mews of the town house nearest them.

"Bless you!" Jules planted a kiss on the shocked man's shiny bald head and tore in that direction like the hounds of hell, or at the very least, a Pekingese, were in pursuit.

And then he came to an abrupt halt.

Because there was indeed a furry creature of some kind, upside down, all four limbs in the air, sprawled on its back in the mews.

It was wearing a blue bow.

Oh, God. His heart sank. From the looks of things, a horse and carriage had knocked into it, perhaps stunned or killed it.

Grief and disappointment sickened and stunned him. He put his hands to his head. He couldn't bear telling her.

He leaned very carefully, very reluctantly toward it.

The cat stretched languidly, pointing all of its toes like a ballerina, exposing a luxuriously fluffy tawny-colored stomach to the sun. It blinked enormous green eyes sleepily, and then closed them again and curled one paw under its chin, looking for all the world like a prone, somnolent pugilist. With a fat, furry, belly.

Adorable!

Christ. He didn't think he'd ever used that word to describe anything in his entire life. Perhaps he ought to rethink his stance on cats. This one had a belly like a . . . like a *cloud* . . . one just yearned to touch it. And the blue satin ribbon tied about its neck was irresistibly whimsical.

For God's sake!

He crept toward it, very slowly, cautiously lest it do something cats were famous for, like bolt. It opened one eye and watched his progress, not so much with alarm as with a sort of dispassionate curiosity. Perhaps it was too drugged from the sun to startle easily.

He saw its fat belly rise and fall with a great cat sigh.

And when he was near, within distance of touching it, he lowered himself slowly into a crouch, crooning nonsense sounds like a looby, happy his knees didn't crack like gunshots and send the beast scrambling.

Slowly, slowly, painstakingly slowly, he extended a hand and—how could he resist?—he succumbed to temptation: he sank his hand gently into that soft fur.

"There, wee Charbydis. Why don't we—"

The cat's limbs snapped closed over his arm like a bear trap and it sunk its teeth into his hand, ears flattened evilly.

Jules screamed like a woman.

The cat seemed to like this. It clung harder. It kicked him like a rabbit with its hind legs.

Jules shot to his feet. Charybdis continued to cling with all four limbs and all twenty claws. The pain was ridiculous. The cat blinked his beautiful eyes at Jules and readjusted its hold on him with jaw, gripping harder with teeth and claw, apparently intending to settle in for a while.

His ears were so flat they looked like bat wings. He met the marquess's eyes with something like equanimity.

This was when he became aware that his scream had brought a crowd of worthy good Samaritans, workmen in caps and heavy boots and aprons, dashing to cluster about him, proving that not all hope was lost for the souls of Londoners.

But they'd all come to abrupt halt at a wary distance. And now they were watching an aristocrat dance around with a cat stuck to his arm as though they'd actually paid to see it.

"Perhaps if you dinna scream, guv," suggested a

man wearing a brown cap and a dirty linen shirt. "I think it encourages him."

"I know it encourages me wife!" one of them in big worn boots said.

Chortles rippled through the crowd. Which maintained a distance, as if they were indeed watching a ring match.

Panting through the burning pain, Jules got a grip on the cat's nape with his other hand and gave a tug. Charybdis's eyes went wide with indignation.

One of the cat arms magically loosened enough to take a wild swipe across his torso.

An impressed roar went up. "Gentleman Jackson has naught on that wee puss!"

The bloody animal had *striped him through his linen shirt*! It burned like mad. He could just imagine the blood welling.

"Ohhh! Get 'im, puss, puss!" someone shouted cheerfully.

Jules was indignant.

"I've another cat you can have, Yer Lordship. Willna fight back! I fear this one will best ye, wee bow and all!"

Inevitably, the wagering began.

"I've got a fiver on the guv!"

"My blunt's on the wee puss!"

Much energetic shouting ensued. The cat's eyes brightened. He adjusted his grip on the marquess, as though he'd only just begun to fight.

"Will . . . any . . . of . . . you . . . *help*?" The marquess supported the cat's furry, pliable spine with one hand and hoisted him up a bit, as it hurt less when the beast wasn't *hanging*. An extravagant plume of a tail swished violently, thumping him in the ribs.

It *was* very soft.

"Well, ye see, Yer Lordship, we're not certain of your goal," said the man in the cap.

"It . . . is . . . the . . . beloved pet of a lady and I . . . *gah* . . . wish to return it to her. Alive. I wish to extract it from my . . . *oh God* . . ." he hissed a breath ". . . flesh. Does that make it any clear . . . clearer?"

The blue satin ribbon had come undone and was dangling almost rakishly, like a cravat.

"Ye've no choice in the matter now, do ye? I think the wee beast is permanently attached to ye."

"Oh, no lady should 'ave a pet like that, sir. I've a badger what'll suit. We can put a wee bow on it, too."

The comedy team of Cap and Boots had everyone laughing merrily again.

"On the contrary," Jules said grimly. "It suits her perfectly. I'll give pound to each of you if you help me extricate this beast from my skin without harming it."

Money turned the conversation serious. Swift discussion regarding strategy and payment ensued, and Charybdis proved no match for three men, who managed to oh-so-carefully pry its claws from Jules's arm. And when a kipper was produced from one man's packed meal, Charybdis was finally persuaded to trade his bite of the marquess's arm for fish. Fish had been the downfall of many a determined cat.

Bleeding and punctured with a variety of little holes, the Marquess now held the untenably fluffy, preternaturally strong cat in his arms like a spring lamb—firmly but without squishing it. Its limbs paddled futilely below his crossed arms, but his bare flesh was out of snapping reach of the feline's jaw.

Charybdis finally seemed resigned to his fate and settled in more or less comfortably, almost agreeably, and ceased thrashing. One might have thought he was the picture of the content feline. Apart, that was, from an occasional unearthly malevolent yodel that seemed to begin in the depths of his body before it emerged from its mouth.

It had the men who'd helped him crossing themselves and backing away uneasily.

"Keep yer pound notes, guv, and best of luck to ye now. I suspect the young lady in question lives in Hades, as that thing is demon spawn in a bow. And as there's hope for my salvation yet, so I willna be takin' yer money."

He bowed, and spun on his big boot heels, and hurried off as fast as his sturdy short legs could carry him.

But the others extended their palms. Which is how Jules gave away his available cash, and had none for a hack to get him to White's, or to anyplace else, for that matter.

He had no choice.

And so the Marquess Dryden walked to White's with an intermittently yodeling cat in his arms.

Chapter 24

How . . . long ago?"

Phoebe's limbs gave way, and she sank down onto a settee and stared blankly into the parlor. She'd returned from her exhilarating ride in The Row on a sunny day to . . . the end of life as she knew it.

Charybdis was gone.

"An hour ago or so. Right out the door he went after molesting the parrot." Having delivered her news, Lady Charlotte drifted out of the room again, dog tucked under her arm.

"One of the maids likely left your chamber door open. We shall fire all of them," Lady Marie assured Phoebe.

Good God.

"That won't solve it," Phoebe said dully.

"It might be amusing to do anyway," Antoinette suggested to her sister. "It would certainly put the fear of God into the rest of the maids."

Phoebe looked up at her, astounded and not entirely certain she was jesting.

"We'll get you another pussycat." Marie patted her knee.

Phoebe turned her head slowly, incredulously,

toward Marie. It was her nightmare, to be stripped this vulnerable in front of these people. People who thought a cat was like a pelisse, and could be replaced by placing an order somewhere.

Her palms were ice. Her stomach a cauldron of misery.

"I have to go looking for him." She stood up. Sat down. Stood up again.

She who fancied herself so *strong* felt cut off at the knees and panicky as a child. Who knew that all that remained between her and helpless devastation was a cat?

"He could be anywhere by now," Marie soothed.

"You must be a joy at funerals, Marie," Phoebe said tightly.

Antoinette frowned faintly at her sister. Then shrugged. It was clear that they hadn't a notion what to do about this sudden interjection of a dreary minor chord into their gaiety.

Lisbeth drifted into the room and game to an abrupt halt, as though she'd noticed a stench. Clearly the atmosphere was funereal.

"What in God's name happened?"

"Phoebe's cat left," Lady Marie explained.

Phoebe jerked her head up. "Left! For God's sake, it wasn't as though he boarded a hack bound for Drury Lane. He seems to have *escaped* from my room and run out the front door."

Ah, she realized. And here it was. In fairy tales and myths, some terrible sacrifice is endured for wanting the forbidden, the out-of-reach. *Please not Charybdis. Please please please.*

"Someone must have left the door to your room open," Lisbeth said mildly, searching out a reflective surface in the room to nervously admire her reflection. "A maid, most likely."

Phoebe looked up at her slowly then.

And *knew*.

Lisbeth's head inevitably drifted back around, drawn by the force of Phoebe's stare.

They stared at each other so long that the Silverton sisters began to shift restlessly.

You have everything, Phoebe thought. *And still you feel so powerless that you had to best me, somehow. You had to take my cat from me. You'll have Jules in the end, and still.*

"I hope someone finds your cat," Lisbeth said very kindly, after a moment. Her stare very fixed.

"You'd best." Phoebe still hadn't blinked.

Gratifyingly, Lisbeth paled and dropped her eyes.

If nothing else, she wanted Lisbeth to worry about sleeping under the same roof with her.

Lisbeth cleared her throat. "Jules is late for our ride in The Row. I hope nothing befell him, too."

Jules. Jules Jules Jules. How Lisbeth loved to use his name.

Use it all you want. Marry him. He'll never really be yours, and you'll never know it.

Or maybe you will.

Lady Silverton drifted into the room again, Franz in her arms. He seemed happy to be safely back in the harbor of the woman's arms and not down on the vast treacherous sea of marble.

"Oh, my dear Miss Redmond, I see that you're dressed for riding. I neglected to tell you that the marquess was here momentarily, but he dashed out again. Is he afraid of dogs, by any chance? Because I fear Franz was barking when he arrived, and he turned around and ran right out the door."

"It seems everyone is fleeing our town house today," Lady Marie chirped.

Twenty minutes later, striding past a series of wide-eyed crowds who crossed the street to avoid him, Jules arrived at White's. Charybdis only stopped making noise when they entered the club. He in fact fell so abruptly silent the marquess glanced down to ensure he hadn't expired from an excess of ill temper.

But no, the cat was looking around curiously with those big intelligent green eyes, for all the world like a prospective member who found the place wanting.

Jules ignored the footman who reached out for his coat and hat, then retracted his hands in shock, eyes bulging, when he saw Jules's bundle.

And as he strode through the place, the cat's fat tail continued switching, which helped clear the omnipresent layer of smoke.

The tail smacked right into Waterburn as he strolled past.

"What the *devil*—" The blond giant swiveled, looking ready to call someone out. His eyes widened.

"Handsome beast," he said to the marquess, in his usual tone of reluctant admiration. "How much did you pay for it?"

"It's surprising what can be had for no cost at all, Waterburn. Why don't you pet it?"

Waterburn stretched out a hand.

"MeeeOWRReeeooooooo*wwwwwwwrrrrrrrr!*"

Multisyllabic, operatic, blood-chilling. It was the sound of a hungry, angry, treed panther preparing to fling itself down onto unsuspecting humans.

Colonel Kefauver shot bolt upright, eyes wild. "Fetch me my blunderbuss at *ONCE*, Haji!" he bellowed. "That *demmed tiger ate those villagers*! We'll get 'im this ti . . ."

He blinked a few times, then slumped and surrendered again to the arms of Morpheus.

It was safe to say that everyone in White's had frozen in mid-motion. Had lowered newspapers. Had paused their drinks on the way to mouths. Even the steam seemed to cease curling from teacups.

Jules would not have been surprised to learn if later one of the gentlemen present wet himself.

Eyes, every last pair of them, were on the marquess and his cat.

The marquess calmly strode to past a frozen Waterburn to where Isaiah Redmond sat. He was equally as riveted as the rest of the club.

Jules's wounds were beginning to itch. *Damn cat.*

In the strange silence, his voice seemed to ring as if he was orating. "My deepest and sincere apologies, Redmond, but I fear I must delay our appointment. I've an urgent errand." He gestured with the cat, as if this was self-explanatory.

"Certainly," Redmond said, after a moment. To the cat. Not to the marquess. He was eye-level with the cat, after all, and its green gaze was as compelling as Isaiah's.

The marquess could still feel the breeze of the tail swishing to and fro. It batted at his ribcage like a stick wielded by a Charlie.

Redmond looked up at Jules searchingly. His eyebrows were a little troubled. But Jules was certain he found the marquess's expression as haughty and impenetrable as usual. If not more so than usual. It was an expression of the *strongly* discouraged questions, even from the likes of Isaiah Redmond. An expression that implied that everything he did was trustworthy and beyond question and above all, *sane*, and was of course rooted in style and sense and purpose.

All balderdash lately, of course. But he still had command of the expression, at least.

Jules bowed, and the cat dipped along with him.

Before he departed, he did one final anomalous thing.

Everyone watched, heads turning in unison, as the Marquess Dryden for the very first time paused by the betting books at White's. He shifted the cat beneath one arm, turned the pages.

The first wager caught his eye because it was so unexpected:

> *Lord Landsdowne wagers Lord Calloway five thousand pounds that he will have Miss Olivia Eversea's hand in marriage before the year is out.*

Only fools and masochists wagered anything regarding Olivia Eversea. It was new, dated yesterday, and the first-ever bet concerning her.

He turned the page, following the sort of instinct that usually preceded winning thousands of pounds. Only this time his suspicions were sinister.

Here were the wagers he wanted to read:

> *Lord Waterburn wagers Sir d'Andre two hundred pounds that M.V. will have a nickname before a fortnight is out.*

> *Sir d'Andre wagers Lord Waterburn five hundred pounds that M.V. will receive hothouse bouquets before a fortnight is out.*

Lord Waterburn wagers Sir d'Andre two thousand pounds that a duel will be fought over M.V. in a fortnight.

The first two wagers were recorded as already settled.

M.V.?

Oh, God.

Miss Vale.

Her success was a result of a fit of aristocratic *whim*. She was a pastime for a pair of bored aristocrats who were profiting from her hunger for beauty, to belong. Waterburn had employed the Emperor's New Clothes stratagem to great effect—she was a sensation because they had made her one.

London society would not take its humiliation lightly if their ruse was revealed.

I never would have had an inspiration if not for you, Waterburn had said to him the night of the Redmond ball.

It was *his fault.* The spotlight was forever on the supposed enigma that was the Marquess Dryden, and this was how he'd, in a moment of weakness, cast the spotlight on Phoebe. And what was it he'd overheard in White's when he'd returned to London? They'd been debating something regarding the hothouse flowers . . . something regarding proof . . . what had they said?

"We'll just ask the girls."

Jules briefly closed his eyes. So the Silverton girls were privy to it, too. Had in all likelihood invited her to London for the express purpose of playing the game.

He stood motionless in the silent club, transfixed by the casual evil of those little bets, the cat's tail whapping against his ribs.

And he turned slowly around again and fixed Waterburn and d'Andre with a gaze so calmly, uncompromisingly black and searching it likely withered the leaves remaining on trees all the way in Holland Park.

The cat gazed green at them.

"Interesting wagers, Waterburn." His voice fair echoed in the room.

Waterburn fidgeted. But then he managed to hoist a pair of fair brows in mock innocence.

"I dislike dull wagers, as well you know."

Jules took some comfort in the conviction that the notion of a duel was absurd. The bloods of the ton often behaved like sheep, but he couldn't imagine anyone rash enough—or bored enough—to shoot each other over Phoebe Vale. At least inside a fortnight.

She would of a certainty be ruined, if a duel was fought over her.

But she was leaving for Africa.

He stared an inscrutable threat at Waterburn. A threat he didn't dare voice. Willed it to sink into Waterburn's very bones. And he thought of Phoebe's glowing face, and her laughter, and he said a prayer, and he wasn't a praying man:

May she never learn of these wagers.

And then he swiveled and exited White's, winding out through the frozen statuary of the crowd. Beneath his arm, a fat fluffy tail continued switching to and fro, to and fro.

It smacked the hand of one of the footmen as he maneuvered past bearing a tray of port.

"Oh! Soft!" The footman exclaimed and smiled.

A murmuring went up and became a buzz after the marquess departed.

Waterburn doubled back to pull a chair up to a table

where d'Andre sat. Turned it around and sat with his arms folded over the back of it. "Why a blue ribbon, do you suppose?"

"I should think it's part of his family crest? The color blue?"

"Perhaps it's a message about fidelity? Blue is for fidelity, after all."

"Why does he have a cat at *all*?"

And so they discussed the Marquess Dryden with the intensity of conspirators against the crown.

Chapter 25

Since he couldn't very well walk back to his town house—which was closer to White's than the Silverton town house, and he couldn't go to the Silverton town house, though his horse was even now stabled there, because of *Lisbeth*, whom he'd abandoned in mad, reflexive pursuit of a cat—he flagged a hackney and gave the driver his direction.

He wanted to be alone with Phoebe when he returned the cat to her. Nothing else mattered right now. And he suffered from impatience, because he could feel her suffering as surely as if it was his own. It howled across his nerve endings.

And so he tolerated the ruminative, cheekily amused stare from the gap-toothed bloke atop the hack.

"Five pounds for a to-and-fro journey. I'll pay you when we arrive at my town house."

The driver skimmed the marquess with an up-and-down glance. Took in the cat, the Hoby boots, the coat, the buttons, the cat . . . and then settled, riveted, upon the expression on the marquess's face.

Whereupon his smile faded, and he shifted in his seat. "At yer service, guv. But that beast best not piss in me hack."

Oh, God. Jules hadn't even considered the possibility of pissing.

"Worse things have happened in this hack, I would wager my life on it."

Fifteen minutes later, during which Charybdis seemed to doze in his arms, he at last stalked up the stairs of his town house.

Marquardt, who'd seen through the window the arrival of a battered hack and the disembarking of the marquess, greeted him at the door.

Jules shifted a now sleepy Charybdis beneath one arm like a parcel. Marquardt followed the motion eyes wide and fascinated, as though his head were leashed to the cat.

Jules began issuing orders. "Send that hack below straightaway to the Silverton place on St. James Square. Tell Miss Vale it's urgent she come. I have her cat. "

"Are we to compose a ransom note to send along, too, then, sir? Would you like to sign it, or shall I spend some time cutting out letters from the newspaper and affixing them to a sheet of foolscap?"

"How much am I paying you to be witty, Marquardt?"

"Not nearly enough, my lord."

"Just ensure it's done quickly, and that the message is delivered verbally only to Miss Vale."

"What if she possesses the wits to refuse to board a carriage that hasn't a crest? What if she isn't in?"

"Ah. This is what I pay you for, Marquardt. Tell her . . . tell her . . ." He couldn't very well send his own carriage or a message sealed with his own seal or written in his own hand into the Silverton household, particularly since Lisbeth was in residence, and he'd abandoned her. He'd *abandoned* her.

"Tell Miss Vale . . . she'll think twice about ever wishing to throw a humidor at me once she sees Charybdis."

Marquardt listened sympathetically, nodding and nodding. He was clearly reviewing the words over and over in his head.

"Had rather a good deal to drink at White's, did you, my lord?" was his careful and sympathetic conclusion.

"No, Marquardt," he said irritably. "I only wish that I had. Have that message delivered to her. Word for word. She'll understand it. And do it *now.*"

"And if she isn't in?"

Charybdis, bestirring himself, and finding himself in new surroundings, growled low in its throat.

Even Marquardt blinked and paled.

"Pray that she is."

A quarter of an hour later, the driver, who'd rehearsed his cryptic message all the way to St. James Square, delivered it personally to Miss Vale. It had taken some negotiation with the stuffy liveried fellow at the door before Miss Vale was fetched, however, which was insulting. Time was money when one drove a hack. And unfortunately, as if they were moons in Miss Vale's orbit, two astonishingly clean, identically lovely women appeared behind her, followed by another one who looked like a painting she was so pretty.

They refused to budge.

It was proving to be one of the strangest days the hackney driver had ever had, and given that this was London, it was not a thing he lightly thought.

"I'm to give the message only to Miss Vale," he tried.

"I'm Miss Vale!" the Silverton sisters chorused. Then giggled.

"I'm Miss Vale," Phoebe said firmly, in her best schoolteacher voice.

Five pounds wasn't enough for this nonsense, the driver decided. He directed his message to Phoebe, as she seemed the least full of silliness.

"I'm to bring ye to yer cat. Summat about a humidor thrown at a head." The delivery was rushed and desultory. He waited.

"Ooooh, how exciting!" Marie and Antoinette clasped their hands beneath their chins and bounced on their toes. "Is it a game played by an admirer? Did someone kidnap wee Charybdis? Ought you to have a care about—"

Phoebe bolted out the door, scrambled down the stairs, her skirts hiked in her hands. She took a soaring leap from the bottom step into the waiting carriage and pulled the door shut behind her. The driver hastened after her, clambering aboard, as the ribbons were cracked over the backs of the horses.

Leaving the Silvertons and Lisbeth gaping in her wake.

The door swung open even before she'd an opportunity to hoist the impressive brass knocker. Revealing a short, unassuming, mostly bald man of indeterminate age, elegantly turned out in black and white. She would have wagered his bemused expression was permanent.

"Told . . . he . . . has . . . my . . . cat . . ."

"Ah," the man said mellifluously. "You must be Miss Vale."

He stepped aside and motioned for her to enter.

He looked her over. His eyebrows twitched but his mouth clearly thought better of frowning. He cleared his throat.

"The marquess has informed me I'm to . . . send you up." His face was composed in carefully bland planes, but he couldn't disguise the faint dubious note. Clearly she wasn't the sort of woman who was usually "sent up" the stairs of the marquess's town house.

She would think about that later.

"And if you would take this to him, Miss Vale? Turn left when you reach the top. Doubtless you'll hear the creature's unearthly yodels."

He handed her a small white rag and a jar meticulously labeled in spidery script no doubt belonging to someone's housekeeper, "St. John's Wort."

Oh, dear. Clearly Charybdis had left his mark.

Charybdis had already recognized her footfall and came running for her, the marquess in pursuit. He came to such an abrupt halt when he saw her that he nearly toppled down the stairs.

She didn't look at him at all. She dove for her cat and swept him up and wrapped her arms around him, holding on tightly, as if the cat was the thing that anchored her to earth. She rubbed her cheek against him. The damn thing purred. And purred and purred. Deafeningly. It did nothing by halves, clearly. It purred with the same gusto with which it growled.

Jules could watch her forever. He greedily drank in the sight of her, her eyes closed, her entire face luminous with joy and relief. At the moment he could think of no finer accomplishment, nothing else he aspired to. *I did that. I made her this happy.* He would consent to be clawed over and over again to put that expression on her face.

"Thank you," she murmured. Her voice was muffled by fur. She hadn't yet quite looked at him. "Thank you, thank you, thank you."

He found he couldn't speak.

She finally looked up and opened her green eyes. And before he knew what he was doing, he reached out and with a thumb brushed away one teardrop glistening in that mauve crescent beneath her eyes.

And then he looked down at his thumb, and rubbed the tear out of existence, right into his skin. As if he could erase any sadness or hurt she'd ever felt that simply. As if he could bear it for her.

She dropped her eyes again, abashed.

For a time there was no sound but absurdly loud purring.

She cleared her throat. "Are you very wounded?" Her voice was soft. Careful. Reminding him that the last they met they'd argued bitterly and parted on a stalemate. "Your man sent me up here with St. John's Wort."

"Mmm . . . D'you know," he mused, "I've been bayoneted, before. But the Frenchman wielding it didn't go *on* stabbing me. This creature is possessed. I would send a message to the archbishop. Perhaps he knows of an exorcist."

She was struggling not to laugh. "Possessed of *tiny teeth and claws*." She held up a great furry mitt illustratively. The thing allowed her to do it, as if it were a stuffed bear, and not a savage predator in an adorable cat suit.

"The beast is misnamed. It should be named for something with talons. A dragon or a phoenix or some such. No—minotaur. There. That's what you should have named it. Minotaur."

She laughed, and turned the now pliant fluffy thing around and kissed him on the orange nose while the marquess looked on with rank disbelief. And then she lowered the beast to the floor, whereupon it strolled over and wrapped his whole sinewy fluffy body, including that tail, around the marquess's shin. And gazed up at him limpidly.

"He's trying to lure me into complacency in preparation for another attack."

"Now you're beginning to sound like poor Colonel Kefauver in White's."

He blinked. "How the devil do *you* know about Colonel—"

"Oh, all the men. Waterburn and d'Andre and the like. They talk."

A silence.

"All the men," he drawled grimly.

She shrugged blithely with one shoulder.

He hesitated. And then he needed to know. "Phoebe . . . did you by any chance receive hothouse flowers today?"

She looked surprised, and there it was that soft, genuine pleasure again lighting her face. "Yes, as a matter of fact. And a bundle of sage, as it so happens."

Which did you prefer? he absurdly wanted to say.

They regarded each other, the air shimmering with unspoken things.

How could he tell her about the wagers? At this point, she might not even believe him. He couldn't bear to be the one to do it. He didn't know whether remaining silent was cowardly or altruistic.

It was definitely selfish. Her joy was his own.

"Go ahead, then. He likes his back rubbed. And his head scratched."

"The creature inflicts grievous wounds upon my person and expects me to forgive it?"

"I expect a lot of creatures inflict grievous wounds and expect forgiveness."

Well. Silence fell like an axe coming down.

They stared at each other again. Phoebe evenly.

The marquess somewhat warily.

"Are you being profound again, Miss Vale? Are you teaching another lesson to me? I expect that was an innuendo, but I am *bleeding*," he said finally with great, and mostly mock self-righteousness.

She arched a single eyebrow.

He sighed. "If you're going to use an *eyebrow* . . ." He bent down and dutifully scratched Charybdis on the top of his head. The cat launched into a fresh bout of purring and rotated his head to and fro so Jules could scratch beneath his chin. The Marquess was disgusted. "Mad, mad fickle beast," he crooned as he scratched.

He stood again and Charybdis slinked under the bed, having satisfied his urge to be fussed over.

They were silent. Without a cat as a buffer, he wondered what there was left to say.

"Did it hurt terribly? The bayonet."

Silly question, they both knew. But he knew when he looked in her eyes that she wanted to undo his wounds the way he wanted to undo hers. That she suffered from the very notion that he had ever suffered.

"It hurt," he said simply. "For a time. And then it healed."

She'd gone paler. She pressed her lips together, drew in a sharp breath.

"Would you like to see my scar?" he tried.

She bit back a smile. "I'm certain that sentence has worked on innumerable ladies."

"Not innumerable. I can innumerate them."

She was smiling in earnest now. "I'm terribly, terribly sorry Charybdis hurt you. But I'm . . . more grateful than I can ever say."

He simply nodded.

And then she asked the most critical question of all. "How *did* you find him?"

He opened his mouth. Then paused. Clearly considering his answer.

"The creature was sunbathing in a mews. On its *back*."

He said it gruffly, turning away from her, toward the window, where the lowering sun was aiming a final, potent golden beam.

The sun nicked sparks of red from his hair.

And she knew for certain: He'd bolted out the door in search of her cat. He'd abandoned Lisbeth, and his dignity . . . for her. Again.

She was making a hash of his life.

He turned back to her. His face inscrutable, apart from two faint furrows across his forehead. He turned to her with something like bemused entreaty on his face. *Save me from myself.*

"Jules," she whispered his name like a prayer of thanksgiving. She laid a hand softly against his cheek before she even knew what she was doing.

She remembered her first glimpse of that fascinating intersection of angle and hollow. She hadn't yet kissed him then. He hadn't been a person to her then, but a series of myths perpetuated by the broadsheets. Lord Ice. And now she knew how it felt when it was chilled, sandy with the beginnings of his beard, when he'd kissed her during their waltz.

Tentatively, almost experimentally, he turned his face into her hand. And raised his hand to cover hers.

And then he sighed.

She watched, mesmerized, the swell and sink of his broad shoulders with his breath, as he surrendered, momentarily, the weight of everything to her, and to the tenderness of her touch. Two people unaccustomed to taking comfort or giving it. And she was so afraid they would only ever find it in each other.

He closed his eyes.

She took the opportunity to hoard details about him while his eyes were closed. The emphatic dark slashes of his eyebrows. Lashes shuddering on his cheeks. A scar, just a nick of a white line, near his jaw.

This. *This* moment, this tenderness, was far more dangerous to either of them than passion. Her heart felt swollen. It wanted to open, to go to him. She kept it bound and tethered, of necessity. He couldn't be trusted with it.

"You're . . . such an idiot," she murmured.

His eyes snapped open in surprise.

Then narrowed.

"You might live through this if you apply the St. John's Wort." She managed to be brisk.

He stared at her. Assessing the change in tone. His jaw was set.

"Very well, then." With startling alacrity he unfastened the buttons of his shirt and shook it off his shoulders, and flung it onto the bed, very much like someone throwing down a gauntlet.

Oh.

It was like a blow. She stopped breathing. Instantly, her head floated off high above her body, and heat rushed her limbs, and her knees, well, they melted. She was grateful for her long skirts, because they disguised the sway nicely.

"Too sudden?" he challenged. He shoved both hands through his hair and pushed it back from his forehead. She watched the play of muscle, complex and poetic and heart-stopping, slide beneath his fair skin as he moved. The seam of dark hair that bisected the planes of his chest and disappeared tantalizingly into the top of his trousers, and cried out for a tongue to follow it downward. The eloquent curve of his shoulder, every valley and angle and slope, seemed designed for a hand to trace.

He still had a bruise on his forehead. It had acquired a greenish cast, but half of it was still purple.

Her voice was a thread, but still she managed to sound acerbic. "I believe it's the *devil's* job to tempt me. Not yours."

"And the difference between the devil and I would be . . . ?"

"None that I can detect." She opened the jar of St. John's Wort and dipped her fingers in. "Show me where it hurts." This was bravado. She wasn't certain she could touch him without surrendering completely.

And now he was the one who looked uncertain. His bluff had been called.

But finally, like a boy, he tentatively extended his arm. She saw a few puncture wounds with bruised edges, puffing up a little now.

She touched them gently. "I'm terribly sorry he wounded you."

He shrugged nonchalantly. He seemed to be holding his breath. She touched gentle fingers to each little wound.

"Better?" she asked.

He simply nodded.

"And here," he said softly. Pointing to his chest.

She hesitated. For a fraught moment her finger only hovered close to his skin. The space between her skin and hers seemed to heat.

And then she moved. She lightly touched him, drew her finger across the beads of blood dried in a perfect little arc across his chest. A violent little rosary left by a little cat whose reflex was to defend himself.

When Jules hissed in a breath between his teeth, it felt like bands of steel going taut beneath satin.

Her finger was trembling. She slowed it. And then stopped. Oh, God. It was no use. It was all she could do not to close her eyes. Her senses were swamped. Sight was suddenly an intrusion. All she wanted was to lose herself in the feel of him.

And then she did close her eyes.

For a moment all she heard was breathing. Hers and his. A subtle storm. She could feel his heart beating, the steady thump of it, beneath her hand.

"Go on," he whispered into the silence. "Do whatever you want to do, Phoebe."

She hesitated only a moment more.

And then with one finger she traced, delicately, wonderingly, slowly, the defined planes of his chest, following the path etched by the swell of his muscles.

Gooseflesh lifted the hairs on his arms. And his nipples became little hard nubs. She fanned open her fingers and dragged her nails lightly, lightly, over them.

His breath snagged in his throat, and his head tipped back. The sound was as erotic as a tongue applied to the back of her neck.

Tension thrummed in him; his skin was fever-hot.

Her own breathing was more labored now.

She opened her hands, dragged them lightly over the swell of his chest, greedy for, wondering at the feel of him. She lingered over his heartbeat. A gratifyingly rapid bass drum inside him. But he kept his arms at his sides. Allowing her to take what she wanted, to explore.

Even as she could feel his cock nudging at her through his trousers.

And she moved infinitesimally closer to him, so that her thighs brushed deliberately against him. *He* was a devil. She, apparently, was a vixen.

Her fingers traveled that alluring seam of hair down, down, down to where his narrow waist disappeared into his trousers.

She paused them at his waistband, just above that impressive bulge.

They breathed in swift and ragged counterpoint. She rested her forehead against his chest. He smelled, of course, like heaven, like sex, like temptation, like home. She shook her head helplessly against him. She thought she tried to move away, but he was opium and she was intoxicated. She almost whimpered. *Help.*

"Do you know what I suspect?" His murmur ruffled her hair. Almost conversational. Impressive for a man so obviously aroused.

She shook her head again. *Don't make me speak.*

Her chest rising and falling, rising and falling, against his. Rather more swiftly. His arms rose, slipped lightly, lightly around her, skimmed up over her shoulder blades. His words were frayed, and low, and slow. It was his mink wrap of a voice, the voice of a sensual mesmerist. "You see, as we've been standing here, I've been thinking about the skin above your stockings, on that very secret place just on the inside of your thighs? Right above your garters. Because . . . I suspect . . . dear God, I suspect it's soft, Phoebe. Like new skin, never touched. The petals of a blossom can only *dream* of being as delicate as this skin. Charybdis has nothing on you. If *you* were to lie on your back in the mews, crowds would gather from all over for one touch, one touch, of that skin."

She tried to laugh. But he'd called every part of her being to life just then. Her skin felt overlaid with fever. The flesh between her thighs burned, burned, as if it knew it was being discussed, was eager to test his hypothesis.

The hammer blows of her heart sent the blood ringing through her ears

And still he spoke. His voice was a resonant near-whisper in her ear, and this, too, was unbearably erotic. "And I think, right now, deep between your legs . . . you're wet, Phoebe, from wanting me, from imagining me touching you, licking you just *there*. If I were to slide my fingers between your legs right now, they would come away drenched. If I were to taste you, my thirst would be slaked."

Oh, God. Oh, God. Oh God.

Her breathing was like bellows now. He'd moved subtly closer; his cock was hard against her belly. His hands slid down to her buttocks and pulled her ever so slightly closer. His restraint was remarkable.

"So . . . *purple*," she gasped, a feeble protest, against his chest.

This took him aback a little. "Oh—my prose? Of course it is. But no less effective for all of that . . . is it, Scheherazade?"

The devil was amused.

"Would you like to wager that I'm right, Phoebe? Lift your skirts in your hands for 'yes.' I want you complicit."

And at first she was afraid her hands wouldn't work at all, and this seemed a terrible dilemma. She tried, but they seemed reluctant to lift from his torso, in case she never touched him again.

There was the murmur again. "Going *once* . . . going *twice* . . ."

She peeled her hands from his torso with a heroic effort and slid them down into the folds of her skirts. And as she furled them up he sank down, down, down, easily, to his knees.

And as the air of the room struck her stockinged legs, that bare place above her garters, his hands cupped the back of her calves. He fanned them, and his fingers combed, leaving ten feathery fiery trails along her skin, lighting tiny scattered bonfires across the entirety of her nervous system. Everything that *could* go erect on her body instantly did so, and an army of gooseflesh likely greeted his fingers when they bypassed her garters and arrived at skin.

She sighed. More accurately, she groaned, softly, shamelessly. She'd never *dreamed* anything could be so exquisite.

And her legs shifted apart, inviting more.

His finger skimmed along the edge of the garter. He dragged his lips softly over, inside her thigh. And she didn't know whether it was this or the anticipation of him opening his mouth, of applying his tongue to her skin, but a great throb of yearning pulsed between her legs.

And then he did part his lips and touch his tongue to her skin, and the blood fled her head, rallying to the new center of her universe farther south.

"I was right. So soft." He sounded intoxicated, too.

Desperation and pleasure and greed and anticipation wrestled, entwined. She didn't know *what* she wanted, only that she did, and he was the one who could give her what she wanted.

Her fingers slipped down to rake into his hair, gripping it, just as his mouth slid a little to the left and his tongue oh-so-delicately flicked between her cleft.

Extraordinary bliss spiked her.

She jerked. She swore extravagantly. Apparently she'd stockpiled filthy words when she was in St. Giles and hadn't had an appropriate excuse for using them again until now.

"You are incredible. And since I was right, I win," he murmured. "For my reward, I want to make you come apart in my hands, and to scream my name."

And his tongue flicked her again.

"Oh, God . . . Jules . . ."

Not a scream. A question, a plea.

He did it again.

She slid her hands over his hair, down to his shoulders, needing him to hold her up, as her knees were useless now. His shoulders were so hard they shocked and thrilled her and almost frightened her; all at once there seemed no give in him at all. It didn't seem inconceivable that he could bear the weight of the world, or that he could break her in two. It was too late now to consider to whom she was surrendering.

Intuitively they moved together to find the rhythm she wanted. The languid heat and velvet of his stroking tongue became more deliberate, more insistent, more precise as they discovered together just what she wanted, and with the last rays of sunlight pouring in the window and warming the back of her neck—she was drugged with pleasure. She was lost. She heard her breath only distantly, a tattered rush of sound. And then he sucked and bliss cleaved her, choking her with a pleasure so violent it was nearly pain.

She shuddered, arching her hips into him. And she moved with him. An icy heat rushed her skin, as if her nerves were recalling every moment of bliss they'd ever known and singing about it.

She dug her nails into his shoulders. Waves of bliss were now as much a part of her as her own heartbeat, as the breath going in and out of her lungs. They built, and rose, cresting, pressed against the very seams of her being. She was going to die. Or scream. Distantly she sensed something coming for her, and she didn't know quite what it was yet. She wanted it, needed it, feared it.

And then his fingers slipped inside her, and crooked, and slid.

"Jules . . . I'm . . . Please!"

A sea of hot stars broke over her, tore her out of her body. Swept her away in an indescribable pleasure, buckling her.

She did indeed scream his name.

She felt his hard arms wrapped around her, holding her fast. She would have fallen.

As it was, she'd dropped her dress over his head.

She seemed to return to her body only in fragments. She was distantly aware of breathing, of hot skin, of sweat, of limbs, of thoughts drifting. She didn't know what belonged to whom. Her senses needed to recongregate, to separate from him.

He fought his way from beneath her dress.

And looked up at her. His hair was mussed from her rummaging her hands about in it.

He stood, slowly. The better to tower over her, she supposed. So fundamentally male her breath was lost all over again.

She looked down. He had a roaring erection. She wondered now if he intended that she give him more, now that he'd given to her. She supposed she was very like a man in that at the moment she wanted nothing more than to flee.

"Where's the cat?" He sounded dazed.

"Under the bed. It's his usual refuge. Why?"

"If I take you now, right here, on this bed, if I make love to you, would he attack me?"

"Why don't you try it and see?"

"Is that an invitation, Miss Vale?"

It took every ounce of strength she possessed to say the following, and yet she knew that she meant it: "Not in the least."

She watched his face, and could almost see him review and reject things to say to her. Assessing whether she could be persuaded. At last he sighed, and reached out and awkwardly swept a strand of wayward hair away from her face and behind her ear. It felt a bit like being pawed by a bear. Tenderness did not come naturally to him. Or rather, it might have, if only he would allow it to, if only he'd surrender to it. He'd be as graceful in that as he was in everything else he *permitted* into his life.

She preferred him when he was awkward and uncertain and finding himself.

He sat down hard on the bed. Tipped his forehead into his hand.

Rediscovered his bruise and swiftly looked up again.

She smoothed her skirts.

Her entire body still tingled with the aftermath of her first-ever release, like an echo of a hallelujah chorus. In the mirror over the bureau she could see that her skin was flushed rose everywhere it was exposed. She looked scrumptious and wanton.

And yet everything about the moment was bittersweet.

"I should love nothing more than to make love to you, Phoebe."

He sounded so miserable, and looked so vulnerable, with the bruise on his head and his little bandolier of a cat scratch and his enormous erection.

"I know."

He cast up a hopeful eye. But when he saw her expression, he quirked his mouth, and his and he shook his head and turned away again, toward the window.

Nobody spoke for a time.

"I'm sorry to leave you . . . in this condition."

Oh, God. The aftermath was so awkward. Yet she might as well make it clear that leaving was what she intended to do.

He gave a short laugh. "I've survived an unused erection before. It's hardly terminal. It's just . . ." His words were halting. "If only you knew how I felt when . . ." He stopped himself. "Because what just happened here was only a hint of how it could be. It would be unbelievably good between us. I *know*, you see . . . for I've experience of these things, whether you'd like to hear about it or not. And I have never . . . *wanted* . . . like this. Never. It has never been this . . . explosive . . . with anyone else."

Wanted? *Loved*, you fool, she wanted to tell him. That was the entire reason. For the bruise and the cat and the desire.

"I know," was all she said.

"And wasn't it good? I didn't know a schoolteacher knew such deliciously filthy words."

She smiled at him. "It was extraordinary," she said gently.

His eyes widened. And then he gave a short laugh, an entirely humorless sound. "It sounds like you're patronizing me."

She shrugged.

"I know how much you want me. *Me*," he urged. He

stood and in one stride was so close she could nearly touch him again. So she could smell him, and of course she wanted to melt into him again. Her arms remained determinedly at her sides. She was strong.

He raised a hand, and then tentatively, gently traced her lips with his thumb, over and over again, brushing over the tiny freckle next to her mouth, lingering there.

"You want *me*," he insisted on a whisper, almost a plea. "No one else."

She felt his breath on her lips. She would be lost if he kissed her.

Kiss me.

Please don't kiss me.

"Who doesn't, Lord Dryden?" She'd tried for brittle flippancy.

He went rigid at her tone.

And then his hand fell from her lips to his side abruptly.

He looked so stung she wanted to comfort him, but then of course, who would comfort her?

Nothing had changed. He had offered nothing new.

"Do you think you can scare up a basket so I can take Charybdis back to the Silverton town house? And hackney fare?"

The cat heard his name, and came slinking sleepily out from under the bed. She knelt and adjusted his bow, which was askew.

The marquess watched. "Is the object of the bow to make that creature look more benign?"

"It's to trap the unsuspecting."

He managed a genuine smile then. They broke her heart freshly every time, his smiles. And then he flung open his wardrobe and found another shirt, one without any bloodstains, slid his arms into it, and deftly buttoned it up. She watched with regret as all of that masculine gloriousness disappeared under linen.

It occurred to her that if she'd been able to spend her life with him she would see this sort of thing all the time. The buttoning of shirts. Shaving. All the less erotic things, nonetheless cherished. The acts of intimacy that knit lives together. She wanted to soothe his wounds and share his burdens and make his life easier, more spontaneous, more passionate.

It hurt. And just as there seemed to be no end to the kinds of pleasure he could give or to the ways in which she loved him, and because of this, no end to the ways he could hurt her, again and again and again.

"And when does your ship leave for Africa?"

"In two weeks."

"And you're going?"

"I cannot think what will keep me here."

His face closed then. Hard, inscrutable. Not unlike Charybdis closing up over a hand reaching for his belly.

He buttoned the shirt.

"Your wounds will heal, my lord."

She kept the tone dry. But he understood all of the meanings in that sentence because he turned around.

"Doubtless," he said finally, coolly. Proving to her that two could play the game of cold distance. "Marquardt will find you a basket. And good luck to you, Miss Vale, wherever you may go."

Chapter 26

They pressed her to explain her mad dash out of the house, the Silverton twins did, but Phoebe laughed and said she could never tell them who'd rescued her cat. Fortunately, their attention spans were very catlike, and they soon abandoned the topic.

And so, for another week, the social whirlwind mercifully continued.

Mercifully, because it was pleasantly numbing not to slow down long enough to feel anything, to recklessly drink and awake thick-headed, to dance with men who didn't want to converse so much as exchange frivolities and gossip, to be admired and envied by those not anointed unto popularity by the Silverton twins and Waterburn and d'Andre. Everything skated over her senses like pleasant music, nothing penetrated. She was loaned the use of an Abigail to care for the dresses she'd brought with her; she was loaned a fine pelisse and a few day dresses to supplement those.

The bouquets continued to arrive after the balls, all addressed to The Original.

And then the first appearance of her name in a broadsheet linked to Lord Camber emerged. It in fact began to appear as if Camber was contemplating embarking upon an actual courtship, such was the consistent profusion of blooms he sent. She rode in his high flyer once more, accompanied by the Silverton sisters and Waterburn and d'Andre. He came to expect a waltz from her at each ball. She knew now he had three sisters, a father who kept his allowance on a tight leash, a love of horses, guns, hunting, and bawdy musicales.

He knew nothing about her apart from the fact that she was The Original and taught school. He'd never asked about her, and she wasn't about to volunteer. All these young men loved to talk about themselves, she'd discovered.

The marquess had wanted to know about *her*.

She'd seen Jules three more times. Each time it was because she'd watched him dance with Lisbeth from across the room. It was like looking at him through a window, watching him move through a parallel life in which he already belonged to Lisbeth. Already lost to her.

Twice he came to the town house to take Lisbeth riding in The Row, and Phoebe always arranged to be in her room at the time, or elsewhere. And bouquets arrived on these days, sent to Lisbeth by the marquess. Always pale pink and white, always a little different, always extraordinarily tasteful.

It struck Phoebe as less a courtship than the stages of penance. But then, she was prejudiced, and she wasn't privy to their conversations. Perhaps they did naught but coo at each other from atop horses.

She doubted it.

No one talks to me the way you do.

But the distance was healing; the distance was *sensible*. And for all she knew, the marquess had quite come to terms with the loss of her and was contemplating with stoic satisfaction a lifetime of supplying Lisbeth with flattery and fine dresses and bearing unbearably beautiful children. And perhaps acquiring a new and fiery mistress somewhere along the way, to cobble together a complete life. Or nearly complete.

No more bundles of sage, or anything like it, appeared for Phoebe.

And so the madness between them was well and truly over. And this was merciful, too.

It was a Friday morning when Lady Marie approached Lisbeth, who was admiring, in turn, her reflection in the back of a silver teapot and the latest bouquet sent by the marquess.

"D'you know, the Settlefield ball is tonight . . . and we all know what that means!"

"Engagements are traditionally announced at the Settlefield ball. At least one per year. Who was it last year . . . ?" Lady Marie turned to her sister.

"Oh, I cannot recall," Lady Antoinette sighed. "I seem to forget the names of people we knew once they're married."

They snickered.

"Except for the ones with the grand, grand titles, of course," they hastened to amend. "The betting books have it that it will be you, Lisbeth."

Phoebe's hand froze, curled round her china cup of coffee. Scorching hot, but she didn't feel it.

"He's meeting with Uncle Isaiah at White's tomorrow," Lisbeth confided with secretive smugness. "One last time, is what he said."

"Likely to have a little chat about settlements," Lady Marie speculated. "After he proposes, of course."

Phoebe found she was holding herself very, very still. As if the contents of her very soul were flammable and she would combust if she moved. But in truth, she knew a brief surge of happiness: Jules would get everything he'd ever lived for to date. She knew he would take pleasure in that: in duty, in completion, in history, in the lands restored to him. Even though she could never understand it.

Nevertheless, it was best not to look at Lisbeth. Because she could trust herself to pretend indifference, she could in fact feign it brilliantly, but not if she was forced to look the death of her dream in its blue, blue eyes.

The girls arrived at the Settlefield ball in their usual fragrant, gleaming cloud and swept up the stairs of the town house. Waterburn and d'Andre met them, attached themselves to their little flock, and descended upon the ballroom proper, as had become their custom.

"What kept you ladies?" Waterburn complained.

"We would have arrived earlier, but Phoebe's cat wanted to play with her ribbon," Lady Marie told him. "And he was so *charming*. He had quite an adventure."

Waterburn went still. "Phoebe's . . . cat?"

"I've a cat," Phoebe confirmed. "I brought it from Sussex."

"Isn't that amusing?" Lady Marie sounded bored.

"Original," Waterburn said cryptically. "What does the cat look like?"

"Very furry. Has a white front and wears a blue bow round its neck. He escaped the other day, you know, but a mysterious benefactor returned it to her. She never would tell us who. Why are you wasting time upon this topic? Fetch us some ratafia at *once*." She playfully tapped him with her fan.

"Straightaway," he said absently, making no attempt

to move. "But first . . . Lisbeth, would you be so gracious as to dance one of the waltzes with me this evening? One never knows. It might be your last before an engagement."

"Well! It's so unlike you to be sentimental, but it suits you! You may have one," she said regally.

Shortly after Waterburn claimed Lisbeth for her waltz, they watched a dancer fling his partner across the room and drop to one knee.

"Almost like he's issuing a proposal," Waterburn reflected. "The one-knee bit."

"We've started a fashion," Lisbeth said loftily.

"We've?"

"The marquess and I."

"Are you sure it's a fashion, Lisbeth? I begin to wonder, truly I do, Lisbeth, if he isn't having one over on us. The man never does anything without a reason, though I'm not always certain what the reason is. Did you know he brought a cat with him into White's?"

She went as rigid and white as a porcelain doll.

The response was exactly what Waterburn hoped for.

"What day was this?" she demanded. Her voice hoarse.

"Oh, a week ago," he said idly, as they swept about in the dance. Phoebe was dancing her requisite waltz with Lord Camber. "I hope you don't mind, but I shan't be flinging you across the room, Lisbeth."

She hadn't heard him. "Was it a striped cat wearing a blue bow?"

"Oh, yes. Handsome beast. Ah! So you're familiar with his cat. If cat familiarity doesn't herald an engagement, I don't know what does. Where did he get it? I should like to have one, too. It *was* his cat, wasn't it?"

When she remained silent he prodded, "Lisbeth?"

"I don't understand. She's just a schoolteacher. She has no family. No money. She's not even *pretty*. Why?"

Her words breathlessly, frantically escalated in pitch and she gripped his hand so tightly he nearly winced. Her face had gone a decidedly unpretty shade of red.

"What on earth are you running on about, Lisbeth? Miss Vale? Why should you worry yourself over her? Talk about having one over on the ton. You know that she's just a lark, right?"

Lisbeth was immediately alert. "What do you mean?"

"Didn't The Twins tell you?"

"I suppose I've been so caught up in the social whirl that I must have forgotten."

Waterburn knew the twins had never said a word to her.

"Well, it's just a bit of fun I hit upon when we attended your house party—to see if we could turn a plain girl with no family into the toast of the ton. To see if we get the bloods to make fools of themselves over her. The Twins got you to introduce them to her and then they invited her to London. We did the rest. And by God, I feel like the Creator himself, because see how well it's worked? Anyhow, the wagers are in the books at White's. d'Andre and I have won quite a pretty sum."

"Oh, of course. Of course I knew. Very clever! I recall now. So she's . . . just a bit of fun," she quoted, repeating him thoughtfully. "She's *nothing*, really," she expounded, sounding as though she was trying to convince herself. "She's . . . a jest."

"She's a lark, Lisbeth! We wagered she would have a nickname and receive hothouse flowers within a fort- night and so forth. Her popularity is *entirely* manufactured. Waterburn giveth, and Waterburn taketh away. You may congratulate me for my cleverness."

"Fiendish," Lisbeth mused. And then after a calculatedly casual pause: "Does the marquess know about it?"

"Oh, I don't believe he does. Though he read the betting books the other day, and he *never* does that. The day he brought in the cat, in fact. But I don't think he's susceptible to that sort of nonsense—he sets rather than follows styles. And he hasn't danced with her even once, has he? He knows the real thing when he sees it, and you, my dear, are the very real thing."

"And he always wants the very best of everything, naturally," Lisbeth reiterated thoughtfully, resembling nothing more than a cat with feathers clinging to its chin.

"Naturally." Even Waterburn was growing irritated by Lisbeth's need to have her supremacy affirmed. "But *imagine* the uproar if word got out. Miss Vale would be ruined."

"I imagine she would," Lisbeth reflected.

And by the time the waltz was over, Waterburn could almost taste the one thousand pounds. He just needed to have a word with one more person: Camber.

Phoebe wasn't terribly surprised when Lord Camber got around to saying, "I should like to show you the garden. It's a very fine one."

Phoebe knew this was a euphemism for, "I should like to steal a kiss and a fondle in the garden because I think we've both had just enough ratafia to enjoy it," and she was surprised and yet not surprised. Camber was a man, after all, dogged, and not timid. He was bound to suggest something of the sort eventually. The difference between aristocrats and the other men of

Pennyroyal Green was all in the confidence and sense of entitlement. All of the bosom gazing during waltzes only fomented it.

"So kind of you to offer. Perhaps another time? I believe there's a bit of a nip in the air." She gave an illustrative shiver.

"Perhaps I can warm you."

Oh. A bit startling. She hadn't expected *persistence*.

"Lord Camber . . ."

"Oh, come now, Miss Vale. Surely someone as original as you is not bound by the usual conventions."

"And those conventions would be . . ."

He laughed. "You know how I admire you. And I *know* you would enjoy kissing me. I excel at it. Don't be prim."

And that's when his hand slid around her wrist and held it fast.

She was too shocked to slip from his grasp in time. She instead stared down at it, astonished. She was shackled by long thick white fingers featuring plenty of hair.

She gave a tug.

He didn't release her.

His face was flushed with the pleasure of touching her, of having her in his control, and from too much drink.

"I swear to you, once we begin, you'll enjoy it. I know you've had a kiss before. Come now." He pulled, and to her horror she was actually dragged a few feet, toward the garden doors.

"I must ask that you remove your hand at once, Lord Camber."

"You ought to know that I never give up quite so easily."

He gave another pull. He was surprisingly strong.

She started to skid, her slippers sliding over the marble. She was mortified. And all at once she was afraid, too.

"*Please* . . . Lord Camber . . ."

She could knee him in the cods, if she got close enough. She could trod on his instep. She wasn't afraid to do *those* things.

"Oh, now. Don't make a scene. One kiss, Miss Vale," he coaxed. "I've seen how you look at me. And I've heard that you don't mind a bit of that sort of thing."

"I look at you with my *eyes*. That's all. And where in God's name would you have heard—"

He released her wrist for an instant. But it turned out it was only because he had new plans for his hand: He slid it up over her kid gloves until his warm, damp fingers were touching her bare skin. He began to close them.

"Lord Camber. I *beg* of you. I must insist you release—"

Lord Camber suddenly levitated three feet off the ground and dropped hard to the marble. He landed with an unnerving thud. His booted feet flew nearly over his head, came down with a smack. He lay stunned.

When he looked up in tandem with Phoebe, he saw the face of the Marquess Dryden. His visage was granite. His eyes were murderous.

"I believe she told you to stop, Camber." The words were evenly measured, terrifyingly quiet.

Camber scrambled to his feet with surprising speed. He stared at Jules, dumbstruck, scarlet with indignation and rage. His broad chest swayed with ragged, furious breaths.

And then he lunged, aiming a fist at Jules like a catapult.

Jules snatched the fist mid-air with shocking speed and spun Camber around and pinning him motionless with his own arm.

Camber's eyes bulged. He was imprisoned against the wall of the marquess's chest. He breathed through his nose like an angry bull.

"*You've* no claim on her, Dryden." He muttered hoarsely.

"Nor do you."

"For God's sake, Dryden. Have you gone mad? Be *sensible*. She's not a lady. She's a schoolteacher. I didn't intend to harm her. I know she *enjoys* doling out favors, I was told."

Phoebe was numb with shock. Her voice came to her from what felt like miles away. "I . . . I swear I *never* . . . by whom?"

Jules's every word was etched in leisurely menace. "I will not allow you to touch her if she does not wish to be touched. Are we clear?"

Camber fumed. He tugged.

Jules jerked his arm farther up his back. "Are we clear?"

Camber hissed in pain. "Yes. Very well. Release me."

Jules unhanded him abruptly and Camber stumbled. He righted himself and then backed away from the marquess, glaring like a man cheated, holding his arm.

Jules reached out a hand for Phoebe; his hand hovered mid-air, stopping himself from touching her in time. "Are you . . ."

". . . Hurt? No. Not really. Thank you. I . . . well, thank you."

She drank in his face, fascinated, her heart swollen. The taut fury, the concern, the possessiveness, the longing that flickered there behind his control.

No one had ever come to her defense before.

And they stared at each other, rapt and speechless. But when Phoebe heard a throat clear she gave a start. It was only then that the two of them noticed the usual ballroom milling had come to a halt around them. A crowd was massed. She saw Lisbeth, and the Silverton twins, and Waterburn and d'Andre move toward them, rats called by the pied piper of scandal.

Oh, God.

She was instantly horrified she hadn't defended herself more effectively. For she saw very clearly that Jules had risked the future he'd so passionately worked toward for so long. She also knew very clearly, and with a sense of despair: the separation she'd thought they'd achieved was an illusion. He could no more help himself from helping her than he could help breathing. He in all likelihood had known where she was in the ballroom at all times.

Jules inhaled at length, a man struggling to settle his temper. To find a neutral expression.

Because Lisbeth's lovely face was part of the crowd, and she was fixedly watching the two of them, mouth a thin white line, jaw tense. Looking for all the world like hard and brittle porcelain.

"Jules . . . ?" Her voice was faint.

Jules took pains to sound bored. "Camber momentarily forgot he was a gentleman, and I reminded him rather emphatically. T'was naught that doesn't typically happen in a ballroom at least once per night. And nothing that Camber will do again."

The heads of the gathered crowd turned in unison toward Phoebe then, eyes glittering like a wolf pack.

Lisbeth's voice rose. Thin, clear, shot through with torment, sounding like a thwarted child.

"But . . . honestly . . . over her? Why should you bother? Don't you know . . . it's all been a *game*, Jules." She gave a tinkling little laugh and cast an inclusive look over the crowd: *aren't men silly?*

"Lisbeth," the marquess said quietly. The word contained an unmistakable warning.

She couldn't seem to stop.

"Surely you've seen the betting books at White's, Jules. She's been nothing but a lark! A wager! An experiment. She's not a *lady* at all, and her popularity is entirely manufactured."

Phoebe swiveled and stared at Jules in horror.

Her hands iced, when she saw that Jules was staring at Lisbeth, stunned, shaking his head. His eyes closed.

Which was when the ground dropped from beneath Phoebe's feet and the very air seemed to warp before her eyes.

"Betting books?" Phoebe's lips were numb. She held her wrist in one hand. It didn't hurt. It was just she wanted something to hold onto, lest the ground swallow her up.

Jules glanced toward her, and stiffened when he saw her touch her wrist. His face went deadly as an ax blade and he fixed Camber with a stare.

"Who suggested you might find Miss Vale *accommodating*, Camber?"

"As if I would tell you." The man lurched away from the marquess as if shoved, and finally disappeared, hurrying off through the ballroom.

The crowd was now layered in rings about them. The low buzz of speculation and commentary sounded like flies about carrion.

Lisbeth wasn't finished. "Oh, yes, the betting books, Phoebe! None of it was meant to be *real*, isn't that right . . . Phoebe?" Lisbeth said blithely, horribly, almost conspiratorially, the shine in her eyes like the light glancing off a blade. "The nickname and so forth. The wager was that they could fool the ton by turning a plain schoolteacher with no family or connections into all the rage. That she would be showered with hot-house flowers and invitations. Hundreds of pounds, they wagered. They've really had one over on the *ton*. The Original and all that. *Honestly*." She wrinkled her nose and gave another little laugh.

Phoebe couldn't speak. She felt peculiarly separate from her body, hovering over the crowd. She looked down at herself, faintly puzzled, as though she was Queen Elizabeth's lady in waiting and had just discovered her dress was poisoned.

And when she looked up with entreaty into the faces of the Silverton twins she saw nothing reflected but the sort of mischievous guilt seen on the faces of three-year-old girls when caught stealing a little cake in the kitchen. They were enchanted with themselves.

Please let it be a dream.

And then Lady Marie shrugged and Lady Antoinette raised her palms.

She waited. She was still in a ballroom, still surrounded by coldly speculative eyes.

"Of course it was," Phoebe's voice was a thread. "It's all been a lark."

She was encircled now, like a deer brought down by wolves. All the men she'd danced with, flirted with, eyed her warily, resentfully, as anyone naturally would if they felt they'd been dealt a counterfeit.

How could she not have *seen*? How could she have been such a fool?

"Who originated this clever plan, Lisbeth?" the marquess's voice was coldly conversational.

Lisbeth looked uncertain. "Waterburn. But you knew about it, didn't you, Jules? Or rather, Waterburn said you read it in the betting books. I thought you knew."

Jules and Waterburn locked eyes. The antipathy that snaked between them was nearly visible.

"Of course," Phoebe managed, through the ringing in her ears. "*I* was in on it all along!" she said brightly. "Didn't you know, Lisbeth?"

Waterburn and d'Andre and The Twins appeared startled by this revelation.

Wary glances ricocheted between them.

"Were you?" Lisbeth's question was uninflected. Entirely disbelieving.

The mutters of the crowd were gathering volume as realization took hold:

"She's a fraud? Miss Vale. Bloody rotten of them. Made fools of us!"

"She's not even very pretty."

A more cheerful one. "Well, I actually I sent her flowers! Bloody good trick, Waterburn! Best wager yet."

"And now that Lisbeth has brought our pantomime to a conclusion, I believe I'll make my exit. Thank you for being such a lovely audience." Phoebe curtsied deeply, theatrically, and blew kisses from her palms, and turned on her heel.

There was a nonplussed pause.

Hesitant, scattered applause. *Pat pat pat pat pat* went hands.

Jules scowled it into silence.

"Is she really an actress?" A man's eager voice came on the periphery of the crowd. "Does she have a protector?"

Jules fancied he could hear the sound of her footfall echoing over the marble, growing ever distant, that he could pick it out from the other ambient sounds. It took every ounce of hard-won control he possessed not to bolt after her. If he waited too long he was certain she would be forever lost to him, slipping into the dark of London, like her cat.

He turned and looked at Lisbeth again. Her hands were white knots against her brilliant blue gown. Her face was bleached of color.

He'd never before today wanted to run a woman through on a pike.

But he should have noticed. He should have been more aware, more sensitive, more careful. She was more astute than he'd given her credit for, and he'd refused to see her as much as she'd refused to see him. He'd dealt with her poorly, even dishonorably. He'd been carelessly at the mercy of his own emotions and needs.

And in a way, he treated her almost like an object.

The way the ton had treated Phoebe.

The way they treated him.

Very nice little vise you've gotten yourself into, Dryden.

"What about the marquess?" someone suggested on the periphery. "He can *act*, too? Was the whole evening a pantomime? The man can do anything."

They were prepared only to admire him, because it was what they'd been told to do. How quickly confusion could spread and rumors grow and the truth become so diffused it could never again be retrieved whole.

Ridiculously, the Sussex waltz started. Lilting and jaunty. It struck Jules as a tastelessly inappropriate theme for the apocalypse.

And then Lisbeth smiled at him. It was the sort of smile that suggested that this was all for his own good. As if she expected to be *congratulated* and thanked for exposing this folly. As if she expected him to be relieved that she'd spared him any more foolishness over a fraud like Miss Vale.

Who, ironically, was the most genuine person in any room.

He realized with a shock he was expected to dance this particular waltz with Lisbeth.

And he knew of a certainty he couldn't bear to touch her.

Chapter 27

Phoebe exited the ballroom through a gauntlet of fascinated eyes. She felt the stares like cinders on her skin. She knew her face was scarlet, which she couldn't help, but she also knew her head was high and her smile regal and brilliant, the smile of a pleased performer. She was grateful she'd had the opportunity to see Signora Licari, because she could imitate that poise.

She would leave them believing she was complicit. Or at least leave them doubting the truth. One little seed of doubt could sprout in innumerable directions, and Waterburn and d'Andre and The Twins would have a time of combating it.

And then when she saw the stairs she lunged for them like a creature bolting for a hole.

Her skirts hiked in her hands, she ran blindly out into the dark, down the steps of the town house, plunging into the London streets, past the rows of identical, judgmental houses. She didn't know where she was going, only that she wanted to run and run until her lungs were aflame in her chest, until her heart exploded, until she gagged with exhaustion. Until she could feel nothing, nothing at all.

And then she saw the Silverton carriage, the driver slumped atop it, sipping at a flask.

She halted immediately. "Take me to the Silverton town house," she demanded imperiously.

He was so astonished he sat bolt upright and cracked the ribbons over the backs of the horses just as she slammed the carriage door behind her.

Tick. Tick. Tick.

He couldn't hear her walking anymore. She could be out of the building. Walking out into the London night—

God. He wouldn't humiliate Lisbeth, despite what she'd done, because he wasn't entirely innocent.

"Do you mind, Lisbeth?" He heard his voice as if it belonged to a stranger, polite, elegant, apologetic. Centuries of breeding had their uses. "I fear I've twisted my wrist persuading Camber to behave like a gentleman. I never could tolerate watching a man treat a woman poorly." He smiled. It irritated him suddenly that his smiles were so very effective. He hated himself for knowing it.

And it worked. She softened. "Oh! Jules. You've gone and hurt yourself, and all over someone who's just a—"

Something she saw in his face stopped her like a hand clapped over her mouth.

There was an uncertain, fraught little pause.

"Your sense of honor is admirable," she concluded hurriedly. Hectic pink moved across her fair face again. *Tick. Tick. Tick.* In his mind he saw Phoebe Vale growing smaller and smaller and smaller, going farther away from him, until she vanished over a horizon.

His jaw ached from being clenched.

He could stand it no longer. "Lisbeth," he said hoarsely.

And suddenly all pretense fell away. She saw it in his

face. She was instantly all panicky entreaty. "Jules . . . please don't . . . you don't want to . . ."

"It's no good, Lisbeth." His voice almost cracked. "I'm more sorry than I can say. I wish you all the best . . . but it's no good. I must—"

She opened her mouth, but said nothing. She closed it again.

He bowed and turned, moved along the perimeter of the ballroom, hardly noticing when some other woman was flung, twirling across the ballroom, while her partner fell to his knees.

Eyes followed him, but he was used to that.

He only allowed himself to run when he reached the stairs.

He stopped short at the entrance, between two footmen. The sky was dark and vast, London was endless, and she could be anywhere.

One of the footmen must have read something in his face and took pity.

"She went that way, my lord," the footman said, pointing.

And so that was the way he ran.

Phoebe threw herself back against the seat of the carriage. And that's when the shaking began. Rage and shame and hurt each fought for a turn with her. She wrapped her arms around herself tightly, to keep herself from retching, closed her eyes, tipped back her head, thumped it slowly again and again against the seat.

"*God* . . ." she moaned.

She kicked the seat in front of her hard. As if it was Lisbeth, or Waterburn, or her own gullible, foolish behind.

And the worst of it was that Jules had *known*. He'd known she was a . . . a *wager*. He'd listened to her rhapsodize about the *men* and the *bouquets* and waltzes, all the while knowing she was being used as the ton's performing dog, an amusement, a novelty.

The ride was short. She sprang out of the carriage, ignoring the proferred arm of the driver.

"Wait here," she ordered him.

She pushed past the sleepy footman who answered the door into the house, nearly vaulted the stairs to her outrageously plush, pink room, and flung everything—so very little she owned, overall—carelessly into her trunk, slamming the lid.

And then she paused for a moment she could ill afford and retched into a chamber pot.

She pressed the palms of her hands over her eyes as if she could blot the ballroom scene out of her mind forever. And she breathed. And breathed. And she tried to reason with herself, to grasp for some place in the roiling chaos to begin rationalizing. It was futile. The pain was in the very air she breathed.

She'd been a pathetic *fool*. Wanting to be wanted so desperately she'd convinced herself she truly was. Wanting to belong so desperately she'd almost believed she did.

She gave her head a toss. They could all go to Hades.

She was going to Africa. And she would never have to think of them or see them again.

And then she went still.

She might be a fool . . . but *now* she was a fool with nothing left to lose. She looked at the fine borrowed pelisse she'd just stripped from her body and flung on her bed, and decided she had plans for it.

She rang for a footman.

"Take my trunk down to the carriage."

She scooped up her cat, which was watching her with deep, fascinated concern, dropped him into his basket.

And ten minutes later slammed the door forever on the Silverton twins' town house.

He'd soon realized the ridiculous futility of roaming a dark St. James Square calling for Phoebe as though she was a lost dog. She was hardly likely to come to him, anyway.

And so he was home again.

The desolation was complete, the taste of it acrid in his mouth. In the library, he shook off his coat and flung it violently away from him. He was tempted to hurl it into the fire, to eradicate memories of the night. He yanked off his cravat as though it were a noose, and threw it, but it didn't flutter far, which made him furious. He unbuttoned his shirt, allowed it to hang open on his torso. His entire life felt confining.

Still, he contemplatively eyed the brandy decanter, and wondered if he could become the sort of man who hurled things in fits of rage.

He was a man who always took swift, precise, perfect action. The action that solved everything, won everything.

Surely, despite everything, he was still that man.

The house was quiet as a tomb. He'd never noticed before, but likely it was always this quiet.

Perhaps I should get a cat, Jules thought.

The bell rang as he was pouring himself a glass of brandy. He froze. Gingerly he settled his full glass down on the table alongside the decanter he'd just spared.

Marquardt was asleep. No one was awake to answer the bell.

In two long steps he was at the window. He swept aside the curtain and peered out.

The lamps were doused for the evening, so he saw only a slight shadowy figure standing on the steps. It could only be a woman. He saw the hulking outline of a large, very fine carriage in the street below.

He took his marble stairs two at a time and flung open the door.

Relief, disbelief made him light-headed.

It unmistakably was her. She looked smaller, but it could have something to do with the pelisse she was wearing, which obviously wasn't hers. It was too large, and it was fur lined, with a collar that swallowed up her slim neck. She'd buttoned it all the way up to her chin.

A meowing basket was at her feet.

She stared at him, her pale eyes glowing. And even in the dark it was apparent she was furious. She fair crackled with it. He could *taste* it in the air, like an approaching storm.

She turned and called down to the driver very coolly, "If you would bring up my trunk?"

Phoebe walked past Jules without looking at him, without waiting for permission. She aimed straight for the staircase, scaled the stairs as quickly as she did nearly everything. He followed her, as if in a dream. He was unable to speak.

He heard the thunk of the trunk dropped in his foyer, and the door closing. The Silverton driver; bless him for remembering to close the door.

She reached his bedroom and settled the basket down and flipped open the lid. Charybdis leaped out, spotted the chair before the fire, and settled in and began nibbling on his hind leg.

Jules found his voice.

"Phoebe . . . I . . . Why are you here? I'm glad that you are, love, but . . ."

She peeled off one glove. Flung it to the floor. She peeled off the other and did the same. She gave it a kick. Beautiful kid gloves went tumbling across the room.

She slipped her feet out of her slippers. She kicked each of them aside and her bare feet curled into his thick rug.

Dear God. He noticed she was trembling. He reached out, tried to touch her. "Phoebe . . . sweetheart . . . You're shaking. You've had a shock. I'll pour a brandy—"

It was as if he hadn't spoken.

"You've wanted me, Dryden. Take me."

He froze. Dumbstruck.

In the silence that followed, the fire spat and popped in sympathy with the temper radiating from her.

His voice was cracked. "Phoebe, I don't . . ."

"Don't *what*? Want me, now that the game is up? Do you even *know* what you really think or really want, or is it all covered over in a carapace of "shoulds"? Don't you dare repeat that to me. I know how ridiculous that sounded. And yes I know very large words like *carapace* and out they come. But it doesn't matter, does it?"

His head was spinning. He didn't know where to begin. "I—"

"I don't *care* whether you want me anymore. Because you were right all along. I. Want. You. The way a woman wants a man. And I will have you tonight."

"Do you even know what you're . . . are you drunk . . . are you . . . please, can we discuss this?"

She was unbuttoning the pelisse.

"Are you a coward, Dryden? Are you *all talk*? It isn't funny anymore, is it? You knew all along. You *knew*. And yet you allowed it to go on. You allowed me to be a mockery. It was in the *bloody betting books*."

She took great relish in spitting out all those *B*'s sequentially.

"Hold. I know that you're angry and hurt, but won't have you falsely condemning me. I *didn't* know. Not at first. I discovered only later. I never go near the damned books. And when I did, *how* could I tell you, Phoebe? I'll admit to selfishness only: the greatest pleasure in my life in seeing you happy, even as it killed me to see you with other men. Breaking your heart would be the same as . . . the same as . . . breaking my own. And you were leaving. You said you were *leaving*. You might never have known."

Well. That stopped her in her tracks. And for an instant he saw wonder, a thrilling yearning flash over her face, a raw hope that stole his breath.

And then she shook her head roughly. Her fury had momentum and she needed to spend it, and she didn't want love or peace. She didn't trust it.

The pelisse was unbuttoned. She shook her arms out of it and let it drop to her feet.

Holy mother of . . .

She was entirely nude.

Chapter 28

His senses took her like a lightning strike. He reeled. Her entire pale white loveliness, long slim legs, the nipped in waist and heavy round breasts.

His breath stopped in his lungs.

A sound at last escaped him. It sounded like "Guh."

She reached up and yanked pins from her hair, one by one, clutched them in her fist, dropped them to the deep carpet, and down her hair tumbled. A pale gleaming waterfall. She gave it a shake.

"Tell me you don't want me." She knew what she saw in his eyes.

He couldn't speak. He stared, unabashedly. Feasted his eyes on her loveliness.

"Not like *this*." He was vehement.

God, he was also tremendously aroused.

"Like what? You don't want me *too willing*? Or are you too cold, Dryden? Do I need to be angrier to offset that glacier you have for a heart? Do I need to start throwing things to really excite you? Or do you need to buy things for me first, to feel like you've earned the right to my body? Am I worthless now to you, who likes only the precious and worthy?"

Her stratagem was primitive, but it was working. It slipped in through his unguarded places, because only she knew them, and lit a touch paper to his temper.

"Have a care, Phoebe."

"You're a coward, Dryden." She stepped toward him. Gave him a little push with one hand, though she of course couldn't budge him. "You didn't tell me about the betting books because you're a *coward*. You couldn't endure my disappointment so you let the charade go on and on. What of *my* pride? Am I really so pathetic?"

She'd wanted him *angry*. And now he was sizzling with it.

"*You* believed them, Phoebe. I'm the only one—*the only one*—who was truthful with you from the very beginning. I have *never* deceived you or misled about what I want or who I am. And dear *God* . . . you are never pathetic. Do not *ever* suggest that to me again. We will talk in the morn—"

"Everything has to be the way you want it, doesn't it? Well, this is the way *I* want it. Are you man enough for this?"

She dodged away when he lunged toward her, stalked toward her, backing her against the end of the bed.

He put his hand on her breastbone and pushed. She toppled backward onto the bed and leaned back on her elbows.

He followed her there, falling forward, bridging her body, propping himself up over her on his hands. He was close enough to taste her breath, which came in furious gusts. Her pupils were large and black.

Christ. His cock was so hard; his body almost vibrated with need. The body he'd dreamed of was now beneath him, nude and gloriously soft and his for the taking.

"Enough, Phoebe." His tone would have given a brave man pause. "You're upset. We can talk in the morning about arrangements . . ."

She twisted and tried for a kick and he dodged in time.

"Don't tell me *how* I am or how I should be! You and your *bloody arrangements*." She swung wildly for his face. "It's now or never."

In a lightning-swift move he shifted and pinned her wrists to the bed.

Her muscles tensed beneath his grip. She tried to move. He saw her eyes widen in surprise when she found she couldn't. At all.

Still, it was an effort to keep her pinned. She was little but surprisingly strong and lithe, like her damned cat. He would bruise her wrists if he didn't loosen his grip, but he wasn't eager to be slapped. Or bitten, for that matter, and it looked like she wasn't above it.

They'd built her up and torn her down and she was a feral creature again, the creature she must have been when she was plucked out the ghetto, a creature like her cat. Hurt and frightened and fighting.

His cock strained at his trousers now, aching. Sweat beaded his forehead, his shoulders. Traced his spine. His control frayed.

She knew.

She arched upward and kissed him, taking his lips hard. Her mouth was supple, angry, demanding. She licked the corners of his lips, and bit the bottom one lightly. Her breasts brushed against his open shirt, and her nipples, bead-hard, grazed against his bare chest.

She opened her legs, wrapped them around his back, pulled him toward her, slid them down along his thighs.

"Go on, Dryden," she murmured against his lips. "Pleasure me. It's what I *want*."

His lips were over hers, and he tried to take control, but her tongue stabbed into his mouth, an entirely carnal invasion. They fought for supremacy, the kiss erotic and nearly violent, and he seized her plush bottom lip lightly between his teeth. She gasped, and when she did he used the momentary advantage and plundered again, taking the kiss savage and deep, a clash of teeth, a duel of tongue, slow, lewd, thorough, and graceless. And as they kissed she brought one leg up beneath him, and dragged her knee slowly once, twice, hard, back and forth, back and forth over his swollen aching cock until he moaned low and savage in his throat, and swore softly, desperately.

He freed her wrists and scooped his hands beneath her back, and her head tipped back. He pressed hot, hard, nearly brutal kisses along her throat, sucking to brand her, and she clung to his shoulders, her fingernails digging in through the linen. He dragged his mouth down to her breasts and licked, then lightly bit one nipple.

Her body writhed beneath him and she reached for the button on his trousers, her hands shaking but nevertheless swift and deft.

He released her again and she fell back against the bed, and he dragged his palms over her body, hungry for the cool smooth feel of her skin, marveling at it. He filled his hands with her breasts, round and taut, and he lowered his head to suck one of them, hard, mercilessly. She gasped the pleasure of it and her body whipped backward, her head thrashed over the pillow, and she swore words no well-bred girl from the ton would ever know, words that would forever be part of her. Begging him, insulting him, inflaming him, urging him on.

He dragged his tongue down the seam of her narrow ribs; he delved it into her navel.

She locked her legs around him, arcing up against him.

And he positioned his body over her, taking his cock in hand, and she wrapped her legs around him, dragging her feet along his thighs.

He hesitated.

"Go on, Dryden." She bowed her body up to him.

His breathing was like bellows, his vision hazed with lust and fury.

"No," he choked.

"I said yes." She tried to pull him down.

"No. Not like this."

"It's like this or not at all."

And then suddenly he rolled away from her, seized her in his arms and pulled her over his body so that she covered him. He wrapped his arms around her. Held her fast. Allowed her to realize that she was at his mercy, no matter how much he wanted her. That he was in control here.

"I want to make love to you."

She shook her head roughly, her breathing tattered now. "No."

"And I want you to make love to me."

The sound of rough breathing. A sawing in-out of breath. "No," she whispered, fighting tears now.

"Ah, but I fear you've no choice," he murmured, almost regretfully, and as though he was talking to himself as well. "No . . . choice . . . at . . . all."

He whispered this last in her ear, soft as a lullaby, as he smoothed his fingers through her hair, again and again. Untangling the fine length of it, as if it was the very source of her wildness. He combed his fingers along the hot silky skin of her back, again and again, as if she were a harp, murmuring to her. As if she was a wild thing to be tamed. She was vibrating with tension, but he was relentlessly tender, relentlessly seductive.

He traced the pearls of her spine with the tips of his fingers, one at a time, savoring, while his lips glided softly to her temple, along her hairline, down to her throat. He kissed her eyebrows, one a time. As if pointing out to her, little by little, the parts of her that had enchanted and enthralled him, showing her the little pleasures that could be had from every part of her, how the entirety of her body was made for pleasure, and he intended to call forth every feeling her body could yield her. Lulling and arousing and memorizing her.

When he kissed her eyelid, he tasted salt. Because that's what happened to fury when tenderness was applied. It dissolved.

And at last she sighed, a sound of frustration, and surrender. She closed her eyes, and he saw tears trembling on her lashes, so he kissed those away. Her breathing was still ragged and swift, but the frantic fury had eased from her, and in place of it a yielding desire.

It excited him extraordinarily, because now he knew that he would at last, at last have her.

He touched his tongue to her ear, and dragged his hands wonderingly down the curves of her again, opening his palms flat, pushing her against his body. God, how he wanted her.

And then she found his lips with hers. A gentle, tentative kiss. Testing. An apology, a prelude. A bump, a slide, a cling. One might have thought it was their very first.

And then it deepened, slowed. Became less a kiss than one more way they could be joined, a rejoicing; he thought he sensed in it elegy, too.

She ended it, and ducked her head briefly, resting it against his chin.

"I *am* afraid." She whispered it. He expected she surprised herself by saying it aloud.

He knew what it cost her to admit it. And he knew what she meant. She wasn't afraid of sex. She was afraid of losing herself, of surrendering to someone, to anyone, of caring enough to open herself up to that kind of pain.

He was afraid, too. She was the only one who had the courage to admit it.

"You're safe with me." It was simply the truth.

She shifted then, slid her body down along his a little so she could kiss his throat, with a searching open mouth. She slid down farther so she could lick a bead of sweat from between the bones at the base of his neck. She slid down to straddle his waist, his cock bumping up against her lush buttocks, and she sat up to push his shirt away from his shoulders. He helped her by lifting his torso and shrugging out of it, flinging it with abandon across the room, startling Charybdis, and she gave a laugh.

And she lowered herself against him, and dragged her cheek along his skin, then gently, one by one, kissed those absurd and precious marks of love, the bruise on his forehead, the scratches dotting his chest. She kissed the mark of war, the thin white scar left by the bayonet. She dragged her tongue down the seam between his ribs while his hands played in her hair, and she could feel in the way his body arched, in the way his breath swayed his chest, in the hard, swift drumming of his heart beneath her body, how much he wanted her. And she slid farther still, raising herself up, sliding down to straddle his thighs, then tugged at his trousers. Another tug freed his cock, and it sprang up almost cheerfully, thick and swollen and curving up toward his belly. She dragged the trousers down, down over his hips, which were slim and white. She skimmed her fingers over the sharp bones while he raised his hips up to help her, but it took some serious tugging before she finally got them all the way off with an awkward yank that made both of them laugh. His thighs were hard as tree trunks and covered with fascinating curling dark hair; the very insides, she could see, were heartbreakingly tender and white, where riding horseback had likely scraped his hair away.

And that's where she bent to kiss him. And she gently pushed his knees apart, and laid her lips, and then her tongue there.

"Good *God*," he gasped approvingly.

She did it again, dragging her nails lightly in the wake of her mouth, her tongue, until he was hissing in air through his teeth, and shifting restlessly. And she could see his cock leaping friskily.

"Please . . . your mouth . . . take me in your mouth . . ." he begged.

She licked the length of his cock and he groaned, long and guttural and primal, as though he was being freshly bayoneted. And then she closed her mouth over the dome of it and slid her lips down.

He hissed in a breath, and swore beneath his breath the filthiest, most appreciative words, and a few suggestions, including "do it again," and curled his fingers into the counterpane. He shifted his hips, rocking them, arching them upward. The cords of his neck were taut and his head tipped back.

She did it again, fascinated by the hot, velvety strength of him, the power she had over him, the ability to give this careful, contained man so much pleasure he was losing his mind. He was so thick she could barely close her mouth around him.

She did it again.

"*Incred* . . . Phoebe . . . *Christ* . . ." He muttered hoarse syllables as his breath came in harsh gusts. He threw one arm over his forehead. His breath sawed in and out. He swallowed audibly, hard.

And then he sat up, propping himself on his elbows, and stared at her.

Seconds later, and she wasn't certain how it had happened, he had her on her back and he was propped on his arms over her, bridging her body.

She dragged her toes along the diamond-hard planes of his calves, and traced, with one finger, the line of those lips.

He ducked to touch his lips to hers, but as he did he deliberately dragged his cock along her cleft. Her body bowed toward him, and she whimpered.

"Wrap your legs around me, Phoebe."

She locked her feet around his back, and he thrust in.

She gasped at the pain of it, and then moaned softly, as the hard length of him filled her.

"Hold on to me, love."

She hardly needed to be told. He moved, and she could tell he was struggling for some kind of finesse, for a prolonging of the pleasure. To be careful with her. But his eyes burned down into her with the ferocity of a conqueror, with a selfish and thrilling and unnerving need. He needed *her*. Pleasure owned him now, and he surrendered, giving his head a little shake, an apology, admitting it was beyond his control now. And all the frustration and longing and desire they'd harbored for a lifetime it seemed spurred him on. He drove his cock deep into her again and again and again, and she moved with him, arching upward to take him deeper, as deeply as she could. She clung to him, fingers digging into his arms. And the tempo accelerated, his white hips drumming, their bodies colliding hard.

Her nails dug into his biceps. The release on the periphery of her awareness, pressing at the very seams of her being, promising cataclysmic pleasure. She knew his must be imminent in the taut line of his jaw, the thrumming tension in his body. The way she'd lost him to his pleasure to the tempo of his body. She thumped his back with her fist, and it spurred him on. Her head thrashed back.

"I . . . Jules . . ."

And she came apart with a scream as he went still over her. His release shuddered through him, shook his big body like a rag, and he spilled into her.

They lay together quietly, side by side, his arms wrapped around her from behind. His rib cage swayed with his breath, which fell softly against her throat. The sweat cooled on their bodies. The fire hissed and popped, burning ever lower. Over in the corner, Charybdis was taking a noisy bath.

But his hands never stopped moving. Softly, slowly, they roamed over her, savoring her. Exploring. Soothing. And then, when she began to ripple again into his touch, his touch became deliberately arousing. She'd never been more grateful for her own skin, for her lips, for her fingertips, for the miraculous variety of pleasure that could be had from it at his hands.

He covered her breasts in his hands and nipped at the back of her neck gently. She rolled in his embrace to face him, sought his lips with hers, opened her body to him, pulling him down to cover her. He tasted dark and sweet as ever; kissing him was like falling through time, endlessly, blissfully. There was only him.

"Here," he whispered.

He rolled her gently onto her stomach, pulled her hips up toward him, and slid his palms along her back. His hard cock brushed against her, then he slid inside, slowly, so that she felt every inch of him. She groaned at the pleasure of it, as he moved this time deliberately, with finesse, finding the places inside her that banked desire into ranging need. He drove himself into her body, and she urged him deeper, and harder, until they screamed together.

They slept like the dead, entangled.

Signora Licari isn't the only one who snores, she thought, smiling faintly.

He did it softly at least, one arm outflung, the other folded protectively across his chest, as though he was guarding his heart. He looked exhausted and spent and happy and very young.

She propped herself up on her elbow and just watched him sleep for a time. What a gift it was to see him this vulnerable, this trusting.

The room was cool; the light easing into it was the pearl gray of dawn.

And she slipped out of bed, and tiptoed across the carpet. She gave Charybdis a good morning kiss, then tiptoed across the carpet, collecting her gloves, her slippers. She gingerly lifted the lid of her trunk and slipped her sketchbook out of it. She lowered it gently to the bed. And then she selected the first dress she found, a worn and wrinkled walking dress, and dropped it over her head. And then she ventured over near the bed to pluck up her pelisse. She bent over.

Which was when one of his arms snapped out and seized her calf.

She gave a little shriek. She tried an experimental tug.

Like a shackle, it was.

"You're leaving." A flat, incredulous statement. A guess.

"Yes," she said softly. "Unhand me please."

He hesitated, and for a moment she thought he wouldn't.

And then he did.

He turned over and folded his hands beneath his head.

The silence was dense.

"Why?" he finally said.

"The only thing that's changed is that we've made love. You want what *you* want and I want what I want. Last night was wonderful. And I am leaving. It's that simple."

"Phoebe . . ."

"Please don't try to stop me. I haven't the strength for it. I do not want to argue. I don't want to be persuaded. We had one perfect night. Let it be enough."

He heard it in her voice. The faint escalating panic.

So many things he could have accused her of then, and he knew he would have been right about all of them. He knew she was still afraid. That she was running away from him and from the fear that she would one day lose him. She was running away from the enormity and uncertainty of all that she felt and all this meant. *He'd* always tried to wrangle uncertainty to fit his notion of how the world should run, to regiment it. When she couldn't control uncertainty with facts . . . she ran.

"I've . . ." he began.

He could have completed that any number of ways:
". . . botched everything." ". . . loved you since I laid eyes
on you." ". . . been a complete idiot for you." ". . . never
deserved you." ". . . been so wrong about everything
that matters in life."

"I love you." He hadn't planned to say it.

She went still.

She kissed her fingers, and laid them on his lips,
stopping him from saying anything more.

"Thank you," she said. "Don't follow me."

Chapter 29

It was inconceivable that she should be gone. He covered his face with his hands, and lay there like one shot in battle, trying to decide how wounded he was, and whether it was terminal.

He could blame his father again, if he wished, for the way he'd attempted to shape life to suit him. He could blame *life*, for so often obliging him. He could blame the ton for perpetuating his myth.

He took his hands away from his face and slid one over to the side of the bed, still warm and mussed. His hands encountered her sketchbook. He pulled it to him, astounded, moved, to encounter versions of himself as seen through her eyes: saturnine, passionate, one that was woefully smeared and green at the corner from grass. She'd tried to capture him.

Emotions are anarchic, she'd told him. *They resist legislation.* He'd never stopped trying to do just that. But his control was both his weakness and his strength. And he was a man who was precise, who did the right thing, the perfect thing.

And of course he hit upon it.

In the end, he knew there was only one way he could live with himself. He might never have her, he might never see her again, but he wanted her to know definitively what she meant to him, how she had changed him, what she had given to him.

The answer was simple.

Peace settled in. And for the first time in a long time he'd thought of his father with some sympathy, because now he thought he understood.

The hush when Dryden walked into White's that afternoon was immediate and total. It was like the aftermath of a cannon shot; a momentary deafness. Reflexively, he handed off his hat and walking stick to the waiting footmen. He stepped forward two feet . . . and slowed when he heard . . .

. . . a meow.

He couldn't entirely rule out Colonel Kefauver meowing in his sleep. But then he looked about . . . and he counted . . . one, two, three, four . . . young men. Holding *cats*. Striped ones.

Mother of *God*.

He closed his eyes, and shook his head. His life was a farce.

And he proceeded through the club, all of them watching him.

"Where's your pussycat, Dryden?" someone ventured.

He didn't turn.

Isaiah Redmond lowered his newspaper, looked up expectantly.

Dryden kept walking.

He found Waterburn at a table in the back. The blond monolith was seated with d'Andre, a number of other young bloods hanging on his every word. "Should have seen her face! Best ruse ever! The whole of the ton fell for it now, didn't they? Hothouse flowers! A nickname!"

They were laughing. "Well, I wager they'll laugh about it one day."

When he realized that his companions had stopped smiling and were staring at a point somewhere over his head. Waterburn swiveled.

Then shot to his feet, nearly knocking over his chair.

"Dryden." After the initial alarm, he allowed a smirk to begin.

"Good afternoon, Waterburn. You're about to earn one thousand pounds."

The smirk arrested. Waterburn's expression flickered between interest and puzzlement and greed.

When realization dawned cold horror settled in.

"Now, Dryden . . ." In an instant he was pale verging on green. "You don't want to do anything foolish . . ."

"I have never done anything foolish in my life." He realized now it was true. Nothing at all was foolish about loving Phoebe Vale. Not even being clocked in the head by his own hat.

"It was just a lark . . ."

"Name your second." He issued the challenge almost conversationally.

The gasp that went up nearly lifted the heavy velvet curtains.

All the other bloods shoved their chairs back and leaped to their feet and stepped backward, as though duel challenges were contagious.

Waterburn choked. ". . . the *devil* . . . Have you gone *mad*, Dryden?"

"Absolutely." Let the broadsheets *try* to make madness fashionable. "I should like to be very specific. I challenge you to a duel with pistols for your slur to the honor of Miss Phoebe Vale. First blood."

Waterburn shook his head roughly in disbelief.
"I . . ." He was stammering now. "Now, one moment,
Dryden . . . it was just a bit of fun. We made a bit of blunt.
And she's just—"

"If you value your life at all, you won't finish that
sentence." The sentence was as hollow and cold as the
barrel of a pistol.

Waterburn clapped his mouth shut.

"Very good. Now, I want the next words out of your
mouth to be the name of your second."

Silence. Apart from the sound of creaking chairs.
Even Colonel Kefauver was awake and staring.

"D'Andre," Waterburn said finally, faintly. He swallowed audibly. "Are you certain you want to . . . That
is, I'm leaving for Sussex tomorrow."

"Perfect." Jules sounded coolly bored. "D'Andre can
meet with my second, Mr. Gideon Cole to discuss par-
ticulars. I suggest the Pennyroyal Green common at
dawn tomorrow. If you *don't* appear, mind you . . ." He
leaned forward almost confidingly, and Waterburn, as
if he was hypnotized, leaned forward, too. "I will hunt
you down. You will never have a moment's rest until
I have satisfaction. And I cannot vouch for whether
I'll take satisfaction honorably. I find that honor has
become rather tiresome, in fact. Because no one, *no one*
makes a fool of someone I love."

Waterburn listened to this, the skin of his face
strangely taut. White lines appeared at either side of his
nostrils. He'd rested a hand atop one of the chairs. Presumably he was clutching it in order to hold himself up.

Jules nodded once, then turned, wove through the
tables, held out his arms for his hat and walking stick
that the footmen appeared to hand to him, then paused
by Isaiah Redmond's table.

Isaiah stared at him as if he'd already committed murder.

"My apologies, Redmond. I had no choice."

"You realize this is the end of it, Dryden."

"A pleasure doing business with you."

And that was all he said. He bowed shallowly.

And everyone watched, riveted, committing to memory to tell their grandchildren, as the Marquess Dryden left White's after doing something he'd sworn he'd never do: follow in his father's footsteps.

The silence settled thickly.

Colonel Kefauver was the first one to speak.

"Well, I think he'll kill you, Waterburn," Colonel Kefauver said admiringly, sounding surprisingly lucid. "Have you seen that boy shoot?"

Julian arrived in Sussex in the early evening, after spending the afternoon cleaning and oiling his dueling pistols. He'd purchased them from Purdey shortly after he'd left Manton's for his own establishment, and he'd practiced with them at least once a month for five years.

Not on men, of course.

Mr. Gideon Cole had promised to join him in Sussex for dinner at the inn and for a celebratory drink after, upon which he would return to London, as the business of arguing in court never ended.

Such was the bravado that preceded duels.

And in Sussex the marquess took a room at an inn. Through his second, Mr. Cole, all parties were informed where he could be found should an apology be forthcoming. He wasn't sure he wanted one.

He rather felt like shooting Waterburn.

He knew the land he wanted, his mother's dowry, everything he'd maneuvered toward to date, was never going to be his. At least while Isaiah Redmond lived. He supposed the novelty of falling on his own sword, which still surprised him, would sustain him through the disappointment.

He had no doubts that he would live, of course.

He had doubts about the quality of his life thereafter, given that it had become fairly clear that Phoebe Vale would not be in it. But he decided to focus on the mundane things that stitched together a day, one moment at a time. Which was also very unlike him, as he was forever planning several moves into the future. He savored each bite of his early supper of a tasty but mysterious stew at the comfortable inn just outside Pennyroyal Green, with Mr. Cole. He savored the sight of a kind autumn sun, lowering on the green, benign Sussex hills unfurling out the window, undulating off toward the sea. The faces of travelers, the simple country clothing they wore.

And he had nearly finished his stew when the door to the inn opened, allowing in a gust of air. He stopped chewing.

Sir d'Andre and Lord Waterburn stood in the doorway.

He swallowed his bite. "Have your pistol loaded, Cole?"

"Of course," Gideon murmured just as casually.

But the two men, Waterburn and d'Andre, looked unusually subdued. The spectre of death would subdue anyone, Jules thought.

"May we have a word, Dryden?" d'Andre, as the second, lifted his voice from the doorway. As if seeking permission to approach.

He hesitated.

"Join us," Jules offered ironically.

The men moved in tandem, weaving through the tables, past the smiling faces of the other diners who were unaware that two of the men had made a gentleman's agreement to attempt to murder each other this evening over a woman.

"I shall say this quickly. I apologize for the offense I gave, Dryden. I was wrong."

Jules looked up into the man's ice blue eyes. "Because you don't want to die this evening?" he asked pleasantly. "The first sensible thing you've done in quite an age, Waterburn."

"It got away from us, please understand. The wagering. I'm not as soulless as you might think."

"Soulless" was an interesting word for a man like Waterburn to produce. And yet he was not entirely prepared to relinquish cynicism when it came to Waterburn.

"Did d'Andre pay you one thousand pounds?"

"A wager is a wager, Lord Dryden, and I honor mine," d'Andre, he of the curls and forelock and tight trousers, said.

"And besides . . ." Waterburn added. "I should like very much to live to see what the ton does with the news that you're in love with a teacher."

A hint of humor. More than a hint of the old antipathy.

But Jules was not a fool. An apology was an apology.

He stared at Waterburn a moment longer, speculatively, thoughtfully. Enough to make both him and d'Andre shift their feet, even as they maintained admirably stoic expressions. He supposed he'd made his point in White's; shooting the man might be superfluous in light of that.

He nodded curtly. "Apology accepted."

Waterburn's shoulders rose and sank in a sigh. "And now we're off to the Pig & Thistle, Dryden. We're wagering on darts this evening, though no one has yet defeated Jonathan Redmond. Join us if you're interested."

Jules watched incredulously as they departed.

He shrugged. And thusly the most dramatic gesture of his life concluded.

They finished their stew, toasted the apology, and Gideon Cole decided to return to London that evening.

Phoebe wasn't new to broken hearts. When her parents had disappeared, one at a time, she'd sobbed herself to sleep for countless nights, only to wake again, heart hammering with terror, feeling the wind of the abyss howling behind her. She could not recall when she'd stopped. Somehow the crying had ceased to be a comfort.

She'd survived. Against all odds, she had in fact thrived.

She would survive this. She could not in truth say her heart was broken, since she'd kept it firmly from the marquess.

And yet the howling wrongness of not being near him consumed her. She moved through her room in a dull haze, a ringing in her ears. She knew the farther away from him she went, the easier it would eventually be, and she, like Jules, took each moment at a time, marking them off the way a prisoner etches marks on the wall of a cell.

She'd indulged in the extravagance of hiring a hack to take her back to Sussex, but she could just afford it, thanks to her winnings from five-card loo. In her rooms at the academy, she settled in at her writing desk, Charybdis sitting atop it staring down at her like a gargoyle, and she finally responded to the letter she'd received the very first day she'd seen Jules in Postlethwaite's.

   Dear Mr. Lunden,

     I should be pleased to join your party of missionaries as a teacher, and am grateful to accept the position. I understand we sail within a fortnight. Until then, you may address particulars to me here at Miss Endicott's academy.

There. It was done. The note that ended one episode of her life and began another.

Charybdis reached down and put a paw on her head.

After Jules bade goodbye to Mr. Cole, he rode out to have one last look at the Sussex property that would never be his. He expected to feel more than he did. As it was, he looked for only a minute. It might have been any piece of land.

And then he turned his horse to stare at Miss Marietta Endicott's academy on the hill. He wheeled his horse about, as if the academy were a pillar of salt, and galloped, headlong, back toward Pennyroyal Green. The chill of the autumn evening stung his skin, and he welcomed it. Filmy clouds obscured a premature half moon. It wasn't quite dark; the sky was a deepening indigo.

He ran his horse mercilessly hard, unlike him, until the two of them were lathered, breathing hard.

And though night hadn't yet officially fallen, the town proper of Pennyroyal Green seemed to have closed for the evening. The storefronts were shuttered; no lamps were hung out on hooks.

He paused on the rise and looked down.

No lights apart from the pub, of course. Cheerful light blazed through every window of the Pig & Thistle, and he could see townspeople milling about inside. He wondered how often Phoebe visited it while she was here.

And that's when something slammed into his body.

The force of it threw him sideways; the reins slipped from his grasp. He fumbled futilely for them, but his limbs seemed peculiarly disobedient. His equilibrium lost, he toppled, slid from the saddle.

Pain.

It was delayed and savage and shocking.

The realization sank in only after he'd landed hard on the ground, one arm over his face, as the hooves of his frightened horse danced over, dodged him:

I've been shot.

He didn't know yet just where he'd been hit. The pain seemed everywhere. Surprising in its consuming totality, raying through him with every beat of his heart. He couldn't remember hearing the sound of the pistol. Perhaps he had. Time seemed to have warped.

And for what felt like minutes, or an eternity he lay on his back in the empty town square, struggling for breath. Listening to the sound of crickets. The way he had the night he'd waltzed with Phoebe.

This thought was surprisingly motivating. He moaned. He heard the sound only distantly, as if it were coming from someone else, or it was the sound of the wind lowing through trees. When the warmth soaked through his shirt, it was a moment before his hand found its way to touch the wound.

And still not a soul appeared; no one stirred in the

square. Whoever had tried to kill him must be satisfied they'd done the job.

I might just die alone.

This thought made him roll, gasping for breath. He struggled to kneel, then rose to his feet. Stumbled and dropped to one knee again.

And in this way, staggering like a drunk, half suspecting he'd never reach it, an eternity later, he arrived at the door of the Pig & Thistle, and swung it open.

Chapter 30

The present . . .

Phoebe heard the footfall only distantly through her concentration. Two pairs of footsteps in the hall, once belonging to Mary Frances, the maid, the other set clearly belonging to a man.

Her door was open, and so the maid knocked on the frame. Her voice was quick and anxious and irritated.

"Miss Vale, you've a visitor. He says it's very urgent and he wouldn't wait downstairs and fol—"

Phoebe shot to her feet so quickly her chair tipped.

But she went still, astonished, when she saw her visitor.

Jonathan Redmond.

"Thank you, Mary Frances," she said faintly. "You may leave us."

Jonathan hadn't removed his gloves or coat or even his hat. He spoke very clearly, very quickly. "I apologize for calling unannounced, Miss Vale, but this is a matter of some urgency. Lord Dryden has been shot. He's been carried into the back room of the Pig & Thistle. And apparently he muttered something about a woman who didn't love him."

Shot.

She felt the blood leave her head. Black began to creep in from the edges of her vision, and her knees buckled.

Jonathan's hand darted out, gripped her arm, and he eased her down to sit on the edge of her bed.

No. No. Please no. "Is he . . ." She wheezed it. She couldn't breathe to speak, very like waking from a nightmare.

"He's alive now. That's all I know."

She looked up, dazed with horror, and in truth, uncertain she should trust him, recalling he was, in fact, a Redmond. "But why are *you* . . . how . . ."

Jonathan was briskly impatient, clearly struggling to remain polite. "He challenged Waterburn to a duel— over you, I might add, Miss Vale. In front of everyone at White's. Waterburn, if you can countenance it, apologized today. He seems innocent of the crime. But no one knows who might have shot the marquess on the common this evening. I came for you straightaway when I heard. I was in the pub."

"But why should *you* be here?"

He hesitated. And then he sighed. "Because . . . Phoebe . . . I know about the gloves."

Shock, a fresh dose of, slapped at her. She glanced guiltily at the trunk in which she'd packed them, then back at Jonathan.

"I . . . I don't understand."

He smiled faintly, but there was little humor in it. "I was there when Lyon bought them in Titweiler & Sons. A one-of-a-kind pair. He was so bloody careful about choosing them. They meant so much to him. But Olivia refused the gift." The word *Olivia* was etched all around in disdain. "And now I can see that he gave them to you. And no, you don't need to explain the circumstances under which he gave them to you. He said you were a good egg." Another smile haunted Jonathan's mouth at the very unromantic way to put it. "No one really knew Lyon, you see. But I do. And there were so few people he confided in. He confided in me, at least some of the time. And there were so few people he held in any esteem. You were one of them. His judge of character is unassailable. And so for the sake of my brother . . . who knows a little something about impossible love . . . I thought you should know about Dryden."

She couldn't take this in.

"But . . . what about Lisbeth . . . that is, surely your family *hates* me . . ."

"My father has sent Lisbeth away to a very stern relative in France, by the way, where she will spend some time in a convent. He's not enchanted with either you or the marquess, but he's appalled by Lisbeth, since she's a member of this family. And we've character, you know. Believe it or not." A glimpse of the impish Jon here, with a new irony. "The Redmonds. He's a complicated man, my father."

He was a terrifying man, as far as Phoebe was concerned.

Her limbs were all-over ice.

Shot.

And then suddenly she made a fist and slammed it into her thigh. And then she did it again. She gulped in breaths, but the air seared her lungs. She hated herself for her cowardice, for the consequences of it. If he died . . . If he *died* . . . Fear was a choking hand round her throat.

She looked up into Jonathan's face, who watched stoically, with sympathy, clearly accustomed to histrionic displays. Then again, he had Violet Redmond for a sister.

She thought: *He'll make a remarkable man one day.* And it was his stoicism that restored a measure of calm and dignity.

"Thank you for telling me. Will you take me to him?" she managed.

She could barely hear her own voice over the roaring in her ears.

Jonathan turned for the door. "That's why I'm here. Come with me."

She burst through the pub door with Jonathan. She blinked in the light, gasped from the warmth.

It seemed a sacrilege that the Pig & Thistle was warm and well lit and filled with laughing, drinking, people, much like any other night, when Jules was lying bleeding, perhaps dying, in the room behind the bar.

"Where is—"

Jonathan pointed. In front of the door to the room behind the bar stood a man she knew to be Captain Chase Eversea—hardly as recognizable as his brother Colin but unmistakable nevertheless. She was uncertain whether he knew her by name.

He barred the entrance of the door and regarded Jonathan coldly.

And received a glare in return.

Jonathan spoke curtly. "This is the woman in question."

This earned upraised eyebrows. "He says you don't love him," Chase said flatly. She suspected it was a test.

"What do *you* think?" she snapped.

He studied her. And then his mouth quirked ruefully and he knocked once on the door, opened the door and gestured her through.

She stopped in the doorway. She'd always thought she was brave, but she was terrified now of what she might find.

She took a deep breath and made herself look.

Oh, but God. He was alive. He looked in fact *very* alive. Jules was naked above the waist, bandaged at the shoulder, reclining on a pallet, sipping at a flask of whiskey, and otherwise looking very alert, and reflective.

He turned and saw her. She was certain he stopped breathing then.

She was also certain only holy relics knew what it was like to be gazed upon the way he was gazing at her.

"Did you have to go and get yourself shot?" She still heard her own voice as if she were underwater.

It was a moment before he could speak, as he didn't seem to be done simply looking at her.

"Clearly, yes. For here you are. Unless, of course, you've stopped off on your way to Africa."

Instantly the room cracked and sizzled with such powerful emotion, nearly visible as fireworks, that even Chase Eversea was taken aback.

More silence of the fraught variety ensued.

Chase cleared his throat. "We'll just leave the two of you alone in—"

Neither of them looked at him.

He backed out of the room and closed the door.

Phoebe stared at him for a dazed moment longer. And then she crumpled.

She sank to her knees next to him. She ducked her head, shuddered, relief wracking her body. "Oh, God. Oh, God, oh, God, oh God . . . . I thought . . ."

He shifted to stroke her hair, and murmured her name, over and over. "Shhhh. Hush now. It's all right. It's all right."

"Are you going to live?"

Then she glanced up from between her hands and had her answer. His voice was strong and he in fact looked quite well, if a bit pale. Now that she was closer, she could see the blood through the bandage. Her head swam, and she closed her eyes again.

"Live? I've already died and gone to heaven, for here you are."

She rolled her eyes at that, trying for insouciance. She could feel hot tears coursing down her cheeks, which embarrassed her. It was a curse to be a woman, sometimes. A very rare *few* times. But when one could make love to someone like the marquess, it was very much a blessing.

"Please don't cry. It makes the pain worse."

This made her laugh, knocking tears away with her fists. "Does it hurt very much?"

"When the whiskey wears off I will know more. They sent the vicar in, that tall handsome fellow—"

"Mr. Sylvaine."

"And it was the strangest thing, but I could swear I felt the pain ease when he touched me on the arm, only briefly."

"I imagine a man of God and a flask of whiskey are bound to take one's pain away."

He smiled. "Likely it was that."

There was a pause.

"I *will* die, however," he said quite seriously, "if you leave me again. Just watch me."

"Jules . . . I've been such an unforgivable coward, but you knew all along that I was afraid. I . . . love you."

"I know," he soothed. "You're forgiven."

She was almost amused he didn't say "I love you," in return.

Almost.

She waited, but it wasn't forthcoming. Very well, then.

"You were right. About everything," she said finally. "About me."

"So were you. About me."

"Both of those statements can't possibly be true."

"Ah, but they are, schoolteacher. I love you so much I can hardly tell my own heart from yours anymore, and I've never said it to another woman in my life as it's never until now been true. It's clear I cannot live without you. There's naught I can do about it. I can't put it in a box, and clearly I'll never behave normally again, or be free of bodily injury, until you're mine, only mine, forever. I surrender. But I want something."

Despite his warning about tears, her eyes were swimming. "Anything," she whispered.

"I want children with you. I want to wake up next to you every day. I want to bicker with you about foolish things and buy you gifts and make love to you every day in a shocking variety of ways. I want to . . ."

Here his glibness failed him abruptly.

He turned to the wall, and said bemused, to himself, "This is harder than I thought it would be. Quite humbling, actually."

He breathed in deeply, turned with resolution toward her.

And when he spoke, his voice was faint, from nerves and emotions and sheer momentousness.

"I should be honored and fortunate beyond all reason if you would consent to be my wife."

Such lovely pomp!

A tentative knock sounded.

They jumped.

"What is it?" they snapped in unison.

Ned Hawthorne opened the door a crack. "Lord Dryden, there's a pair of stricken gentlemen here who have something to say to you. And I think you'd better speak with them straightaway. *Straight*away."

Jules exchanged a glance with Phoebe. "Send them in, then."

Two men stood in the doorway. A ruddy, stocky, country squire, gray-faced and resolute, mud on his boots. The other a young man, lean as a sapling, dressed in fashionable clothes, young enough to feature a few spots on his complexion . . . sporting a long forelock that dropped down over his eyes.

They bowed low.

"Lord Dryden, I am Mr. Frederick Hart, and this is my son, Jem. Tell him, Jem," the older man ordered grimly.

The young man swallowed, his Adam's apple bobbing. He looked near to casting his accounts.

"Were you shot with a .45 caliber pistol, Lord Dryden?" His voice shook. The hat in his hands trembled violently in his grip.

The marquess frowned warningly, began to sit up, winced, and Phoebe put a protective arm over him, preventing him from moving.

Jem opened his palm, and inside was a ball the precise match of the one they'd taken out of him.

The expression on Jules's face had the boy taking a step back.

He stammered, his words clicking from dry-mouthed nerves. "We were taking target practice, sir, you see . . . I'm an excellent shot, most days . . . the light was dying and I know we should have stopped, and my hair . . ." he lifted up his forelock "; . . . well, it fell into my eyes as I fired. I fired wide, and the ball in all likelihood ricocheted . . ." He closed his eyes and swallowed. "Would that I'd shot myself instead!" He was anguished. "Are you very injured? I cannot tell you how sorry I am."

"Damned foolish hair on the fast young men these days," his father muttered. "That ridiculous hairstyle. When we heard what befell you—word travels fast here, you ought to know, in a small town—I insisted he accept the consequences. I couldn't bear it otherwise. And nor could he, am I right, son?"

The young man hesitated, then nodded his head miserably.

Jules was frozen with incredulity. In truth, he could not speak. He was touched by the display of honor in two country squires, and by the humbling—in truth, *hilarious*—definitive evidence that some things *were* beyond his control. And life knew what was best for him better than he did, and had brought to him, not with graceful precision, but with magnificent, ridiculous poetry.

"Well," he said quietly, very sternly, when he could speak, "the consequences will be grave, indeed. I shall need restitution."

The young man closed his eyes and swallowed. His face was the color of parchment, and his father had a white-fingered grip on his arm, lest his son fall to his knees.

The young man deflated before their eyes. "Name it, my lord," the young man said, his voice gravelly with resignation.

"I'd like you to cut off that damned forelock."

There was a silence.

"Is that . . . all, my lord?" his father ventured.

"Yes."

The boy looked about wildly, as if he'd lunge for a pair of scissors immediately. "Straightaway, sir."

Jules suddenly envisioned a ton full of young men who'd shaved their hairlines. He sighed.

"That will be all," he told them. Every inch the imperious, impersonal marquess, icily intimidating, entirely certain they would do precisely what he wished when he wished it.

They instantly leaped to do just that. "If we can ever do anything for you . . ."

"Oh, you have. That will be *all*," he reiterated. "You may leave."

They bobbed their heads frantically and bowed and backed out of the room, lighter in step.

The father muttered something they didn't hear. But they heard the son's reply.

". . . don't know, Da. Read in the broadsheets he might be going crackers. Something about a cat . . . ?"

He turned to Phoebe, whose eyes were watering and brilliant. Mirth or tears or some combination of emotions.

She was biting her lip.

"I'm going to bronze the pistol ball Chase Eversea took out of me. Because it brought you to me. Speaking of which . . . come here," he whispered.

He cupped the back of her head with his hand, eased her face down to him.

The kiss was lingering, desperate, joyous, searching.

And when he ended it, his fingers played in the hair at her nape.

"So . . . ?" he whispered against her lips.

"Yes," she whispered. "Oh, yes. I should be delighted beyond all reason to be your wife."

He closed his eyes against an enormous wave of relief, and shook his head wonderingly on a smile that near broke her heart. He took a few deep breaths.

"*How* did I get so lucky?" His voice cracked. He gave a short laugh.

She kissed the fading bruise on his forehead. She kissed his cat scratches. She kissed the bound wound on his arm. She kissed his eyelids. She laid her head over his beating heart. He covered it with his hand, and sighed. They would take care of each other from now on.

And as he eased into sleep, Phoebe murmured, "I *knew* you were meant for me."

Epilogue

The marquess arranged the next part of his life as swiftly and purposefully as he arranged the first part of it. A special license was discreetly obtained and they were married in London just days after he was shot. Marquardt was kept busy dispatching messages to the members of the marquess's family informing them he now had a wife. Given Phoebe's experience with recalcitrant girls, he had no doubts at all she would be able to command servants, not to mention cope ably with his family. A skilled modiste named Madame Marceau (recommended by his friend, Mr. Cole) was enlisted to provide Phoebe with a glorious wardrobe befitting the wife of a marquess.

Before they departed from Sussex for London, however, Phoebe needed to finalize matters at Miss Endicott's academy.

Phoebe wrote to Mr. Lunden and told him she would not, after all, be accompanying his group on their mission. And Miss Endicott, when informed that the reason for Phoebe's departure from the academy now involved a marquess and not a trip to Africa absorbed it with her usual alacrity.

"All of our girls eventually make triumphant matches," she said easily. "I expected you to do no less, eventually. And much like a catapult, my dear, the lower you begin in life, the higher you can eventually fly. All it requires is the right person to, shall we say, effect the launch."

And then . . . did . . .

Did Miss Endicott *wink* at her?

Phoebe believed she did!

She wondered suspiciously, then, if Miss Endicott had sent her upstairs with the marquess deliberately. But Miss Endicott was as enigmatic, in her way, as she was indomitable. Phoebe would never know.

Her next stop was to bid farewell to her pupils, including Miss Runyon and Miss Carew, who would never forget their encounter with the legendary marquess, and had indeed turned it into a sort of fairy tale they told to the other girls around the fire at night.

Phoebe gathered them around, dispensed hugs and cheek kisses, and told them her news.

The girls were bug-eyed and worshipful and rapt as she delivered one final lecture.

"And if you are virtuous and disciplined and hardworking, if you are kind to others and respectful of your elders, if you complete your lessons on time, if you learn your languages and Marcus Aurelius thoroughly, and if you are very good and virtuous—then you, too, might grow up to marry a devastatingly handsome marquess."

The girls released a collective sigh.

"Is that how *you* won the marquess, Miss Vale?" Miss Carew breathed. "Because you are good and virtuous?"

"It is indeed." Phoebe crossed her fingers in the folds of her skirt. The lie was her final gift to Miss Endicott. It was incentive enough for the girls to behave for a good long while.

* * *

A week after his wedding—during which he and his wife had not once left his London town house, had in fact only seldom visited the lower floors of the house, and had lost themselves thoroughly in sensual abandon—the marquess appeared in White's to share a drink with his friend Mr. Gideon Cole. He'd chosen an hour when he knew Waterburn and d'Andre would not be present.

For he had unfinished business to address.

The moment he appeared, the merry hum of conversation came to an astonished halt. For an instant the only sound was the ambient one of Colonel Kefauver snoring. Seconds later, it started up again, reincarnated as low, excited murmuring. For despite the discretion with which they'd married, word had indeed escaped. Had he changed, they wondered? Was he domesticated, any less intimidating, formidable?

But if *that* were true, why were they all shifting in their seats and nervously awaiting his first words?

He handed off his coat and hat to the footman. "Congratulations are in order, I understand, Lord Dryden," the footman murmured. "I wish you joy in your marriage."

"Thank you."

He took up his position in the bay window, accepted an ale, and waited for Mr. Cole to arrive and have a sip of his own drink before he leaned forward, raised his voice, and said into the relative hush of the club:

"Do you know, Gideon, it's the strangest thing, but lately I find it very unfashionable to be fashionable?"

Turmoil ensued.

His words were repeated, analyzed, worried over, passed from person to person to person. The fast set wobbled about rudderless, nervous and testy, casting suspicious looks at each other, wondering who was more "fashionable" and dreading to be accused of such a thing. The Row was a hostile, uneasy place, as everyone in high flyers felt suddenly unutterably self-conscious and a scramble was made to obtain ordinary horses, not the sort with matching socks and whatnot. Ballrooms were scenes of tension. Dinner parties, long ago planned and anticipated, were now comprised of long awkward silences and accusatory stares, for no one knew whether they were in the presence of some-one unfashionably fashionable.

Phoebe seemed unaware, apart from one obser-vation. "You seem unusually gleeful," she told her husband.

"Do I?" he said absently. "You bring it out in me."

The marquess enjoyed this for a few weeks, and then with his usual impeccable timing, deployed the second tier of his plan.

"Although . . ." he mused to Mr. Gideon Cole in White's, in a voice that hardly needed to be raised, given that everyone was straining to hear it, anyway, "I believe *original* ought to be fashionable, don't you agree? Uniquely lovely and interesting things and *people*, for instance." He paused for delivering his coup de grâce, casually. "In fact, I can't imagine anything more tragic and absurd than being a twin." He gave a short, pitying laugh. "What could be *less* original than two *identical people*?"

Well.

A wave of relief rippled through the London soci-ety. Nearly prostrate with gratitude to be *finally* given something of a direction, it was tacitly decided that those heretofore considered the *most* fashionable of them would now be considered the least, and the ton set about shunning the Silverton twins, Waterburn, d'Andre, and Camber good and proper, until Waterburn and d'Andre were said to be considering enlisting in a foreign army to avoid the humiliation, à la Byron, whilst the Silverton twins were rumored to be touring convents out of desperation to be away from London.

And when he appeared with his wife in The Row, at first they beamed at her, because she was original and because they didn't dare do otherwise given who she'd married. And then they beamed at her because it was nearly impossible not to melt in the rays of her obvious radiant happiness.

The marquess still made them a little nervous.

Satisfied he'd used his powers for good, the marquess settled into married life with Phoebe. At night, Charybdis slept beside them.

And when he allowed the marquess to pet his *belly* . . . well, Jules's happiness was complete.